Praise for *Chainbreaker*:

"You won't be able to put this one down."

—*Huffington Post*

"*Chainbreaker* is an elaborate tale of magic, gods, and the beautiful, unfortunate humans caught in an ancient titanic struggle. You'll cheer. You'll cry. And once you enter this world, you'll never want to leave."

—Traci Chee, *New York Times* bestselling author of *The Reader*

"Mysterious, compelling, and urgent, *Chainbreaker*'s scintillating prose, complex and multi-dimensional characters, and quick pace will pull you in till it leaves you breathless and transformed."

—Aditi Khorana, author of *The Library of Fates* and *Mirror in the Sky*

"Expands on the universe created in *Timekeeper*, with new mythology, character development and international intrigue that really highlights Tara's talent for world-building. *Chainbreaker* combines factual historical research with a believable and original magic mythology to create a world that feels wholly real. With pacing and action running like clockwork, this is a startlingly unique series with a truly golden set of diverse characters."

—Lauren James, author of *The Next Together*

"A wonderfully diverse read with unforgettable characters you can't help but root for."

—*Bustle*

"Riveting and complex . . . Tara Sim's newest fascinating tale full of magic, intrigue, and clocks will hook you."

—*TheMarySue.com*

"An imaginative and action-packed novel set against the backdrop of Indian uprisings against the British occupation."

—*Book Riot*

"Our most anticipated sequel of the year."

—*Paste* Magazine

"Sim continues to offer an action-packed adventure for her lovely queer couple, but *Chainbreaker* features a particularly vivid environment and dynamic new characters thanks to the author's personal cultural experiences."

—*BookMarked*

Praise for *Timekeeper*:

*A Paste Magazine: Best Book 2016

*A Barnes & Noble Teen Blog Best Queer Fantasy 2016

"*Timekeeper* is an extraordinary debut, at once familiar and utterly original. Between its compelling world, its lovely prose, and its wonderful characters, the pages flew by."

—Victoria Schwab, #1 *New York Times* bestselling author

"Alive with myth, mystery, and glorious romance, *Timekeeper* will keep hearts pounding and pages turning til the stunning conclusion. Reader beware—there's magic in these pages."

—Heidi Heilig, author of *The Girl from Everywhere*

"*Timekeeper* is a triumph . . . If you read only one such book . . . let it be this one."

—*Bustle*

"*Timekeeper's* premise is original and its world unique."

—*EW.com*

"While the world is wildly interesting and fantastic, with broken clock towers that have left towns frozen in time, it's the emotional impact and diverse cast of characters that make this book soar . . . The resulting story is an exciting and inclusive one, drawing in elements of magic, mystical spirits, swoon-filled romance, and just so much more."

—*BookRiot*

"Part mystery and part romance, this fantasy novel delves into what it means to grow up and make important decisions. With an easily relatable main character struggling to fit in, the novel has a realistic and contemplative voice. VERDICT: A must-have richly written fantasy novel that will have readers eagerly anticipating the next volume."

—*School Library Journal*

"Sim creates a cast of complex and diverse characters, as well as a mythology to explain how the clock towers came to exist . . . an enjoyable, well-realized tale."

—*Publishers Weekly*

"Mystery, LGBTQ romance, and supernatural tale of clock spirits and sabotage that explores how far people might go for those they love. Its strongest elements are the time-related mythology and the supernatural gay romance."

—*Booklist*

"This LGBTQ steampunk romance sports a killer premise and admirably thorough worldbuilding, helpfully annotated in the author's afterword. The characters—even the bad guys—are sympathetically drawn and commendably diverse in sexuality and gender."

—*Kirkus Reviews*

"An enjoyable start to a promising new trilogy."

—*BookPage*

FIRESTARTER

BOOK THREE OF THE TIMEKEEPER TRILOGY

TARA SIM

Sky Pony Press
New York

Sky Pony® is a registered trademark of Skyhorse Publishing, Inc®, a Delaware corporation.

Visit our website at skyponypress.com

10 9 8 7 6 5 4 3 2 1
Library of Congress Cataloging-in-Publication Data available on file

Print ISBN: 978-15107-0620-0
eBook ISBN 978-1-5107-0624-8

Cover design by Sammy Yuen

Printed in the United States of America

Interior design by Joshua Barnaby

For those who thought they couldn't go on,
and who went on anyway.

And for you, Father. I miss you every day.

"Love is the emblem of eternity; it confounds all notion of time, effaces all memory of a beginning, all fear of an end."

— Madame de Staël

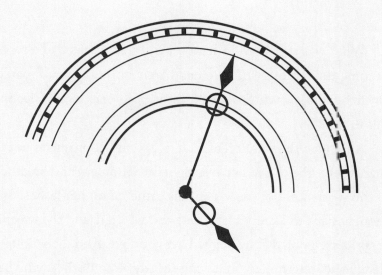

London, January 1877

Snowflakes fell in lazy spirals through the dim evening light and collected on Cassie's hair. The street was quiet except for the crunch and squeak of snow beneath her boots, and she could hear her own breathing, a strangely intimate noise that made her feel as if she were the only living thing on earth.

The sound of an airship engine purred overhead, but she couldn't see it beyond the clouds, the sky a riot of gray streaked with veins of white. There were more and more airships these days.

Hands deep in her coat pockets, she walked the length of the street until she reached the familiar fence. Looking grimly at the surname on the gate, she cursed under her breath.

"Damn you, Danny. You should be here."

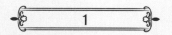

What was supposed to have taken three weeks had already become three months. There had barely been any word, barely any news. Enfield was Stopped. Colton had gone to India. Danny was in trouble.

And there she was, full of secrets, and full of promises not to share them. She closed her eyes tight for a moment and breathed in the sharp scent of snow as flakes gathered on her lashes. She thought back to Danny's face, pale and worried, and the way his arms had trembled as he hugged her goodbye. And then Colton, steady and determined, following shortly after. Both leaving her with a fear she now had to face alone.

Well, not alone. Danny's parents had to face it, too.

There was a crunch behind her, the sound loud after the silence of the snow. She turned to find a man standing across the street looking at the Harts' house. Scowling, Cassie took a step toward him, but the man barely paid her any mind. He made a show of looking at his timepiece and slowly walked down the street, as though his behavior wasn't the least bit suspicious.

"Little bleeder," she muttered. Shivering, she headed for the Harts' front door.

Danny's mother tried to smile when she saw Cassie, but it seemed her mouth didn't want to cooperate. "Cassie, dear, come in."

"Thank you, Mrs. Hart. Is now a good time?"

"Yes, of course. For you, always."

Leila stepped back and let her inside. The furnace was on,

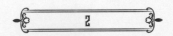

but a draft from outside made Leila shudder. She took Cassie's coat and hung it up.

"Let me put on the kettle."

Cassie caught a glimpse of herself in the mirror near the door and swept the snow from her auburn hair before following Leila into the kitchen, where it was much warmer. She wondered if it was still hot in India, or if they had a winter season like England did.

"Chris, Cassie's here," Leila said as she bustled to the stove.

Christopher Hart, sitting at the kitchen table, graced Cassie with his own feeble attempt at a smile. There was no doubt he and Danny were father and son; they shared the same messy dark hair, the same green eyes, the same long limbs. Only the sharpness of Danny's face hinted at his mother's side.

"Hello, Cass."

"Hello, Mr. Hart." She sat at the table. "How have you been?"

Danny's parents exchanged a look. Cassie, who had been over several times since Danny had departed for India, recognized this look. They had been having a discussion of some importance before she'd arrived.

She noticed a familiar piece of paper near Christopher's hand: a telegraph. It had arrived just days ago from the clock mechanics' office. The message was simple yet hopeful: *Christopher's son is alive and well.*

Judging from Christopher's and Leila's expressions, and from the dark feeling swirling in her gut, no one believed it.

"We've certainly been better," Christopher finally answered.

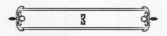

"Have you asked to send a wire to Danny in Agra?"

"The office won't allow it," Christopher sighed. "Official news only."

Cassie grunted. "Rubbish."

Danny's father touched the edge of the telegraph, his eyes heavy and sad. Cassie hadn't seen him this way for many years, not since they'd received word that Danny's grandfather had passed. What a turn—the father Danny had lost now mourning a lost son.

He isn't lost, she told herself firmly. *He said he would come back. Colton said he would bring him back.*

"After everything that's happened," Christopher said, "we've grown more and more convinced something is wrong. The Indian rebels trying to rise up again, Enfield targeted . . ." His face hardened. "And Colton gone."

Cassie tried not to flinch. "But Colton left a letter. He said he was coming back."

"Who's to say he was the one who left it? What if someone took him?" Christopher banged a fist against the table, making Leila and Cassie jump. "Damn these clock spirits. Never thinking about the consequences of what they do."

"Chris . . ." The kettle shrieked, and Leila took it off the stove. "We've discussed this. Maybe Colton just went back to Enfield."

"I don't believe that. For all we know, he could be in India!"

Again, Cassie resisted the urge to fidget. Clearing her throat, she said, "I know it might be nothing, but I saw a strange bloke outside."

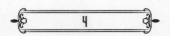

"Oh, *him*." Leila huffed and poured three cups. "We've both seen him. Comes around like clockwork every two days. We thought he was a salesman at first."

"But every time we see him or try to talk to him, he leaves." Christopher accepted his tea with quiet thanks. "Obviously he's spying on us. Might know something about Colton."

"Maybe," Cassie said uneasily. She had only just raised the teacup to her lips when the front door rattled under a pounding fist. Leila's hand shot to her throat in surprise.

"Who on earth—?" She hurried from the kitchen, her curls bouncing. Christopher and Cassie scraped their chairs back and followed. In the hallway, Leila opened the door to reveal three large men wearing the blue of the London authorities.

One tipped his cap. "Mrs. Hart, is it?"

Leila seemed spooked into silence, so Christopher stepped forward. "This is the Hart residence, yes. May we help you, officers?"

The man's gaze traveled from Christopher to Leila, sparing only a glance at Cassie. "Christopher Hart and Leila Hart? Parents of Daniel Hart?"

Leila heaved a shuddering gasp. There was usually one reason why the police showed up at your door with your son's name on their lips.

"No," Cassie whispered, shrinking back against the wall. *He's dead. He promised he'd come back, and now he's dead.*

Christopher gripped his wife's thin shoulders, his knuckles white. "What about our son?"

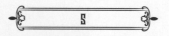

The constable signaled the other two before they barreled into the house. One clomped up the stairs while the other brushed past Cassie into the sitting room.

"Wait just a minute!" Christopher yelled. "You can't barge into someone's home—"

"Actually, sir, we can," the constable said. "And I'm charged with asking you a few questions about Daniel, such as when you last spoke to him and where he was last seen."

"We haven't seen him in months!"

"Please," Leila whispered. Her dark eyes shone with tears. "Has there been news? What's happened to Danny? Please, don't tell me he's . . ."

The constable sighed, and Christopher tightened his grip on his wife's shoulders. Cassie could hear the crash of furniture being overturned, drawers being pulled out of the desk upstairs, the ruffling of papers, all of it a distant clamor under the pounding of her heart.

"By order of Her Majesty the Queen," the constable said, "Mr. Daniel Hart is to be apprehended and tried for treason."

The coast of Bali

The sea was restless. The normally turquoise waters churned a frothy gray, reflecting the clouds overhead. Waves rose and fell like small, doomed empires.

Zavier breathed in the humid, salty air and closed his eyes. He tried to focus on that tentative thread stretching between him

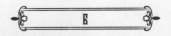

and the sea, the small link that would connect him to Aetas. As he expected, the connection was thin here. They were too far away from the god's prison to feel him in Bali.

But he could feel another. He waded into the surf, deep enough that the tide licked at his shins. Bending, he cupped a handful of water, then pressed it to his forehead as if baptizing himself.

"Oceana," he murmured, "you're anxious today."

Zavier had seen her only once, but that one time was enough. He'd been younger then, more a slave to his heartbreak. He'd stood upon the shore, and Oceana upon the water, and looking into her eyes had been like searching all the sea's uncharted depths.

She had spoken in that voice that wasn't a voice, telling him a story, one of gods and rage and time. All of the tales were real, just as he'd always envisioned them: the battle between the god of time, Aetas, and his creator, Chronos.

The lie—the only piece of the story that was false—was that her brother Aetas hadn't died.

The god of time was trapped, and longing for release.

Zavier wouldn't have known had it not been for Oceana. And because she had given him this revelation, he knew he could never back down. He had to free Aetas and bring back time. No more clock towers. No more barriers. Just time: free, simple, fluid as the water he stood in.

He had promised.

"Zavier." Edmund had left the aircraft he was repairing so

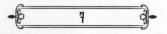

they could return to the *Prometheus*. As he approached, the tall young man looked worried, and with good reason. Another plane had landed near the secluded beach.

"They're from the *Kalki*," he said. "Looks like it's just the two of them."

"Be on guard," Zavier told him. The *Kalki* Indian rebels knew to leave their crew alone, but there was no telling what they would do now that their second rebellion had failed. A couple of small dealings in the past weren't enough to convince their group that the *Prometheus* crew wasn't another threat to their cause.

Even if that cause was already dying. The *Kalki*'s crew had failed to assassinate Viceroy Lytton; what else did they have planned? Zavier thought, *Probably not enough.*

He and Edmund watched as two Indian men approached. The sand shifted under their feet as wind tugged at their clothing. Halfway to the shore, one of them said something to the other, then continued forward on his own.

He was a young man with brown eyes and thick hair, dressed in an aviator jumpsuit with goggles hanging around his neck. Warily, he stopped before Zavier and Edmund.

"You look a tad familiar," Edmund said before the newcomer could speak. "Have we met before?"

"No, not that I know of." His accent coated the English words like warm syrup. "My name is Akash Kapoor."

"From the *Kalki*," Zavier said, a half question. Akash gave a half shrug. "Are you a clock mechanic?"

"No, but my sister is."

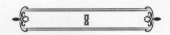

"I see." Zavier wanted to glance at Edmund, but stifled the impulse. "And where is your sister?"

Akash's face hardened. "On your ship. As a prisoner."

This time he did exchange a glance with Edmund. "Your sister is Meena, then." Akash nodded stiffly. Zavier breathed in deep, letting the briny air settle his thoughts before he spoke again. "You may see your sister on one condition. You both help our cause. You cannot return to the *Kalki,* nor can Meena."

"She's not a rebel," Akash mumbled.

"Are you?" Again, a half shrug. "Well, whatever you may be, you're a part of the *Prometheus*'s crew now, and you will help me convince your sister to join us."

"There's no other way I can see her?"

"She's a talented clock mechanic. We need her."

The young man thought for a moment, then nodded. "All right."

"Thank you. Edmund, we'll need to radio the ship. Mr. Kapoor, tell your friend over there that you won't be returning with him."

Akash turned away, jaw clenched at the order.

What was it that Aunt Jo kept saying? Be more likable. That was how to win people over. So far, Zavier hadn't quite gotten the hang of it.

He noticed Edmund watching him. "What is it?"

"Nothing. You seem tired."

Zavier waved his friend's concern away. "I'm fine, Ed." He realized he was still standing in the water and walked back to shore, shivering. "Just have a lot on my mind."

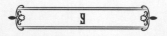

"Bit of an understatement, that," Edmund muttered. "You sure we can trust this one, Z? I mean, he did come with the rebels."

"He doesn't seem an essential member of their group. Might only be a supporter." Zavier checked his timepiece, the second hand chipping away precious time he could be spending on other matters.

"Hurry up with the radio, Ed. We need to get back and check on our other prisoners."

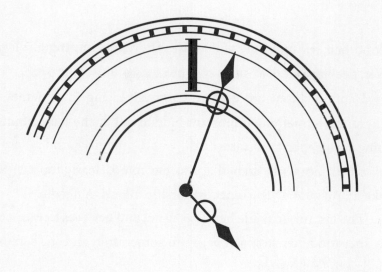

Daphne woke with a start, her heart pounding and her veins throbbing with terror. Her eyes were wide and glassy as they stared at the ceiling far above her.

Something beyond her consciousness had screamed at her to wake up, to recognize what had scared her. But nothing emerged from the shadows. Nothing slithered from underneath the bed. Nothing latched onto her arms and legs or dragged her across the room.

Blinking, she turned her head toward a round window. Beyond the thick glass was a purplish haze, like the thickest sludge of her dreams. If she crawled out the window and into that murky twilight, would she be lost in it? Or would she find a new home among the stars just starting to appear?

Rising onto her elbows, she shook her head. She felt funny, insubstantial. Slowly, she moved to the edge of the bed. Her

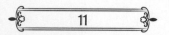

blond hair fell on either side of her face as she swung her legs over, peeking out of a long nightgown.

Daphne closed her eyes and swayed, trying to remember. There was something important hidden under the haze, something she needed to recall.

Small moments flashed across her mind, nearly too fast to take in. An auto. Dust. Tents. An airship. Blood. A needle.

The last image made her gasp again, and her eyes flew open. As she stood, her stomach began to somersault, and she scrambled to the rubbish bin.

After heaving out the pitiful contents of her stomach, she pushed the bin away and leaned against the bed, panting. She wiped the saliva from her mouth and grimaced.

They drugged me, she thought, perhaps the first coherent thought she'd had in days. *Over and over, they drugged me.*

It all came trickling back. Colton had run off into the camp to search for Danny, but so had Captain Harris. Partha had taken her and Meena into the city. Then, the gut-churning sound of guns—so many guns, all firing at once. The crumbling clock tower. The cannon blast of an airship. Her and Meena being taken.

Then came the wave of confusion, the fear. Looking out the window and seeing the ocean far below. Screaming. People she didn't know trying to calm her. Raking her nails against someone's face. And then, the needle that promised sleep.

A couple of crew members had tried to speak to her. Their words were lost, hidden somewhere in her mind. She didn't know

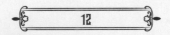

who they were, or what they wanted with her. But the panic had settled now into uneasy determination. She wanted answers.

Gritting her teeth, Daphne rose to unsteady feet and tottered toward the door. Locked, of course.

"Water," she called through the metal door. "I need water."

The door opened with a slight squeak and she looked up. A mousy girl, short and thin, stood on the threshold with a tray in her hands. When she saw Daphne, she smiled with pale lips.

The girl was perhaps Meena's age, or younger. She kept her hair in twin braids that roped behind her ears and ended in small tufts at her shoulders. Her eyes were gray, almost silver.

The girl placed the tray on the bed beside Daphne. Daphne looked it over with mild interest. Bread, ham, potatoes. And water. She grabbed the glass and gulped it down, soothing the burn in her throat.

As Daphne gasped for air, the girl nodded once and turned to leave.

"Wait!" Daphne put the glass down. "Please don't go. You have to tell me where I am."

The girl stopped. Biting her lip, she made complicated motions with her fingers.

"I . . . what?" The girl did the sequence again, pointed to her throat, and shook her head. "Oh. Oh! I'm so sorry, I didn't realize . . ."

The girl pointed at her eyes, then her lips, then her ear. "You can understand what I say?" The girl nodded with a "so-so" gesture. "I see. Well, I . . . I need to know where I am. Please."

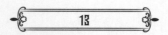

The girl held up a finger, signaling her to wait. She went into the hall, waved, and came back. A few seconds later, the Indian woman who'd greeted her the first time she woke in this cell appeared.

"You're up again." She didn't sound too happy about it. "How do you feel?"

"Awful," Daphne said. "Where am I?"

The young woman cleared her throat. "You're on the *Prometheus*. My name is Prema, if you do not remember"—Daphne didn't—"and this is Sally." She gestured to the girl. "We know that you are Daphne Richards, and that you are a clock mechanic."

Daphne's heart tripped a little in her chest. "And what exactly do you want with me?"

"Zavier has spoken to you before. Do you not remember?"

"No, that drug you stuck in me probably addled my memory."

Prema shifted. "I'm sorry for your discomfort. If you like, I can bring Zavier here to speak with you again. He's out at the moment, but should be back soon. Until then, is there anything you would like?"

Anger, hot and tight, rose to choke her. She was a prisoner here, and they were trying to pretend she was a guest.

"I don't care about *Zavier*. I want to know why I'm here and what's happened to Meena."

"Meena is safe, as are the others."

"Others?"

Sally's eyes widened and she glanced at Prema. In a flash, Daphne understood. They weren't supposed to reveal that detail.

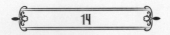

"You have Danny," Daphne guessed. "He's here, isn't he?" The women remained silent. "*Isn't he?*"

"Why don't you eat up before—"

"Tell me where he is!"

"Daphne—"

"Is Colton here, too? What about Akash? Harris? Partha? *Where are they?*"

"I promise we'll explain everything," Prema said, taking Sally by the elbow and making for the door. "But we're not allowed to speak of any of this until Zavier's returned. Until then, please eat and recover your strength."

Daphne rushed at them, but her weakness made her trip. The door slammed shut and a key scraped in the lock.

Daphne banged on the door. "Just tell me they're all right!" she yelled through the metal. "Please!"

She slid to the floor, shaking and cold. Once she had calmed down, she wiped her face and struggled back to the bed. Despite her fear and her anger, she was starving.

She stared at the wall as she mechanically chewed. The ham was rubbery in her mouth, but she needed to fill her stomach. She needed enough strength to get through the next few moments.

The others were here, she was sure of it. There was no telling about Harris and Partha, but Danny . . .

Danny had been kidnapped weeks ago. An airship, very much like this one, had attacked them on their way to India. It only seemed right to put the two incidents together.

But then what had happened to Akash? He'd gone off to find Danny, but had he succeeded?

She touched the diamond tattoo at the corner of her eye. God, Akash. What if he had gotten tangled up in this as well? What if these people had found him, and hurt him?

Strength. She needed strength.

Packing her doubts and fears into a small box in her mind, she scanned the room. She nearly laughed as she studied the food tray. Someone had been stupid enough to give her a toothpick.

Kneeling in front of the door, Daphne carefully inserted the pick into the lock. She had to be careful; the wood would break if she used too much force. But the tumblers were hard to find, and she cursed under her breath, feeling for them blindly.

Her mother had locked her in her room enough times for Daphne to learn this particular trick. But the lock before her was different, one she wasn't used to, and it took several minutes before she heard a hopeful *click*.

Breathing out a relieved sigh, Daphne palmed the toothpick, remaining on her knees as she slowly eased open the door. It would be just her luck if Sally or Prema were standing guard. Thankfully, she saw no one through the small crack. Opening the door farther, she peered into the hallway. Clear.

She stood and hurried down the corridor, covering her mouth in an attempt to stifle her loud breathing. Her nightgown fluttered around her ankles, whispering as she moved. When she heard voices up ahead, she darted behind the corner, waiting for them to pass. Surprisingly, the speakers had German accents, but she had no time to wonder about it.

I'll be caught at this rate, she thought bleakly, listening as their footsteps retreated down the hall. *And then they'll drug me again.*

She moved down a flight of stairs, down endless corridors. How big was this airship? Passing a set of doors, she could hear the sound of metal pounding on metal.

As she descended another flight of stairs, something began to tug at her. The familiar sensation lodged itself in her midsection and urged her onward like a boat being pulled in from the tide before it could be lost at sea.

It was darker down here, and colder. Daphne found herself at the mouth of a corridor closed off by a heavy door. Heart pounding, she looked through the small porthole in the door, but the other side was dark.

Taking slow, even breaths, she pushed the door open and walked inside. She wrapped her arms around herself, feeling like a ghost in her pale nightgown. That familiar sensation tugged her forward, icy metal kissing her bare feet with every step she took.

There: a small, barely perceptible glow.

Daphne hurried forward. Bars lined the walls on either side, doors leading into cells. And in one of those cells—

"Colton!" she whispered sharply.

The clock spirit looked dead. He sat leaning against a wall, his head hanging forward. Colton had always had the image of a teenage boy, his hair blond and his skin bronze like the metal of his clockwork. But now his skin was pale, his hair lackluster, the faint glow of his body gone. In fact, she realized he was partially transparent.

Daphne fell to her knees and gripped the cold metal bars. "Colton! Colton, please wake up!" He didn't respond. Daphne looked around and spotted his central cog, tucked into the power-magnifying holder that Christopher Hart had built for him before he'd left England in search of Danny. Daphne grabbed it and pushed it through the bars, as far toward Colton as she could manage.

He twitched. A faint glow returned to his body. When he raised his chin, his bright amber eyes were open.

"Daphne," he murmured.

"Yes, it's me." She reached through the bars. "I came for you."

He touched his fingertips to hers. A small shock traveled through her, as if time had jumped across her skin. The hairs on her arms stood on end.

Colton pulled the cog holder closer, pressing it to his chest. He made a relieved sound.

"I'm going to get you out of here," Daphne said, studying the lock above her head. A flimsy toothpick couldn't trigger the tumblers on this one. She would probably have to come back with something sturdier, if not with the key itself.

"Daphne."

Something about Colton's voice made her look at him warily. His face was grim, his lips pressed together. It still awed her that a clock spirit, only a pale imitation of a human, could look so . . . well, human. But here he was, thousands of miles from his clock tower in Enfield, still living. But barely.

The thought terrified her. What if he died before they could bring him back home?

"Daphne," Colton said again. "Do you know where they took Danny?"

"No, but I'm going to find him. And Meena, and anyone else these bastards took. Then we'll all escape. Together."

But Colton slowly shook his head. "They won't tell me what happened to him. I don't know if he . . ." His voice wavered, and although clock spirits couldn't cry, Daphne could practically see his eyes welling with tears.

"If he what?"

Colton hugged the cog holder tighter. "They shot him. They shot Danny."

Daphne's senses grew muted, as if traveling through a funnel. In her mind, she saw Partha shooting Lieutenant Crosby, the blood spraying from his body. She remembered the blood-soaked clothes of the boy with the tinted goggles. The smell surrounded her, metallic and dusky.

"Is Danny alive?" she whispered.

"I don't know. They won't tell me anything." Colton closed his eyes. "Daphne, what if he—There was so much blood. And the look on his face. The pain he must have felt." Colton hid his face with a sound like a small, wounded animal.

She reached through the bars again to touch his sleeve. "You can't think like that. I'm sure he's all right. If I go and look for him, I can—"

A throat cleared behind her, and she flinched. Colton looked up with an expression she had never seen him wear before, raw and stark and visceral.

Pure hatred.

She turned to find a young man regarding her from the doorway. He carried a lantern, which cast a sickly yellow light across the floor.

The young man looked between her and Colton with a mixture of exasperation and pity. His eyes were gray, almost silver.

"I was wondering if you'd made your way down here, Miss Richards. I have to admit, you impress me more every time I encounter you."

She grimaced. "And how many times would that be?"

He touched the back of his head. "Three. The first, you clobbered me with a pipe. The second, you nearly gouged out my eyes. The third"— he gestured to the scene before him—"I find you orchestrating a prison break."

The blood-soaked clothes. The tinted goggles. "You're the one who tried to get Danny killed on the *Notus*."

"I wasn't going to kill him." The young man set the lantern down and walked to where she remained crouched. She scrambled closer to Colton, who grabbed her hand as if he could protect her even from behind bars. "I assure you, I only wanted him to help us."

"And where is he now?" Colton demanded.

"I'll answer all of your questions in time. Miss Richards, I want to help you. Now that you're stable again, I want to give you an opportunity."

She gripped Colton's hand tighter. "What sort of opportunity?"

"The chance to talk with Meena."

Her face went slack. *Meena.*

"If you would like to speak with her, please follow me. If not, then I'll have to escort you back to your room."

Daphne took three deep breaths before nodding.

Colton tugged at her hand. "Danny," he said urgently. "What about Danny?"

"I want to speak with him, too," she demanded.

"I'm afraid that's impossible at the moment. But if you wish to see Meena, you have to come with me."

Daphne looked at Colton, an apology in her eyes. "I'll find out where he is."

She stood on unsteady legs. The young man made to help her, but she shied from his touch.

"Daphne, please don't leave," Colton begged. "Not with him. Please."

"I'm sorry, Colton. I promise I'll come back."

The spirit's face crumpled, and she had to turn her back before she could give in to guilt. She needed answers, and as far as she knew, this was the only way to get them.

The young man picked up his lantern without so much as a

glance at Colton. Daphne followed him out, her body slow and heavy.

"Who are you, anyway?" she asked.

"I'm sure I've told you my name before," the young man said, "but perhaps you were too . . . indisposed to remember. I'm Zavier Holmes." He glanced at her, and she spotted the fading scratch marks on his cheek. "Would you like to change before seeing Miss Kapoor?"

"I'm fine." He'd already seen her in her nightgown; she didn't have the presence of mind to be embarrassed.

"I'm sorry for all the trouble we've put you through."

Daphne barked a mirthless laugh. "Don't bother. I'm never forgiving any of you for this."

He opened his mouth as if to contest it, then thought better of it and gave an unconvincing shrug. "Fair enough."

Zavier led her to a room guarded by a large Indian man wearing a turban.

"No disturbances?" Zavier asked. "Has he come yet?"

"Not yet," the man said in a startlingly deep voice.

"Good." Zavier gestured to the room. "You'll find her inside. Let us know if you need anything."

Daphne gave them both a cool stare and walked inside; the door closed gently after her. The room was different from the one in which she'd awoken, more of a sitting room with a table by the window surrounded by three chairs. In one of these chairs sat an Indian girl with a dark braid resting over her shoulder.

"Meena," Daphne whispered.

The girl looked up, her eyes widening as she rose. "Daphne!"

They hugged each other with desperation, with relief. How many days had they been on this airship? How many times had Daphne been drugged? How long had she been alone?

Meena stepped back and looked Daphne up and down. "Where are your clothes?" The Indian clock mechanic was wearing her traditional salwar kameez, and she even had a red bindi on her forehead. Daphne, in her nightgown and her hair a mess, suddenly wished she had taken Zavier's offer to change.

"I was trying to find everyone."

Meena motioned for her to sit. A pot of tea rested on the table, and Meena poured her a steaming cup. A clock ticked somewhere in the room, but Daphne didn't bother to check the time.

"What do you mean, trying to find everyone? I heard that you were . . . resisting them. I did, too, but then they explained."

"Explained what?"

Meena sighed and sat beside her. Daphne glanced at the healing burn mark on the girl's face, received when the Meerut clock tower had exploded. "We're prisoners on this ship, but they don't want us to be. These people, they're the ones who have been bombing towers around India. They say they know how to make time continue on without them, though they haven't explained how yet. They want us to help, but . . ." Meena shrugged. "I think your answer will be the same as mine."

Daphne took a sip of tea, nearly burning her mouth. "They're the terrorists."

"Yes."

"And they want *us* to help?"

Meena grimaced. "Yes."

"What did you tell them?"

"I kicked a man named Edmund in the shin and tried to strangle the redheaded girl."

Daphne hid her smile in her teacup. "I gave that Zavier bloke the scratches on his cheek."

Meena's eyes twinkled, then her expression grew somber again. "Daphne, we have to find a way off this ship."

"You think I don't know that? I was trying to plan a way to escape when Zavier found me. They have Colton in a cell. They're purposely keeping him weak, but I don't know why."

"That poor spirit." Meena hesitated, chewing her bottom lip. "And Danny?"

"I don't know."

Meena lowered her eyes, and Daphne continued to drink her tea. The thought of Danny was making her palms sweat. No one would tell her where he was, and if he wasn't on the *Prometheus*, then where exactly was he?

Not dead, she told herself firmly. *He's not dead.*

"How do you think we can escape?" Meena whispered.

Before Daphne could answer, the door opened. Thinking it was Zavier coming to tell them their time was up, Daphne turned with a scowl.

"Akash!"

Meena bounded from the table and into her brother's arms.

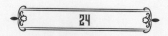

He held her tightly as they swayed on their feet, whispering in quick Hindi that Daphne couldn't translate.

Daphne stood slowly, once again wishing she had taken Zavier up on his offer to change. When Akash saw her, she flushed, but his smile outweighed her embarrassment, and more than anything she wanted to copy Meena and fly into his arms. She remembered how well they fit around her body, how good it felt to be held by him.

He was in his jumpsuit, his hair windblown, his face radiant. But there was something in his dark eyes that made her take pause. Something she'd never seen there before.

"Daphne," he said. Her face grew even warmer; he'd never called her by her first name before. She liked the sound of it on his tongue.

"Akash. I . . . I'm glad you're all right." It was the mildest of what she wanted to say, but the rest could wait.

"I didn't know they took you, too," Meena said, worriedly fixing his hair.

Suddenly he wasn't looking at either of them. "They didn't take me. I'm here on my own."

The silence after his words was piercing.

"On your own?" Meena repeated. "How?"

"I doubt you could have strolled up and asked to come aboard," Daphne said. "Did you strike up a deal with them? Can you get us out of here?" He only stared at the floor. A horrible, sinking feeling opened in the pit of her stomach. "You're working for them."

Akash flinched. "I'm not—"

"The truth, Akash."

He fiddled with his goggles. "The truth? The truth is that these people knew I was a supporter of the rebels, so they let me onboard. To talk to you." He looked at Meena beseechingly. "But only because I wanted to help you, behan. I knew they'd taken you, and I had to find you. So I made a deal. You and I work for them, and I get to stay here, with you."

Meena's face, so alive just a moment before, was now hard and cold. Akash took a step toward her, saying something in Hindi.

"Nahi!" She backed away from him, her eyes furious. "You didn't tell me this, Akash. You didn't tell me you were a supporter of the rebels."

"Only because I want the British to leave our home. You *know* that. You want them gone as much as I do."

"But at what price?" Meena demanded, her voice starting to shake. "Killing men left and right? I heard about the assassination attempt on Viceroy Lytton. I've heard your rants, Akash. You wanted the man dead."

Akash's silence was answer enough. The cogs in Daphne's mind had been turning slowly, disbelievingly, but now they sped up again.

"Danny wired us to tell us he was trying to help the viceroy," she said quietly. "He knew what was going to happen. Were you there with him?" Akash finally met her gaze, his eyes wide and wet. He nodded. "And you did nothing to stop it. You were too much of a coward to do anything. And because you were a cow-ard, Danny was shot."

Meena's jaw dropped. "Danny was *shot*?"

"And now no one knows if he's alive or dead," Daphne snarled, coming closer. "Because no one helped him!"

Akash raised his hands. "Daphne—"

"*No!* You have no right to call me that."

"I did try to help him! I tried to get him out of that camp, but he insisted—"

"You could have told him you were with the rebels! You could have told him the truth!"

"And where would that have gotten me? Surrounded by British soldiers? A bullet to the head? You may be one of us, but you're more British than you are Indian. Your skin and your accent are a privilege. You seem to forget that."

Daphne reeled back, stung. They stared at each other, fury and frustration twisting between them. Daphne finally turned back to the table, crossing her arms over her stomach. A weighted dread settled over her, and something else she had tasted often enough before—grief.

"You disappoint me, Akash," she heard Meena say, her voice soft. "I have no desire to see you right now. Please leave us."

"Meena!"

She yelled at him in Hindi, screamed until she was hoarse and crying.

Daphne heard the door close. She turned to find Meena on the floor, rocking back and forth as she wept into her hands.

She knelt beside the younger girl, steadying her. "I'm sorry, Meena. I'm so sorry."

"How are we going to get away now?" the girl sobbed. "How am I ever going to forgive him?"

"We'll find a way." But as she tried to convince herself of the truth in her words, she could only think of Colton in his cell, his life fading with every tick of the clock.

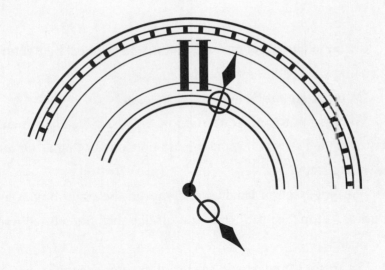

C olton. Colton!"

He opened his eyes and smiled. Castor was leaning over him, the sun behind him casting a halo around his dark hair as he grinned.

Colton lifted a hand and touched the side of Castor's face. "You look like an angel."

The grin widened. "Do I? You look like a tomato."

"What?" Castor tweaked his nose, and he yelped in pain.

"You were sleeping in the sun for so long, it burned you right up."

Colton groaned and rolled onto his knees. "I told Abi to wake me!" The fact that his sister hadn't done so immediately triggered his worry. "Where is she?"

"She went off with a couple of her friends."

The worry shifted into annoyance. "That's not like her."

Castor laughed and mussed Colton's hair. "She'll be a young woman soon. She'll want more independence."

"What about me?"

"What about you? You're almost eighteen. Nearly a man." Castor smiled slyly and snuck a hand up Colton's thigh. "Or are you one already?"

Blushing, Colton laughed and shoved the other boy away. "I guess I didn't expect her to run off like that. She's usually so responsible."

"So are you, but you still sneak out to come see me."

Colton frowned. "You don't think she's seeing a boy, do you?"

Castor's eyebrows rose. "I hope not. If we're going to move to London, she shouldn't get too attached to any Enfield boys. Or girls," he added with a knowing grin.

The thought sent a small stab of panic through Colton's chest. Castor had been pestering him about moving to London for months, and even when he argued that he couldn't leave Abigail, Castor insisted that she should come, too. Colton's younger sister, regularly burdened with sickness, had been growing stronger in the last few weeks, which had only bolstered Castor's planning.

It wasn't as if Colton didn't like London. Rather, he didn't like the thought of leaving Enfield. Of leaving his home, his parents, his old life. He loved this town in a way Castor never had. In a way Castor never would.

"Maybe," Colton murmured. He grabbed hold of the fence behind him to stand, then hissed between his teeth. He'd scraped his finger against a splinter.

"Let me see." Castor took his hand and studied the small cut, already welling with blood. Without a second thought, he popped the finger into his mouth to suck the blood clean.

"Castor! You can't do things like that." Colton pulled his finger back and looked around, but hidden in the garden behind the house, no one could see them.

"No one's home." Castor pulled Colton in closer, a happy light dancing in his brown eyes. "I just get so excited talking about the future—a future where we can be together." He combed his fingers through Colton's hair, the light in his eyes changing to something else, softer but just as passionate. "That's all I want, Colton. More than anything else. You and me, free."

Their bodies met, and so did their lips. Colton could taste the hint of copper in Castor's mouth, an echo of his own blood. It thrummed within his body, beating against Castor's hands. *I am alive*, his blood sang. *Alive, and with him.*

It was those green eyes that had made him curious from the start. He thought, at first, that he had never seen a shade so green before. But something tickled his memory; maybe he had, once. In a dream.

Colton had watched the clock mechanic climb his tower's stairs, a package resting on his shoulder, eyes focused on his feet until his gaze rose to take in the clockwork—*his* clockwork. The way those eyes regarded him, the way they examined and

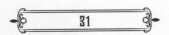

questioned, caused something to shift. Or maybe it had been the sadness in those eyes, the heavy weight of hopelessness.

Maybe that was why he'd shown himself the first time. Maybe he had helped because he knew no one else would come. That the clock mechanic was on his own. That that was how he lived: facing the world on his own when he didn't have to. Maybe it was why he had spoken to him, asked about his life, tried to make him smile.

Maybe it was why he had kissed him. The mechanic had knelt there, in front of Colton's clockwork, those green eyes cataloging every piece and gear and cog like it was the most important thing on earth. That was when Colton knew. And when those same eyes had looked up, so green and bright and sad, he'd had to kiss him.

He had felt the thrum of the mechanic's blood, the beat of his pulse in his lips. The promise of life, the feeling that this would never end. Just the two of them, and between their bodies, a single heartbeat.

He couldn't move from the pain. His body ached, his side hurt, and his mind was sluggish. They had taken away his cog holder again. It was propped against the opposite wall, out of reach.

It had been a couple of days since Colton had seen Daphne. She had promised to come back, but she hadn't. No one had come except Zavier, and that was only to take his cog holder away.

He was alone, trapped. Just as he had been in his tower.

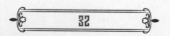

Except there, he could move. There, at least, he could see Danny.

The pain of his memories made Colton clench his jaw. They came every so often now, these brief hauntings. He wanted to make them stop, but he also wanted more. He wanted to see and remember his mother and father, his sister Abigail, his town . . . and Castor.

They had been time servants, once. They had been loyal to the Gaian god Aetas, Timekeeper over mankind. Through their meditation, time was maintained around the world. Colton liked those memories the most. They gave him something to hold onto. They made him remember how his life had once been, and understand how it was now.

At least, he thought he understood.

He had been killed to create Enfield's clock tower. All clock towers—all spirits—were merely the result of sacrifice when Aetas died, when time spiraled out of anyone's control. Only Colton's death, and the deaths of thousands like him, had prevented time from ripping the world apart.

And here he was now, sitting in a dark cell, leagues away from Enfield. It was enough to make him want to laugh, bitter and tired. But he didn't move. He barely moved anymore.

The door down the corridor opened. Zavier had returned.

The young man stopped before Colton's cell, hands loosely gripping the bars as he studied the clock spirit. His brown hair was perfectly styled, his clothes without a wrinkle. Colton detested the sight of him.

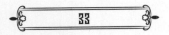

There was a word he thought he'd never use. *Detest.*

"What do you want now?" Colton mumbled.

"I was wondering if you wanted a break from this place. See the ship, meet some of the others."

Colton frowned. It had to be a trick, but he wasn't sure how. His new memories brought little pockets of his old persona, the boy he used to be when he was alive. Right now that boy was telling him that Zavier had some ulterior motive.

"Why would I want that when I'm so comfortable in here?" Colton drawled.

Zavier raised his eyebrows. "Have a sense of humor, do you? Interesting. I didn't know clock spirits spoke this way with humans."

Because I'm not a clock spirit. I'm a human. Or I was. That other Colton was coming more and more to the forefront of his mind, tearing apart the naïve, cheerful spirit he had been in his tower. He had been so ignorant, then. So stupid.

Zavier dug out a key from his pocket. "Regardless of your answer, I would still like you to come with me." He unlocked the cell door and stood there, waiting. But Colton remained right where he was, glaring. "You're too weak, aren't you?"

Colton looked toward his cog holder. Zavier carefully handed it to him, eyeing the central cog that was Colton's only link to this world. Hundreds of years ago, his life's blood had been spilled on this cog.

He slipped his arms through the straps and let the cogs settle on his back. Relief, warm and golden, spread throughout his limbs. He closed his eyes in gratitude.

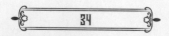

"I hope you can stand now?" Zavier asked, voice dripping with contempt.

It was difficult, but he managed to get to his feet. He felt off-kilter, like leaning too much one way or the other would send him toppling to the floor.

He followed Zavier into the corridor. His side panged him, and he pressed a hand against it. Back in Enfield, his tower's right wall had taken damage, and his own right side sported a mirror wound.

"Why are you doing this?" Colton asked Zavier's back. The young man's shoulders were broad, the nape of his neck pale.

"I want you to answer some of our questions," Zavier said. He looked back over his shoulder at Colton. "The fact that you're here is nothing short of astounding. There are a few other clock mechanics on the *Prometheus*. We'd like to understand you better."

Hope flared briefly within him. "Will Danny be there?"

"No, but Miss Richards will."

That was something. Colton took in his surroundings as they walked through hallway after hallway, absently brushing a hand down the front of his vest. It was Danny's vest, but it had long since stopped smelling like him. The walls on either side of them were a metallic gray, the floor echoing their footsteps. He could almost sense the air parting on either side of the ship, the smooth currents of time hugging the vessel as it cut through the sky.

Colton touched the cog in his trouser pocket. Big Ben had given it to him before he'd left London, as if the spirit had known he would have need of it. Back in that cell, separated from his cog holder, that small cog had been the only thing keeping him alive.

They reached a door that was already half-open. Colton could hear voices on the other side, ones he didn't recognize, and he shrank back.

Zavier hesitated, straightening the cuff of his shirt. "I know what we're doing is right," he said suddenly, almost as if to himself. "Important things are being set in motion, Colton. Things that can change the course of history." He paused again, refusing to meet his eyes. "I just wanted you to know that I find your place in these events regrettable."

Colton wasn't sure what to say to that, so he said nothing at all.

Zavier gestured to the half-open door with his metal hand. "I promise it won't last long."

"Eager to get me back to my cell?" He brushed past Zavier and into the room. It was cluttered with occupied chairs, ranging from spindly metal stools to a plush love seat. Sitting on the latter were two faces he knew.

"Colton!" Daphne sprang up and put her hands on his shoulders. She was dressed in her typical clothes now, her blond hair hanging in a braid. "Are you all right? I'm sorry I didn't come. They wouldn't let me."

"It's all right," he said. "I knew they wouldn't." Colton saw the Indian girl behind Daphne. "Meena," he said with a smile. She smiled back.

"Blimey, this him, then?"

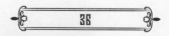

Someone grabbed him and spun him around. Colton lashed out in surprise, and Daphne pulled him back toward her.

The girl who had touched him held up her hands. "Tetchy, aren't you?" She had red hair and her face was splattered with freckles, her body pleasantly plump. "Wasn't gonna do nothing."

"Careful, Liddy," said a man. "He's a clock spirit. We dinna know all his properties yet."

"And that's what brings us here today." Zavier closed the door and signaled everyone to sit. Only he, Colton, and Daphne remained on their feet. Daphne pulled Colton closer, a protective hand wrapped around his arm. He would be lying if he said it wasn't a comfort.

"This isn't an interrogation," Zavier said. "Please, sit."

Daphne glanced at Colton, who nodded slightly. He lowered himself onto the love seat with Meena on his right, Daphne on his left, pretending not to notice the way everyone's eyes bored into him. He leaned back far enough that the cog holder pressed against his spine.

The group had left Zavier a padded seat near the door, which he took, completing the circle of clock mechanics with Colton at its center.

"Well, Colton," Zavier said with a smile that didn't touch his eyes, "this is somewhat of a miracle. For the first time in history—or history as we know it, anyway—a clock spirit has traveled far from his clock tower. How do you feel?"

Colton couldn't help a small laugh. "You're asking me how I *feel*?" He wondered how Danny would answer. "Bloody awful.

But I have you to thank for that." The tremor of suppressed laughter in Daphne's body told him that Danny would have approved.

Before Zavier could reply, a girl sprawled on a chair to his right snorted. She was picking at her fingernails with a dagger, her feet propped on the lap of an Indian girl beside her who had a hand placed rather familiarly on her calf. The girl's brown eyes flashed in Colton's direction.

"That accent." The dagger girl huffed. "Of course the clock spirit 'as to be *British*." Her own accent was throaty, almost nasal, and Colton couldn't place it.

"Shocking," drawled the redhead, Liddy. "A clock spirit whose tower is in England—and he's British! Who would've thought?"

"All right." Zavier held his hands up, signaling them to stop bickering. "Let me start with an offer for you, Colton. Now that we know the extent to which you rely on those cogs, we can have our smith make them stronger."

Meena shifted. "You can do that?"

"Yes, but we need to study the holder more." Zavier returned his attention to Colton. "Your tower was attacked, yes?" Colton nodded. "How much damage was there?"

Colton was tempted to lift his shirt to show the long, ropy scar that went from underarm to hip, but thought better of it. "The right side was hit, and the tower nearly fell. I Stopped the town before it could."

A murmur ran through the room. The man who'd scolded Liddy earlier whistled through his teeth, watching Colton with fascination. "So if ye restarted time," he said, "the tower would fall, and the town would just Stop again anyway."

"Unless we could prevent it somehow," Zavier corrected.

"How do ye suppose we do that?"

"I'm not entirely sure." Zavier turned back to Colton. "Do you know how long you've been a spirit?"

If Colton still had a heart, it would be pounding. He studied the others—these strangers watching him, waiting impatiently for his answer. Should he lie? Tell the truth?

No—not the truth. Not yet.

"I don't know," he said instead.

"You have no memories of your . . . conception? How you came to be?"

"No."

The questions came in a steady stream after that, mostly from Zavier, but sometimes from one of the other mechanics: What did he do in his tower? How much control did he have over his powers? How much were his senses affected? How did his spirit body work? And finally, when Colton thought he couldn't take any more, the questioning turned to Danny.

"It seems strange for an entity such as yourself to become so attached to a human," Zavier said. In his time, he and Castor would have been punished if they'd been caught together. Now it didn't seem to faze anyone. Then again, judging by how close the girl with the dagger—Astrid—and the other Indian girl were, perhaps it wasn't anything noteworthy.

"How exactly does that, er, work?" Liddy asked.

Colton pressed his lips together, and Daphne scooted forward. "I don't see how that's any of your business," she said.

Zavier shot Liddy an exasperated look, and she flopped back in her chair with a small *hmph*. "What we really want to know is how Danny was able to save Enfield," he said.

Daphne's breath caught. It was a tiny sound, barely audible, but Colton heard it and worried Zavier had, too.

"What do you mean?" Colton asked, feigning ignorance.

"You know exactly what I mean. Matthias—you recall him, I hope?—was bombing towers around London. He'd planned to attack yours next, until your central cog was stolen." He glanced at Colton's cog holder, then at Daphne, who went pink. She, of course, had been the one who had stolen it.

"Danny somehow prevented Matthias from exchanging your central cog with that of Maldon's clock spirit all on his own. To me, this seems implausible. Unless . . ." Zavier leaned forward, his chair creaking loudly. "Unless he did something unexpected. Or had help."

"I don't know how he did it," Colton lied, trying to avoid his penetrating gaze.

Of course he knew. Danny had told him, and more than that, Colton had seen it. Felt it. The small cog Colton had given Danny—just as Big Ben had given Colton one of his own small cogs—had reacted strangely to Danny's blood. Danny had been able to start and stop the time in Enfield, so long as that connection held fast.

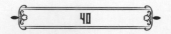

It was the same phenomenon Colton had discovered in his own time. Knowing that secret had led to his death and the building of the clock towers. Colton didn't want to imagine what Zavier would do with the information.

That's why they're holding Danny, he thought. *They could be torturing him right now.*

"Are you sure about your answer, Colton?" Zavier asked slowly, a threat lurking beneath each word.

"I don't know what else you want me to say. I don't know."

They stared at each other. Finally, Zavier sighed, then nodded to the others as he stood. "That's all our questions for now. Thank you for providing what answers you could." Judging by the set of his eyebrows, he was frustrated he hadn't learned more. Colton felt a vindicated sort of satisfaction.

The other clock mechanics filed out. When Zavier approached him, Colton stayed firmly seated.

"I want to speak to Daphne alone," Colton said. "And Meena."

"Why?"

"Because they're my friends, and I want to make sure they're all right."

"You can see for yourself that they're fine."

Colton fisted his hands on his knees. "If you want me to answer more questions in the future, you'll let me speak to them. *Alone.*"

Zavier weighed this for a moment before nodding. "You have two minutes. I'll be waiting outside." He closed the door behind him.

Daphne knelt before Colton. "What's wrong? What aren't you telling them?"

"We can help you with whatever you need," Meena whispered beside him.

Colton gathered his strength, but it was quickly fading. He could feel one of his unconscious spells coming on. Before it hit, he had to tell them all he knew.

It came out slowly at first. His words were uncertain, abrupt. But the more he spun out his story, the more fluid it became.

"They knew that blood could control time, and with Aetas gone, they had to use it." He closed his eyes. "They picked me. I was their sacrifice, Enfield's sacrifice. They used my . . . my blood, to build the tower. To give the cogs my power over time.

"I'm not just a spirit. I'm—rather, I was—human. And I'm remembering who I used to be. It's fighting with who I am now. I don't know who *Colton* is, or if I ever really existed, or if I exist *now*. I don't know what I am anymore."

When he opened his eyes, he knew from the look on her face that Daphne didn't believe him. He was too scared to look at Meena, so he studied his lap instead.

"Colton . . . that's . . ." Daphne swallowed. "I don't know what to think."

"Clock towers weren't built that way," Meena argued. "We would know if they were."

"But no one knows how they were built," Daphne said fairly. "We tried to build a new tower near Maldon to restart the town, and it didn't do anything." Her hand hovered above Colton's, debating whether to touch him or not. "Are you sure about this? Are you sure it wasn't just a bad dream?"

"The clock spirit Danny and I met in Meerut was having strange dreams," Meena said. "And you said the spirit in Lucknow was having dreams as well."

Daphne nodded. "It could be something affecting all the spirits." She finally placed her hand on top of Colton's. "I don't think—"

There was an unexpected flash, like lightning striking metal. A painful jolt rocked his body, making the scar on his right side burn. A gasp tore through the air.

"Daphne!"

She staggered away from him, bracing herself against the wall as she retched. Meena moved to her side and started rubbing her back.

Colton remained in his seat, stunned, until Daphne turned back to face him, her eyes wet. Her face was the color of sour milk.

"Colton," she whispered. "Oh, God . . ."

He knew. When she had touched him, she had seen his memories. They had raced through his mind in a blur, landing painfully on his final moment. She'd seen the knife. She'd seen his blood.

Daphne fell to her knees, stifling a sob behind her hand. Meena looked between them, gaping.

Zavier chose that instant to open the door. "What—?" He stopped short, then frowned at Colton. "What's going on?"

"She . . ." Meena hesitated, still startled by the outburst. "She's overcome with all that's happened. She needs rest."

Daphne's eyes locked with Colton's across the room. With a look, he tried to tell her that he was sorry, that he hadn't meant for her to see. Her own gaze said she understood. And in an instant, Daphne's expression had hardened again. The resolve in her eyes had tripled.

Zavier's eyes shifted warily to each of them. "I'll escort Miss Richards to her room. Colton, you'll be taken to a more comfortable room as well. No more cell for you."

Colton wasn't sure if Zavier expected thanks for this "kindness"; he certainly wasn't getting any. Cell, room—in this place, they were the same.

"We're doing this for your own good," Zavier said when Colton reached the door. "You'll see that, in time."

If Colton survived that long.

W hat happened?" Meena demanded as she stood by the window, arms crossed. The midmorning light gave her hair a reddish glow.

Daphne sat on her bed, holding her head in her hands. Zavier had been cross after the meeting yesterday, and hadn't given them the chance to talk about her revelation about Colton. Daphne doubted she could have been coherent, anyway; she'd been reeling ever since touching Colton's hand.

That one small touch had transferred something to her— something electric and terrifying. In her mind, she had seen Colton as someone else entirely. Someone who might have been the human he insisted he was. And then, the blood . . .

A small voice chanted in the back of her head: *It can't be true. It can't be true. It can't—*

But she had seen it. *Smelled* it. Coppery and inescapable.

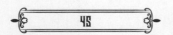

"I don't know how to explain it," Daphne mumbled. She began twisting her fingers together in an effort not to tap them against her thighs. That was a warning sign, the tapping; it meant she needed to smoke.

"Colton *did* something to you. I saw it."

"He didn't do anything to me. Not intentionally, I don't think." Daphne swallowed the lump in her throat. "Meena . . . what he said was true. All of it."

The girl shook her head. "The towers—"

"I *saw* it!" Daphne rubbed her aching temple. "Damn it, I *saw* what they did to him!"

She related it all as best she could, from the churning ocean Colton had waded into to the glint of sun on the knife that had ended him.

The mattress dipped as Meena settled beside her. "But . . . why?"

"It was the only way. After Aetas died, time had to be controlled somehow."

Meena tugged on her braid. Pull, pull. Pause. Pull. "Do you think they know?" she whispered, nodding to the door. "Do you think this is the reason they're taking down the towers?"

"No. They can't, or else Colton wouldn't have kept it a secret." Daphne knuckled her forehead with a frown. "Zavier said something about Aetas. About 'freeing' him. Whatever it is they're working toward, that's at its center."

"Do you think Akash might know what they're planning?"

There was hesitation in Meena's voice that echoed the rage

in Daphne's heart. For the past week, Daphne had been left to her own devices. In that time, she had kept a lookout for some means of escape. She'd found the galley, a room full of plants, and a smithy run by an irritable smith named Dae, but nothing in the ways of a viable route.

Then, yesterday after Colton's interrogation, Daphne had finally spotted something: a hangar door. Her stomach had leapt at the sight of it, but before she could creep nearer, she had been stopped by a familiar voice.

Akash.

He had come to speak to her through her bedroom door earlier in the week, to apologize for what he'd said and done. She had covered her ears until he went away.

But in that moment, she had felt rooted.

"Daphne, we need to talk."

"I told you not to call me that."

Akash sighed, running his hands violently through his hair. "Will you please listen to what I have to say?"

"I've already heard it."

"Then let me hear what you have to say. You can yell at me all you like, call me whatever names you think I deserve."

Daphne didn't respond. Her grief made her tired, and it was too much effort to stoke her rage. So she merely continued walking down the corridor, determined to map out the hallways leading to the hangar door.

"Da—Miss Richards, please!" Akash begged. "Say something, even if it's that you hate me!"

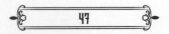

She hadn't even given him that.

Meena had had similar run-ins with her brother, but she wouldn't tell Daphne about them. The redness of the girl's eyes was enough for Daphne to guess.

"No," Daphne said in answer to Meena's question. "I don't think they would tell him."

Meena hummed in agreement. "What did he mean," she asked, "when he said you were more British than Indian?"

Heat crawled up Daphne's neck. "Only that my father was half-Indian. I told him about my parents when we were stationed in Lucknow."

Meena blinked at her. "Oh. You . . . don't look it."

Daphne sighed; she wondered how many times she'd heard those words, and how many more times she would have to face them. "I know."

"That's wonderful, though. I had no idea." Meena hesitated, as if debating on whether or not to hug her. Instead, she cleared her throat and played with the hem of her kameez. "Well, whatever Zavier's goal is, I think they have something planned for us. I keep seeing them in little groups, whispering."

Daphne could sense it, too. Something taut, expectant. Like a rubber band about to snap.

"We have to get away before they act on their plans," Daphne said softly. "As soon as we find Danny, we'll create a distraction and head for the hangar. I found a route we can take, but we'll need a way to break the lock on the hangar door."

"I'll try to get my gun back from them. I can shoot the lock off."

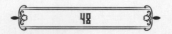

"Good. Then we just need to get in there and . . ." She sighed. "Try to fly the plane back to Agra, I suppose."

Meena made a skeptical noise. They both knew it was imperfect, but what other choice did they have?

There was a sudden knock at the door, and they both jumped. It swung open to reveal Zavier on the other side. "I'd like you both to come with me."

"Why?" Meena demanded.

"It's time we had an important discussion."

Meena stiffened beside her, but Daphne felt oddly calm. Something about Zavier's posture, his expression, made her curious.

"We've been putting it off out of necessity, but we can't delay any longer," Zavier continued.

Daphne wrapped her hand around Meena's and squeezed gently. "As long as it doesn't take all day," she said.

Zavier pressed his lips into a thin line. "We wouldn't want that."

They followed Zavier into the belly of the airship. The space was eerie, much too large for a dozen people. Earlier that week, Zavier's aunt Jo had told her it belonged to her late husband, and that it had once served in warfare.

Daphne didn't like the implications of that.

Zavier stopped at a door and let his hand hover over the handle. Edmund and another crewmember, a Sikh man named Anish, stood guard on either side. When Zavier sent Edmund a questioning gaze, Edmund nodded in response. Zavier took a deep breath and opened the door.

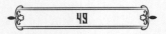

Sunlight illuminated a scratched table surrounded by chairs and glinted off a pitcher, the water droplets on its tin surface spangling like tiny flecks of gold.

A young man dressed in a tan jumpsuit sat at the table. He had dark, somewhat shaggy hair, as if he'd gone without a haircut for a couple months. He leaned back in the chair, his scuffed boots resting casually on the tabletop, his arms folded across his chest. He'd been glaring at the opposite wall, but turned as they entered the room.

Daphne gasped.

The young man shot to his feet. It was no wonder she hadn't recognized him; he was taller, tanner, his face a little more defined, as if he had aged three years in three months.

"Daphne," he said.

Before she could open her mouth to respond, he jumped over the chair and gathered her in his arms. She squawked, but held him just as tightly. *Thank God. Thank God . . .*

He stepped back and took in her face. His now-golden complexion made his eyes even greener.

"Danny." She touched the sleeve of his jumpsuit. "It *is* Danny, isn't it?"

"Last I checked," he said with a goofy smile. His eyes flicked behind her and then widened. "Meena!"

"I was so afraid," Meena said, her words muffled in his shoulder as she hugged him. "No one knew what had happened to you!"

"Well." He eased back and gestured to the walls. "This is what

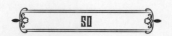

happened to me." As Danny noticed Zavier for the first time, his eyes hardened. "And him."

"We're on our way to being best mates," Zavier said dryly before slapping a file onto the table. "Please, sit."

"Are you all right?" Danny murmured as they took their seats. He'd seen the burn scar on Meena's cheek. "Who's hurt you?"

"No one. We're fine." Daphne caught Meena's eye and they shared a nod. They would need to find a way to speak to him, to share their plan, without being overheard. "We're all right, Danny."

He didn't look convinced.

Zavier cleared his throat. "I feel compelled to remind you three that there are others outside the room, so please don't get any ideas." Danny clucked his tongue. "I've been waiting for Danny to return so that we might have this meeting. I can't tell you how relieved I am to finally get this underway."

Daphne could tell. Zavier's muscles were looser, his eyes brighter. He even seemed . . . *happy.*

"Wait. Danny, where have you been?" Daphne demanded. "We were told you were shot!"

He grimaced and touched a spot high on his chest, near his clavicle. "I was." He unbuttoned the collar of the jumpsuit and pushed it far enough down his shoulder to expose the wound. Meena inhaled sharply. The surrounding skin was swollen and red, but the actual bullet hole was a dark pink.

"He's been in recovery," Zavier said impatiently as Danny refastened the jumpsuit. "Anyway, Danny knows more about this than the two of you, so let me briefly fill you in. You know the creation of the clock towers happened after the death of Aetas, correct?" They nodded, but Daphne's insides squirmed. She could still smell coppery blood. Colton's blood.

The story flew out of Zavier's mouth, almost too fast for Daphne to follow. Chronos, the creator of time, had designated responsibilities to each of the Gaian gods he made: Terra for earth, Caelum for sky, Oceana for sea, and Aetas for time. But Chronos hadn't expected Aetas to give some of this power to humans, the time servants who helped stabilize that power.

"Chronos was enraged," Zavier explained. "He trapped Aetas in a prison beneath the ocean. But without Aetas to guide it, time slipped out of control, and so the clock towers were built in an attempt to restore order."

Daphne squirmed again as Colton's memories flashed through her mind. She pressed a hand to her stomach and spared a glance at Danny, but his eyes were fixed on the water pitcher, his face carefully blank.

"Chronos made us believe Aetas was dead. Chronos had grown tired of his role, and he wanted humans to drive themselves to extinction. I don't think he wants this responsibility anymore, watching over the earth. But he didn't count on the time servants—now the clock mechanics—to do the work for him. And," he said, voice quivering with excitement, "we no longer have to."

Zavier explained he was a follower of Oceana as well as Aetas. He had prayed to her as often as he had prayed to a god he once thought dead. And one day, she had answered. She had

called him to the ocean. She had given him a clue to Aetas's prison.

And there, where the water flowed, he had found the secret to freeing time.

"It's right there," he said, hands flat against the tabletop. "Right in our grasp. If we free Aetas, time is freed with him. No more clock towers, no more fear of Stopped cities, no more loved ones trapped forever." He glanced meaningfully at Danny. "If we find a way to free Aetas, this can all be over."

Danny snorted. "Over? You think it could ever be that simple? Our entire lifestyle will change. The world itself will change."

"For the better," Zavier stressed. "Danny, I know you did something to time when you saved Enfield. It could very well be the thing we need to release Aetas from his prison!"

Danny made a rude gesture. "Sod off."

Daphne's hands curled into fists under the table. Danny's words—*our entire lifestyle will change*—soured her stomach. For years she had fought for normalcy. For a life that, if not ideal, was at least *stable*. Working for the Mechanics Union had provided that for her. She maintained her parents' empty house, she worked hard, and she made sure her mother was kept comfortable in St. Agnes' Home for Women.

London was all she had. It was her home, her haven, the place where her past and future waited, and she would do everything in her power to return.

She couldn't afford for Zavier's goals to touch hers.

"It sounds mad." Meena shook her head. "I don't like this."

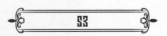

Taking a deep breath, Zavier composed himself again. "You don't have to like it, Miss Kapoor. But you will have to accept it."

"And what does that mean?" Daphne demanded.

"It means that I'm putting you three to work. Tomorrow."

They looked at one another before Danny cleared his throat. "Come again?"

"We have a mission. Since Danny isn't willing to tell me his secret, we'll be using the water we've collected from Aetas's prison to free a city from its tower. I believe this demonstration will help you all understand the importance of what the *Prometheus* is doing firsthand."

"Absolutely not," Daphne said. "I'm not taking part in that."

"Me, neither," Meena added.

"What makes you think any of us will?" Danny gave a pitying little laugh. "Come off it."

Zavier carefully smoothed back his hair, examining the table-top. "I have one good reason."

Daphne's stomach dropped. She knew what he would say before the words even crossed his lips.

Zavier locked eyes with Danny. "We have Colton."

For a moment, the room was utterly still. Even the sunlight seemed dimmer.

Danny's body had gone rigid. "What?" The word was quiet, strangled.

"He's here. On the *Prometheus*." Zavier let that sink in for a second. "As our hostage."

Meena screamed as Danny threw his chair back, coming at

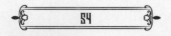

Zavier so fast that the boy could barely put up a defense. Danny successfully landed a blow before Zavier caught his arm and twisted it behind his back, making him cry out. The door flew open and Anish ran in, Edmund on his heels.

Anish dragged a thrashing Danny away with little effort. Danny struggled, his face red.

Zavier gingerly touched his jaw. One lock of hair had fallen out of place. "I should have expected that."

"Where is he?" Danny's voice was low and raw, his chest heaving with every breath. "Show me!"

Zavier lowered his hand. "I can't, Danny. Colton's our hostage for a reason."

Daphne swore. She should have seen Zavier's plan sooner.

"If you refuse to help with our mission," Zavier said, walking around the table to where Danny was still being restrained by Anish, "and if you don't tell me about what you did to the time in Enfield, then . . ." He sighed, and it almost sounded like he felt an ounce of regret. "Well, then Colton will be the one paying the price."

Danny stared at Zavier with such hatred that it transformed him into something else, hot and fatal, like a dying star. Daphne heard his ragged breaths, his desperate swallow.

"If you agree to help us," Zavier said quietly, "then we won't lay a finger on him. I give you my word." He bent his head forward slightly. "Well? Do you accept?"

Daphne balled her hands into fists. She mentally begged him not to give in. There had to be another way.

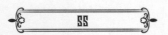

But even she couldn't see one.

Danny finally sagged in Anish's arms. "Yes," he whispered to the floor. "I accept."

The clang of metal against metal echoed in Danny's ears. It wasn't enough—not nearly loud enough. He grabbed the tin cup from the table and threw it after the pitcher, striking the wall with a dull crash.

Left with nothing else to throw, he punched the door and kicked the walls.

"Fucking—gormless—*bastard*!"

How could he be in this room, in here, when Colton was out *there?* He put his face in his hands and groaned. He was going to crack open. His body would split and tear apart and there would be Danny chunks all over the walls and *Colton was on the ship.*

Shaking too hard to stand, he crumpled to the floor. The air was hot and he could barely breathe. Panic. Elation. Rage.

Colton.

"Where are you?" he whispered to the floor.

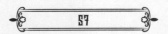

He drew the small cog from his pocket. It was about the size of a sixpence, bronze, and dull from lack of polishing. It had come from Colton's clock tower, from when a mechanic had forgotten it there. Colton had given it to Danny after an argument they'd had in what seemed another lifetime.

As he touched it, there was a small quiver of recognition, as if the cog knew that Colton was near.

Danny rubbed his thumb against the metal. Zavier wanted his secret, a secret connected to this cog. When his blood had touched it a year ago, he'd been able to control Enfield's time, however briefly.

Armed with that knowledge, Zavier might be able to use it for his own means, whatever that entailed. If the blood of a clock mechanic was strong enough to break Aetas's prison . . .

The clock spirits would vanish.

Colton would die.

Danny closed his eyes and clutched the cog, pressing his knuckles to his forehead. He was faint, his body oddly light. He had been told not to overexert himself. His gunshot wound throbbed as a painful reminder.

He wasn't sure how much time had passed since he'd been shot. A week? Two? Zavier had taken him to a nursing station in a small southern Indian village staffed by volunteers from Europe. They had watched over Danny while he was subjected to surgery, fever, pain. Truthfully, he didn't remember much beyond the smell of blood, the nurses' white caps, and the heat.

When his fever had broken and he could walk around well

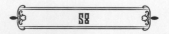

enough on his own, Zavier had returned to claim him. Danny had considered running, finding the nearest cantonment where he could wire for help, but Zavier had contacts at the nursing station as well. Danny had been guarded day and night.

Now here he was, muddled and infuriated. Still wounded. And now *this*.

Danny staggered back to his feet and pounded on the door again. Maybe if he yelled loud enough, Colton would hear him. Wouldn't it just be that sadist's way, putting Colton in a room nearby, so close and yet so far.

He wrenched at the handle and kicked the door until it flew open. Danny staggered back and nearly toppled onto the bed.

"Bloody racket you're making in here," Edmund said. "What's gotten into you?"

"What's gotten *into* me?" Danny panted. "You're holding Colton and everyone else hostage, you're forcing me to do your work, I was *shot*, and you're asking *what's gotten into me?*"

"All right, settle down." Edmund closed the door, but stationed himself between it and Danny. "There anything I can help with?"

Danny laughed hollowly. "Yes. Tell Zavier to land this ship and let us all go."

Edmund rolled his eyes. Danny had to admit that they were nice eyes. Dark blue, like navy ink.

"I know it's difficult, but I promise there's a good reason for it all."

"You have no idea," Danny snapped. "No idea what this is like. I can't even see my—!"

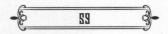

His what? Was there even a word, a title, that would properly describe what Colton was to him?

Edmund continued more softly. "Look, I'm sorry. Truly. Z can be a little, er . . . impassioned."

"A bastard, more like."

Edmund grinned. "Yes, that too."

Danny stared at him, a thousand questions racing through his mind. He waited to see which would reach the finish line first. "Why are you even here? You're not a clock mechanic."

"I've been mates with Zavier for a long time. Me and Liddy both. I'm doing this for him."

"*Why?* He's horrible."

Edmund shook his head. "He's not, I promise. Zavier's only doing this because he thinks it'll help everyone in the long run."

"What about me? What about Colton and the other clock spirits?" He thought about Aditi in Meerut as her tower fell. "What about them? They don't deserve this."

The young man took a deep breath and let it out with a little grunt. "That's between you and Z, to be frank. But"—he scratched at his shaggy hair and pursed his lips—"I'll see what I can do, yeah? For Colton."

"Will you please let me see him? Please?"

"Z wants you to do the mission first." Before Danny could protest, Edmund turned to the door. "You look peaky. I'll bring something up for you."

Danny sat on the bed, his strength dissolving. Edmund gave

him a once-over, a worried line forming between his eyebrows. "When Zavier's ready, he'll tell you."

"Tell me what?"

"His other reason for doing all this." Then he left.

Danny lay back and stared at the ceiling. He lifted the cog, now hot and damp from being trapped in his hand, and pressed it against his chest. Over his heart.

Zavier chose Lyallpur for the mission. It was located in the northwest of India, the area referred to as the Punjab. Some of the crew had already scoped it out and drawn a comprehensive map. One look and Danny knew this was going to be far more difficult than he'd imagined.

They waited until midnight. Jo warned them to be safe before the Scottish mechanic, Ivor, took her hands and brought them to his lips as he said goodbye. Danny raised an eyebrow. Were they . . . together? Judging by the uncomfortable look on Zavier's face, it was a safe assumption.

Daphne and Meena were led off by Ivor. Daphne looked over her shoulder at Danny before disappearing into the ship's hangar. He wanted to tell her to be safe, too, but the look in her eyes told him that he needed the luck more than she did.

As Zavier ushered the others to the second hangar, Danny pulled him aside.

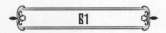

"You're going to kill them," Danny said. "The spirit."

"It's not killing. We're freeing them." Zavier made a shooing motion, and Danny had no choice but to follow the others into the hangar—rather, he was pushed inside—and comforted himself with the image of Zavier falling off the clock tower.

Although Danny could sometimes forget he was on an airship while aboard the *Prometheus*, a smaller plane like the one they flew over the Punjabi plains couldn't conceal the turbulence that churned his stomach. They landed a mile from the city, under cover of darkness. As the others unpacked their equipment, Danny staggered off and vomited. It wasn't just the plane ride; it was the whole idea of what they were about to do. What Zavier was about to do.

I can't let him. I have to stop it somehow.

But Colton . . .

He startled as Prema touched his back and handed him a canteen of water. "We're ready."

After rinsing out his mouth, he followed them into the city. Lights winked in the windows and at the top of tall buildings. Domed roofs rose over the crooked streets, arches leading to uninhabited alleyways.

A few British officers patrolled the streets. At the sight of them, Danny's heart leapt hopefully, but one look at Zavier crushed his hope like a grape under his heel. There were still Daphne and Meena to think of, and Colton. And Akash, wherever he was.

Besides, if he revealed what they'd come to do, he'd probably be lumped in with the rest of Zavier's lot and labeled a terrorist.

There was an invisible leash that led from Danny's neck to Zavier's hand, and everyone knew it.

Eight streets connected to the circular clearing around the clock tower, the layout of the city purposefully modeled after the Union Jack. When Zavier had gone over the plan with the crew yesterday, he'd pointed out the clearing on the map. "There are eight bazaars around the tower, each connected to one of these streets, which means they're never empty. It'll be near to impossible to sneak into the tower without being seen."

"So," Edmund had picked up, clapping his hands together with glee, "there'll be a lively show in Street Number Three starring Anish, Astrid, and me." The French girl had sneered as she played with her knives. Or maybe she'd smiled. It was hard to tell.

When they reached the tower, Danny couldn't help but be impressed by the size and construction of it. Columned arches adorned all four sides, windows cut between molded beams, topped with an elaborate domed roof with small spires on each corner. Four clock faces shone over Lyallpur so that everyone in the surrounding streets could see the time. Decorative fountains added the final detail to the beautiful scene.

"People call it the Ghanta Ghar," Prema whispered at his side. "The Hour House. And that red stone? It was brought from the Sangla Hills."

Danny forced himself to swallow. "And you're going to tear it down."

There was a glimmer of regret in her eyes. "Yes."

Zavier hadn't lied about the hub being a busy place. Indian men congregated around the bazaars, which were still open even at this hour, while British residents and servants went on about their business. Danny couldn't help the sensation that everyone who passed was staring at him.

Zavier motioned the crew toward one of the bazaars, and they gathered around a silk stand, where Prema pretended to feel some of the cloth and made sounds of interest for the sake of the vendor who eyed their party.

"When will they begin?" Felix whispered to Zavier, his Austrian accent a strange contrast to their surroundings. An ex-grenadier in his thirties, Felix had been recruited by Zavier and Jo for his specific and deadly skill with explosives.

"Soon. Just give them time to prepare."

The group lingered at the stall for a few minutes more. Prema asked the vendor questions in Urdu as Danny looked around constantly, counting the number of soldiers. Sweat dampened his undershirt. It was cooler here than it had been in the south, and the breeze made him shiver.

He jumped at the crack of gunfire. Several people cried out in surprise, and the soldiers ran toward the street where the sound had come from. Away from them.

The vendor began to pack up his wares in a hurry. Others did the same, and curious bystanders followed the soldiers toward the distraction.

"Now," Zavier whispered sharply.

The group slunk across the clearing, using the thinning

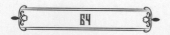

crowd as cover, until they reached the clock tower. Zavier darted to the door and found it locked; a quick moment with a pick and it swung open. Prema pulled Danny past the threshold.

Zavier motioned for them to duck to the floor as he peered out a window. Their harsh breaths were drowned out by the clock's loud ticking. The tower exuded a power that seemed to ooze down the very walls, dripping onto the back of Danny's neck and traveling down his spine. A shudder wracked his body.

"We're all right," Zavier whispered. "No one saw us."

The others followed him to the stairs that led up to the clockwork. Danny had to brace himself against the wall, trailing at a slower pace. The stairs creaked under their weight, and a dark, swaying shadow made him start before he realized it was only the pendulum.

He thought about Colton's tower, the smell of wood and dust and metal, the familiar chimes, the light of sunset gleaming through the large clock face. The Lyallpur tower felt different—aloof and cold. Wary.

As Felix made for the clock room to set up the bomb, Zavier turned back to Danny, his gray eyes piercing through the dimness.

"Talk to it," Zavier ordered.

Ivor had placed Daphne and Meena on opposite windows of the plane, their role being to watch the sky for any other aircraft. But Daphne kept looking over her shoulder at Ivor and the way he

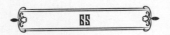

flipped through the controls, skilled at keeping the plane at a low yet unsuspecting altitude.

He'd told them his job was to wait for the signal from the clock tower, whatever that meant. Then he would fly over and drop the water stored in the underbelly of the plane, the same water that floated above Aetas's prison, dense with magical properties. Daphne could feel it sloshing below her feet, warm and restless.

Although the plane rumbled its steady mechanical song, the silence began to eat at her. "Why are you with Zavier and the others?" she asked. Meena turned at the question, equally curious.

Ivor glanced back at them, surprised. "Well, ah . . . bit of a long story, that, but I s'pose I've taken a fancy to Jo."

"There has to be another reason than that."

Ivor was silent for a while, focused on the gentle circles he was flying above Lyallpur. "It's no easy thing, being a mechanic from Scotland. Not since the rebellion, I reckon."

He must have meant the Jacobite uprising a century before, when the Scots had tried to put their own monarch on the English throne. Much like the Indian rebellion, the uprising had failed, sending a bloody, violent wave across the country. If Daphne remembered her history textbooks correctly, there had been another, much smaller attempt at uprising nearly fifty years ago, but that too had failed.

"Your Mechanics Union set the basis for ours," Ivor went on. "We have a similar setup, but it's not as well organized. Besides that, the English Union controls everythin' we do. Bet I couldn't even scratch my own arse without being told first."

Meena's shoulders shook as if she wanted to laugh. "I know the feeling," she said.

"So, what, this is your personal brand of rebellion?" Daphne asked.

"When ye put it like that it sounds rather trite." He shrugged. "If the towers were gone, if the mechanics were gone, it'd be one less thing my country has to worry about, ken?"

Meena seemed thoughtful, but Daphne stiffened. *If the towers were gone, if the mechanics were gone . . .* That was the one thing she couldn't have happen. She looked over at Meena, wondering if they ought to try to knock out Ivor and steal the plane, but the Indian girl caught her eye and shook her head.

Danny, she mouthed.

Frustrated, Daphne sat back and glared out the window, wondering if he was faring any better.

Danny watched the gears of the Lyallpur tower turn and reached for the small cog in his pocket. *Talk to it*, Zavier had told him, as if it were that easy. But when he opened his mouth to speak, he found his voice had fled.

When Zavier had first told him his role, Danny had refused, arguing vehemently against it. In the end, Zavier had simply turned to Edmund. "Bring one of the spirit's cogs," he'd said, "and a hammer and chisel."

Danny had given in before they could carry out the threat.

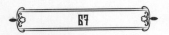

Now in the tower, with his fingers wrapped around the small cog, he took a deep breath. "I know you're in here," he said, quietly, almost to himself. "I know the spirit of this clock tower is here. Please, I need to speak with you. Will you show yourself?"

There was no response. Danny took out the cog and fiddled with it, listening to the sounds of Felix setting up his device above. Zavier tensely watched the stairs, motioning for Danny to continue, to keep the spirit distracted while Felix worked.

After another quiet moment, Danny said, "Aap khatare mein hain."

Prema looked at him, confused. Zavier's brow furrowed.

"What was that?" he demanded. "Prema, what did he say?"

But before she could answer, they were suddenly aware of another presence in the room. Maybe it was the word *danger* that had made the difference—Danny had asked Meena to teach him the phrase—because now a man stood a few feet away from them, glaring. His skin was brownish red, his hair copper, his eyes amber. A faint glow illuminated his body.

"Hello," Danny whispered. "I'm not here to hurt you. I just want to speak with you."

The spirit looked up the stairs, then said something in an Indian dialect.

"I'm sorry, what?"

Prema responded in Hindi, to which the spirit replied sharply. "I told him we're here to check on the mechanism," she said with a grimace. "He told us to get out."

Danny smirked. "Fancy that."

"What did you say to the spirit, Danny?" Zavier demanded. "What made him finally appear?"

Danny met Prema's gaze with a challenge, and she sighed. "He told the spirit he was in danger."

Zavier hissed between his teeth. "You unbelievable *idiot*."

The spirit started yelling, gesturing sharply at them. Danny didn't need Prema to translate that the spirit was ordering them all out of his tower.

"Did you really think I would stand by and watch?" Danny said over the yelling. "Look, he's terrified! His tower is beautiful, it's— it's *life*. And you want to snuff it out just to chase after a myth!"

Prema was trying to calm the spirit. Danny, hoping he'd be understood, turned and yelled, "They're going to destroy your tower!"

Silence fell, swift and tense. Even Felix stopped moving above. Then the spirit glowed brighter, and the clock faces above began to glow with him.

Zavier swore and ran up the stairs. "Felix, quickly!"

The spirit winked out, reappearing at the top of the stairs. He knocked Zavier back with a sweep of his arm. Zavier tumbled down the stairs, and Felix grabbed his bag before racing down after him. The tower's energy swelled, *tick tocks* booming in the confined space as the hands of the four clock faces swung in separate directions.

"Scheisse!" Felix cursed.

"Everyone out!" Zavier called as he struggled to his feet. He turned to glare at Danny, who was laughing. "Don't think this setback changes anything."

The tower rumbled as the spirit screamed above. Time distorted around them, making them stagger. Danny's limbs felt as if they were being pulled from his body, his heart racing too fast and making his vision blacken.

"I'm not leaving," Danny yelled over the noise, over the pain. Zavier yelled in vexation and punched him in the stomach with his metal hand. Danny doubled over, choking as he tried to breathe. Zavier hoisted him over his shoulder.

"Let's go!"

Everything jumped and rattled. Danny bit his tongue and tasted blood. The street was a dizzying blur of light and sound, and everything was bathed in red. Water sprinkled the back of his neck. *Rain?*

"Ivor dropped the water! Go!"

Being jostled on Zavier's shoulder made his stomach burn, and his bullet wound raked claws across his shoulder and chest. He tried to fight his way free, but Zavier only held him tighter as he ran.

And then Danny heard it: the roar of fire, the crumbling of stone.

He twisted around and saw the tower's clock faces explode in sprays of glass. Flames licked the inside of the tower as its foundation caved and the structure teetered. A golden light rose from the wet stone around it.

"No!" He fought against Zavier's grip again. "*No!*"

Danny didn't know what happened next; a strange tingling took over his body, followed by darkness. When he woke in the small aircraft, his head and stomach were sore, his mouth paper-dry.

It took all his strength, but he turned his head and looked out the window. A plume of smoke rose from the heart of the city like a funeral pyre. Lyallpur was running on time. No gray barrier. No clock tower.

"I'm going to kill you," he mumbled. Zavier, flying the plane, pretended not to hear.

When they returned to the *Prometheus*, the others were already waiting outside the hangar. Everyone looked fine, although Daphne was frighteningly pale and Edmund sported a black eye.

The buzzing in Danny's body turned to liquid energy. He threw himself at Zavier, wanting to pound him within an inch of his life. Before he could so much as grab him, Zavier pushed him to the ground, yanking his arm up behind his back. Daphne and Meena raced forward.

"Stop!" Zavier shouted. "Everyone, just—stop!"

And they did. All eyes were fixed on Zavier and Danny, some with horror, some with curiosity. Daphne breathed hard through bared teeth, her blue eyes crackling.

"Let him go," she demanded.

"Not until he understands." Grabbing a fistful of Danny's hair in his free hand, Zavier yanked his head up, making Danny wince. "I didn't just bring you on the mission to distract the

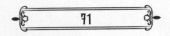

spirit. You needed to see what we're capable of. If you don't tell me what you're hiding, this will happen again and again until I get answers. You may think the spirits are defenseless, but they're not. They could extinguish us in an instant if they so wanted to, as demonstrated tonight. And you believe that even with all that power, *they're* the ones in danger?

"You don't know anything, Danny. That spirit was going to kill us—even you." Zavier released his grip so suddenly that Danny toppled over. Daphne hurried to his side. "The world can survive without the spirits if Aetas is freed. So consider this: either we blow up the towers the messy way, or we free Aetas and let time resume its course without the fuss. You could be the difference, Danny. What you know about time, what you did in Enfield . . ." Zavier flexed his metal hand. "It could be the answer to freeing our lost god."

Danny was shaking too hard to stand, and had to lean on Daphne just to stay propped on his knees. "Do you expect me to let you keep destroying towers, to make me go on these bloody missions, when I know what will happen in the end? Colton will disappear. He'll *die*, and you'll be the one to kill him!"

"It doesn't have to be that way," Zavier replied calmly.

"There's no other option! You said so yourself—"

"I'm willing to strike a bargain with you, one that will benefit us both. If you'll listen."

It hurt to breathe, but Daphne and her familiar scent of bergamot helped calm him down, if only slightly.

"What bargain?" Danny asked.

Zavier cleared his throat and nodded to Jo, who looked on nearby. "Would you please make peppermint tea for Danny? I'll need a whiskey."

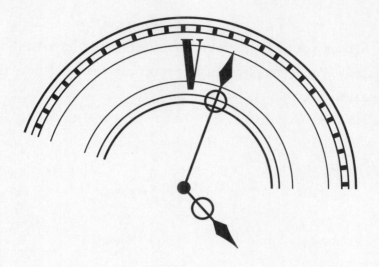

His memories sometimes blurred together, and it became diffi-cult to pick them apart again. He knew that Abigail had never been to the ocean, though he'd wanted to take her so many times. Yet he dreamed that she stood on the shore, the wind tugging at her dress, her hair flying about her in eerie silence. No coughing, no rattling breaths, no fever. Just Abi—his Abi—and the sea.

Colton struggled with consciousness, losing himself over and over to the darkness that went hand in hand with weakness. There was Castor, fooling about behind Instructor Beele's back as they learned more about Aetas and time. Castor kissing him, promising that everything he'd ever wanted would come true. His mother and father working endlessly, smiling at him when-ever he could help.

"Please stop," Colton whispered to the memories. "I can't take any more."

"Haven't done anything yet."

He opened his eyes, taking in a young man with olive skin, his hair a cloud of dark curls, wearing an apron over his clothes. He looked Colton over with interest.

"First time I've actually seen you awake," the young man said. "How d'you feel?"

Colton tried to move, and was glad when he could. He sat up and remembered—again—that he was no longer in a cell. Zavier had been true to his word, and though the room was small and bare, it was infinitely better than metal bars.

Colton swung his legs over the side of the bed and looked up at the stranger. "I suppose I feel the same."

"Hm." The young man glanced at Colton's cog holder. "My name's Dae. I've been trying to find a way to strengthen your conductor."

"My . . . what?"

"*Conductor.* The getup on your back. It's a conductor for your power, isn't it?"

Colton slowly nodded. "I call it a cog holder."

"Right. Well, whatever it is, Zave told me I need to take another look at it."

"I can't be too far from it."

"Then come with me to the smithy."

The smithy, as it turned out, was a lot more interesting than Colton had expected. He recalled the blacksmiths in Enfield, the ringing of their hammers at their forges, making weapons and cookware and all sorts of common tools.

This place was something entirely different. Here, there were . . . *things*. Things he didn't recognize. Peculiar things. A star-shaped device spun on the wall, a tipping scale was making tinny sounds, and a man-shaped automaton without a head slumped in one corner. Every so often the automaton lifted a finger, as if about to say something important, before its arm fell with a clatter.

"What on earth?" Colton touched the scale, which began to rock back and forth with increasingly agitated noises. "What is all this?"

"My inventions," Dae said. "Or the starts of them. Most are failures, but some turned out all right." He gestured at Colton. "The conductor, please."

Colton hesitated, but when Dae remained standing there, hand extended, he carefully slipped the cog holder off and handed it to him. Dae accepted it with grave caution.

"I'll do nothing to the cogs themselves," Dae said, "but I need to study them. D'you mind?"

Colton shook his head, then sat on the floor. If he ended up passing out, it would be easier to do it down there. Dae seemed to forget the clock spirit was even there while he pondered the device that Christopher Hart and the smiths in London had built.

At the thought, Colton's mind flared with guilt. Christopher was no doubt furious with him for leaving, and anxious about Danny. Colton had once promised he'd do nothing to put Danny in jeopardy, but it seemed that promise—like so many others—had been in vain.

Colton leaned against the anvil near the currently banked forge. He longed to close his eyes, but kept them trained on Dae as the inventor made gentle taps against the cog holder with a small hammer, each tap causing an odd buzzing sensation down his spine.

"I like your hair," Colton said.

"Uh. Thanks." Dae frowned. "It's from my mother. She was Greek."

Colton rubbed a thumb over a white smudge on his trousers. "I like Greek things. Or I think I do. I like Greek stories."

Dae glanced at him, eyebrows raised. "Myths, you mean?"

"Yes. Like Perseus, and Psyche, and Troy."

The inventor smiled. It was small, but it took years from his face. "I like them, too. My mother used to tell them to me." He bent back over the cog holder. "Zave likes them, too. The ship is called the *Prometheus*, after all."

Colton stiffened. He knew that story. The Titan Prometheus, stealing fire for the humans, imprisoned by an angry Zeus.

"It's like Aetas," Colton said to himself. "He gave humans the power to control time, so Chronos had him killed."

Dae paused. "You believe Aetas was killed?"

"He *was* killed."

"Zave didn't tell you? Aetas isn't dead." With a shrug, Dae turned back to the cog holder. "That's why we're all here. To free him from the prison Chronos created."

"The prison . . ." Colton's voice faded away. Aetas, imprisoned like Prometheus.

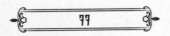

Aetas, freed.

When the smithy door opened, he didn't bother to look over his shoulder.

"There you are."

Colton scowled at Zavier's familiar baritone.

"Colton, I need you to come with me."

It took all his willpower not to say something rude. "Why?"

"Please don't be difficult."

Dae looked from the door to Colton. "I'm done for the moment, anyway, but I'll need another look soon," he said as he handed the holder back.

"Thank you." Colton stood with difficulty and slipped it on.

"Follow me," Zavier said before disappearing into the hall. Colton clenched his teeth and did what he was told, because what other alternative was there? Still, Dae's words refused to leave him alone.

"Is it true?" Colton blurted. "About Aetas. About freeing him."

Zavier hesitated before giving a tiny nod. "It would be much easier to believe he was gone, wouldn't it? But instead, he's trapped beneath the earth. We intend to change that." He hesitated again, but he must have known he had no reason to keep going. The return of Aetas could only mean one thing.

The return of time.

Colton felt . . . hollow. Used. The men from London who had stormed his town had claimed the god of time was dead, that only a sacrifice could restore time to Enfield. All of that undone with just a few words from Dae and Zavier.

His entire history, a sham.

Colton and Zavier arrived at a different room than the one in which Colton had been questioned, but he didn't ask about it. He didn't care anymore.

Zavier drew in a breath to say something, but in the end merely shook his head and, with a sigh, opened the door. He motioned for Colton to enter.

Colton complied without complaint. The sooner they got this over with, the better.

Danny stood as soon as the door opened. He'd been sitting on the edge of the settee, foot tapping impatiently on the faded cream rug, heart beating a nervous rhythm in his chest. His pulse drowned out all other sound. All that existed of him was the loud *thump thump* in his ears.

Until he saw him.

Colton walked into the room and stopped. His eyes were wide, his face strangely pale. But those eyes—they were the same amber shade, bright and otherworldly.

The door closed behind him.

They stared at each other, incapable of anything else. Colton's blond hair was disheveled, his stance wary. And his *clothes*. Danny realized with a blush that they were his own clothes. Colton took him in with the same strange look on his face that must have been on Danny's own. They stayed like that for some time, neither saying a word as they took stock of the other—noticing what was the same, what had changed.

Finally, Danny took a tentative step forward, and Colton mirrored the action. Another careful step, and another. Fear gripped his throat, choking his breaths and stinging his eyes. He was terrified this would end in a puff of smoke, that he would wake up in bed and find he was alone.

But when he raised his hand and touched it to Colton's cheek, there was no puff of smoke. No jolt awake. Danny exhaled a shaking sigh and lifted his other hand to frame Colton's face. Colton trailed his fingertips down Danny's cheeks, across his jaw, over his throat.

For a long while they stood there, leaning their foreheads together, Danny's breaths warm on Colton's mouth. They had been the same height before Danny left. Now Danny was an inch taller. Even that small difference hurt.

Colton put his hand on Danny's chest. Over his heart.

"Danny," he whispered.

"Colton," he whispered back.

Just like that, the spell was broken and Danny kissed him with all the force of his relief. They clutched each other tighter, harder, until it was impossible to breathe.

The world tipped and spun and danced. Lights exploded behind his eyes. Time wrapped Danny in its comfortable sleeve, forcing him to be aware of their bodies, the airship, the ground miles and miles below. And Colton's lips, urgent and familiar against his own.

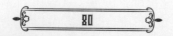

"Danny," Colton murmured against his mouth between kisses, as if he could only subside on the shape of his name, the feel of his lips. "Danny."

Happy, dizzy, Danny didn't dare tell Colton to stop. His need for air was overlooked until he forced himself to break away, gasping. Alarmed, the spirit guided him to sit on the settee and knelt before him. Spots swam in his vision, but he kept his eyes open on Colton.

"Sorry, forgot you had lungs. Are you all right?" Colton asked.

Danny nodded with a laugh that startled him for its brightness, its ringing, golden sound. "Yes. Yes, I'm all right." He swept back Colton's hair and kissed his forehead. "I'm all right, now."

He didn't know he was crying until Colton wiped a tear away. Danny rubbed a sleeve across his eyes. "You're really here."

Colton smiled weakly. "So are you."

They laughed. Their hands drifted together, their eyes locked. Then Colton began to unfasten the top of Danny's jumpsuit.

Danny wasn't sure whether to stop him or not. He sat frozen while Colton unbuttoned the jumpsuit down to his navel, pulled his arms through, and slid his undershirt off his body. Danny's heart beat even faster—until he realized Colton's intent.

The spirit's eyes landed on the bullet wound. Sadly, gently, he traced the skin around it with a finger.

"I saw this happen," Colton whispered. "I tried so hard to get to you, but you ran, and . . ."

Danny *had* seen him there. He hadn't just dreamed it. That moment had been a sword above his neck, inching closer, about

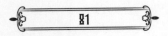

to cut him no matter which direction he ran. He'd had no choice but to turn from Colton, from his outstretched hand and the promise of safety, to save the viceroy from assassination. It had been painful enough, being shot; what hurt worse was that Colton had seen the whole thing happen.

"I'm so sorry." Colton leaned in and kissed the wound. Danny shuddered. "I'm sorry I couldn't save you."

"Colton." Danny buried a hand in the spirit's hair. "You traveled all the way to bloody India for me."

"But it still wasn't enough. I didn't get there in time to do anything useful."

"Wait." Danny leaned back a little. "Why *did* you come to India? I heard about Enfield being Stopped, but I thought you were in London. With my parents." Pain blossomed behind his breastbone as he wondered if he would ever see them again, or Cassie.

Guilt flashed in Colton's eyes. "I was."

"So why did you come after me?"

"The note. I found it in your room. The one that said you were being watched. And when I was in London, I got one, too. It said you were in danger, and that if I wanted to save you, I needed to come to India. They . . . They sent a photograph. Of you. Of someone pointing a gun at you."

Danny paled. Suddenly cold, he put his undershirt back on and pushed his arms through the sleeves of the jumpsuit.

"And this?" He touched the contraption on Colton's back.

"It holds the cogs I took with me from Enfield. Your father

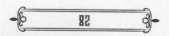

helped make it. I'm so sorry I left them, but I had no choice." He brushed a thumb over Danny's collarbone. "I didn't want them to hurt you."

"Well, they seem to be pretty decent at it."

Colton looked up sharply. "What do you mean?"

"You must have realized by now. They didn't lead you here to save me. They need leverage. If I don't do what Zavier says, he'll harm you. And he knows that hurting you is . . ." Danny swallowed. "He knows I'd never let anything hurt you."

"You shouldn't worry about me. I'll be fine."

Danny laughed, but this time the sound was bleak and gray. He hid his face in his hands. "You don't understand."

"What don't I understand?"

The tone was bitter, challenging. Danny dropped his hands and stared. Colton stared back. There was something new about him, something different. An awareness in his eyes that hadn't been there before.

"I just meant that you don't know the whole story."

"Then tell me."

Danny closed his eyes and the words tumbled out—Zavier's plan, the missions, the way Danny had been pulled into everything—all because of what he'd done to stop Matthias in Enfield over a year before.

When he opened his eyes again, Colton was on his feet, standing a few feet away. His eyes were fixed on nothing, his face blank.

Frightened, Danny stood. "Colton—"

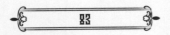

"You went with them. You went to the tower they destroyed."

"Not willingly! I don't want them to do this, but I have no choice. Zavier's forcing me to do this because of you. If I don't, then they'll do something to you, or your tower, or Enfield. And Zavier said—" He pressed his lips together, hating himself even for saying it out loud. "Zavier said that if I do these missions, he'll let you go. He'll leave Enfield alone, and tell the Indian rebels to leave it alone, too."

"And if Aetas really is imprisoned, and not dead? Will your blood be the key to free him? Is that why Zavier wants your secret?"

How did Colton know all of this already? "I-I won't tell them about the blood."

"He'll find out eventually."

"How?" But Colton remained silent, staring off into nothing again. "Colton, you're scaring me. What aren't you telling me?"

"If Aetas is freed, then I'll be gone."

"No. No, I swear it won't come to that."

"Why? Because Zavier promised?" Danny clenched his jaw, and Colton scoffed. "You're really going to trust *him*?"

"What's wrong with you? You're acting strange."

"*Nothing's* wrong with me." Now Colton sounded angry. Not irritated, or frustrated, as he had in the past. *Angry*. At Danny.

"I'm not the villain here," Danny said.

"Are you sure about that? You're helping him. You're going on missions to tear down clock towers, to destroy the spirits who live in them."

"What do you want me to do, Colton? I have no choice!"

"You *do* have a choice!"

"Yes—destroy everyone, or destroy everyone but you. Do you really think if I had a chance to save you, I wouldn't take it?"

"It's not right!" Colton began to turn away, but Danny caught his arm. He yanked it free.

"What would you do in my place?" Danny demanded. "What would you choose? Would you just let me die?"

"Danny—"

"*Would you?*"

"I'M ALREADY DEAD!"

The words reverberated off the metal walls. Danny stood motionless as Colton walked to the far end of the room, arms crossed low over his chest.

The silence roared in Danny's ears. He wanted to speak, but found his voice wouldn't work.

Finally, Colton turned back to him, his eyes old and tired.

Danny attempted to say his name, but only his lips moved. After a minute, he tried again. "What?"

Colton walked back to him, dread weighing every step he took. "I know the truth now. About the clock towers."

"What are you talking about?"

"I have to show you."

Danny shook his head and backed away, but Colton grabbed his arms.

"I'm sorry, Danny."

The room twisted. Colors faded in and out. Danny saw places and people flash by—far away, remote, like he could run for eternity and still never reach them.

He saw Enfield. Old, small, simple. A man and a woman, and between them, a boy.

The boy had freckles, and his bottom row of teeth was crooked, but when he smiled it was as if the entire room lit from floor to ceiling. His brown hair flopped over his forehead, his blue eyes bright and inquisitive.

The ocean, the roar of waves. A tall, lanky man lecturing about the properties of time and how each and every one of them should give thanks to Aetas. The blue-eyed boy, dripping wet and shivering, bowing to the sea.

It's Colton, Danny thought in wonder. *That boy is Colton.*

He saw a girl, sick in bed. Colton tending to her and kissing her forehead, spooning broth into her mouth, reciting stories. His mother crying downstairs, and Colton hugging her tightly. His father broodingly smoking a pipe.

Another boy, tall and handsome, racing into an alley alongside with Colton. They were laughing, their faces flushed, their eyes lit with inner fire. The boy taking Colton in his arms and kissing him deeply in the shadows of the alley.

Danny flinched back. *I don't want to see that.*

Colton resting his head on the other boy's chest as they lay in bed, the boy running his fingers through Colton's hair. Talking of London, of the future.

I don't want to see this!

It all came so fast, like spinning in endless circles. Colton testing his blood in a timepiece, eyes widening with surprise. Time distorting. Aetas proclaimed dead.

"This world will end if we don't find a way to control time."

"I can only hope our God in Heaven will forgive us."

"Take him."

"It has to be all his blood. Every drop."

No.

Colton screaming, eyes fastened to a knife that glinted in the red light of dusk. The blood. The smell of copper. The *pain.*

No.

"The throat, too."

No!

Blood dribbling from Colton's mouth, staining the cogs underneath him crimson.

NO!

Danny screamed the word as he wrenched himself away with a sob. Falling to his knees, he heaved, but nothing came up.

His vision was black—or maybe his eyes were closed. He pressed his forehead to the old rug beneath him, which smelled dirt and dust. Anything to take away the burning scent of blood.

"Colton," he rasped. "Colton . . . Please . . ."

Danny didn't even know what he was pleading for. To be told it wasn't true. To have the memories wiped away.

Colton knelt beside him and put a hand on his back. Danny flinched at the touch.

"I'm sorry. I'm sorry you had to see, but I need you to

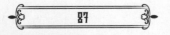

understand what happened, how I became like this. I was human, once. And now I'm not."

The hand slipped away. Danny took in a shuddering breath and sat back on his heels. "They killed you."

Colton nodded.

Danny wanted to claw his eyes out. Claw his brains out. Anything to make the memories stop repeating in his mind.

He reached for Colton's hand and grasped it tightly. "I should have known. All the clock mechanics need to know. Why didn't you tell me before?"

"I didn't know until recently. All the clock spirits may have already died, but that doesn't mean they're not alive right now, like me. It doesn't mean they have to be subjected to what Zavier's doing. They deserve better. Wanting to save me alone is selfish."

Danny's voice wavered and broke. "I can't lose you."

"You need to stop Zavier."

"I *can't*. If I don't do this, he'll—"

"Danny." Colton paused, as if searching for the strength to push the words out. "My tower was attacked. When I go back to Enfield, it will fall. There's nothing more he can do to me." He wrapped his fingers around Danny's wrists. "Don't let Zavier do this. We'll find another way."

Desperation tightened Danny's chest. Zavier had already named his price. Danny would help him, and Colton would be spared, even from Aetas. If he didn't comply, or if he went back on that bargain, they would break Colton's central cog.

"I can't," Danny whispered. "I can't, Colton. I'm sorry. I can't."

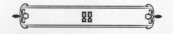

He made to grab or hug him, to drive the awful sight of Colton's torn throat from his mind, but the clock spirit leaned away. There was betrayal in his eyes, and it cut deeper than the knife had.

"Fine." Colton stood. "Do what Zavier says. Let him control you."

"You think I haven't tried stopping him? He promised that you would be safe if I went along with it for now. There's nothing else I can do!"

Colton's hands curled into fists. "I promised my sister that I would never leave her. I promised Castor that everything would be all right. Promises are easily broken, Danny. I thought you knew that."

He left the room without looking back.

Danny didn't try to follow. He slumped to the floor, shaking so hard his teeth rattled. The spray of blood flashed across his eyes. The sounds of Colton's screams echoed in his ears.

He lay there and longed for that knife to kill him, too.

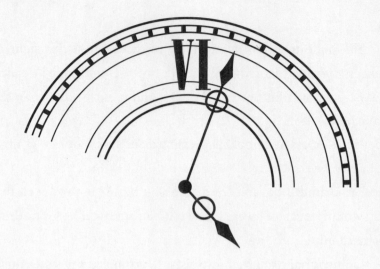

The sight of the ocean was like all of Colton's memories combined. The wind tugged his hair, skimmed the surface of the water. Sand shifted under his feet, and it took all of his control not to fall to his knees and bury his hands in it.

Instead, he bent down and scooped up a handful, allowing it to slowly trickle from his palm, the grains scattering at his feet.

"Make sure he doesn't bolt," Zavier ordered the two crew members flanking Colton, Anish and Ivor.

But even had they not been there, he wouldn't dare leave the gray-crested waves or the clouds overhead, or the gulls wheeling and crying near the rocks. It was too familiar. It felt like home.

He and Castor would have stood here and prayed to Aetas. They would have played in the surf, laughing as they hid from Instructor Beele.

You can't have that anymore, he reminded himself. *Zavier is going to use you. You need to focus.*

More questions had been asked of him in the last couple of days. As Colton had explained his trip from London to Agra, there was one detail in particular that fascinated Zavier.

"You were able to stay at the bottom of the riverbed for an extended amount of time?"

Colton had just told them how he'd been chased on a train with no other option than to jump. "Yes."

The young man had exchanged looks with a few of the others. Colton had found this ominous, but didn't dare ask about it.

He'd found out soon enough. Zavier had told him that the airship would be landing off the coast of South Africa, and they would be making a trip to the ocean, Colton included. Most of the crew were here: Anish and Ivor; Edmund and Prema, who stood watching Zavier with worry; Liddy and Astrid, whispering together; and even Daphne and Meena, guarded just as closely as he was.

And Danny. He stood where Edmund could keep an eye on him, hands bound. The metal looked particularly cruel against the fragile bones of his wrists. Danny swayed slightly, his entire body radiating exhaustion. His face was thin and pale, green eyes trained on the ground. Carefully not looking in Colton's direction.

They had once talked of going to the ocean, back when they'd spent their days in the musty air of his tower. It had always been an impossible but fond daydream. Now here they were, in the middle of a waking nightmare.

Regret seeped through him. Some part of him longed to run to Danny's side and hold him tightly, to kiss the cool, pale curve of his cheek and whisper that everything would be fine. But a new part wished to turn his back to him, no matter the pain it would cause them both.

Danny had worried, once, that he was following in Matthias's footsteps, sacrificing too much for his own personal happiness. Tending to only one rose while the rest of the garden withered. Colton could see now that he'd been right to fear it.

You would do the same.

The thought didn't help.

Zavier stood before Colton, gray eyes determined. "I know you're wondering why I brought you here today."

"For the view, I hope."

Ivor sniggered. Zavier glared at him before returning his attention to Colton. He took a deep breath; he actually seemed nervous, the fingers of his metallic hand twitching. "Somewhere off this coast lies Aetas's prison."

Liddy and Astrid stopped whispering, and Daphne's eyes bored into Zavier. Danny frowned at the sand.

"We know what it looks like from above," Zavier continued, "but not up close. If we're going to get there someday, we need more information. And you're the best suited to help us."

Colton glanced at the waves. "You aren't worried I'll be swept away? Or run off?"

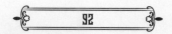

Zavier gave him a razor-thin smile. "You won't run." He looked in Danny's direction.

And he was right, damn him.

"How will I find it?" Colton asked. "If it even exists."

"It does exist. And Oceana will show you."

Colton tensed. Oceana, sister of Aetas. Ruler of oceans.

"Let's not waste time," Zavier said, stepping aside.

"No. I won't be your errand boy."

Zavier took another deep breath, as if fighting to keep a lock on his temper, then turned to Edmund with a nod.

With some hesitation, Edmund unholstered the gun at his belt. He pushed Danny to his knees and pressed the barrel to the back of his head.

"No!" Colton rushed forward, but Anish blocked him. Daphne and Meena tried to move closer, but Liddy and Astrid held them back. Danny's eyes were wide, his breathing rapid.

Colton whirled toward Zavier, whose face was carefully blank. "You wouldn't kill him. You still need him to talk."

Zavier shrugged. "You know the secret, too."

The words were so simple, said so calmly, but they still had their desired effect. Zavier only needed one of them: Danny or Colton. Not both.

"I'll go," Colton said, his voice shaking. "Just, please—don't do anything to him."

Danny looked up, his eyes rimmed in red. Beseeching. Colton had to turn away before he lost all his strength.

He took slow steps, but as he neared the surf, he felt an

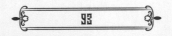

all-encompassing urge to disappear under the surface, to remember what it was like to be surrounded by dark water. The tide splashed around his ankles, then swallowed his legs, his hips, his chest, until he was completely devoured.

Colton opened his eyes—he wasn't aware of having closed them—and remembered at the last minute not to open his mouth in wonder.

Everything was *blue*. The world had been replaced with murky dimness, but it was beautiful, like permanent dusk.

The sand and silt shifted under his feet as he moved forward, slippery plants brushing against his hands. Fish with shiny green scales darted ahead of him. A small school of red fish erupted from behind a rock when he passed.

He wished he could stay down here forever.

Eventually, he began his search for the prison. Zavier insisted that Aetas was trapped here, under the ocean, but Colton still wasn't sure he believed it. Why would Chronos trap Aetas and allow time to unravel? Why wouldn't he have stepped in or reclaimed the power of time as his own?

Colton felt as if he'd been asleep for years, only to wake up and find the world a different place. In a sense, that was exactly what had happened.

Something moved in the corner of his eye. He turned slowly.

A woman stood regarding him from only a few feet away. She was abnormally tall, her body willowy under a flowing gown of blue seaweed. Her oval face was expressionless and pale, her eyes a piercing green, like a cat's when a light shines on them.

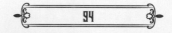

Colton remained perfectly still. The woman moved her head slightly, and her long, floating hair moved with her.

You have come to see him?

The voice in his mind was low and feminine with a hint of something trickling, like water over rocks. It seemed as natural as the ocean life around them.

I've heard that Aetas can be found here, Colton replied.

Oceana bowed her head. *You are one of his own.*

Images of the sea. Aetas's web of time. Castor.

I was.

I am truly sorry for what has happened to you. Oceana lifted a slender, gray-green hand, motioning him to follow. *Come. I will show you.*

He wordlessly trailed behind her. The train of her gown was threaded with seashells and sand dollars. Tiny fish swam through her hair. All around her was a glow, as murky and blue as the waters over which she reigned, brightening the dark of the ocean floor.

Oceana stepped to one side to allow Colton to take in their destination. A large circle had been cut into the bedrock, surrounded by a ring of golden light that rose like a beacon toward the surface of the ocean. Around the circle was a latticework of earth, looking very much like the bars of his former cell.

Colton approached the opening, peering inside, but all he could see past the golden light was darkness. He *felt* something, though—a strange sharpness, somehow both comforting and disturbing. The cogs strapped to his back began to hum and glow.

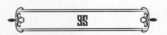

How far down does it go? he asked.

Far enough.

He examined the god again, wonder and dread warring within him. Oceana's face was eerily still, but the rest of her was in constant motion; the slow, graceful movements of water.

How did this happen?

It was many years ago. Aetas gave humans too much power, and Chronos was not happy. She paused. *Chronos is rarely happy. Things were once simpler, or so he said.*

She turned back to the circle. *Aetas was pleased to learn the secrets of time, and to control it as he liked. But it is difficult. I could see how it strained him. Giving some of the responsibility to the humans helped.*

Looking at him again, her blue lips formed a slight smile. *Aetas loved his followers. But when Chronos heard of what he had done, he banished him here. And here he has remained.*

You want him to be freed.

Yes. I do not have many followers left. Those I do have, I spoke to in their dreams. One has listened and understood. Through the humans my brother was punished for helping, my brother may be freed.

But if that happens . . .

Oceana's gaze met Colton's, sea foam and frothing tide. *Aetas never wanted this. To see beings like you existing, knowing how you perished, would upset him. He will reward you with sleep.*

I don't want sleep.

Then what do you want?

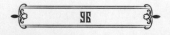

Colton watched bubbles rise from the golden circle. *A heartbeat.*

When Colton emerged from the waves, Zavier and the others hurried to meet him. Most of them, anyway; Danny was still being held at gunpoint.

"Get that away from him," Colton demanded. "Then I'll tell you what I saw."

Zavier nodded to Edmund, who put the gun away with a look of relief. Danny gratefully closed his eyes.

"What did you see?" Zavier asked softly.

Colton stared at Danny, who was hunched against the wind, his face still turned away.

"An ending," Colton said.

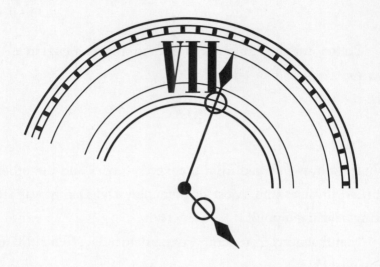

She found Danny in one of the unused corridors. It was dark with the lights turned off and no portholes cut into the metal walls. The crew had been allowing Daphne to wander now, and thanks to that, she and Meena had devised a way to execute their plan.

But first, she needed to check on Danny.

He sat in a shadowed corner, his legs drawn up, his head resting on his knees. He didn't move when she settled beside him, the metal cold against her back. Danny's hair was a mess. It usually was, but now more so than ever, like he'd run his hands through it too many times.

Sighing, Daphne drew two cigarettes from her pocket. They were presents from Jo after she'd seen Daphne's irritable tapping, and she'd handed them over with a wink. Daphne struck a match and lit the ends of both, then held one out. "Here."

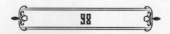

Danny finally lifted his head. He looked awful. His face was drawn, with deep, sleepless bruises under his tired eyes. When she pressed the cigarette toward him, he took it between shaking fingers.

"When was the last time you ate?" she asked, taking a drag.

He shook his head. He didn't know.

Daphne blew the smoke from her mouth with a relieved sigh and closed her eyes. "God, I needed that."

Danny, uncertain, imitated her, putting the cigarette to his lips. He held the smoke in his mouth until Daphne motioned for him to exhale. When he did, he immediately started coughing. Daphne tried not to laugh.

"How can you and my mother stand these things? They're disgusting."

Good; he was talking. "It helps. I know I shouldn't, but I got into the habit after my own mother . . ."

She trailed off, knowing she would choke on her own emotions if she said another word. It pained her to think of her mother at St. Agnes's, wondering why Daphne hadn't visited, maybe even worrying herself sicker because of it. If she ended up being the reason for her mother's condition getting worse . . .

Daphne took a deep, shaking breath, nursing her cigarette like a lifeline.

Danny eyed his own before taking another, smaller pull. "It does help. It reminds me of home." Then he buried his head again, his pale, spidery hand dangling the smoking cigarette between his fingers.

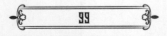

"I'm sorry, Danny," she whispered. "For everything."

Gossip flew fast on the ship. Everyone knew about Danny and Colton's meeting, even if they didn't know exactly what had transpired between them. But Colton had stormed out and Danny had been in a tight-lipped stupor since. Now, after the trip to the ocean, Colton was locked again in his room under Zavier's orders.

Back on the shore, Daphne had wanted to run in after him, hold him back. But when he'd returned, dripping and safe, she knew that he brought danger on his heels: he had seen Aetas's prison.

Zavier's story was true.

It seemed that no matter how hard she tried to clutch onto the constants of her life, they kept spinning out of her hands. Her father, dead. Her mother, sick. Matthias, a fraud. Akash, a liar. Now Zavier was trying to take away the rest of it—the Union, the clock towers, the one force on this earth worthy of the term *magic*.

If Zavier got his way and freed the god of time, her life as she knew it would disappear for good.

The cigarette was about to burn down to Danny's fingers. She plucked it away and snuffed it out.

"He showed you." It wasn't a question, and the words made Danny raise his head again. His eyes were unfocused, wary. "He showed me, too. But not on purpose."

"You saw. You saw what they did to him."

Daphne shuddered. "Yes."

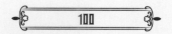

Danny leaned his head against the wall and exhaled brokenly. His eyes began to water.

"I had no idea," he murmured. "Our entire history was built on a lie. No, worse—they didn't even tell us how the towers were built. But it makes so much sense now. In Shere, when I got this—" he touched the scar on his chin—"I was bleeding all over, and time flickered. I thought I'd just been fast on the repairs, but it was something more. And Lucas in the failed Maldon tower . . . his blood made time restart for a moment."

Danny reached into his pocket, where Daphne knew he carried the small cog. "The power of our blood is the secret Zavier wants. Something powerful enough to break open the prison. But if he releases Aetas using blood . . ."

"Do you think it'll require another sacrifice?" she asked in a hushed voice.

"I don't know." His face grew stony. "We can't let him find out about it. Any of it."

"Agreed."

They sat in silence as Daphne finished her smoke. She thought about Narayan, the clock spirit she'd befriended in Lucknow. He had told her about his dreams, his memories. He, too, had been a human sacrifice so a clock tower could rise. And that little girl in Dover . . .

"How could they do this?" she whispered. "How could they kill all those people?"

"They were desperate. They thought the world was ending."

"It's no excuse. And Colton . . . God, I can't imagine how he must feel. He was *human*. He was just a normal boy with a family who loved him."

Danny broke. It was a quiet breaking, like eroding stone. His body curled in, agonized.

Daphne's hand hovered over him, uncertain. Finally, she touched his hair. She was surprised by how soft it was. "This must be hard for you."

"I can't even be with him, or talk to him. He hates me."

"Because you told him about Zavier's threat?" Danny nodded. "You can't help that. He has to understand what's at stake, here."

"He doesn't care. He'd rather die than let any more towers suffer. But he's . . ."

Already dead.

The words didn't have to be said. They were already carved into their minds, on the walls of the dark corridor.

Daphne snuffed out her cigarette.

"Danny," she said softly, "we're going to get off this ship. Tomorrow."

They waited until the crew was busy with lunch.

Meena had noticed the shift rotations pinned up in the galley one morning, every day and meal assigned to different members of the crew. She'd memorized the shifts for today, which put Liddy and Prema on lunch duty.

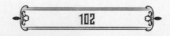

"Liddy's the one who took my gun," she had told Daphne the other day. "I'll steal into her room and get it back while you and Danny figure out the rest."

Which was how Daphne found herself loitering in the hallway closest to the hangar, constantly peeking around the corner for the signal from Danny. She had discovered a bunker-like door several corridors down, identical to others throughout the *Prometheus* that were able to cordon off certain sections of the ship. It had taken her a couple of days to figure out how to close and lock it, their best bet for keeping the crew from reaching the hangar quickly. That was what Danny was doing while Daphne kept lookout, ready to deal with whoever thought to come near.

"Da—Miss Richards, what are you doing?"

Daphne froze. She had expected Zavier, Edmund, one of the other pilots. Not Akash.

She turned and met his confused gaze. His goggles hung around his neck, his hair disheveled. He looked as if he had just rolled out of bed after a restless nap.

She forced her brain to whir into motion. "Decided to spy for them too, have you?" she bit out. "Are you going to tell Zavier what hallways I'm roaming?"

Irritation crossed his face. "No."

"Then what I'm doing is no business of yours."

He sighed, running a hand through his thick hair. "Will you listen to me for just two minutes? Not even that—thirty seconds."

Daphne itched to look around the corner, to see if Danny or Meena had returned. "Thirty seconds," she agreed, heart racing.

Taken aback by her consent, he wasted a few of those seconds figuring out where to start. "I . . . I'm not with the rebels anymore. I mean, I wasn't to begin with—I was more of a supporter, someone they could use to pass on a message or two."

"That sounds like enough involvement to be considered one of them," Daphne replied, crossing her arms. Had Danny locked the door yet? Had Meena been caught?

Akash frowned, but he didn't seem angry at the barb. "I won't deny that. I wanted—I still want—the British out of India. My parents talk about the first rebellion with fear and scorn. I don't believe this is right, to force the British culture on my country. But . . . after speaking with Danny, I know the reverse is true as well. It also wasn't right to use bloodshed and violence against the innocent."

Though Daphne's arms were still crossed, she could feel herself softening. His words didn't hold the note of desperation they'd had before, as if he could win forgiveness so long as he said the right things. This time, his words were slow and heavy, like he had to drag them out into the open.

"I never wanted you or Meena to get caught up in this. *I* didn't want to get caught up in it. But here we are." He glanced at the metallic wall, then rubbed his hands over his face. He looked so tired. "I don't know what to think about Zavier's plan, but since Meena doesn't like it, I do not like it either. The only thing I can do on this damn ship is try to protect you. So . . . that's what I'll do. If you will let me."

Daphne didn't respond, and her ears buzzed with the silence.

Akash, hands burrowed deep in his jumpsuit pockets, tried not to look at her.

"I don't need protecting," she said at last. "Nor does Meena. You should know that by now."

"I only mean that these people are unpredictable. What they want is . . . well, I don't quite understand it," he admitted, rubbing the back of his neck sheepishly. "But I know it means trouble."

"And you think you're the best candidate to sniff out trouble? You knew that there would be an assassination attempt on Viceroy Lytton. The chapati in Lucknow had a message stamped on it, and you knew exactly what it meant. You lied to me."

His dark eyes flinched. "Yes."

"You lied to Danny."

"Yes."

"Did you want Lytton to die?"

Akash sighed. "*No.* He is not a good man, but—"

"But you were right there in that camp with Danny," she snarled as she took a step forward, the plan momentarily forgotten in her wave of anger. "You were *right there*, and you did *nothing*! Danny was willing to risk everything to stop it and you had the answer the whole time. And for his efforts, he got *shot*. Danny could have died because of you."

Akash studied the ground between them. The distance was only a foot, but it felt like so much more. "Yes. You're right. And I am sorry."

"Have you told Danny that? Have you even tried to see him?"

"Not yet, but I will."

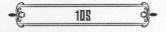

"It's up to him whether or not to forgive you. Until then, I can't give you an answer." *Except he'll be off this ship with the rest of us soon.*

She had asked Meena, tentatively, if she wanted to include Akash in their escape. Meena had thought it over, then shaken her head with remorse.

"They won't hurt him," she'd said. "He's already in their good graces. He can leave anytime he wishes."

Still, Daphne could feel something tremble inside her at the thought of leaving him here.

Akash opened his mouth, brows furrowed, but stopped himself. Taking a deep breath, he swallowed with a nod.

"That's fair," he mumbled. He finally met her eyes again, and Daphne wished he hadn't; his gaze seemed to delve straight into her chest, tightening it to the point of pain. She couldn't help but remember what it felt like to hold him under the stars, the safety that had enveloped her as his mouth found hers. Akash took a hesitant step toward her, because he could read her all too well. She burned with both fury and grief, wanting so badly to touch him, and also wanting to keep him away.

Before she could make up her mind, the ship lurched and they stumbled into each other.

"What the—?"

It happened again. Sirens began to blast through the speaker systems.

"Is the ship under attack?" Akash turned to her, but she was already running down the hall. "Da—Miss Richards! Wait!"

She hid around a corner, waiting for Akash to pass her. Then she ran to where Danny had gone, nearly colliding into him a minute later. His eyes were wild, his face ghostly pale.

"Did you do something?" he panted.

"No, I thought you did!"

"Then Meena—"

But the girl joined them then, out of breath as she rested her hands on her knees. "That girl's room is a den of terrors," Meena gasped. "But I found my gun. What is this ghastly noise?"

"I don't know, but we can't waste the distraction," Daphne said. "Get to the hangar."

The siren was loud enough to partly cover Meena shooting at the lock. When it broke away, Daphne pushed the door open and hastened the other two inside. Danny paused on the threshold, staring down the hall. His face was contorted with pain.

When she had first told him about escaping, he had demanded to bring Colton with them.

"He'll be locked in his room," Daphne had pointed out. "And Zavier keeps the key. He never shows up to meals, so there would be no way to sneak it off him."

"I won't leave without Colton."

"Danny." She had gripped his arms, looking him straight in the eye. "When we leave, we'll find the British army and get all of their airships to attack the *Prometheus*. We *will* free him, I promise."

But now Danny had started to breathe strangely, like his panic was strangling him. Daphne touched his arm.

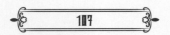

"I'm leaving Akash here," she said softly. "But I plan to drag him from this ship once we attack with real soldiers and a real defense."

Danny didn't look convinced. "You two go and find help. I'll stay here with Colton."

Footsteps sounded nearby. Daphne squeezed Danny's arm tighter. "We don't have time for this," she hissed, pulling him along behind her. "Come on."

The hangar was unmanned, and Daphne pushed Danny inside as Meena blocked the door.

"We can't leave him here!" Danny yelled. He tried to shove past Meena with no success.

The door to the landing plane was open. Daphne hopped inside and was immediately dizzied by the controls. Her hands hovered uncertainly above the panel.

"Can you start it?" Meena called, hands pushing against Danny's chest.

"I can try." Thankfully, when Ivor had taken her and Meena up in the plane during the Lyallpur mission, she had been paying attention to what he was doing. After tinkering with the controls, it came alive with a rumble beneath her.

After wrestling Danny into the back, Meena and Daphne closed the doors and strapped themselves in.

"Daphne, I swear to God," Danny was yelling. She ignored him as she flipped the control to open the hangar door.

"Are you sure you can fly it?" Meena asked as the sky revealed itself before them. Her eyes were wide, her hands trembling. She must have gone up in planes countless times with her brother, but Daphne at the helm was an entirely different matter.

"I'm fairly sure." Daphne eased the plane forward and her stomach jolted with fear and elation.

Danny cursed as the plane rolled out of the hangar, dropping a few feet. Meena shrieked, but Daphne pulled up and leveled out. Her entire body seemed to come alive with the motions, as if she were meant for open air and singing wind. A smile came unbidden to her face, full of victory and delight. They had made it.

Daphne was one step closer to home.

Her breath was beginning to come more evenly when it was stolen again by what she saw.

In the sky, two behemoths were engaged in battle. The *Prometheus*, dark and brooding, against a newer airship, sharper and leaner. Sinister. The boom of a cannon reverberated through the air, making their tiny craft shudder.

"Who are *they*?" Meena asked.

Focused on the controls, Daphne couldn't get a good look at the scene playing out behind them. She wasn't sure where they were going, and glanced at the compass every three seconds. Alarm quickly replaced her elation.

Danny had twisted around to stare back at the ships. He suddenly lurched forward. "Look out!"

Something slammed into the hull of the plane. Daphne yelped as she tried to steady the aircraft, but they were losing altitude fast.

"Do we have parachutes?" she called out to Meena.

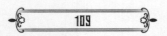

"I—"

The plane shuddered again as it took another hit. Another plane, smaller than their own, had risen from the clouds to ram them. Daphne couldn't see the pilot, but she didn't need to. The plane wasn't one of the *Prometheus*'s.

"Daphne!" Danny yelled.

"Hold on!" She flipped a couple of switches and tried to climb higher, but the other plane knocked into them again. Something tore into the hull.

"Oh God oh God oh God." She couldn't tell if the chant was coming from Danny or her own lips, Meena yelling in Hindi beside her. Daphne struggled to keep her sweaty hands on the controls.

Another hit. Another scream.

"Daphne!"

The controls were too erratic, the plane's nose dipping toward the ground.

They plummeted to the trees below.

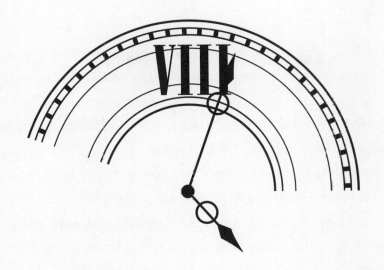

Something sharp poked Danny's cheek. His eyelids fluttered open, and he released a low groan. His head was *killing* him.

For a long time he just lay there, cheek pressed into the prickly ground. He had no idea where he was or how he had gotten there; the only thing he could process was the firm earth beneath him.

As his blurry vision cleared, something caught his attention: a tan snake slithering through the undergrowth not two feet away from him.

Danny jumped up, almost blacking out again. Gagging and gasping, he scuttled as far away as he could from the vile thing and watched it glide soundlessly through the forest floor.

Forest?

Blinking, he looked up. He was under the shade of tall coniferous trees, the tops of which were illuminated with bright

sunshine. Down here, however, the light was filtered through the branches into something more ominous. And it was cold as hell.

Danny blew warm breath onto his chapped hands. His palms and face were scratched and stinging, no doubt from falling through the branches. They'd been passing over India, hadn't they? Maybe they were north. Very, very north.

God, his head. He touched it carefully and, sure enough, found a tender bump near his temple. He must have hit it when . . .

"Shit!" He looked around again. There was no sign of Daphne or Meena, or even the plane.

What if they were stranded? What if they were hurt?

Calm down. I'm sure they're around here somewhere.

Danny leaned against a tree until his head stopped spinning. Then, feeling fuzzy and strange, he walked slowly through the trees and around large gray rocks, dried needles and twigs crunching under his boots. Birdcalls echoed through the canopy above him. The spot would have been peaceful had it not been for the jitters coursing through his body and the heavy sense of dread welling in his chest.

Walking helped cut the bite of the air a little, but a forest was never truly quiet, and every so often a rustle would make his shoulders tighten. He startled at a sound right above him, looking up just in time to see two beige monkeys leaping from branch to branch. He had never seen monkeys outside of the London Zoo. They were furry and snub-nosed, almost comical.

But there were probably more lethal creatures lurking out here, like that snake. He alternated between keeping his eyes on the ground and scanning the trees, searching for signs of Daphne and Meena.

One of the boulders looked different than the others, and Danny moved closer to inspect it. Someone had carved a likeness into the rock, a long face with closed eyes and extended earlobes. It looked familiar, like something Meena would have pointed out to him. The Buddha, perhaps.

He put a hand on the Buddha's cold nose. "Think you could help me find the others?" he asked of him. The stone was silent. "Thought not."

Something crunched to his left, the unmistakable sound of a footfall. His heart leapt as he turned.

"Daphne?" he called. "Meena?"

Three people emerged from the trees. They wore jumpsuits like Danny's, only theirs were more like uniforms, better fitted and a dusky blue. The person leading the group was a woman with blond hair cut like a man's. The two men who flanked her looked like they would be a match for Anish.

The woman gave him a brief smile, but it was all wrong and didn't reach her brown eyes. Newly awakened dread shot up Danny's spine, freezing him where he stood.

"Hello there," the woman said in a smoky voice, her accent English. "I'm assuming you're from the *Prometheus*?"

Danny's eyes darted among the three figures. "You certainly aren't."

Which meant they were from that other airship—the one attacking Zavier and the others.

But why? Was it a rescue attempt? Had Major Dryden called for reinforcements to take down the *Prometheus*? But if that were the case, why would they attack their plane?

"Who are you?" Danny demanded.

The woman gave him that chilling smile again. Instead of answering, she signaled the other two to step forward.

Danny backed up until the Buddha's nose was digging into his back. Heart pounding, he looked left and right, but there was no way he could outrun these men.

A shot rang out, making Danny jump. One of the men staggered back with a curse. Before Danny could figure out what had happened, a small hand grabbed his wrist and tugged.

"Run!" Meena shouted. They bolted from the Buddha and into the tree cover.

"Where's Daphne?" Danny gasped.

"Don't waste your breath. Come on!"

His head throbbed, and when he stumbled, Meena wrapped an arm around his waist and pushed him to keep going. When they reached another large boulder, they fell behind it. Meena sat on top of him, pressing her hand against his chest to keep him down. "Shh!" She looked up, tense and waiting. Her gun glinted in her other hand, the same one she'd used to shoot Zavier on the train from Agra.

The sound of heavy boots went past their boulder, then paused.

"Split up," the woman ordered. Three separate pairs of feet went off in different directions.

After a minute, Meena exhaled. She shifted off of Danny and sat him up against the boulder. "How's your head?"

"Let's just say there are two of you right now."

She clucked her tongue. "I don't know where Daphne landed. I grabbed onto a branch to break my fall." There was a gash on her arm, but the wound was already clotting.

Danny peered around the boulder, but even that small motion hurt. "Who are they? Do you know?"

"No, but I very much doubt they're here to save us." Meena pointed to the left. "We should go this way. None of them went in that direction."

But before they could even move, someone broke through the trees, running right at them. Meena gasped.

"Akash!"

The young man was out of breath, his black hair disheveled. "Come quickly, they'll be back any moment!"

"Who are they?" Danny demanded.

"I'm not sure, but Zavier says they mean us harm. Meena, chalo!" He held out a hand.

Danny saw her hesitate. He hadn't spoken to Meena's brother since they'd been in the Queen's camp weeks ago, and he still wasn't sure what to think about his betrayal. He couldn't imagine what Meena was feeling.

But then Akash drew in a sharp breath. "Daphne. Where is she?"

"We haven't found her yet," Meena said.

Akash scanned the trees, scowling. "Go that way," he said, pointing. "The *Silver Hawk* is there. I'll find Daphne."

"I'm coming with you," Danny said firmly.

"I don't think—"

The sound of running decided it for them. Meena grabbed Danny's wrist again as Akash bolted in the opposite direction.

"Meena, stop! I have to go with him!"

"He may be a liar," she panted, "but he would never harm Daphne."

They found the *Silver Hawk* in a sloped valley near a small river. The sunlight reflecting off the metal forced him to squint as they tripped over clods of earth. The door to the aircraft was open, and running toward them was—

"*No!*" Danny skidded to a stop, but Zavier still grabbed him.

"We don't have time for this. Come on, both of you!"

Meena growled as he reached for her arm, but at that instant, their pursuers broke through the tree line. One of them bled from the shoulder, darkening his blue jumpsuit to his waist.

"Quickly!" Zavier pushed them toward the *Silver Hawk*. The engine roared in the valley like a hundred angry beehives.

Astrid leaned out of the door, her hair loose and dancing in the breeze, her eyes narrowed as a set of small knives bloomed between her fingers. With a quick movement, she threw one of her blades. A pained groan behind Danny told him it landed. She flicked her wrist again, and the woman's scream followed.

Danny fumbled with the ladder, hands slipping as he hauled

himself up into the plane. When Meena, Zavier, and he were onboard, he poked his head back out.

Akash ran from the trees with Daphne hanging limp in his arms. "Hurry!" Danny shouted as the three assailants stirred in the grass.

The blond woman yanked the knife from her arm and flung it at Akash as he raced by, nicking his calf. He stumbled, but kept going as Zavier reached down to grab Daphne. As soon as Akash pulled himself inside the plane, Zavier slammed the door shut. Akash jumped into the pilot seat, still panting as sweat ran down his temples.

Danny scrambled to Daphne's side, sliding with her across the floor as the plane lifted into the sky. Her hair was littered with small twigs and leaves, her face as scratched Meena's and his own. Danny checked her breathing.

"She'll be all right," Zavier said after looking her over. "We'll have our medic, Charlotte, take a look when we get back."

Meena glared at him. "Who attacked the ship? Why were they after us?"

Zavier remained silent, but Danny knew something was terribly wrong. His eyes burned like silver fire, his jaw clenched tight. Calm, composed Zavier had been taken off guard.

The *Prometheus* swallowed the plane in one of its hangars, and Akash made a sloppy landing. Shaken up as they were, it hardly mattered.

Akash insisted on carrying Daphne to the infirmary himself. Danny and Meena trailed behind, limping into the hall where the rest of the crew was already waiting. The crew rushed forward with loud questions, asking if they were hurt, if Daphne was all right.

Why were they this worried about their prisoners, prisoners that had just tried to run away? Danny could only stare as Prema checked him over for injuries, silent and stunned with all that had happened.

And then he saw him—Colton. He stood in the back, Edmund's hand around his arm to keep him in place. Colton's amber eyes drank Danny in with concern.

Danny forgot about anger and compromise and threats. In that slowed down moment, it was easy to see how different the spirit was among the rest of them; something other, something almost untouchable. It was in the way he stood, the weight of uncountable years in his gaze, the impossible magic that clung to his skin. A beckoning and a warning.

Danny pushed past the others until they were standing face-to-face. Colton looked straight into his eyes, *through* his eyes, into whatever internal mechanism made Danny tick.

Something lay broken at their feet—a crevice, a crack wide enough to swallow them both. But Colton lifted a hand and crossed that distance, cupping the side of Danny's face, his fingers tracing the cuts that marred it. It took all of Danny's strength not to lean into that hand, to not remind them both how desperately he ached.

"Zavier, will you *please* tell us what's going on?"

Reluctantly, Danny turned.

Zavier had his arms crossed tight, biting furiously on a thumbnail. Jo put a hand on his shoulder as the others crowded closer. Prema had been the one to ask the question, and Danny could see it echoed in the confused gazes of the other crew members.

Finally, Zavier turned with a yell and punched the wall with his metal hand, denting the surface. "They're going to ruin everything!"

"*Who* is?" Ivor demanded.

"Zavier, calm down," Jo ordered. "We'll figure this out." She looked across the hall at Danny. "And . . . I think it's time you told them the whole story."

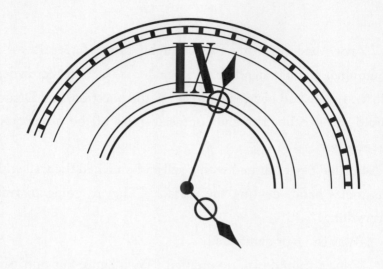

In the infirmary, Charlotte, the Austrian woman married to Felix, used her cache of medicines to treat Meena's gash and Danny's spinning head. Danny had to drink a foul assortment of herbs disguised as "tea." His nose wrinkled with every sip.

Daphne flitted in and out of consciousness, and Akash hovered over her, dark eyes pinched with worry. When Charlotte waved smelling salts under Daphne's nose, Daphne's eyes flew open with a strangled gasp.

"There we are," Charlotte said pleasantly. "Follow my finger, if you please."

"Where—?" Daphne turned her head and winced.

Danny woozily left his bed for hers. He touched her clammy hand. "I'm here, and so is Meena."

Daphne sighed in relief. When she noticed Akash on her other side, though, she seemed to grow paler.

"Akash saved us, you know," Danny murmured. "He carried you to the ship and got a knife thrown at him for his trouble."

"What? Where?" Charlotte bustled Akash off to take a look at his leg.

Daphne watched as Charlotte drew a privacy screen, hiding Akash's embarrassed expression. "Did he really?"

Danny nodded. Before he could say any more, Jo slipped into the room. "Good, you're all on the mend. Zavier wants to see you three in the meeting room."

"Can't it wait?" Meena asked.

"He insists on doing it now, before he holds an assembly with the crew."

Danny helped Daphne to stand, and she leaned against him for support. Together they walked to the room where Danny had reunited with Daphne and Meena. And where Danny had learned that Colton was onboard the ship. He still felt Colton's touch, the ghostlike imprints of the spirit's fingertips on his skin.

Zavier sat at the table, hunched over a mug of what looked like whiskey. At his side sat a girl not much younger than Meena, with light brown hair and gray eyes. Daphne made a little "oh" sound.

"Here they are," Jo said as she closed the door. Danny helped Daphne settle into a chair. "It'll just be us, yes?"

"Yes." Zavier cleared his throat. He looked haggard, and the girl watched him with worry. Danny remembered seeing her a couple of times on the ship—Zavier's sister, Sally.

Jo touched Zavier's shoulder. "Go ahead. Tell them."

He took a deep breath, looking . . . young. Helpless.

"I want to free Aetas," he began, his voice slow and cracked, "because my mother is trapped in a Stopped town." He gestured to Sally. "*Our* mother."

No one spoke. Danny looked between them, noting the same gray eyes, the same strong nose.

I have an interest. It was what Zavier had told him, once, when Danny had asked him why he was so invested in this implausible scheme.

"It was during the Austro-Prussian War," Zavier went on, addressing his mug. "I was thirteen, Sally was about seven. Our mother was—is—a nurse. When she was stationed in Kaplice, in Bohemia, a bomb dropped on the tower and destroyed it. She's been trapped there ever since."

Danny was momentarily transported out of the room, returning to that moment when Leila stood hunched over the phone, eyes wide with terror. The sound of his mother crying. Standing before the gray barrier that separated him from his father. *Your fault.*

"Mechanics have tried to free Kaplice, of course," Zavier murmured. "But they've had about as much luck as they did with Maldon." He met Danny's eye. "In this instance, there is no runaway spirit. It's either freeing time itself, or nothing."

Sally signed something, and Zavier nodded. "Sally and I lived with our father after that, but a couple years later he died in a mining accident." He paused to take a swig from his mug. "Then we stayed with Aunt Jo and our late uncle. I vowed to do whatever it took to free our mother, and Aunt Jo said she would help however she could." He looked at her, and she gave him an encouraging nod to go on.

"During that time, I prayed to Aetas. I prayed to Oceana. Hell, I prayed to any god who would listen. I just wanted to believe in something. I wanted to believe that I could save her. And then, one day, Oceana called me to the ocean. Aunt Jo didn't understand why I needed to go, but . . ."

Jo's eyes were glazed with memory. "I took him anyway," she said in a faraway voice. "Didn't know he'd be coming face-to-face with a goddess, of all things."

"I hardly believed it, even when she stood before me." Zavier swallowed. "She told me . . . told me that I could help. That there *was* a way to save my mother. Once I found out the truth about Aetas, I knew I had to free him."

Danny risked a glance at the others. Daphne was listing to one side, wearing a strange frown. Meena stared at the table's surface.

"I've always hated the clock towers. If they were gone, if their hold on time were dissolved, then no one else would have to suffer what we went through." He glanced meaningfully at Danny. "So I gathered my crew, and here we are. I didn't want Sally to tag along, but she insisted." He raised an eyebrow at her, and she shrugged. "We want our mother back. We want everyone in every Stopped town to be freed. We want the world to go on as it used to."

The room fell into uneasy silence. Danny listened to his own breathing, short and shallow.

"And your arm?" Meena asked in a croaking whisper.

"What about it?"

"When you said you've always hated clock towers, you glanced at it."

A wry smile lifted a corner of his mouth. He flexed his metallic fingers. "An accident. I am—was—a clock mechanic, just like you three. But I was terrified of the towers after what happened to my mother. I wasn't paying attention, and my arm got caught in the gears."

Danny felt Daphne shudder against his side.

"The towers are unnatural," Zavier said. "Every second of every day is a countdown to when they'll malfunction next. If we want to see the world progress, we must cut our connection with them. Danny, you have to understand. You know what it's like to have a parent trapped. Wouldn't you have done *anything* to free your father? Weren't you desperate to find a way?"

"Yes, but . . ."

Colton.

"I realize that you're concerned about the spirits," Zavier went on, "but you have to let them go. They're not living entities. Millions of people will benefit from time being restored. If we want to help the world, there must be sacrifices."

"You said you could save him," Danny rasped.

"If there's a way to save him, we will. We'll do whatever we can to keep Colton for you. We can make a deal with Aetas, maybe. But the others . . ."

Daphne leaned forward. She was looking at Sally, talking

directly to her. "Look, I'm sorry for your loss, but do you really believe in this cause? Do you really want to bring down the towers, and free Aetas, if that's even possible?"

Jo interpreted some of what Daphne said, but once Sally understood, she nodded.

"She says she loves her brother and wants to free her mother as much as he does," Jo translated as Sally signed, "but she agrees that Zavier has been . . . mean." Sally gave her brother a small shove, and he scowled at her in response. "She apologizes for his behavior."

Zavier scoffed and slid a book toward Danny. It was old and battered, the spine cracked and the corners rubbed raw. "That's *Prometheus Unbound,* by Percy Shelley," he explained. "I want you to read it. Maybe then you'll understand the importance of our mission a little better."

"But who were those people who attacked us?" Daphne demanded.

"I'll explain to everyone later," Zavier replied. "And about you three taking off in one of our planes—which was destroyed, by the way—"

"Official pardons all around," Jo said with a wiggle of her fingers. Zavier swung his glare toward her. "You all need a break, Zavier. You've told them what they need to know, and now I'm going to take them back to the infirmary."

"Fine," Zavier muttered, sounding for all the world like a child denied his favorite toy.

Danny stood, the thin book heavy in his hand. Zavier held

his gaze for a moment. There was something more than cold determination in those eyes. Something Danny knew all too well.

Desperation.

Out in the hall, as Meena supported Daphne with an arm around her waist, Daphne took one look at him and scoffed. "Don't you dare," she said.

"Don't I dare what?"

"Start siding with him. He's trying to get your sympathy."

"If he wanted to play that angle, he'd have told me at the beginning. Besides, I *do* understand. My father was trapped in Maldon for three bloody years. I know what it's like."

"Why are you even letting him do this?" Daphne demanded of Jo. "Why do you go along with whatever he says?"

"It's been a long time since I've seen my sister. My niece and nephew need a mother. I'm not trying to justify what he's done, but give his words some thought, all right?"

They reluctantly followed her down the corridor, but Danny stopped, taking another look at the book in his hands.

"I'll catch up to you later," he said.

Jo let him go without questions, which was precisely why she was the only one on this blasted airship he liked. He turned and headed in the opposite direction.

Liddy was standing guard outside Colton's door. Well, sitting guard; she was slouched against the wall, whittling a piece of wood. When Danny came around the corner, she hopped to her feet.

"Yes?" she drawled. "And what does our escape artist need, hm?"

"Just let me in," he mumbled. "Please."

Liddy took out the key, jangling it in his face. "You two are like magnets. I'm locking you in for one minute, but that's all. Got it?"

Colton was sitting on the edge of the low bed, head bent as he examined something in his hand. He lifted his face in surprise when Danny walked in. The sight of him sent a blow through Danny's chest. Colton was too damn beautiful for his own good.

Danny was stricken speechless for a moment, his tongue dry. Colton stood and pocketed what he had been studying: a tiny cog.

"What's that?"

"From Big Ben," the spirit said. Vague, cold.

"Oh." Heart racing, he reached into his pocket and touched the cog Colton had given him. He glanced at Colton's neck, remembering what the knife had done there. Wincing, he let the cog go.

"Zavier gave this to me," Danny said, lifting the copy of *Prometheus Unbound*. "I was wondering . . . I mean, since you like . . . since we both . . . Do you want to read it? Together?" *Like we used to?*

Colton's face crumpled, but in a blink it turned back to that uncharacteristic stoniness. "I don't think that's a very good idea."

Danny resisted the urge to hold the book to his chest, as if to use it as a shield. His body ached. His mind ached. He wanted to lie down and never get back up again.

"Are you sure?" Danny whispered. He didn't know what had compelled him to say the words, but now he wished he hadn't. He quickly turned for the door, eyes burning.

But the door opened before he could reach it. Dae stepped back, surprised to see Danny there.

"Oh, it's you." Quick as that, he dismissed Danny and turned to Colton. "I think I've completed it. The new holder."

Danny watched, fascinated and forgotten, as Dae transferred Colton's cogs from the holder Christopher Hart had made into a new one. The cogs glowed faintly, and when Colton put on the holder, he looked even more substantial. More human.

Colton made a surprised sound. "I feel great."

"Better than the other one?"

"Definitely. Thank you, Dae."

Danny couldn't tolerate another second of seeing Colton smile at someone who wasn't him. Liddy tried to say something as he left the room, but he silently continued down the hall, taking refuge in his room.

An hour later, Prema came to collect him for Zavier's assembly.

The crew gathered on the observation deck. Though he had learned the plane they'd stolen had crashed in the Himalayan forest, Danny had no idea where the airship was at the moment, and didn't particularly care.

"You're all wondering who those people were," Zavier said.

"The airship that attacked us is a class-A registered ship, the type usually commanded by the military. From the intelligence we've gathered in the past few weeks, I believe I know who it belongs to. The group calls themselves the Builders. They've tracked our progress taking down clock towers, and they want to stop us. But they aren't military, so far as we know. It's like they're a separate entity altogether. It could be they've received under-the-table government funding, but it's hard to say.

"What I do know is"—he paused, frustration passing like a wave across his face—"they're rebuilding the towers we destroy."

The crew erupted in shocked protests. Zavier waited for the chatter to die down before continuing.

"The Builders have only succeeded once so far, in Khurja. That was the second town we liberated, and time was going strong when we left, thanks to the water from Aetas's prison."

A dark realization grew in the pit of Danny's stomach. He turned and met Daphne's eye. Her face was white, frozen with horror. Like Danny, she knew how the tower had been rebuilt.

Blood. Sacrifice.

"We're not sure how the Builders are doing this," Zavier went on, "but we can't let them distract us. We *will* free Aetas. Until then, we'll be vigilant—and we'll fight back."

"How?" Felix asked.

"With a demonstration. An open declaration of war." Zavier's steely determination lit his gray eyes, turning them to storm clouds. "We're going to take out the astronomical clock in Prague."

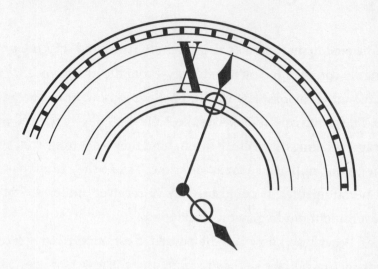

The musty wallpaper smelled of spice and vinegar, as if someone had spilled wine on it a hundred years ago. Danny leaned his head against it as he cradled *Prometheus Unbound* in his lap, occasionally running his fingers along the old, crinkled pages. The spindly chair he sat on was uncomfortable, but the only other option was the bed by the window, already claimed by Edmund.

The apartment Zavier had rented was small, with barely enough space to squeeze in the two beds, a stove, a hearth, and a water closet with the tiniest tub Danny had ever laid eyes on. Somehow, he was meant to share this space with Zavier, Edmund, and Felix. None were too happy about it.

The ship had dropped them off a few miles from the city, and they'd hitched a ride on the back of a wagon that was carrying goods to market. Liddy, Astrid, Daphne, and Meena had come too, holed up in their own apartment down the street. Everyone else was on the *Prometheus*, awaiting orders.

Danny had considered jumping from the wagon or escaping into the streets of Prague, but Colton was still on that airship, and Zavier's threat still clamped around his neck like a collar.

"Can't win," Danny muttered.

Edmund looked away from the window. "What's that?"

"Nothing." Danny returned to the book—Zavier's book. He'd hoped to find something hidden there, something beneath the story of Prometheus being freed.

The door opened and Zavier walked in, unraveling a blue scarf from his neck. He looked tired, his face pink from the cold. "Just did a preliminary search," he said, throwing the scarf on the bed where Felix had spread out. "The security is lax. I think this will be easier than we thought, but we'll still need to be careful, especially with the clock being where it is."

Danny had only caught a glimpse of the tower when they'd arrived earlier that afternoon. The astronomical clock—known as the Orloj clock—stood tall, dark, and proud in the Old Town Square. He could see what Zavier meant about it being so out in the open.

"What's the plan, then?" Edmund asked.

"We'll split up tomorrow to gather as much information as we can. Street layouts, in case we need to run. Details about the square and the clock. Anything we don't already know. You'll be helping us with that," Zavier said, noticing Danny in the corner.

"Allow me to show you how surprised I am." Danny returned

to the book. Edmund laughed, but it turned into a cough as Zavier cast him a withering glance.

"You'll be escorted at all times while we're here," Zavier said. "I mean it, Danny. No more running."

"Hard as it is to believe," Danny replied, "I actually want to return to the *Prometheus*. You are, unfortunately, my only way back there." *That I know of.* "But I won't be going inside the tower."

Zavier barely thought it over. "Agreed. Now, let's get dinner from downstairs and call it a night."

"Er, one thing," Edmund said, lifting a finger. "One of us has to share a bed with him." He pointed at Danny, who flushed.

"What, are you saying I smell?"

"No, it's only . . . well . . ."

Zavier rubbed his face with a gloved hand. "Yes, Ed, he likes other men. That doesn't mean he likes *you*."

"Wasn't suggesting it—I mean, I'd be flattered—It's just, wouldn't it be uncomfortable for you?" he asked of Danny.

"I'll sleep on the bloody floor," Danny snapped. "Heaven forbid you're *uncomfortable*."

"No, you won't," Zavier interrupted. "I'll get some extra blankets and *I'll* sleep on the floor. Ed, you share with Felix. Sorry, Felix." The man sighed.

"I'm not taking an entire bed for myself," Danny argued, but Zavier held up a hand to silence him.

"You are, and that's the end of it."

Danny shrank farther into the corner, using the book as a feeble barrier between himself and the others. He was nothing but an oddity to them, a specimen they didn't understand. It didn't help that Zavier kept watching his progress with the book like a hungry hawk.

That night, curled up alone while Felix and Edmund snored in the other bed, Danny remembered when Colton had snuck out of his tower to come to his cottage. How much better he had felt holding the clock spirit in his arms, knowing he would be right there when he woke up.

But Colton wasn't there as the sun rose over Prague the next morning. Colton was miles away, and wanted nothing to do with him.

People milled about the Old Town Square among rococo buildings painted in soft colors. They were elegantly designed with asymmetrical scrollwork and shell-like curves, windows and roofs arching toward an overcast sky. A tall church brooded to one side, its black spires stabbing upward, like something out of a Gothic novel.

But what stole Danny's attention was the clock. The tower itself was simple, built of pale brick with a small, black clock face at the top. Despite its humble appearance, he sensed the power emanating from it, rippling up his spine. He almost thought he could feel the cog in his pocket grow warmer.

Zavier and the others had spread out; to stay in a group would be to attract attention. But Danny still needed an escort, and today that duty had fallen to Edmund. Though Danny was prickly about the previous night, Edmund acted as if nothing had happened.

The wind whipped through the square, and Danny huddled deeper into his coat. Zavier had managed to get him dark trousers, a white shirt, a dark waistcoat, a long black coat, and a gray scarf. Only his boots were his own, the only piece left from his life before.

"It's not very impressive," Danny remarked of the tower.

"You haven't seen it all," Edmund replied with a smirk. "Come here."

Danny followed, watching the metal rod at Edmund's hip sway with each step. Dae had made the device, which the *Prometheus* crew called tasers. Zavier had used one on Danny before, sending painful electrical currents through his body. His fingers twitched with the memory. He knew that if he tried to run, Edmund would use the rod without hesitation.

They walked around to the tower's left side. Danny gasped.

It was *beautiful*.

He had never seen anything like it. There were two large faces unlike the one above their heads, the top one black with golden numerals and astrological symbols; there was even a face within the face with oddly shaped hands. The one below consisted of golden pictures framing a castle or a church at its center.

They were both framed with black iron molding, flocked on either side with statues of angels and apostles and a dark-boned skeleton. Family crests adorned the brick wall leading around to the front of the tower. High above the black and gold faces, a gilded rooster perched in a niche.

"God," Danny breathed. It was the most breathtaking clock he'd ever seen.

"I'd only seen drawings before," Edmund said beside him. His eyes, too, were wide with wonder. "The real thing is . . . It can't even compare."

Danny curled his cold hands into fists. Zavier wanted to destroy this tower, this beautiful creation.

Edmund, sensing his sudden hostility, sighed. "I don't like it either, you know. It doesn't seem fair, but I know what Zavier's going through, and he's desperate. I wager you'd have done anything to help your father."

"What do you mean, you know what he's going through?"

Edmund breathed into his hands to warm them, then said, very softly, "He saved me."

Danny frowned, not sure he'd heard right.

"We grew up in Exeter together, us and Liddy. The two of them were clock mechanic apprentices, but I don't have the, ah, gift." From the way Edmund was gazing up at the astronomical clock, Danny wondered if he wished he did. "Z lived close by and we became friends. I was allowed at his aunt's house whenever my father . . ." He shrugged. "Then dear old Dad got himself stabbed down at the pub, and my mum died a little later of consumption. Jo, Zavier, and Sally took me in."

Danny chewed on the inside of his cheek, feeling guilty for the less-than-kind thoughts he'd had toward Edmund. "I'm sorry."

Edmund shrugged again. "Wouldn't have got through it without Z. When he asked me to help him free his mum, of course I said yes. Only seemed fair." Edmund jerked his chin up to the face within a face, where a hand shaped like a sun pointed to an astrological symbol. "You know the thing above is called an astrolabe? It tells the positions of the sun, planets, stars. Can't read a wink of it myself, but isn't that something?"

"You know an awful lot about clocks for someone who isn't a mechanic."

Edmund flushed. Before he could respond, a young woman with dark hair in two long braids stopped to admire the clock. She clutched a rose-colored shawl around her shoulders. When she caught Danny looking at her, she smiled and said something in Czech.

"Sorry, English," Edmund replied.

"I was asking if you knew the story of the clock," she said with a throaty accent. "You look as if you are seeing it for the first time."

"We are, indeed," Edmund said as Danny's stomach writhed. The story of the clock? Did she know? How could she possibly—?

"The counselors of Prague wanted the best," the young woman explained, "so they hired clockmaker Hanuš to design it many, many years ago. They didn't just want a structure to measure time, but to measure the stars' passing. Hanuš designed exactly that."

She gestured to the astronomical faces. "It was perfect in every way, but the counselors were frightened of Hanuš's talent.

They did not want him to make a tower more impressive than Prague's for another city. So in the night, they had him blinded with a piece of hot iron."

Edmund inhaled through his teeth. Danny winced.

"Hanuš, after healing, took his best pupil and went to the heart of the clock." Her dark eyes trailed upward. "The pupil, following his master's instructions, stopped the clock. And since Hanuš was the only one who knew how his particular clock worked, no one could restart it. Prague was trapped in time for a hundred years because of Hanuš's revenge."

Danny had heard a variant of this story before; mechanics whispered of the mysterious hundred years Prague had lost to time. It was no wonder the city felt so old, its citizens running an entire century behind most of the rest of the world. Danny wondered when the young woman beside them had been born.

"Of course, someone—perhaps Hanuš, perhaps his pupil, perhaps another clockmaker—made it run again," the young woman said. "And thank goodness for that."

"There haven't been any other problems with the tower since then?" Edmund asked.

"No, we care for it well. It's said that the ghost of Hanuš haunts this tower. Anyone who tries to disrupt the clock suffers a tragic death or goes insane."

"Lovely," Danny muttered low enough that the young woman wouldn't hear. "Think Zavier knows?"

Edmund rolled his eyes. "Like that would stop him."

He was getting tired of Edmund being right all the time.

At noon they crossed paths with Daphne and Liddy near the Gothic church across the square. Liddy carried another of Dae's taser devices. Daphne seemed to have recovered well enough, but dark circles still shadowed her eyes. She was dressed in trousers and a long, thick tunic, over which she wore a fitted dark blue coat.

"How are you?" Danny asked her as Liddy and Edmund exchanged a word.

"Liddy farts in her sleep. How do you think I am?"

Danny snorted around a laugh. "Felix isn't much better. His snores could tear down the walls of Prague."

"Maybe combined they can take down the tower before Zavier can even come near it."

They shouldn't have been laughing, and they both knew it. But seeing Daphne and talking to her after his lonely night was a tiny lifeboat in a sea of doubt.

"Danny," she whispered when they'd calmed down, "do you think Zavier will find out about the blood from the Builders? Would it be better if he finds out from us instead?

"We can't do that!"

"I know, it's just . . ." She looked around the square, lost. "I don't know what else to do."

"We'll think of something."

"All right, enough chitchat," Liddy said, breaking them apart. "Ed, you and Danny go back and jot down what you've learned. Daphne, we have more scouting to do."

Daphne shot Danny a quick "kill me" look before following Liddy.

At the apartment they shared a meal of pork, dumplings,

and sauerkraut, then passed the afternoon hours sketching and making notes. By the time Zavier and Felix returned, Danny was reading the last of *Prometheus Unbound*.

There was one passage he kept returning to. Asia, whom Prometheus loved, says that Zeus is to blame for all the problems of the world. Prometheus, on the other hand, gave the humans fire, and therefore advanced their civilization. Between the two of them, Prometheus was the greatest asset to humans.

In the same passage, the character Demogorgon says, "All things are subject to eternal Love."

He was fairly certain Zavier hadn't intended him to find any meaning in this, but it made him pause nonetheless. Zavier thought the spirits were evil, manipulative . . . but they still had thoughts, emotions, even memories.

Colton was right. They deserved better.

Danny lay wide awake that night as thin moonlight slanted through the window, projecting a beam of silver over his stomach.

There was another quote from the book that kept twisting inside him: *Soul meets soul on lovers' lips.*

He ran his fingers over his own lips, remembering all too well the feeling of Colton's mouth, the warmth of his lips, the shape of his soul.

Danny sat up. He quietly crawled to the end of the bed, where he had left his boots. He could tiptoe out of the room and go back to the clock, study it more thoroughly. Maybe even go inside, though he'd told Zavier he refused to, in order to warn the spirit as he had in Lyallpur.

Reaching down for his boots, he froze. Zavier sat against the wall directly between him and the door.

But he wasn't looking at Danny. His head rested on his arms, the metal one glinting in the moonlight.

Danny hesitated. He leaned back, thinking to return to bed, but the mattress creaked and Zavier looked up. Their eyes met, and Danny knew he'd intruded on a private moment. Zavier's face was no longer stiff and cold; it was soft and vulnerable. Young.

All things are subject to love.

Danny tried to read those eyes, but Zavier looked away, embarrassed, wrapping himself in his blankets and pretending to go back to sleep. Danny waited a moment, then did the same. Pulling the blanket over his shoulders, he wondered if Zavier suffered the same nightmares he did.

As luck would have it, Danny was paired with Zavier the next day. He knew in a heartbeat that it was no coincidence.

As they wandered the square, Zavier jotted down notes and drew details and blueprints, the connecting streets of an alleyway or the white crosses in the ground before Town Hall. The crosses were said to memorialize the executions of leaders of the Rebellion of the Czech Estates against the Habsburgs. Danny didn't know a lick of Czech history, so listening to Zavier was akin to browsing a textbook.

"A bunch of men were killed here," Danny said as he tapped

his toe against one of the crosses, "and the clockmaker haunts the tower. This is the most morbid town square I've ever set foot in."

Zavier made a small choking sound; Danny later realized he'd been stifling a laugh.

Around noon, they sat on a bench by the fountain in the middle of the square where they watched people running errands, or holding hands as they strolled, or stopping to gaze at the astronomical clock.

"Does it bother you?" Zavier asked suddenly, hunched over his notebook.

"Does what bother me?"

"Your wound."

"Oh." Danny touched his left shoulder. "A little. Right now it's only a dull ache I've learned to ignore."

A humorless smile flashed across Zavier's face. "You've had to put up with plenty of those, haven't you?"

There he was, being metaphorical again. "Does it bother you, then?" Danny asked, gesturing at Zavier's arm.

Zavier glanced at it, surprised, before returning to his notes. "It did at first. But as I've come to learn, given enough time, you can get used to any pain."

Danny shifted on the bench. "I finished *Prometheus Unbound*, but I'm not sure what you wanted me to take away from it, to be honest."

Zavier raised his gaze to the clock tower radiating its stable power across all of Prague. "Aetas's story closely resembles that of Prometheus's in the myth. Chronos made him to oversee time,

but was displeased with his efforts, especially after he gave some of that power to humans, just like Prometheus gave humans fire.

"There are arguments that humanity no longer has need of Zeus, but Prometheus remains necessary. If Aetas were freed, would he have more to offer humanity than Chronos? We wouldn't need to rely on clock towers. We'd live off what Aetas has given us."

"So, what, you fancy yourself some sort of Heracles?" Danny snorted. "You think you're going to free Aetas all on your own?"

"If it has to come to that. Hopefully by then I'll know how."

Danny turned away. He didn't want to remember the sight or smell of blood.

"You know that anyone who tries to tamper with that clock dies or goes insane, don't you?" Danny asked.

"Seems like someone's been listening to the local legends. They also say that if the skeleton on the clock nods, the country is in peril. Superstition, Danny. It goes a long way."

"You're going to hurt these people," Danny whispered. "They love this clock. Hell, I've been here a day and I love it, too."

"Danny . . ." Zavier closed his notebook. "This isn't just about a vendetta, or showing you what we're capable of. This is making our message clearer. These Builders"—his face twisted—"and anyone who tries to oppose us are going to learn a hard lesson. They can't rebuild this clock, not as the original clockmaker did. I doubt the Prague citizens would even let them try. This plan isn't a feeble attempt to bring you around or to free time. This is a declaration of war."

Danny shook his head and watched a small girl run after her parents, clutching at her father's coattails. The father laughed as he leaned down to whisk her up, her curls bouncing. The mother tickled her leg, making her laugh.

"And," Zavier added softly, watching them, "one step closer to my mother."

In the afternoon, Zavier passed Danny off to Liddy so that he could plan with Felix. Walking Prague's streets, Danny was amazed by just how old this city was. London was old, too, of course, but its roots had been partially hidden by technology; Prague's were still visible under its foundation. The city's ancient history had seeped into the cobblestones and crooked streets and aged buildings.

"You miss your bloke?" Liddy asked as she twirled the taser in her hand like a baton. Danny had never been particularly fond of her, but she wasn't exactly malicious. Just annoying.

"Why did you join Zavier?" Danny countered. "Edmund told me you're both from Exeter, but there has to be another reason."

She paused. "I was a mechanic with him, sure. Couple years younger than he is, but we were in a lot of the same classes. He helped me with the coursework, sometimes. When he asked if I would help him with all this, I said sure."

"Just like that? If you're a clock mechanic, doesn't that . . . I don't know . . . didn't that seem wrong to you?"

A faint blush touched her face. "No."

"No?"

"*No.*" But when Danny kept staring at her, she sighed. "I was sacked, all right?"

"What? Why?"

"It's not about what I *did*. I just . . . couldn't keep up. I didn't learn like the others, yeah? Mum and Gran hadn't taught me to read, I barely knew my numbers. The others called me out on it all the bleeding time, made me into a joke. The Lead couldn't let me continue since I was so far behind, so—" She made a scissor-like motion with her fingers.

"That's ridiculous. They should have let you retake the courses, given you a tutor."

Liddy snorted. "Our little branch isn't like yours in London. Not the same funding, staff, resources. Zavier tried, but . . . it wasn't enough." She narrowed her blue eyes at Danny. "I'm not even sure why I'm telling you this, other than to make you understand that I've no ties with the Mechanics Union anymore. And anyway, they'll be out of commission soon enough."

"So this is just revenge to you?"

"'Course not. When Zavier first told me what he'd planned, I called him a nutter." She started to swing her taser in circles again. "But he and Ed talked me 'round. And I want to free his and Sally's mum, too." She gave his shoulder a good-natured shove; he nearly stumbled into passersby. "We'll keep your bloke safe. Zavier'll find a way."

He rubbed his arm. "How long is this mission going to last, anyway?"

"Oh, not much longer. They should be setting everything up tonight."

Danny stopped in his tracks. "*Tonight?*"

"Thought you were impatient to get back to the ship."

He needed more time to devise a plan if he had any chance of saving the clock. He'd tried before in Lyallpur, and that had blown up in his face. Literally.

Danny noticed a shop on their left. Bottles of every color filled the window, along with dried herbs dangling from strings and small figurines of stars and suns. The table was covered with a pale lavender cloth, a stack of long cards positioned at its center.

A woman was seated at the table, her long dark hair tied back with a blue kerchief. She watched Danny with curious eyes, but said or did nothing to call him over. Still, he felt the urge to approach her, like a moth inextricably drawn to light.

"Hey," Liddy called. "Danny. Oy!"

He ignored her, stopping before the woman and her table. The woman stared back at him, one eyebrow quirked ever so slightly upward.

Eventually, she touched the cards with a slim, pale finger. "I read the cards for you?" she asked.

"Danny," Liddy growled at his side, "this is just a bunch of nonsense. You don't believe in this stuff, do you?"

"Not really," he murmured. But he nodded to the woman anyway. She began shuffling her deck, then asked him to cut the

cards into three piles. Touching the cards seemed strangely intimate, as if giving them permission to peruse his soul.

The woman pointed to the stack on his right. "This is past. The middle is present. This one, future." She collected the cards again with the present deck on top. After more fiddling, she looked up at him with an enigmatic smile.

She put one card on the table. Then two. When five cards had been laid out before him, she returned to the first and turned it over. It showed a man with a golden crown sitting on a throne holding a scepter.

"This, your past—the Hierophant. You have struggled between what is right and what is wrong. The answer will come. The answer is within you."

She turned over the second card. It was flipped, but even upside down he could see a man and a woman holding goblets beneath a winged lion.

"The present desires," she said with another small smile. "The Two of Cups. It usually means love, but because it is inverted, you may also be feeling doubt, perhaps about a certain person. A strong card, a powerful omen. There is still love waiting for you."

Liddy sniggered, and Danny went pink. He hoped beyond everything the woman's words were true.

The third card was turned. It featured a man standing at a table with the symbol of infinity above his head. "This, the unexpected future. The Magician. It is a card of great power. You are on the path to something momentous. It will show you how much power you possess."

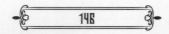

Now Liddy cast him a sideways glance. Danny's eyes never left the cards.

The woman turned over the fourth, which showed a crumbling fortress struck by lightning. The sight of it made his stomach twist.

"The Tower," she said, her voice quiet. "A great change is coming, and soon. Things you have known, things you trust to stay—it will all change."

His heart beat furiously in his chest, his fingertips numb. He could no longer hear the babble of people on the street, or sense Liddy's presence at his side. It was only him and the cards.

The woman watched him a moment, her smile gone. With the utmost gravity she put her fingers on the fifth and final card.

"The outcome," she said, then turned it over.

A man dangled from a beam of wood covered in ivy. He was suspended by one foot, his head shrouded in a halo of gold, hands tied behind his back. Danny had noticed all of the cards were printed with Roman numerals at the top; this one bore the number XII, like the apex of a clock.

"The Hanged Man," she said.

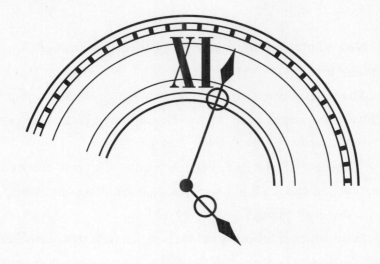

They were finally ready to set up the explosives. Everyone squeezed into the boys' apartment as Felix and Zavier explained how the mission would work. Danny barely paid attention. He stared at his knees, occasionally catching Daphne's or Meena's eye.

They wanted to do something. They wanted *him* to do something. But he was caught in a net, and every twist and turn he made to free himself only ensnared him more.

Twelve *bongs* echoed across the square. With the lamps turned down and unsuspecting residents of Prague asleep in their beds, the group quietly filed out into the street. Danny had left his coat behind, and he shivered in the February air.

Six months since he'd left home.

Zavier issued silent orders and Liddy and Edmund stalked on ahead, scouting the square and the surrounding alleyways. The

rest waited until they returned with the all clear, then quickly made for the tower. Zavier took out familiar metallic discs like those he'd used during his first unfortunate meeting with Danny on the *Notus*.

At the astronomical clock, Zavier flung a disc up toward the metal grating, releasing the thin, sturdy rope hidden within. He held onto one end, giving it a tug to be sure that it was secured above.

"Liddy and Ed will patrol the square and give an alert if anyone's coming," Zavier whispered. "If you hear a high whistle, hide. A low whistle means false alarm."

"'Ide where?" Astrid said without bothering to lower her voice. "'Ow am I to shove these three into an alleyway in time?"

"Let's put it this way. If any of us are caught, we'll be facing the same sentence, so take your pick: the ship or a Czech prison."

Felix scaled the rope first, hauling the equipment on his back as he had in Lyallpur. Zavier checked the street and followed. Pale moonlight fell across the cobblestones of the square, and Danny thought he caught a glimpse of Edmund by the church.

Felix and Zavier wrenched open a metal door cut deep within the wall next to the clock. When they disappeared inside, Astrid sighed.

"It's said the windows up there led to a prison for aristocrats." She sniffed. "If you ask me, better to use a dungeon."

"Of course you'd think that," Daphne muttered as Meena stared up at the faintly glowing clock faces with unease. "Where's the *Prometheus*? Don't you have to drop the water from Aetas's prison around the tower?"

"That will come," Astrid said with a lazy wave of her hand. "Perhaps your Indian boy will be the one to deliver it."

Even in the semidarkness, Daphne's blush was visible.

Danny cleared his throat. "What are we supposed to do in the meantime?"

"We watch. And wait."

He reached into his pocket and rubbed the small cog. He would go mad just standing there, waiting for the inevitable, finding out once again that he was too weak to make a difference; too weak to put a stop to this.

"Edmund and Liddy told me how they came to be on the *Prometheus*," he said to fill the growing silence. "What about you?"

Astrid was quiet a long moment, and Danny was sure she was ignoring his question. But slowly, the story spun out of her. She'd grown up in a village in northern France, always knowing she had the gift to connect to time. She'd been training with the local mechanics guild until she turned fourteen, when she confessed to her mother and father that she wasn't the son they thought they had, but rather a daughter.

"They kicked me out." Astrid shrugged as if to dismiss it, but Danny could see the tightness around her eyes, the way she swallowed hard. "I was on my own. I'll spare you a long story—I eventually found a troupe, a uh . . . cirque itinérant? I learned to throw knives. Crowds loved it. I did that for a couple of years, until Prema and the others found me. She 'ad run away, because she did not want her family to know she preferred kissing girls.

She was with the crew then, and knew I 'ad the same gift for time, though I was untrained. I was tired of the troupe, so I begged Prema and Zavier to let me join the crew instead. I kept the knives, though." She fingered one with a sharp smile.

"You don't care about what Zavier's doing?" Daphne asked.

"Non. I may 'ave the gift, but I am not a . . . mechanic. Towers, no towers"—she tilted her knife from one side to the other—"it makes no difference."

Danny clenched his jaw, fixing his eyes on the clock. He watched the strange hands, the ones ending with a small sun and moon that tracked the movement of the celestial bodies. Time was so strong here, so exact. He felt it against his skin, not quite a push, but a firm embrace. It made the cog in his pocket vibrate with power.

Danny bit his lip and took out the cog. He stared at it and thought about Aditi's tower in Meerut just before it had been blown to bits. Before it had given Meena the burn on her cheek.

He'd used his blood, just a little, to force the spirit to come out. If he did it again . . .

But Zavier was so close, and Astrid kept darting warning glances in Danny's direction, as if she could sense his restlessness. Daphne and Meena had retreated further into the shadows and were whispering to each other, no doubt scheming up a way they could knock Astrid unconscious and steal away before the other two returned.

Before Danny could join them, something tugged his eyes upward. He tried to focus on the highest clock face, but his vision became distorted, as if he were looking through a thick lens. After blinking a few times, he finally figured out what was skewing his vision.

A black mass stood in front of the face. Not blocking the light, but absorbing it.

A chill ran down Danny's spine as time skittered across his skin and over the nape of his exposed neck. The more he peered at it, the more the figure resolved into a human shape. But it was unlike any clock spirit Danny had ever seen. The spirit's skin was jet, hardly distinguishable from the black glass of the astronomical clock. Its eyes, piercingly bright by contrast, were a golden-amber.

It was looking straight at Danny.

He immediately let go of the cog and took a step back. Astrid saw the movement and followed his gaze. She gasped.

Daphne edged toward Danny, but didn't take her eyes off of the clock. "Is that the spirit?" she whispered. "What does he want?"

Danny shook his head. He didn't know. He remembered the fury of the Lyallpur spirit and how he'd tried to destroy them for demolishing his tower. Did this one know what Zavier and Felix were doing inside?

Astrid mumbled something in French, followed by, "Make it go away."

"I don't know how." His voice sounded distant, like the spirit could absorb that, too.

As if the spirit had heard them, it suddenly vanished.

"That wasn't normal," Daphne said. "It felt . . . stronger than usual. Warped."

"Do you think it's because of this?" Meena asked, pointing to the astrological clock faces. "Maybe they give it more power. Make it different than the others."

"Maybe," Danny murmured. As much as the spirit had scared him, he wanted it to come back. To speak to it. Warn it.

He wondered who the spirit had been before they'd died for Prague.

Or who the new spirit would be if the Builders rebuilt this clock.

"I do not like this." Astrid sheathed her dagger. "I will go check on the others. You three stay 'ere."

But as soon as she started for the clock, it tolled one. They froze, watching the spectacle of the clock's performance. A small bell chimed continuously as two windows opened above. Figures of the apostles peeked through each window, gliding on a mechanical track. When they were gone, the golden rooster above the clock faces crowed, followed by one clear, deep knell.

Afterward, the square was deathly silent. The four stood unmoving, waiting for something more to happen. Astrid was the first to shake herself out of her stupor.

"It is taking too long," she said, moving toward the still-dangling rope.

That's when they heard it: a high whistle.

They looked across the square. Figures were moving toward them; not Edmund and Liddy, but two police officers, with thick

double-breasted coats and flat caps. The officers hadn't seen them yet, but it was only a matter of time before they noticed four teenagers loitering in front of the clock.

Quicker than any of them could register, Meena darted for the policemen.

Astrid swore and took off after her. She caught Meena within seconds, tackling her to the cobblestone and muffling her cries with a hand. Fumbling with the taser at her belt, she sent a bolt of electricity through Meena.

"Stop it!" Daphne grabbed at Astrid, but the French girl whipped around, knocking her feet out from under her. Daphne landed with a cry.

The policemen called out something in Czech. Danny hesitated, glancing between the girls, the clock, and the policemen. He ran out into the square, waving his arms above his head.

"Help! They're going to—"

A figure lunged from the shadows at one of the policemen. The man jerked with a strangled yelp before falling to the ground, twitching. The other raised his baton before Edmund also zapped him with his taser.

Danny and Edmund stood panting, glaring at each other with nothing but moonlight and a couple of bodies between them. Danny feinted right, then ran left, but Edmund didn't fall for it. He was tackled to the ground as Edmund rammed the taser into his back, sending an excruciating bolt of electricity up his spine. Danny screamed. It felt like he writhed and choked for an eternity, every nerve, every cell of his body on fire.

"Christ, Danny," Edmund said above him. "You just don't learn."

Liddy ran up to them. "We have to go."

"We're just leaving these blokes here?"

"We have to! Where's Zavier?"

Edmund yanked Danny upright and tugged him along, Danny's movements jerky. Around the corner, against the glow of the astronomical clock, the shadowed forms of Zavier and Felix climbed back down.

"There's something wrong with the devices," Zavier said, panting. "We have to abort and come back." He saw Meena slumped on the ground, Daphne hovering over her, while Edmund supported Danny. "What happened?"

"What d'you think? Bleeders tried to run again," Liddy said, leaning over to spit.

Zavier's face clouded, but Edmund waved him off. "There's no time for that now. We ought to go."

Zavier clenched his jaw and nodded. "We'll try again later. Let's regroup."

As soon as they were back in the apartment, Zavier grabbed Danny by the collar.

"You said you wouldn't do this again," he growled. "You know the stakes, Danny. We made a bargain!"

Danny opened his mouth to shout back. Zavier had no clue what would happen if they destroyed another tower, if they

allowed the Builders to sacrifice another victim. But he couldn't do it, not with the secret hanging between them, thick as blood.

"The clock's a symbol for these people," Danny croaked, Zavier's knuckles against his throat. "And you're about to take it away from them."

"This isn't about them!" Zavier pushed Danny away and tried to pace, but the room was too crowded. "This isn't about you, or Prague, or even the Builders—"

"No, it's about *you*. You and your personal mission. You've roped all these people into your stupid ideals—"

"It's not about me, either. Or Sally, or my mother. It's about Aetas, and the way it's supposed to be. Believe it or not, freeing him will *save* people. Yes, Prague will lose its clock, but they can always build a new one."

"It won't be the same," Danny muttered.

Zavier released an inarticulate cry and kicked the nearest pack. Felix winced; it was his.

"Z, let's just focus on contacting Dae," Edmund said. "The sooner we get the issue with the bomb sorted, the sooner we can leave."

"They'll be looking for us now," Astrid agreed. "They'll 'ave more guards."

Zavier caught his breath, fixed his hair, and nodded. He dug through his own pack for the clunky radio he'd brought from the *Prometheus*, then fiddled with the mechanism until crackling filled the apartment. Zavier glanced at the door before mumbling into the device.

Danny sunk onto the bed and clutched his head in his hands. After a moment, he felt a touch on his shoulder. He looked up at Daphne's face, pale and drawn.

"Are you all right?" she whispered. "Does it still hurt?"

"I'm fine."

"Dae! Hello?"

Another loud crackle, then Dae's muted voice came from the radio, as if he spoke through a thick wall. *"Zave? What happened?"*

"The explosives wouldn't activate. I think something got switched around in transit. Hold off on the water until we can figure out what to do next."

"What you did was stupid." Liddy frowned down at Danny and Meena.

"I'm trying to stop you from making a huge mistake."

"That isn't your decision," she said.

Zavier handed the radio to Felix, who rattled off a string of jargon, then nodded and passed the device back.

"Think it can be fixed by tomorrow night?" Zavier asked into the radio.

"Absolutely."

"Thanks, Dae." Zavier glanced at Danny. "Do me a favor? Put the spirit on."

" . . . All right."

Danny tensed. He stared at Zavier, who met his eyes with a challenge. Daphne put a warning hand on Danny's shoulder.

There was some rustling and crackling from the radio, then a sweeter voice, achingly familiar: *"Danny?"*

He jumped up and grabbed the radio from Zavier's out-stretched hand. "Are you all right? What are they doing to you?"

"Calm down, they aren't doing anything."

Colton sounded different. Tired. Danny turned his back to the others and held the radio closer to his mouth. "You aren't wearing the cog holder."

"No. I was, but they took it off." Colton paused. *"I think they're going to do something to it."*

A reminder of what he had to lose if he didn't comply. Danny glared over his shoulder at Zavier, leaning against the wall and watching him.

"Danny, don't do this," Colton whispered, his soft words nearly eaten by static. *"I don't care what they do to me. It's—"*

Zavier plucked the radio from Danny's hand. "He might not care, but you do. Don't you, Danny?"

"You've already proven your point," Danny said, voice low. "Just give him back the cog holder."

Zavier mumbled the order into the radio. He nodded once at Danny. "This will happen one way or another. I'm sorry, but that's just how it is."

"You're not sorry at all. You *like* playing god and making everyone scramble for your sake."

"That goes to show how little you know me." Zavier turned away to speak with Felix.

Danny felt so heavy, he was amazed he didn't break through the floor. No one was looking at him now.

Daphne and Meena joined him. "You'll see him soon," Daphne said.

When he didn't answer, Meena asked, "What do we do?"

"You're asking me?"

"Astrid already told Liddy and Edmund about the spirit you saw. Zavier's going to find out, but I doubt it'll stop him. Do you think it's . . . malicious?"

He thought about the shadowy figure and shuddered. It felt so different from the bright, warm presence of Colton and his tower.

"I don't know. But if it is," he said with a glance over his shoulder at the others, "maybe it'll stop Zavier for us."

After a night of troubled sleep, Danny woke to low murmuring. Opening his eyes, he noticed a new addition to the room, as if it weren't crowded enough.

As Danny sat up, Akash turned from his conversation with Zavier. He settled beside Danny with a small, sheepish smile.

"What are you doing here?" Danny demanded.

"I was told to drop the water over the tower early this morning, when the guards were changing shifts. I landed the *Silver Hawk* outside the city afterward."

"You're really becoming part of their crew, aren't you?"

"It isn't like that. I volunteered so I can see my sister. So I can make sure she's safe."

"And Daphne?"

Akash looked down.

"She still hasn't forgiven you. Hell, I'm not even sure if I've forgiven you yet."

"I know. I . . ." Akash wrung his hands together between his knees. "I should have helped you. I should have done something to prevent you from getting hurt. I'm sorry, Danny. I mean that."

Danny sighed. Really, who was he to judge him? Akash had done what he thought was right. More than that, what he was doing now—agreeing to help Zavier so he could stay close to Meena and Daphne—was exactly what Danny was doing for Colton.

"I forgive you," he finally said.

A relieved grin broke across Akash's face, smoothing the worried divot between his brows.

Danny glanced out the window. The sky was tinged pink, just past dawn. "So, what now? You've dropped the water already."

"The power in that water will last a day or so," Zavier said, cutting in. "According to Ed, there've been more guards around the square, but I suspect security will return to normal when there's no further disturbance."

"Just a bunch of pranksters," Edmund said cheerily. "That's all they'll think we are."

The memory of Colton's words, begging him to stop this, tightened his chest. But what could he do?

With Edmund as their escort, they walked to the girls' apartment. Akash fidgeted with his goggles, and it was only then that Danny realized he'd put a lot of thought into his appearance. His hair was combed, his clothes freshly laundered. Danny couldn't help but feel a little sorry for him.

Liddy opened the door, eyes twinkling when she saw Akash. "You have a visitor," she called into the apartment.

Meena's dark eyes widened at the sight of her brother. "Akash!" She started forward, then paused. After a small shake of her head, she hugged him tightly, his body sinking into her embrace. They exchanged a few words in Hindi before she took a step back. He gently touched the burn on her cheek. His eyes darted to Daphne, who stood by the door with her arms crossed. Not angry, but wary.

"Miss Richards," Akash greeted her. "How are they treating you?"

"Barring the electric shock incident, it's been all sunshine and roses," she said. Danny rolled his eyes.

"I need to get back to Z," Edmund said. "Can you and Astrid look after these four?"

But Astrid refused to come along.

"She's pining for Prema," Liddy said, ducking as a knife embedded itself in the door above her head.

Their destination was the church, where Danny could hopefully keep an eye on the clock. As they crossed the square, Danny noticed a couple of policemen, but they didn't look particularly worried. He felt the water, though—that sharp, intense power he'd first noticed in Khurja.

The Gothic church rose tall and imposing, topped by two black spires. The others seemed impressed, the wistful look on Meena's face reminding him that she'd probably gone a long time without an idol to bow to. Much to Danny's annoyance, there were a couple of buildings between the church and the square, which limited his view of the clock.

Inside, the pews were lined perfectly between high molded gables. The organ above their heads was black and gold, much like the astronomical clock across the square. The columns ended in elegant black structures framing gilded figures of biblical myth, and above the altar posed a triumphant angel.

Devout churchgoers sat in the pews, quietly praying in search of something they didn't understand. An answer, maybe, to some unspoken question. Danny thought back to the tarot cards and each enigmatic image: the Magician, the Tower, the Hanged Man.

He looked up and saw a sculpted portrayal of a man above a tomb. The name sounded vaguely familiar: Tycho Brahe.

"He was an astronomer," Liddy said at his shoulder. "Did you know the poor bloke lost part of his nose in a duel? Not over a woman or anything exciting like that. A mathematical formula, of all things."

Danny almost smiled. "Must have been quite the formula."

"It says touching his right cheek helps get rid of toothaches." She pressed two fingertips to Tycho's cheek. "Not that I have one, but maybe it'll prevent one down the road."

"Good idea." Danny shook himself. Their interaction had felt almost normal; he was letting his guard down. Ignoring her confused look, he continued walking through the church.

Spotting Daphne and Akash in a small niche, Danny hid

behind one of the columns. Daphne's arms were crossed tightly over her chest, her blue eyes cold and hard. Akash's hands were buried deep within his pockets.

"I said I was sorry. And yes, I told Danny. He's forgiven me."

"Bully for Danny."

"I don't know what else you want from me," Akash whispered. "I would do anything for you. If I could go back to that moment and tell Danny what would happen, I would. But I was frozen. I could do nothing. I feel shame for that every day."

Daphne looked down. They stayed wrapped in silence for a moment, neither of them moving. Eventually, she sighed softly.

"I want to forgive you. I want to forget that most of this even happened. But . . . I can't."

"Why not?" It wasn't a demand. It was a fragile, broken whisper, and it seemed to hit Daphne like an arrow, making her hunch her shoulders.

"You did everything you thought was right," she said. "And I can't blame you for that. But I . . . I'm not sure I can trust you again. Matthias was my mentor, back in the Union, but he convinced me to do something out of my blind trust for him, something that ended up harming a lot of people. He abused that trust. I can't handle that again. I can't."

Akash almost reached out to her, then thought better of it and dropped his hand.

"I miss London," she said softly. "I miss my home. I miss my mother, and . . . and having a predictable life. A *stable* life." Daphne pressed the heel of her hand to her eye, her lashes

glittering with unshed tears. "Everything is changing, and I can't stop it. It started when Matthias betrayed me—maybe it even started when my own mother tried to hurt me, so that she wouldn't be the only one hurting. I don't know. But it seems that everyone turns on me eventually."

"I won't."

"You have."

Akash flinched, unable to hide from the truth of that simple statement. "What can I do to prove that I'm not that person anymore?" he asked. "What would earn back your trust?"

"I don't *know*, Akash. I just . . . Everything is happening at once, and I can't stand it. I need time." She turned to walk away, but paused. "Thank you. For before."

As Daphne wandered off to another corner of the church, Danny caught a glimpse of Meena, who'd witnessed the whole thing. She shared a look with Danny, then went to comfort her brother.

Danny thought of Colton turning him away, the painful longing and frustration in his expression. Had some pivotal trust between them been severed?

There was more to grief than words and promises. Time, after all, could not mend everything.

Zavier returned to the boys' apartment with Edmund and Felix after the others had eaten.

"When are you going to do it?" Danny asked.

Zavier spared him a glance before turning back to his new purchases. "That's no longer your concern. You're not coming this time. Too much of a liability."

Danny clenched his hands into fists. "I won't run again."

"I think that's the fifth time you've made that promise," Edmund said.

Danny grabbed Zavier by the arm. It was the metal one, solid and cold beneath his grip. "I'm coming. You can't keep me locked in this bloody room any longer."

Zavier regarded him coolly. Finally, he nodded. "I thought you might be stubborn about it. Fine, you can come."

"And me," Daphne said.

"Me also," Meena added.

"Meena, no," Akash argued. "You might be hurt or caught."

"That is a risk," Zavier agreed. "Ed, why don't you make everyone some tea? Then we can all sit and plan it out."

The room was crammed with uneasy energy. Akash kept glancing at Daphne and Meena. Both looked just as stubborn as Danny felt. He *had* to go back to that clock. He had to see that spirit again and—what? Convince it to attack Zavier? Plead with it to back down? Which would Colton want most?

The tea Edmund made was hot and tart, but Danny eagerly drank it anyway. It should have woken him up, but every minute he felt drowsier and drowsier. By the time he was down to the dregs, he could barely keep his eyes open.

Oh, hell.

"You bastard," he hissed, trying to rise from the bed. Daphne was already slumping toward the headboard, her blond hair falling across the pillow. Meena's head drooped as the cup slipped from her fingers.

Zavier took the cup from Danny's heavy hands. "No need to worry. By the time you wake up, it'll be over."

He pushed Danny back onto the bed. Danny struggled, but it was useless; sleep sang its siren song, pulling him under. He briefly caught Akash's worried question before his head rolled against Daphne's and he surrendered completely.

As Danny's consciousness floated back toward the surface, his first thought was to look out the window. It was the heavy dark of midnight, with little moonlight to relieve the oppressive blackness.

His eyes snapped open. Zavier. The Orloj clock.

He'd been sleeping against Daphne, who was also beginning to stir. Danny pushed himself up and accidentally elbowed her in the stomach. She grunted.

"What—?" Her voice was scratchy and slurred. "Danny?"

"I'm going to kill him," he growled. "I'm going to fucking kill him."

He nearly fell off the bed, steadying himself against the other one, where Akash sat next to Meena's sleeping body. Akash jumped up to help.

"Lie back down," he said, but Danny pushed him away.

"You bloody—let them—"

"I didn't know the tea was drugged! They told me that I could keep you three safe if I watched over you."

Meena groaned, pushing up on her elbows. *"What time is it?"* she asked in sleepy Hindi.

Danny lunged toward the door, stumbling and cursing, his vision swimming dangerously.

"Danny, wait!" Daphne called.

"What is going on?" Meena asked.

Out on the street, the cold night air helped sober him. He shook his head and hurried to the square where the power kept pulsing, writhing, skipping beats like an irregular heartbeat. His own heart pounded in tempo, one-two-three, one-two-three.

Someone called his name, but he kept running; or, tried to run as he glanced off the sides of buildings. He could see the glow of the astronomical clock ahead, and the shadows of people fighting below. Edmund and Felix were taking on three or four policemen on their own. There was no sign of Zavier.

Suddenly, the power pulsed hard. Danny nearly fell to his knees, and the cog in his pocket shivered. Looking up, he choked on a gasp.

The black and gold spirit stood between the two windows where the apostles made their hourly appearance, its feet balanced on the sills. Its golden eyes blazed with hatred, its ebony hands clutching the metallic rope Zavier had used to climb the clock faces.

And there he was, dangling under the XII—Zavier, with the rope around his neck, legs flailing as his hands scrabbled at his throat.

The Hanged Man.

Danny ran for the clock, hand diving into his pocket. Without thinking—without quite understanding what he was doing—he dug the cog's spokes into his wrist, his blood flowing over the metal.

Reaching the tower, he slammed the bloody cog against the lowest clock face.

The world was sucked away in a scream. He hurtled into a dark unknown, zooming over a bridge of stars. They brushed against his fingers, hot dust and blazing light, the stuff of dreams and the end of the world. The giant weight of a planet caught his side, red and swirling, a distant blue moon, the roar of the sun behind him, endless black.

The spirit shrieked above him, causing the tower, the ground, the very air to vibrate with electric power. Danny gasped as he returned to his body, keeping the cog pressed against the face. The surge of power jumped over his skin, *under* his skin, making his teeth ache and his heart nearly explode from its force.

Zavier dropped to the ground in a heap. Coughing and wheezing, he tugged the rope from his neck as Edmund and Felix were beaten back by guards, who'd seemed to take no notice of the struggle nearby.

Then the Orloj spirit was right before him. Danny snatched the cog away just before it grabbed him by the throat, lifting him off the ground. He choked and scratched at the spirit's hand, but it was like attacking stone. The spirit's golden-amber eyes bored straight into him, its black lips curled back, baring its teeth.

Zavier slammed into the spirit's legs. The spirit dropped Danny and turned to attack, but something stole its attention. It looked up at the clock, where the bell began to announce the next hour.

"The bomb!" Felix yelled. "It's set to go off at one!"

The clock was just about to toll one o'clock.

The spirit shrieked again and disappeared into its tower. Zavier collapsed. Danny pushed to his feet as the others raced from the square.

"Get up!" he yelled, tugging on Zavier's arm. "Hurry!"

The windows opened. The apostles began their familiar path.

Danny pulled a half-conscious Zavier from the ground, groaning as his body protested. The bells kept ringing, the windows beginning to close. Danny pushed Zavier as hard as he could toward the square as the tower struck one.

The street erupted into shards of glass.

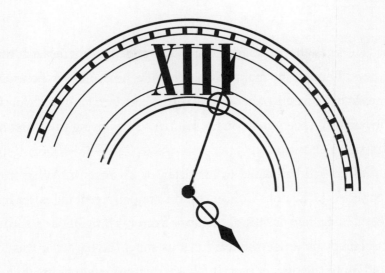

XIII

Colton went through a cycle of caretakers while the others were gone. Currently he was being watched by Charlotte. He couldn't complain; she was kind and didn't treat him like a prisoner. And she let him into the plant nursery where she liked to spend her time.

He brushed his fingers over verdant leaves and thought about the garden behind his house. His mother would hum to herself as she planted new vegetables, or insist his sister Abigail sit near the hedgerows for some fresh air.

Colton leaned over a plant with wide leaves. "This one smells nice," he said.

Charlotte looked up from pruning. "That's basil. We use it in the kitchens." She took a deep breath. "I love the smell of this place. It's so soothing."

He knew her husband, Felix, had gone to Prague with the others. Though she maintained her smile, he could see the small lines at the corners of her eyes, the first hair-thin cracks of worry. He had often seen them on his mother's face during the worst of Abigail's sickness.

What had happened to his sister, or his parents? What had happened to Castor? Colton couldn't remember much after his death, just a few flashes of memory from his long life as a spirit. It seemed the longer he lived in this state, the harder it was to hold on to the distant past. It felt nearly impossible to imagine a future. He existed only now, in the present.

"You're not a clock mechanic, are you?" he asked.

"I am not. But Felix, he knows his way around explosives." She frowned slightly. "He was a grenadier in the Austrian army. He knew Zavier's uncle, before he passed. Felix owed him a favor and Zavier called it in."

"Why did you come with him?"

A small laugh escaped her. "I have my uses, too. Felix was a grenadier, but I was a surgeon, and they needed someone with my skills. Besides, it's not that simple to leave behind the one you love."

Colton bowed his head, focusing on the sounds of Charlotte pruning behind him. Though he was mired in the present, he still felt the insistent tug of the future wrapped in the scents of his past. He was blurred at the edges, boy and spirit and love and loathing.

An alarm blared overhead. Charlotte gasped and dropped

her shears. As the alarm cut off, Ivor's voice crackled out of the speakers.

"Landing party returned. Requesting emergency medical assistance."

Charlotte went pale. "Felix," she whispered, hurrying to the door.

Colton followed close behind, thankful for the strength from Dae's new cog holder. Charlotte wove through the corridors toward the hangar. The landing party was stumbling off the plane; a few other crewmembers crowded around, eager to help. Prema rushed forward to embrace Astrid when she stepped into the hall.

Edmund and Felix limped out with Zavier supported between them. They all looked battered, but Zavier had received the brunt of whatever had attacked them; his face was scratched, his throat bruised, and there were bloody splatters over his right side.

Jo hurried to support him, Sally on her heels. "What happened?" she demanded.

Zavier tried to speak, but all he could manage was a weak gasping sound. Charlotte quickly checked his pulse, muttering to Ed to carry him to the infirmary. She threw her arms around her husband, letting out a relieved sob into his shoulder.

Daphne and Meena followed after them. They didn't look hurt, but their expressions quashed the small relief that had begun to form inside him. The two of them were speckled with blood, but it didn't look to be their own. Colton soon saw why.

Akash ducked out of the hangar, Danny barely conscious in his arms. Danny was deathly pale, a shocking contrast to the bright blood that oozed from his left shoulder. He was jerking and fighting for breath, eyes open but glassy. Someone had tied a scarf around his shoulder, but that did little to stop the blood. Red seeped onto the floor, over Akash's boots, dripping from Danny's fingers.

"Mein Gott." Charlotte gestured them to follow her. "We have to be quick, he's already in shock."

Their actions and words were hazy, distorted, muted. Colton stood frozen as they rushed past, leaving nothing but a trail of blood behind. The smell was metallic, powerful. He could remember being drenched in it, could feel it leaving his own body as that terrible magic claimed him. His own gasps like Danny's, those desperate gulps for life.

His body hummed. His vision darkened. Danny's blood, pooled on the ground, sang to him. He stared at it until someone tugged at his hand.

"Come on, Colton," Daphne whispered. She led him down the corridor, Meena on his other side. They were silent, lost in their own private, if less violent, shock.

Crew members crowded the infirmary door. Liddy shooed them away so that Daphne, Meena, and Colton could pass.

Zavier was laid out on a bed, half-awake. Sally held his hand as Prema examined him, hissing to herself about the state of the bruises circling his throat. Jo stood at the foot of his bed, eyes darting between her nephew and the boy a couple of beds down.

That other boy had Colton's full attention. Charlotte had torn his shirt and tourniquet away, revealing a bloody torso already marred with a bullet wound. The new wound, a couple inches higher, was a jagged rent of flesh so deep Colton could see a hint of bone. The sheets and mattress were already soaked red.

Danny was still now, his eyes closed. He didn't even appear to be breathing. His head was tilted away to one side, revealing the pale slope of his bloodstained jaw, the vulnerable expanse of his throat.

Daphne made a small noise of pain. Colton realized he was squeezing her hand too tight and let go.

"He'll be all right," she said, but her voice was fragile.

"What happened?" Jo asked again.

Edmund took a deep, shaky breath. "We were trying the fix the explosives inside the tower, but police came as we were leaving. Someone must have seen us slip inside. As we were trying to get away, the—the clock spirit attacked us. It grabbed Zavier and tried to . . . hang him."

Prema inhaled sharply.

"Danny was running toward the clock. We'd put them under so they wouldn't get underfoot, but I guess the dose wasn't strong enough." Edmund's Adam's apple bobbed as he swallowed. "Danny did something, I didn't see what, but then the spirit was attacking him. The explosives were set to go off at one o'clock, and when it turned one, Danny grabbed Z and shoved him out of the way. The glass still got him, though. He was right in the middle of the blast."

Meena whimpered and put a hand to her cheek, where the

burn mark was. Akash stood off to the side, dazed and bloody, but at his sister's distress he put an arm around her shoulders.

"He saved me." It took a second to realize that Zavier had spoken, his voice low and hoarse. He painfully turned his head toward Danny, gray eyes half-open. "He didn't have to. He could have left me there to die."

"Shows how little you know him," Daphne replied coldly.

"Charlotte," Jo asked, "will he make it?"

The surgeon was concentrating, her arms stained to the wrists with Danny's precious blood. She'd wrapped the wound as best she could—the bleeding had slowed some—and now she pushed the syringe Felix handed her into Danny's vein. "Time will tell," she murmured. "He needs rest. He may go into shock again, but we'll have to see."

Now realizing how crowded the infirmary had become, Charlotte shooed the observers out. Edmund gave Danny one last look, squeezed Zavier's arm, and left the room. Meena tugged a still-dazed Akash to his feet. Daphne watched him, her eyebrows set in a worried frown.

"He was right behind Danny," she told Colton. "He pulled him out of the debris and carried him all the way back to the ship." She sighed deeply. "Colton? Speak to me. Please."

He met her eyes, but couldn't think of anything to say. Jo and Sally remained by Zavier's side, even though Prema assured them he'd be fine. Felix left to get Charlotte hot water and more bandages.

The infirmary was far from empty, but as Colton turned,

it was just Danny and him. His limbs felt frozen, but somehow he made it to Danny's bedside. He could still smell the tang of blood, so bitter compared to the earthiness of the basil. The blood felt . . . sharp. Magnetic. It called to him, as though it had come from his own body.

He touched the side of Danny's face, but he remained still. And cold.

Felix returned with a bowl of water and some cloths. Charlotte wet one of the cloths, but when she moved to wipe the blood from Danny's skin, Colton grabbed the rag away in a dizzying onrush of anger.

"I'll do it."

She nodded and left him to it.

"She's trying to help, Colton," Daphne scolded.

He knew that. He'd apologize later. Right now, there was only Danny. He dabbed at his chest, wiping away the offending blood. Danny didn't even stir.

"He feels dead," Colton whispered.

"He isn't dead. And he *won't* die. You know he's too stubborn for that."

Colton wrung the cloth over the bowl, turning the water from clear to crimson. His hands buzzed and the cogs on his back gently vibrated. If Daphne noticed he was glowing brighter, she didn't comment on it.

When he was finished, he pulled off Danny's boots, careful not to jostle his body too much, then covered him with the blankets Felix had brought. Danny still felt cold to the touch.

"Danny," Colton called softly, brushing the hair from Danny's forehead. "Danny, please wake up. It's me. It's Colton. Please, open your eyes . . ."

But he didn't stir. Colton couldn't even feel his heartbeat, it was so faint. He sobbed quietly, tearlessly, and rested his forehead against Danny's. He called Danny's name over and over, hoping if he heard it enough times, he would remember to wake up—remember who he was leaving behind.

He didn't know how long they stayed in the infirmary. Time meant nothing to him anymore. Visitors came and left. Charlotte made regular checkups.

One of those visitors was Zavier. He still looked wrung-through, the bruises on his neck a wreath of purple and black. Sally helped him stand, her thin arm around her brother's waist for balance.

He looked at Danny with something like regret. He caught Colton's eye.

"I owe him my life," Zavier said, voice still raspy.

"And yet he sacrificed his own for yours."

"He shouldn't have." Zavier took a deep breath and winced. "Look after him. You're free to do what you want on this ship. Just . . . make sure he lives."

Colton eyed him, suspicious, but Zavier actually seemed sincere. Zavier let Sally lead him out of the infirmary, and when he was

gone, Colton turned back to Danny. He'd hoped to hear some sort of sarcastic reply behind him—"Careful Zavier, don't want to let on that you actually have a heart"—but Danny hadn't even twitched.

Eventually, minutes or hours or days later, Charlotte said that Danny could be moved back to his bedroom.

"His body is responsive," Charlotte said as she tested Danny's reflexes, poking each fingertip with a needle. "And it seems like he wants to wake up. The risk of going into shock again is over, I think."

"I'll look after him," Colton said.

So he took residence in the room they'd given Danny. It was such an impersonal room, but at least it smelled like him. Colton sat in a chair beside the bed, staring at Danny's chest, willing him to breathe deeper, pump blood faster. All the things Colton couldn't do.

Danny woke the next day while Charlotte was performing one of her checkups.

"Gott sei dank! Can you hear me, Danny?"

His green eyes were distant underneath heavy eyelids, but he nodded slightly.

"Follow my finger." She moved it left then right. "Very good. Do you know where you are?"

He looked around, stiffening when he saw Colton. His lips parted, but he said nothing.

Colton was similarly frozen. He'd imagined all he'd do when Danny woke up: hug him, kiss him, make him promise to never leave his side again. But all he could manage was to sit and stare back.

"Danny?" Charlotte gently prompted.

Danny blinked and turned back to her. "We're on the ship." He tried to move, but cried out sharply.

"You have a bad tear on your shoulder. You need to rest a few days more before you'll be back on your feet." She hesitated, plucking at a wrinkle in his sheets. "They say you saved Zavier in the explosion. That was very brave of you."

Danny closed his eyes with a grimace. Charlotte smiled and touched his forehead.

"Sweet boy. Go back to sleep; you'll heal faster." She nodded to Colton and left.

A strained silence filled the room. Colton waited for Danny to look at him again, but his eyes remained shut.

There was a tear beyond the one in Danny's shoulder, and they both felt how deep it went.

Colton stood. He couldn't be here right now, not when his mind was so crowded with warring thoughts. Danny finally looked at him, helpless and tired. He was so pale, but his eyes were still that beautiful bright green.

Without thinking, Colton grabbed Danny's hand, relieved to find it warm. He lifted it to his mouth, kissing the center of his palm. Danny moved his hand to stroke Colton's cheek, and he leaned into the touch for just a moment before turning to the door.

He needed to think.

He needed to strike a deal with Zavier.

XIV

Thinking ended up taking a lot longer than Colton had anticipated. He'd spent an eternity in his tower doing nothing *but* thinking. This was different, though; this was thinking that would lead to an inevitable end, not thinking of things that had already been.

Since Zavier had given him full access to the ship, he holed himself up in a wing no one used. He was still angry with everyone, angry with himself. There was no way he could have controlled what had happened to him; he had died and then lived a second life. A lesser life. A life he couldn't in good conscience give to Danny, to whom he wanted to give the world.

It didn't seem fair.

But with Zavier's plan, he wouldn't even have that option. He would be abandoning Danny, just as he'd abandoned Castor.

God, Castor. That needed thinking about, too.

Finally, he left his dark solitude to seek out Zavier. He found him in his office, sitting at his desk and staring blankly at a book.

Zavier looked up when Colton entered. There were dark circles under his eyes, and his hair didn't look as neat as it usually did. He seemed deflated. Drained.

"We were wondering if you'd jumped ship," Zavier said. "Danny's been asking for you, but no one knew where to find you."

"I needed some time to myself." Colton sat in the chair before Zavier's desk, not bothering to wait for permission. "And to figure out what sort of deal to make with you."

Zavier's eyebrows lifted, and his eyes flashed with a hint of his old energy. "A deal?"

"Let me make one thing very clear. You dragged Danny into your plans and forced him to do what you asked. And he did it, because you held the winning piece—me. But when you were in danger and about to die, he saved you. He put you before himself. Even before me." Briefly he thought of Danny turning away from him in the Queen's camp to save the viceroy, the decision that had led them all here. "He didn't have to, but he did. And he very nearly died because of it. You may still have your winning piece, but you owe him, and me."

Zavier listened, head cocked to one side. When Colton was finished, he took a deep breath. "I don't understand why he did it either, to be honest. But . . . you're right. I owe him my life and more."

"Then will you listen to my offer?"

"Yes."

"No more tower attacks."

Zavier sat very still, frowning at his desk. "Do you plan on giving me the answer I'm looking for, then? The secret you and Danny are keeping from me?"

"No."

"Then what the hell do you expect me to do?" He slammed his metal hand down. "We're going to free Aetas, whether you like it or not. We're already looking for ways to keep you and your tower safe so that you and Danny can stay together. What more do you want?"

"I want the spirits to have a peaceful death. Oceana said . . . She said if he's freed, we would all be able to sleep. It sounds a lot better than being ended by fire and smoke."

"Sleep?" Zavier sat back. "An odd choice of words. What does it mean?"

"I don't know," he lied.

Zavier took a minute to think it over. "The spirit of the Prague tower . . ." He carefully touched his neck, still mottled with impressive bruises. "It didn't act like you did. It was . . . more. Too powerful for its own good."

"It doesn't matter now, does it? That spirit is dead."

Zavier sighed. "Yes."

"The authorities will be looking for this airship, after all the damage you've caused. So why not stop all this and let me help you in a different way? A less violent one?"

That caught Zavier's interest. "How?"

"The Builders." Colton had heard whispers of them after their attack on the *Prometheus*. If they were rebuilding towers, that could only mean one thing.

He closed his eyes against the memories.

"Colton?" Zavier stood and walked around the desk, leaning against the corner. "What are you suggesting?"

"Instead of destroying the towers, spy on the Builders. Figure out what they're doing, and where, and why."

"And find out how they're rebuilding the towers," Zavier finished slowly. "Which might lead to the information I need to free Aetas. And you'd be willing to help?" Zavier asked, skeptical.

"Yes, if you agree to stop demolishing towers. And if you promise not to involve Danny again."

Zavier nodded. "Deal."

Colton didn't smile. He didn't feel relieved. He'd actually done very little, and he was damned either way.

"One more thing," Colton said, standing. Zavier was taller than him, but he still managed to look the young man straight in the eye. This wasn't usual for him, this coldness and calculation. He didn't know who he was anymore.

But he did know one thing: he had to protect Danny at any cost.

"You won't lay a hand on him again," Colton said softly. "The power I have, that you're so afraid of? If you put Danny in danger again, or so much as touch him, I'll make you sorry."

Zavier watched him unflinchingly, and Colton was afraid his words hadn't had the effect he'd hoped for. Then he noticed that Zavier's eyes were pinched; he hid it well, but he was unnerved.

"I don't plan on putting Danny in danger again."

"Good." Colton turned toward the door, but Zavier had more to say.

"We had reports about you. You seemed docile. Innocent. We didn't expect you to fight back."

Colton hesitated with his hand on the doorknob. He thought about the boy he'd been, soft-spoken and easily awed, and of the loneliness of his tower. How people were constantly trying to take away the things that mattered most to him.

"I'm not just Colton anymore," he said. "I am also Evaline, and Ben, and every clock spirit in the world. I speak and fight for them, because they can't."

He opened the door and glanced back over his shoulder. "I am also Danny Hart. Everything you do to one, you do to the other. Remember that."

When he reached Danny's room, Colton was confused to see Danny sitting on the side of his bed with Charlotte hovering over him. His shirt was off, as were his bandages, revealing the sinister slant of his new wound. The skin around it was red and angry, the wound itself puffy. By contrast, the rest of Danny's skin was milk-pale.

They looked up when Colton entered. Danny's eyes flashed with fear.

"Good, you're here." Charlotte beckoned Colton inside. "You'll need to support his weight."

"Support his weight? For what?"

She held up a long, curved needle. It looked like a fishhook.

"I'll have to suture his wound," she explained. "We have to be sure the flesh knits."

Danny's breathing sounded strained, his back muscles tense. "How . . . How many sutures?"

Charlotte examined his wound again. "Maybe thirty?"

He let out a shaky breath. "I only needed four, here." He touched the scar on his chin.

"I'm sorry, but it must be done."

Colton watched as she prepared the sutures, his head cocked to one side. He noticed Danny looking at him, and he straightened his neck.

"All right," she said, touching the side of Danny's face. "This will be uncomfortable."

Danny closed his eyes as she started threading the hooked needle through his flesh. He gripped the edge of the bed with white knuckles.

Colton moved to his side and grabbed his hand. Danny looked up, startled, but squeezed tightly as a sound of pain hummed in his throat. Colton unthinkingly smoothed his fingers through Danny's hair, a gesture familiar to them both. A little of the tension drained from Danny's body.

He moved his hand down Danny's back, pressing his palm to skin. It was so warm. He traced lines and circles over his spine and shoulder blades, and Danny sighed at his touch.

"All done," Charlotte said after she snipped the thread and tied a tight bandage around his shoulder. "Thank you, Colton. Danny, how do you feel?"

"Bloody awful."

"It'll be better in a few days." She began to collect her equipment. "You should wash up, as long as you make sure not to get those stitches wet."

"I'll take him," Colton said, startling everyone, including himself.

"I'll leave you in his capable hands, then."

After she left, neither of them moved for a while. Colton realized he still had his hand pressed to Danny's back.

"Can you stand?" he asked.

Danny gained his feet but wobbled, and plopped back down to the bed moaning and rubbing his head. "No."

Colton almost cocked his head again, but stopped himself. "Come here."

"What—? Hey!"

Colton was pleased to find his new strength allowed him to lift Danny from the bed, one arm under his legs, another behind his back. Danny squirmed, but gasped when the motion tugged his wound.

"P-Put me down," he said, eyes wild.

"You need to bathe, and you can't walk. What else do you expect me to do?"

Colton grabbed clean trousers on their way out. Danny was too weak to put up a fight for much longer, resting his head against Colton's chest instead.

After a few turns, Colton found his way to the washroom. It was a metallic room with benches near the walls and three copper tubs sunk into the floor. He carefully set Danny into one of the tubs.

"It's cold," Danny complained, but his eyes were half-closed, his words low. He'd already used up a lot of energy. Colton hoped he wouldn't drown in the bathwater.

"Just give me a moment." Colton climbed into the tub to undress him completely, but Danny grunted in protest.

"You want to bathe with your trousers on?" Colton asked, arching an eyebrow.

"At least let me do it," Danny mumbled.

It took a couple of painful minutes and some swearing, but Danny managed to disrobe himself. Panting with the exertion, he sat back and closed his eyes as Colton threw the clothes toward the nearest bench before he turned back to examine the tub's faucet.

Colton turned a dial and a jet of water sprayed out, making him jump. It was ice-cold, and Danny yelped.

"Sorry, sorry!" Colton fiddled with the other dial until the water was too hot.

"Are you planning on boiling me alive?"

"Hold *on*." Colton tried turning the dials halfway each, and the water became soothingly warm, like standing in a beam of sunshine. "There."

He climbed out, his legs wet, and waited until the water was up to Danny's chest before twisting the dials again to shut off the stream. The gentle sound of lapping water filled the room, and thin, hazy steam rose from the tub. Danny's face was flushed, and he'd closed his eyes again, making sure to keep his shoulder away from the water.

They sat in silence as Danny soaked, each wrapped in their separate thoughts.

Danny eventually sighed. "I thought you weren't speaking to me."

"I can't let you die. I promised your father I'd bring you home."

Danny opened his eyes, fixing Colton with a familiar green stare. It was the look he reserved for puzzles and card games. "Is that the only reason?"

"You know it's not." He got up to fold Danny's trousers.

"Are you still angry with me? I tried to stop him, Colton."

"I know you did. Instead, you saved him."

Danny turned his head and the water rippled. "Would you have preferred I left him to die?"

"No, of course not." Colton set the trousers on the bench and returned to the tub, sitting cross-legged by the rim. "I know you wouldn't stand by and let someone else suffer."

"But I'm making you suffer," Danny said. "I know you don't care what happens to you if I disobey Zavier, but *I* do. And that's selfish, maybe, but—"

"Danny, stop. There aren't going to be any more bombings."

He frowned. "What?"

Colton explained the deal he'd made with Zavier, and Danny's mouth dropped open. As he spoke, he grabbed a nearby bar of soap, lathering it before picking up Danny's good arm and beginning to scrub.

"But how can they get intelligence on the Builders?" Danny asked. "Do they even know where they are?"

"No, but they'll be looking. And I agreed to help."

"You shouldn't get involved."

Colton smiled ruefully. "I'm already very much involved."

Danny grabbed the soap from him. "But what if they find out about the blood? What'll you tell them if they ask?"

"I'm going to keep the truth from them as long as I can. I don't want Aetas released, but . . ." He smoothed a lock of Danny's hair away from his face as a drop of water rolled down his forehead. "Maybe they really will find a way to save my tower."

"I thought . . ." Danny looked down at his hands, clutching the bar of soap between them. "I thought you didn't want that."

"I want to be with you, Danny. And that's the truth."

After Danny was through washing, Colton drained the tub and gently toweled him dry, Danny's dark hair sticking up in chaotic tufts. He couldn't stop himself from touching Danny's warm, damp skin, from the crook of his elbow to the hollow of his throat.

Danny watched him languidly. Waiting. Anticipating. Colton leaned into him as he dried his back, eyes fixed on Danny's lips. He touched them with a fingertip and saw them part.

But they were still so scared.

Colton helped him out of the tub and into clean trousers. Cleaned, dressed, and falling asleep, Danny easily sank into Colton's arms as the spirit carried him back to bed. He savored this; the heat of Danny's body, the smell of him, the soft breaths that made his chest rise and fall. Colton set him down and pulled the covers over him.

"Colton," Danny called sleepily. "Please don't go. You need to stay here. Keep safe."

"I'll be safe." He stroked the back of his finger over Danny's cheek. "I promise."

Danny looked ready to protest again, but he was losing the battle with sleep.

"I'm sorry," he whispered.

"I'm sorry, too," Colton whispered back.

As Danny fell asleep, Colton remembered the story he and Castor had told his sister Abi so long ago, the one about the princess trapped in her tower and the prince who fought to find her. When the prince lay wounded on the battlefield, she took up his sword and fought in his place.

He would protect Danny no matter what.

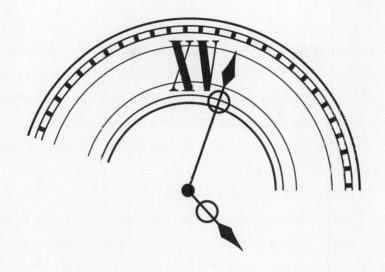

Khurja's streets were flooded with people meandering to and from the bazaar. It made Colton feel as if he stood in the middle of a cyclone of sound, surrounded by chatter and yelling and bartering. As the only person with white skin, eyes naturally went to him, and he had to fight the urge to run into the nearest building.

What if someone knew what he was?

"Don't worry," said Prema. "You look very human. It's just that you also look British."

"I am British."

"You know what I mean. They've been uneasy after the rebels tried to attack the viceroy."

Colton frowned; it was the reason why Danny had been shot. Akash, on his left, shifted uncomfortably.

The young Indian pilot had flown Prema, Anish, and him to Khurja. Though he was still getting used to the crush of the city,

Colton was fascinated by all that was for sale and wanted to take a closer look at everything. They wandered toward the heart of the city, which didn't take long despite Colton desperately taking in everything they passed: the people, the buildings, even the sky. He'd spent most of his long life in close quarters, shuttered from the world. Now here he was, actually a part of it.

If only Danny could be at his side.

They navigated onto a smaller side street littered with trash, but full of incredible smells of food vendors peddling from wooden carts. Colton never felt hunger, but suddenly wished he could.

As they walked, they tuned their ears to the gossip around them in hopes of catching mention of the Builders. Colton grew increasingly frustrated that he didn't understand the language. As they passed a group of women outside a small, whitewashed building, Akash's head turned sharply, but he didn't say what he'd overheard.

Colton sidestepped into an alley, waiting for them to follow. Anish was a silent shadow watching the street.

"What did you hear?" Colton demanded.

Akash ruffled his hair. "It's not related, exactly, but the women were talking about the new British officers harassing people. Some women have been followed home. One has even disappeared."

Prema frowned. "There aren't any British officers here. They must mean the Builders. Danny said they wore some sort of uniform."

"Do you think they're still here?" Colton asked.

"If they are, I'm sure we'll find them near the new tower," Prema said.

Colton didn't want to go near the new tower. Khurja already felt odd, like a train not completely running on its tracks. The air smelled sharp, and the cogs, hidden by their leather cover, vibrated gently against his back.

"How do we get near it?" Akash asked. "Won't it be guarded?"

"Almost certainly. But we'll have to try regardless."

It was almost evening, the azure sky gradually bleeding into crimson sunset. Prema bought food as they waited out dusk, each of them quiet and keeping to their own thoughts.

Colton couldn't help but notice Akash's mournful look. Finally, he turned and asked, "Do you fancy Daphne?"

Akash's eyes widened. "What?"

"You really upset everyone with what you did. I should be upset with you, too, but . . . I've learned that you can't change what's in the past. The important thing is what you intend to do in the future. So, do you fancy her?"

Akash looked away. "I . . . yes. I do."

"Then do you plan on helping Danny and me, or do you plan on helping Zavier?"

"You. Of course you." Akash lowered his voice, darting a quick glance at Prema, who was watching the street with Anish.

"Do you think Aetas should be freed?"

Akash fiddled with his goggles. "I don't know. It seems like something the ghadi wallahs ought to figure out among

themselves. What Zavier says makes sense, but it also seems wrong. And if Meena and Daphne don't like it, I trust their judgment."

"I think you're a good person, Akash. Just make sure Daphne sees it, all right? She can be stubborn."

"You say that as if I don't already know," Akash mumbled.

"And thank you. For helping Danny in Prague."

"I wasn't—" Akash thought over his words before continuing. "I didn't do it to make up for not helping him in the durbar. I helped Danny because he's my friend."

"I know." They shared a small smile before Prema stood, dusting off her hands.

"It's getting dark," she said. "Shall we?"

The clearing where the tower stood had guards posted at every street. Colton and the others stood to the side to survey the scene. The wrongness felt strongest here. Colton rubbed his arms and made a face, feeling a prickle between his shoulder blades. It was . . . bitter. That was the only way he could describe it.

"How ugly," Prema remarked, her voice the perfect match for the darkness settling over Khurja. "That's the best they could do?"

The tower was short and squat, built of a simple, rough limestone. Instead of a spire on top, they'd used brown shingles. The solitary clock face was small and had no numerals, only hands.

"They were in a hurry, looks like," Akash said.

Colton could only stare in distaste. It was more an imitation of a clock tower, any chance of grace or beauty replaced with

an almost industrial-like minimalism. The bitterness in the air emanated from the tower—if it could even be called that—and skittered over the cogs he wore. He took a step back and shook his head. "I don't want to go in there," he said.

"You made an agreement with Zavier," Prema reminded him. "Don't worry, I'll go with you."

"But how do we get past the guards?" Akash nodded toward the clearing. There were three total, two white and one Indian, all carrying long guns. Colton wondered what would happen if they shot him. He wouldn't bleed, he knew that much, but would he still die?

The memories rose again and he closed his eyes, hand grasping at his throat.

"Colton, are you all right?"

No, he was not all right. If it was as he suspected, the horrible tower before them was a grave marker.

Come.

His eyes snapped open. That voice— *What?*

Who are you?

He gaped at the tower. It couldn't be . . . but somehow it was. The spirit was sensing him, reaching out.

What sort of strength did this spirit possess to do such a thing?

"We need a diversion," Prema said. "Then Colton and I can run in through that door in the front."

"And how do you propose to get back out?" Akash asked.

"We'll have to be very, very fast."

Akash and Anish doubled back, finding a roundabout path to end up on the street opposite Prema and Colton. They waited for a couple of tense minutes, Prema chewing on a thumbnail, as the sky overhead dimmed.

Colton was still rattled. Before he could reach out to the spirit again, a red flare flashed across the clearing. The three guards called out as they ran for the street where Akash and Anish had set off the flare.

"Go!" Prema pulled Colton's arm and they sprinted to the tower, the power intensifying as they drew closer. Prema tried the door. Locked.

"Hold on." Colton banged on the wood until it cracked. He reached in and undid the lock, and they hurried inside. Prema closed the door and they were plunged into darkness.

Not total darkness; a faint glow came from the small flight of wooden stairs. Prema gestured him to go ahead of her. Bracing himself, fighting the urge to run back outside, he took the steps slowly.

His body shivered and his hands jerked. Being in Big Ben's tower had never been like this. There, he'd felt stronger, like he could do anything. Here, it was as though the power was rejecting him.

A platform had been built before a small pendulum. The clockwork and gear train rose high above, attached to the pole turning the clock's hands. Colton watched the solemn movement of the cogs, his own vibrating faster.

Turning, he came face-to-face with a young woman.

He backed up a few steps. The young woman's nose was slightly too big for her face, but her body was petite. She had dull copper-colored skin, light brown hair, and eyes like his—amber-gold.

They stared at each other. The young woman cocked her head to one side, and he did the same.

"Who are you?" she repeated.

"I'm . . . like you. I think. My name is Colton. What's yours?"

Her eyes shifted as she tried to remember. "Lalita."

"Lalita. It's a pretty name." She smiled shyly. "May I ask you some questions?" His voice was calm, but everything in him told him to run. He wanted to forget Zavier, forget India, but he couldn't abandon the others. He was doing this for Danny, not himself.

Lalita nodded. Colton studied her pitiful tower again, fighting back a curse.

He remembered Akash's remark about a missing woman and shuddered.

"How long have you been here?" he asked.

"I do not know."

"Do you have any memories? Dreams, maybe?"

She shook her head. "No. No memories. I am just Lalita, and I've always been here. Where do you come from?"

Colton spared a glance at Prema, who stood gawking to one side. "A long way away."

"Can I go places, too?" She looked up at the clock face. "I would like to go outside, but it feels bad when I do. I become very weak."

He toyed with the idea of telling her to take apart her own clockwork, rip out her central cog. But that would Stop Khurja, and he couldn't be responsible for that. Not after Enfield.

"I wouldn't recommend it," he said. "Lalita, I have just one more question. Has anyone come into your tower? Besides us, I mean."

The young woman tilted her head again. Colton almost did, too, then caught himself.

"A few people," she said at last. "They wear funny clothes, all one piece, with belts and big boots. One is a woman. She came a lot, but she's not here anymore."

Colton nodded, then turned to Prema. "Is that enough?"

Prema blinked and cleared her throat. "I . . . thought you didn't speak Hindi."

"I don't."

"She's speaking Hindi. And you're answering in the same language."

"Am I?" He touched his throat. He hadn't been able to understand anyone on the streets, but he could understand Lalita just fine. Perhaps there was no set tongue among clock spirits; time had no language barriers.

"Lalita." He took her hands in his. "I'm so sorry. I wish I could help you."

She looked confused. "Help?"

"Just . . ." He squeezed her hands. "I'm sorry."

Prema peered down the stairs. "We need to leave. I think I hear voices."

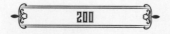

Khurja's clock spirit didn't try to stop them, but she looked sad about them leaving. Colton thought about her blood staining the ground this tower was built upon. Had they ripped her throat open? Had they plunged a knife into her body, too?

He wanted to ask her more. He wanted to know what the Builders had done to make Lalita powerful enough to worm her way into his mind.

"Colton, hurry!" Prema urged.

He glanced once more at the spirit before following Prema down. They paused at the door, listening for guards on the other side. Through the crack he'd made, Colton saw movement.

"Ready?" Prema pushed the door open. "Run!"

Zavier leaned against the wall, gray eyes leveled at Colton as Prema debriefed him about the new Khurja tower. Colton didn't meet his gaze. Instead, he looked around the office, adorned with few personal touches. A book of Greek myths rested on the bookshelf, and Colton's fingers twitched to open it.

"So she had no recollection," Zavier repeated. "Like she'd been born out of nothing. And yet Colton was able to speak to her in Hindi."

"I didn't know I could do that," he said in his defense.

"But you knew you could break the door."

Colton rolled his eyes and looked away.

"Clock spirits are strong," Zavier murmured, touching his still-bruised throat. "The question is, how strong?"

Zavier went to his desk, jotting something on a piece of paper. "None of the clock spirits remember how they were made,

but this one was just *there*, and made her own bubble of time around Khurja. How? The Maldon tower built last year didn't work—it had no spirit. So how did the Builders manage it?"

He glanced up at Colton again, but this time Colton didn't look away.

"The spirit said there was a woman who came often," Zavier mumbled, tapping his pen against the paper, leaving behind blotches of ink. "And we saw a woman with the Builders when they tried to take Danny and the others. Are they the same?"

Edmund had been lurking by the door, and now interrupted. "We need more information. Z, tell them."

"Tell us what?" Prema asked.

"We have a lead." Zavier smiled briefly, but it was cold. "Builders have been seen in Austria. Near Dürnstein."

"There's an impressive clock tower there," Edmund added. "They might be setting up a preemptive attack in case we head that way, or maybe they're studying it."

"Whatever their motive, I agree we need more information." Zavier pointed the pen at Colton. "Speak to the Dürnstein spirit and report back with what they say."

Colton nodded once and left the office. Daphne was waiting outside, nervously tapping her fingers on her thighs. She straightened when she saw him.

"How's Danny?" he asked before she could ask about the mission.

She sighed. "Feverish. Charlotte is looking at him now." Daphne hesitated. "He's been asking for you."

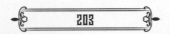

He looked down the hall to his left. Toward Danny's room.

"I've been given another assignment," he said. "Austria, this time."

She made an aggravated noise, but whether it was toward Zavier's assignment or Colton leaving, he couldn't be sure. "What do I tell Danny when he wakes up and asks for you again?"

"Tell him . . ." The words wouldn't come; there were too many he wanted to voice, and too many that refused to be spoken. "Tell him I'll be back soon."

Akash flew them to the outer edges of Dürnstein once the *Prometheus* was close enough. They stayed well back from the river, unwilling to expose themselves in such a small town, especially one overrun by Builders.

As in Khurja, Zavier chose the landing party to best blend into their surroundings. Felix, a native Austrian, had been asked to go, but Charlotte had made the point that he'd been through enough on the Prague mission. Instead, Akash stayed by the *Silver Hawk* as Colton, Edmund, and Liddy strolled into town, which was situated by a wide, dark river and cradled on its other side by craggy, tree-covered hills. Across the river were vast fields of what Colton thought might be grapevines.

Even from a distance, he could see the clock tower rising over the small, quaint buildings dotting the river's edge.

"It's blue," he said in surprise.

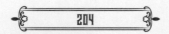

"All the better to stand out." Edmund touched the metallic rod at his belt, looking uneasy. "Remember, look like you belong here. Anyone gives us so much as a sideways glance, we'll need to pop out."

"Zavier said to gather as much information as we can before that," Liddy reminded him.

"We will, don't get your knickers in a bunch."

Zavier had wanted to come on the mission himself, but Jo had put her foot down, claiming he needed time to recover. It seemed there was at least *one* person who could give Zavier orders.

Colton liked the look of the town. High above the brown-shingled roofs he could see a crumbling ruin perched on a hill, a remnant of the past.

"That's the old castle," Edmund said, following his gaze. "Odd, isn't it? Such a tiny place having its own castle."

Colton imagined Enfield with its own castle. He ached at the thought of his town, and worried about the state he'd left it in.

All these months will feel like a second to them, he thought sadly. *All this life they're missing . . .*

It started to rain lightly as they entered the town proper. The streets were narrow, the buildings pressing in on them from every side. They followed the river down a dirt path, ducking behind a pink building with a clear view of the clock tower.

From far away it was impressive, but up close, it was astounding. It was sculpted with grand flourishes and molding, the light blue exterior trimmed in white. There were two sets of clock faces: a small black one halfway up, and a larger, more elaborate one at

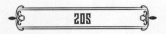

the top, white with golden numerals and hands, surrounded on either side by carvings and sculptures of men he didn't recognize. The building was topped with a large cross.

Other statues decorated the tower, gray and weathered. A few cherubs frolicked around the courtyard, their small legs dangling over the railing or hanging onto the platforms where the statues stood.

"It's beautiful," Colton said. He was immensely glad Zavier had agreed to not destroy this one.

"It is a gawker," Edmund agreed. "But those two bleeders are marring the scene a bit. Think they're Builders?"

Two men—flesh, not stone—stood in the tower's courtyard. They wore jumpsuits a few shades darker than the tower, along with wide belts and tall boots. One of them carried a gun.

"They look like they're waiting for someone to come out," Liddy said. "More of them inside, probably."

"Damn." Edmund leaned against the building and raked his wet hair back. "Guess we'll have to wait."

Colton looked at the tower again, taking in all its details and carvings and potential footholds.

"Oy, what're you doing?" Liddy whispered sharply as Colton darted forward.

"You want information on the Builders, don't you?"

The others shared a look. "Colton," Liddy began, but Edmund held up a hand to stop her.

"Let him go." He nodded toward the tower. "Just be careful, all right? And make sure you aren't seen."

"I won't be."

Colton moved around the buildings, following the river, eyes always on the tower. Beneath each of the clock faces were dark windows he could easily fit through.

When he reached the base of the tower, he peered around the corner. The two Builders were still waiting, looking bored. One of them poked at a cherub with his gun and said something that made the other laugh.

Colton found his first handhold and pushed himself up, reveling in the lightness of his body, the surety of knowing exactly where he planned to go. He'd climbed around his own tower so often that the movements were easy, familiar. The only tricky part was not being seen.

No alarm was raised, so he continued ascending. His hair and clothes were damp from the rain, and his hands slipped more than once. When he got to the window, the wind picked up, and he clung harder to the small ledge just under it.

He carefully crouched on the ledge and pressed his face to the dark glass. He thought he could make out the shape of two people looking up at the softly glowing clock faces. Colton tensed, but they didn't appear to notice him. After a few minutes, they moved toward the stairs.

Once they were gone, he opened the window as quietly as he could. He hopped soundlessly down and crept toward the darkened staircase.

"How did you make the other one come out?" asked a man below.

"You have to threaten it somehow," replied a woman with a deep voice. "It might just be shy. No matter—as soon as the tower's torn down, we'll get a new one."

"Will those children come running when we do?"

"I'm still waiting for my contact to confirm, but I believe so. Until then, we'll continue the work in Prague and see what we come up with."

"About that . . . The citizens are resisting our rebuilding efforts."

The woman didn't say anything for some time. "We'll have to delay the mission here so that I may pay the city a visit, then," she said at last. "And show how their beloved clockmaker pales in comparison to what we can provide them." The sound of a door opening and closing echoed up the stairs.

The back of Colton's neck prickled, and he whirled around. A middle-aged man stood across the room, staring inquisitively at him. His skin was pale, almost blue, but his hair was silver and his eyes were amber. He wore a simple homespun shirt and dark trousers.

"What are you doing here?" the man demanded. Like in Khurja, Colton understood him, though the spirit's words were heavily accented.

"I came to say hello," Colton said slowly, "and to ask what you know about those people who just left."

The spirit scowled. "If you are with them, get out of my tower."

"No, I'm not with them. I'm like you. Can't you can feel that?"

The man examined him, eyes trailing up and down his body. "Strange."

"Yes, it is, isn't it?" Colton swept the wet hair from his forehead. "What did they want?"

The spirit raised his eyes to the clock faces. "They wanted to speak to me, but I didn't reveal myself, not even when one drew blood."

Dread pooled inside him. So they *did* know.

"It felt . . . wrong," the spirit whispered. "The blood."

Colton thought back to Danny's blood in the *Prometheus*'s hallway, the buzzing warning of it. "What did they want to speak to you about?"

"They asked if I had dreams, and what they were about."

"And do you? Have dreams?"

"Sometimes." The spirit looked up again, sad. "I dream about a family. A little girl who sits on my shoulders. And I dream of leaves and vines."

Colton thought of the vineyards across the river. "If those people come back, you can't tell them anything. These are *our* secrets. They want to do something to your tower, and we can't let them."

The spirit's eyes flashed. "I will protect my tower."

"Good." Colton hesitated, not wanting to ask, but still needing to know. "Are there any bad dreams? Anything with—with time or . . . or violence?"

The spirit's thick eyebrows drew together. "No," he said

eventually. "Not that I can remember. Except . . . I did dream, once, of an axe. And pain."

Colton shuddered. "Thank you."

He wondered if he ought to go back down the way he'd come, but decided enough time had passed since the Builders left. He crept down the stairs, past the swinging pendulum, to the door. Opening it a crack, he cautiously looked for signs of the Builders, but they were all gone.

The rain had created puddles in the courtyard. Crossing it, he looked back up, marveling at the beauty of the tower. His own tower seemed so ugly by comparison, especially with the damage it had sustained.

Touching his right side, he started down the path when his neck prickled again. He turned back slowly, wondering if the spirit had recalled something more, but received a worse shock: one of the Builders was standing in the middle of the road.

Staring straight at him.

Damn.

Colton took off running. The Builder shouted and gave chase, boots kicking up mud and water. Colton dove around the corner of the building where he'd left Edmund and Liddy.

"They saw me," he said.

Edmund cursed as he and Liddy ran behind him. "Now what?" Liddy called.

"Colton, you wait for the Builder at the end of the street. Liddy, come here." Edmund pulled her into a tiny alley.

Colton wanted to protest, but the Builder rounded the corner and grinned. "Nowhere to run now," he said, advancing on Colton. "I have some questions for you."

Before he could come any closer, Edmund and Liddy jumped out from the alley and grabbed him. The man struggled, but Edmund was bigger and forced him to his knees on the wet cobblestone while Liddy quickly tied his arms together with metallic rope.

Edmund dragged the man to the nearest building and pushed him up against it. The man sat in a dirty puddle, coughing and sputtering.

"Now," Edmund said, taking out his taser, "you'll be answering some of *our* questions."

The man bared his teeth. He looked young, maybe in his twenties, with thin brown hair and hazel eyes.

"You think you can get me to say anything?" His accent was English.

Liddy pulled out a gun. Cocking back the hammer, she pointed it at him with a sweet smile. The man's eyes widened. "Go ahead, stay silent for all we care."

"No," Colton said, grabbing the gun from her. "No wounding or killing." Liddy scowled.

But the man was looking at him now. His mouth sagged open. "Wait," he whispered. "Wait, you can't be . . ."

Edmund glanced at Colton, suddenly uneasy. "You recognize him?"

"No, but I know what he is. A clock spirit. But how can you be here, outside your tower?" He looked past them, to the blue and white tower. "And your accent . . ."

"Never mind that." Edmund kicked the man's boot. "Who are the Builders?"

The man's gaze lingered on Colton. "Not too hard to figure that out, eh? We heard the Indian clock towers were falling, so some of the dignitaries from England and the continent funded us to rebuild them."

"But you're not part of the Mechanics Union?"

"Do we look like we're from the sodding Union?"

Liddy wrinkled her nose. "So you're nothing but a bunch of tower fanatics."

"We like tradition."

"What you built in Khurja wasn't a clock tower." Colton curled his hands into fists. "It's a monstrosity."

The man shrugged. "I'd beg to differ. It's simple, sure, but it's efficient, and that's what matters."

"How was the tower made?" Edmund asked, but the man ignored him, blinking against the rain.

"Who's your leader?" Liddy tried.

"You haven't been doing your research, have you? Not too hard to find what you're after if you ask the right people." Liddy pulled out a second, smaller gun and drew back the hammer. The man sighed. "Her name is Phoebe Archer. She's the one who got us our backing. After what you did in Prague, she's been in a right state. That clock was one of a kind, and you went and blew it up." He clucked his tongue. "She's one for punishment, Miss Archer is."

Edmund brandished the taser at him. "Answer my question. How exactly was the new tower in Khurja built?"

"Why not ask him?" The man grinned at Colton.

"Hey, there!"

The other Builders had found them. The man laughed as Colton and the others bolted for the town's outskirts.

"Damn it, damn it, *damn it*!" Edmund looked over his shoulder. "Little gormless—"

"Not now, Ed!" Liddy pointed to the *Silver Hawk*. "Let's get the hell out of here first, yeah?"

Akash had already fired up the plane's engine. As they climbed inside, Builders fired at the hull.

"Stop shooting at my plane!" Akash yelled as he pushed forward. The *Silver Hawk* rattled over the bumpy ground before climbing awkwardly into the sky. "Bloody Brits."

"Oy," Liddy said.

Edmund spun Colton around, gripping his shoulders. "What did he mean back there? Do you know how the towers are made? How *yours* was made?"

Colton shook his head, speechless.

"You know something. The sooner you tell Zavier, the sooner this can end."

"Has he found a way to save my tower?" he shot back. "When he figures that out, *then* this can end."

No one said anything more. Once onboard the *Prometheus*, they marched Colton to Zavier's office.

He was surprisingly receptive to the news. "At least now we know the leader's name," Zavier said. "Phoebe Archer. I swear I've heard her name before."

"She also said something about a contact who might be tracking us," Colton said.

Zavier's eyebrows furrowed. "I bet she has many of those. In any case, we'll have to lie low until we figure out a strategy."

Colton had bought them a little more time, at least. He would have to make the most of it while he still could.

Colton opened the door without knocking. Danny was sitting on the edge of the bed, an old, battered book open on his lap. He was dressed, his left arm in a sling.

Danny looked up and froze. The green of his eyes deepened, his lips parted. His dark hair was a mess, as usual. Colton wanted to run his hands through it. Make it even messier. He wanted to trace those lips with his own, make Danny sigh his name.

They stared at each other for a long time. Colton could see the pulse in Danny's neck, fast and strong. The way his eyelids lowered slightly in understanding.

Slowly, Colton closed the door behind him.

If anyone noticed that Colton now stayed in Danny's room, no one said anything about it. There were a few raised eyebrows and smirks, but Danny was too lost in his stupor to care, feeling—for the first time in months—happy.

Colton had put so much distance between them he'd been afraid that everything they'd built would just end. Colton had confessed, that first night, that he'd also been afraid, but now there was some time to figure things out.

And time for other things, too.

Danny had watched, mesmerized, as Colton closed the door that night before crossing the room. He'd come in so confidently, so grave and intense, it had stolen Danny's breath. Colton had cupped Danny's face in his hands, their eyes meeting in a moment that shattered and remade him.

Then Colton had kissed him, hard and full of need. The book had slid off of Danny's lap, toppling to the floor; he hadn't even noticed. He'd been too busy pulling Colton closer, feeling as much of him as he could, pain and ecstasy digging shallow trenches within him, filling him with light.

They'd fallen back onto the bed. Colton had climbed over him, kissing every square inch of skin, nipping the racing pulse at his neck. Danny whispered his name, murmured it against his lips, arched his hips against his. Colton had gently removed the sling and slowly unbuttoned his shirt. He'd kissed the wound, counting every stitch with his tongue. Had kissed down his sternum, his stomach, lower.

Danny sat dazed and embarrassed in the mess hall the next morning. He hardly came here, but Colton had urged him to come.

"I want them to see us together," Colton had said. "The more they understand us, see us together, the more guilty they'll feel."

"When did you become so calculating?"

"Oh, I've always been calculating. Don't you remember when we first met?"

Danny smiled, finding the memory of Colton pretending to be his assistant funny now, though he'd been beyond flustered at the time.

They held hands beneath the table as Danny picked at his breakfast, sneaking glances at Colton that were returned with secretive smiles.

"When's the wedding?"

Daphne sat across from them, looking between them with a faintly amused set to her mouth.

"June," Colton said. Danny blushed, unable to tell if he was joking or not.

"I guess you two made up." She cradled a mug of tea between her hands. "I can practically see little hearts forming in the air above you."

Danny looked away while Colton laughed brightly. The sound was different outside his tower; it held less humming power. It was more human. "She's just jealous," Colton said, brushing his thumb against the sensitive underside of his wrist.

Daphne rolled her eyes. "It's about time you two were talking again."

Danny snuck a glance at Colton and was a little surprised to find the clock spirit doing the same. They both smiled sheepishly and looked away.

"I didn't even need to bother with sugar in my tea," Daphne grumbled. "Danny, your hair's a mess."

"It's always a mess," he argued.

"More than usual. Why don't you let me cut it for you?"

He blinked. "You know how to cut hair?"

"I've cut the hair for a neighbor's son a few times, and my mother's." Her voice softened on the last word. "I won't make you look ridiculous, if that's what you're worried about. Well, no more ridiculous."

"Har." His hair *was* irritating him lately; it kept falling into his eyes. "All right, why not."

"Good. Come along, then." She stood.

"What, right now?"

Colton nudged him. "Go on. I'll read the book in your room."

Danny made to stand, but Colton grabbed the back of his neck and planted a firm kiss on his mouth first. Edmund, Liddy, Jo, and Ivor started cheering at a nearby table. Danny broke away, his face hot enough to melt iron.

Daphne shook her head with an "are you done?" look on her face.

Danny cleared his throat and followed her out, glancing over his shoulder at Colton, who waved cheerily.

Charlotte loaned them a pair of scissors, and they continued on to Daphne's room. Meena was knocking on the door when they arrived.

"Oh, there you are." She saw the scissors. "What's this?"

"We're cutting Danny's hair."

"Ooh!"

Danny didn't know why this was such an exciting event, but the girls seemed content to fuss over him, so he sat back in a chair and let his eyes glaze over. Meena tugged on a lock.

"You have very good hair. Nice and thick."

"Er . . ."

"It's a compliment," Daphne said, comparing the length of different strands. "Now, sit still."

When she made the first snip, he jerked. She *tsk*ed and swatted his arm.

"You *are* afraid of me cutting your hair!"

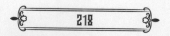

"I'm not! I just haven't had it cut in a while."

Meena sat on the bed and watched them, grinning. "Should I gasp and make faces so Danny knows how funny he looks?"

"That will be quite unnecessary," Daphne said, cutting another strand.

Danny sighed and closed his eyes. He remembered sitting on a large kitchen chair as a child while his mother toyed with his hair, complaining about how it remained obstinately messy no matter what she did with it. She had even cut it as short as possible once, to his and his father's horror, but it had only grown out as much a mess as ever.

Still, the feeling of his mother combing his hair with her fingers and her familiar scent of perfume and cigarette smoke had soothed him. He almost thought he could smell it now, but realized it was only Daphne's bergamot.

"Danny," Daphne said softly behind him, "what did Colton see? In Khurja?"

He opened his eyes. Meena's smile was gone. He thought back to what Colton had told him the night before.

"It was terrible, Danny," Colton had whispered, his voice nearly lost in the inky darkness of the room. Danny had only been able to make out a blue silhouette and the soft glow of amber eyes. "The new tower was . . . it wasn't right, barely even a clock tower. It had all the parts—I don't know how they made them so quickly—but it almost had no life to it."

Danny had traced the curve of Colton's neck to his shoulder. "Was there a spirit?"

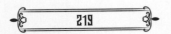

"Yes." Colton closed his eyes. "A young woman had gone missing in Khurja right before the tower was built. I saw her in the tower. The spirit seemed to . . . reach out to me, somehow, as if her words were in my mind. She didn't know how she'd gotten there, just like me in my tower. I had no memories when I was made into this. It was like being born again, starting with an empty slate."

"Tabula rasa," Danny had murmured.

He'd watched Colton's eyes lower, the gentle silence rolling over them with a promise that it wouldn't be gentle for long.

"I used to be alive," Colton had whispered. "I used to be so much more than I am now."

Danny's hand had tightened on his arm. "Don't say that."

But the silence had stretched again, long and dark like a shadow in autumn.

"They can't keep doing this," Colton had said eventually. "Someone has to stop them."

Which made the difficult situation that much more complicated. If Aetas were freed, the clock spirits would disappear. If he wasn't, clock mechanics would die.

And Danny and Colton were caught right in the middle.

Danny told the girls what Colton had shared, and what had happened in Dürnstein. Daphne stopped cutting to listen, and Meena's face grew hard.

"They might do the same thing in Prague, don't you think?" Daphne asked.

"Maybe," he said, "but Zavier's right that the people might not let them. That's what Colton overheard, too."

"It's still a possibility." Meena touched her burnt cheek. "I wonder if they'll try to build a new tower in Meerut as well." Her eyes were pinched, likely thinking about Aditi. "Colton is right: we have to stop them."

"But how? Zavier won't let us do anything. Hang on . . ." Daphne came around to face Danny. "How did all the spirits start remembering their past at once? Colton said the spirit in Dürnstein did, too. He remembered an axe."

"Maybe because of what Zavier's doing," Danny said. "When he destroyed that first tower using Aetas's power, it could have triggered something in the spirits. We've already seen how much they seem to be connected to one another."

They speculated a little more, then fell into silence broken only by the occasional snip of the scissors. Danny watched dark clumps fall on either side of him, crumbling away the foundation of who he'd built himself into over the last few months, trying to chip him back into the Danny he once was.

But he didn't think that was possible anymore.

"All done." Daphne made him stand and turn toward the small mirror above her dresser. He almost didn't recognize himself. He did look a bit more as he once had, but there was something else there, too. Something in the shadow of his cheekbones, in the curve of his eyes.

"You look very handsome," Meena assured him.

"Yes," Daphne agreed, rubbing a hand over his head to shake off loose hairs. "I think Colton will like it."

She shared a smile with Meena, but Danny only stared at his reflection, thinking how much he looked like his father.

Danny didn't have time to ask if Colton liked the haircut. As soon as he was through the door, Colton pounced on him.

"You didn't—even—look," Danny said between kisses.

Colton leaned back for a second. "It's nice," he said, pressing Danny against the door.

He had no idea if clock spirits had . . . urges, but whatever drove Colton now, Danny couldn't complain. They fell to the bed laughing and fumbling, but Danny put a hand on Colton's arm to stop him when he moved to undo his shirt.

"You got to undress me last night," he said. "I want to do it this time."

Colton looked surprised, but he sat back on his knees. Suddenly he seemed uncertain.

"I told you I can't feel anything. Not like that."

"I know. But I want to see you."

Colton smiled softly. Danny removed the cog holder, both of them watching for any signs of weakness. Colton was all right so long as it was beside them. Danny slowly unbuttoned his vest—a vest he'd taken from Danny—and then the shirt underneath.

As soon as he slid them off Colton's shoulders, he gasped.

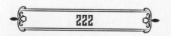

Colton's right side bore a long scar, red and ropy from underarm to hip.

"How did that happen?" he whispered. "Why didn't you tell me?"

"It happened when my tower was hit. It's not very painful at the moment."

Zavier had told him that Indian rebels had hit Colton's tower to Stop Enfield's time, therefore stopping the production of rifles. Danny touched the scar and Colton flinched.

Being as gentle as possible, he laid Colton down. "I promise I'll fix your tower. We'll make it beautiful, hire the best architects, and people will come from all over just to wonder at it." He kissed up the twisted scar, lips barely brushing it, as he touched the central cog with reverent fingers. "We'll find a way."

Colton watched Danny a moment, eyes unreadable. Then he flipped Danny over and pressed their noses together.

"I know we will."

It was a little awkward, with Danny's arm in a sling. They tried moving around, but most positions made him hiss in pain.

"Come here," Colton said, lying flat on his back.

Danny uneasily straddled him. "Like this?"

"Yes." Colton's eyes shone. He ran his hands over Danny's chest and stomach, over his thighs. Colton's skin was like sun-warmed satin under Danny's fingertips.

Danny closed his eyes to focus on the sweet and aching sensation. He tried not to be tense, tried to act as if this was all very natural. They'd done this before. But not like this, when Colton could look up at him and gauge his every reaction. When nothing could be hidden. Danny flushed as Colton met his eyes. As Colton's fingers found their mark. He gasped and rocked forward.

"Yes?" Colton asked.

Breathless, he nodded and pressed his good hand to the wall behind the bed. Time was nothing while Danny was caught between his hands, being teased and being adored and being delirious with it all.

He arched his back and made a sound as if he were becoming undone. And he was—the corkscrew spiral of sensation was winding tighter, threatening to unravel for several feverish seconds until, finally, it did.

When he climbed down from the high, he was surprised by how tired he was. Colton was clutching his hips.

"Was that all right?" Colton asked. His eyes were even brighter, sparks of golden flint.

Danny tumbled over a breathy laugh and lay beside him. His body was pulsing and hot and heavy. Colton pulled him in closer, kissing his neck.

"More than all right," Danny murmured. He twined his fingers into Colton's hair, his lips drifting across the spirit's skin in constellations of his own making. Being so near him made Danny dizzy with want, so full of affection his chest could barely contain it. Without warning, his eyes burned, and he closed them tight to keep hold of this feeling a little longer, so that Colton wouldn't see just how badly he craved him.

They had enough pain.

He lay with his head tucked under Colton's chin. Colton traced little circles on his shoulder. With one hand curled over Colton's hip, he thought this might be what normal felt like.

"Where did you even learn that?" Danny asked sleepily. He'd always been surprised by Colton's knowledge, but a clock spirit had a lot of time to kill, and his natural curiosity had likely led him to peek into the secret lives of Enfield lovers.

But Colton's silence hinted at something more. Danny remembered the memories he'd seen, the ones Colton had transferred to him.

"Oh."

Colton sat up. "Danny . . ." He swept a newly cut lock of hair from Danny's forehead. "It was a very long time ago. Castor's gone."

Castor. The tall boy with chestnut hair and brown eyes, an easy sense of humor, and natural charisma. The boy who was everything he wasn't.

Danny thought about those revealing memories, each one making a small nick in his already wounded chest.

"You still love him."

Colton's eyes widened, but he didn't reply.

"Then what the hell am I?" he murmured. "A replacement."

He regretted the words as soon as they were spoken, and

wondered why he had bothered to speak them at all. But thinking back to those intimate memories he had glimpsed, he couldn't ignore the way they poked into him like needles.

"How can you say that? That's not true." Colton turned his gaze away. "Besides, what does it matter? I don't even know what happened to him. Or my sister. Or my parents. They're all dead. Long gone." There was a frightening distance in Colton's expression. "He was left behind, while I . . ."

Colton paused to gather his words. "I don't know how he could stand it, after. He saw me dragged away. Probably saw my body, too. He certainly saw that tower and knew what it meant. I didn't want to leave him." He cradled the side of Danny's face. "Just like I don't want to leave you."

Danny put his hand on top of Colton's. He wanted to forget the whole thing, to apologize, change the topic to something lighter. But it had latched on, draining his happiness like a leech. He couldn't forget the look in Castor's eyes, or the way Colton's heart had once beat faster at the sight of him.

Danny held Colton's hand tighter. "But you still love him." Colton turned away again. "If we were standing side by side, me and him, who would you even choose?"

"That's not fair," Colton said in a voice so fierce that Danny dropped his hand. "How could I ever make a choice like that? I've already . . . I've caused you both so much pain. Pain I can't undo." He buried his face in his hands. "I can't do anything to make it better, and I'm just going to keep hurting you."

Danny sat up, hating himself. "Colton, no. You're not hurting me."

"I can't forget how I felt about him, but that doesn't mean—"

"I know. I'm sorry. I'm an idiot." He pried Colton's hands away and laid Colton's head on his uninjured shoulder. "You're not hurting me, I promise."

"I am. I will."

"You aren't. You won't." He pressed his lips to the top of Colton's head, splaying a hand against his back, smooth and warm. "I don't know what came over me. Forgive me. Please."

Colton touched his fingers to Danny's wound, circling the bullet scar underneath it, both inches from Danny's heart.

"I always do."

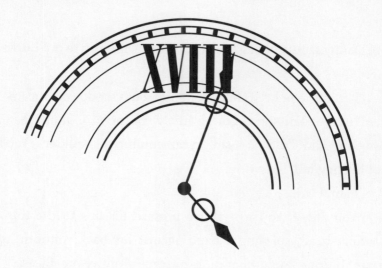

XVIII

The *Prometheus* hovered over the Indian Ocean. Whenever another airship could be seen in the distance or a sea ship came into sight down below, one of the pilots would simply drift upward, losing the ship among the clouds. Daphne liked to watch this maneuver from the observation deck, standing before the glass wall as the ocean disappeared and they were suddenly surrounded by white.

It was a good place to think, and that's what she most needed to do. It seemed everyone aboard the *Prometheus* was thinking—especially Zavier, who sought intelligence from contacts in Meerut and Prague. No new towers yet, but Builders had been spotted in both cities.

The only ones who didn't seem to be furiously lost in planning were Danny and Colton. She knew they both needed the distraction, and it was refreshing to see them finally together.

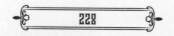

Still, it sometimes aggravated her to see their silly smiles when the world was cracking around them.

They ate in the mess hall most mornings. Meena joined them, though Akash was suspiciously absent. Meena told her it was because he didn't feel comfortable around the others yet, but Daphne had glimpsed him talking to Danny and Colton in the corridors on several occasions.

So it's just me, she thought with a pinch of guilt.

It would be a relief to be able to speak to him again. But something held her back—pride, anger, she didn't know.

"People who can't forgive other people usually can't forgive themselves," Meena said loftily at the mess table one morning.

Daphne snorted. "What am I forgiving myself for? Being righteously angry?"

"*I'm* the one who got shot," Danny cut in. "And I've forgiven him."

"Good for you. Go get me tea."

"You've just had tea!"

"Get me some more."

Danny rolled his eyes and let go of Colton's hand. As he walked to the kitchen, she noticed Colton's eyes on his backside.

"You're incorrigible," she said. The spirit grinned. "*Anyway,* that's not the most pressing issue here. What do you think Zavier's going to do, now? Focus on stopping the Builders or freeing Aetas?"

"*Daphne,*" Meena groaned, "I've barely finished breakfast. Can we talk about this later?"

The girl shrugged. "You can have more than one home."

The other two left her outside the doorway, her fingers pressed to the cold metal wall. Home had always been an image to her, a unique feeling—the loud melancholy of London. Gray soot and copper gears and white steam. A hint of gold when she sensed the time threads running through the city, that familiar constant.

She tried to imagine a home of green palms and blue skies and golden temple domes. Wondered, if only for a fleeting moment, if that were even possible.

Akash still stood at the large window looking out at the clouds. She remembered the sight of him carrying Danny back from Prague, the way his shirt had stuck to him as the blood dried, his wide vacant stare. He almost looked that way again, like he wanted to run, too.

But there was nowhere to go. And this silence had gone on long enough.

Daphne closed the door behind her and walked toward the window, keeping a few feet between them. She put her hand against the cool glass, wondering what those clouds must feel like.

"When I was little, I thought they were like candy floss." She nodded at the clouds. "I wanted my father to get some for me so I could try it. He just laughed."

A tentative smile crept across Akash's face, but it fell almost immediately. "Miss Richards, I . . ." He blew out a frustrated breath. "I would apologize again, but I've apologized enough."

"You're right." Dropping her hand, she turned to face him. He looked tired, his dark eyes seeking out hers with something akin to hope. "It's me who should be apologizing. I've been unfair to you. I'm sorry."

He took a moment to gaze at the clouds, her words hanging over them like condensation. "I did try to stop Danny. But it's also true that I didn't help him."

"You couldn't control what would happen. You couldn't predict what he'd do." One of her eyebrows lifted. "No one can."

"He seems happy now. With Colton. They were so sad before. In some ways, they still are." Akash slipped his hands into his pockets. "I didn't know what I wanted. I hate the British. After the way they've treated me in the past, like I'm some savage who miraculously learned how to fly a plane . . . and after what they did to Meena . . ." He clenched his jaw. "We're just bodies for them to shove about. But then I met you, and you were so different. You respect our culture, wanted to understand it more. You're part of it in a way they never will be.

"I didn't know if I wanted the rebels to succeed or not. After getting to know you, I . . . I didn't think I wanted that any longer. But Daphne's England is different from their England."

"It's a little less crowded in mine."

He laughed, a soft miracle. They stood in contemplative silence, the silence of the clouds swallowing them, secluding them from an angry world. They stood in a new country, neither India nor England. They were their own nation.

You can have more than one home. Daphne thought she understood, now.

Akash moved closer, and she let him. He raised callused

fingers to her jaw, tracing it with the lightest touch. "Do you forgive me?"

"Yes. I'm sorry I took so long."

He moved his fingers up, touching the diamond tattoo by her eye, then skimmed her cheek in a way that made her eyes flutter.

"Miss Richards . . ."

"Daphne."

He smiled. "Daphne."

He leaned in and kissed her.

Something swooped in her stomach, like a plane taking an unexpected dive—frightening and exhilarating. Akash's lips were soft, his mouth warm and tasting vaguely of cinnamon. She wrapped her arms around his neck and drank him in, the fresh smell of him, the solidness of his body. If they walked out into those clouds right now she would be in danger of drifting off, and he would anchor her.

He kissed her tattoo, her jaw, the spot under her ear. Eyes closed, she existed for each fleeting touch, to feel every little spot he found. Her hand dove into his thick hair, down the column of his neck, and he shivered.

"I was so afraid," he murmured between kisses. "I thought I had ruined everything, that you would never talk to me again."

She wanted to tell him that was ridiculous, especially when they were doing much more than talking, but something snagged in her mind.

Talking.

Her eyes flew open. "I have an idea."

He leaned back, surprised. "You do?"

"I've just thought of something we can try." He blushed, and heat rushed to her face. "Oh, God, no! I didn't mean—"

Akash laughed nervously and ruffled his hair before smoothing it again. "Why don't you tell me what you *do* mean?"

"It's complicated. Find Meena. I'll meet you at her room." She pulled him back down for another kiss. It took a minute for them to part, and when they did, she felt dizzy. "I'll be there in a moment."

She hurried down the corridors, touching her lips, which had formed a small smile. Her chest and stomach felt weightless and hollow, like nothing filled her body except for light and clouds.

But she had to put that feeling aside for now. She knocked three times on Danny's door, then bit her thumb to keep from pacing the hall.

The door opened to reveal a mostly naked Colton on the other side, his blond hair disheveled, kept decent only by the pillow he held to his hips. But what flustered her more was the large scar on his side.

"What on earth are you doing?" She held up a hand. "Stop, never mind. Don't answer that. Where's Danny?"

"He's indecent," Colton said. An embarrassed groan came from inside the room.

"Well, I need both of you dressed. I just thought of something we can try to get one up on the Builders."

Colton's amber eyes flashed. "What is it?"

"Put your trousers on and you'll see."

A few minutes later, they joined her in the hall. Danny's face was red as a lobster, though Colton seemed unfazed as he held Danny's hand. Daphne wondered if he possessed any shame.

When they reached Meena's room, they all shared a confused look. Akash's gaze lingered on her, and she turned as red as Danny before she cleared her throat.

"The residue of Aetas's water is still on the plane, yes?" she asked Akash. He nodded; he'd delivered the last of it to Prague. "Colton, Danny told me about what happened in Khurja. How you could hear the spirit's voice in your mind. What if you could speak to the clock spirits through the water?"

Colton leaned back on his heels as Danny frowned. "How?"

"I don't know—I'm not sure if it would even work—but something struck me as odd. You were able to speak to the foreign clock spirits without knowing their languages. You could hear them even though you weren't in their towers. What if that's because of Aetas's power? What if it gives all spirits the ability to communicate with one another, like how you all started remembering your pasts at once? If you were close to the water—"

"No."

Danny's blush was gone, and he met Daphne's gaze straight on. His shoulders were squared as if ready for a fight.

"He's not going near that water. You don't know what it could do to him."

"It's only the tower that would be affected, right?" Meena broke in. "Wouldn't Colton be safe?"

"But how would that even help us? Would he be spying on the Builders?"

"Essentially," Daphne said.

Danny shook his head. "I'm not going to risk—"

"I want to try it."

They all turned to Colton, who was looking thoughtfully at the floor. He lifted his eyes to Daphne.

"I'd like to try it."

"Colton—" Danny began, but the spirit put his hand on his arm.

"I'll be all right. I think Meena's correct. The water might only react if it came near my tower. I won't even touch it."

Danny took a deep breath. He looked miserable, but also like he didn't want to weather another argument.

Akash led them to the storage tanks in the belly of the ship. With little outside light, they stumbled around as Akash tried to remember which turns to take.

"They had a special hose I attached to the *Silver Hawk* that connected to a smaller tank," he whispered, his voice echoing slightly against the metal walls. "They had to fill it from the bigger tanks. I think they're in here."

He opened a set of double doors and looked for a light. Meena found and lit a gas lamp in the corner. The room was cast in shadow, but the two large metal tanks before them shone eerily in the darkness. The glow was faint, like Colton away from his tower, but Daphne felt the strange, sharp pull of the power inside of them.

"There's only a little left," Akash said, rapping a knuckle against the side of one of the tanks. If Daphne listened hard enough, she could hear the last of the water sloshing with the subtle motions of the *Prometheus*. "How would Colton use it, Daphne?"

Danny raised both eyebrows at the use of her Christian name. He mouthed Daphne's name at her knowingly, and she scowled.

"I thought maybe if he just touches the tank." She turned to the spirit. "What do you think?"

Colton started to tilt his head to one side, but snapped it straight again. "I think that'll be enough. I won't touch the water," he assured Danny when he opened his mouth to protest. "What should I do? Just think about another spirit?"

"Maybe one you've already met."

Colton nodded and approached the nearest tank.

Meena came up behind her. "Did you and my brother . . . ?"

She snapped her head around. *"What?"*

"I keep seeing the looks you two give each other." Meena gave a Cheshire cat grin. "You two made up, didn't you?"

"Not important right now."

"Oh, I disagree—"

"If you'd like me to concentrate," Colton said over his shoulder, "gossiping should probably wait."

Sufficiently admonished, they lapsed into silence as Colton placed his hands on the softly glowing tank. He waited a moment, and although nothing substantial happened, the cogs on his back glowed a little brighter.

Danny released a tense breath.

They waited while Colton bowed his head and closed his eyes in concentration. The light of the tank pulsed a few times, and Colton jerked. Danny made to go to him, but Daphne held him back.

Finally, after about fifteen minutes, Colton lowered his hands and staggered away from the tank. Akash caught him before he collapsed, but Danny was there in a second, wrapping his arm protectively around Colton's waist.

"What happened?" Meena asked. "Did you find another spirit?"

Colton looked dazed. Danny gripped his chin so he could see his face. When Colton's eyes cleared, he turned to take in the rest of the group.

"I found her. The one in Khurja. Her name is Lalita."

"The one you spoke to before," Daphne clarified. "The . . . new spirit."

"Yes. I asked her about the Builders, though she doesn't know what they're called. I asked about their leader, Phoebe Archer. The name didn't sound familiar, but she told me about a woman with short yellow hair." He nodded to Danny. "The one you saw before, right?"

"Right. But what's she doing there? I thought she'd be in Prague by now."

"Lalita told me this Archer woman was having a conversation the other day while inspecting her tower. She said something about it being the first success, and that they had permission to begin the next tower."

Daphne's stomach tightened. "The next tower . . . where?"

"I think she said Meerut."

Frowning, Meena touched her scar, and Akash put a hand on her shoulder.

"So they're going to kill another mechanic in Meerut." Daphne took a deep breath. "I think we need to tell Zavier."

Danny reluctantly nodded. "I think we do, too."

Zavier wasn't very happy to learn about what they'd done.

"I gave you clearance to roam freely about the ship, but that doesn't mean you can poke your noses in places you shouldn't," he complained. Sally was in the office, too, her gray eyes flitting between their mouths as they spoke. If Daphne didn't know any better, she'd say the girl was amused. "Why the hell did you go down there, anyway?"

Colton took a step forward. "I spoke with the new Khurja clock spirit," he said.

Zavier stared at him as if he'd just declared himself the next Tsar of Russia.

Danny sighed. "What he means is that he used the power of Aetas's water to communicate with her. Through their minds."

"She was a little taken aback, and it was hard to hear, but I got through eventually," Colton explained. "Anyway, this Archer woman was at her tower recently, and said something about a new tower in Meerut."

Zavier's head jerked back as if someone had taken a swing at him. Sally frowned and looked at her brother.

"Meerut? I thought you overheard her saying she was going to Prague?"

"Maybe her plans changed."

"Whatever may have happened, we have to stop them," Daphne said. "We can't let them create another area of time."

Zavier ran a hand over his neat hair, narrowing his eyes. "I agree they should be stopped, but I'm a little confused about why you're not defending them. If past experience is anything to go by, you lot don't want Aetas freed."

She shared a look with Danny. "Not like this. We don't want these new, ugly towers built. We don't want new spirits being created just to die when you release Aetas."

When Zavier looked at Colton again, it was with a hint of guilt. Then he turned his focus to Danny, who stared back defiantly.

"I'm only agreeing to this because I want to know how they're building the towers. We'll try to get our hands on Archer herself. Then"—he glanced between Danny and Colton—"we'll see who can tell me their secret first."

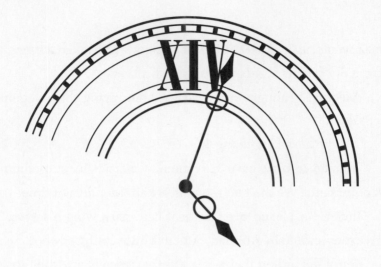

After Zavier announced to the rest of the crew that they'd be returning to Meerut, Colton tugged Danny's arm and led him back to his room. It was getting late, and Danny looked tired.

As Colton closed the door, Danny took out his timepiece and set it on the nightstand, staring at it for a melancholy moment. Colton knew his father had given it to him a long time ago.

Colton came up behind him and wrapped his arms around Danny's waist. "You'll see them soon."

Danny closed his eyes. Colton leaned in and kissed the scar on his chin.

"You need sleep," he said.

But sleep wasn't only what Colton had in mind. He laid Danny back and stole his thoughts away with kisses. Still, there was a heaviness in his touch, in the way Danny kissed him back. Colton brushed his lips across Danny's throat and he made a

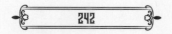

small sound, an intimate vibration against his mouth. He felt that sound as a beginning to something bigger, a distant peal of thunder, the pulse beating on his tongue like the rhythm of the tide.

When Danny finally fell asleep, Colton outlined his body in lines and grooves and contours, filling in the shadows and the soft falls of his hair. He studied the way Danny's eyelashes quivered against his cheek, the softness of his mouth when he wasn't frowning. The heartbreaking way his fingers curled inward toward his palm, as if trying to grasp something intangible.

Colton wanted to keep him this way forever, to trap him in amber and force time to stop moving, if only to stay like this.

But it had to end, and dawn eventually broke the spell. Danny opened his eyes, smiling to see Colton beside him.

"I dreamed we were back in Enfield," he murmured as he stretched. "It was peaceful."

Colton brushed a thumb against his cheek. "That does sound nice."

Danny heard the sadness in his voice. "Don't worry, we're going back soon."

If it was even possible. Colton clung to so little; he couldn't even grasp at the hope that they could both came out of this whole, alive, together. The weight of all that could and could not be descended on him, and would have stolen his breath away had he any to be stolen, that simple yet unfathomable currency that came with *being human*.

He wanted to remind Danny just how impossible it was to ever return to how they had once been, but that would be cruel.

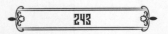

Instead, he continued to caress the side of his face, trying to memorize this moment while it lasted. "I know we will."

Frowning at the tone in his voice, Danny sat up. "Colton . . . are you only humoring me?"

Colton suppressed a wince, answering the question with silence.

Danny ran his hands through his hair with a mirthless laugh. "Do you *want* to be swept away like all the other spirits when Aetas is freed?"

"I never said that."

"Then why isn't your heart in this fight, Colton? You should be doing this for yourself, not for me!"

"I don't *have* a heart." The spirit pressed a hand to his still chest. "I'm not human anymore. I'm not like you. If I . . . Even if Zavier found a way, and I stayed safe, what would happen?"

"We would be together," Danny said, voice rough.

"Yes, but for how long? A few years? A few decades? Danny, you'll grow old. You'll *die*. And I won't. I'll be stuck in that tower, back to where I started. Alone." The terrifying promise of it touched the edges of him, and he shivered. He couldn't face that gaping stretch of loneliness again. He refused to.

"After enough time, you'll forget about me," Danny mumbled to his hands. "In hundreds of years, I won't have even existed to you."

If Colton did have a heart, it would have broken. He touched the side of Danny's face. "I would never forget you."

"Colton . . . please, just—just let me be selfish. Let me keep your tower."

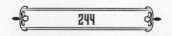

"It's not your tower. It's mine."

Danny looked like he'd been slapped. He shrank, eyes dropping to the wrinkled covers. "You once said it was mine, too."

"That's before I knew—" Colton shook his head. "You *know* I want to be with you. But"—he touched his central cog, lying forlorn on the bed beside him—"why should I be the only one to survive? What about Ben and Evaline and Lalita? What makes me more deserving than any of them?"

"Because I need you," Danny whispered.

"No, you don't. You think you do, but if I were gone, you'd find someone else. A human someone."

"God, not this again!"

"Yes, this again. I want you to be *happy*."

"Well, this isn't making me bloody happy!" Danny made to get up from the bed, but Colton grabbed his arms. "Let go of me!"

"Let go? You don't even know what letting go means. These memories . . ." Colton pushed back against the images in his mind, forcing him to look at his past, to remember all he'd lost. "I've accepted my own death, and now you need to—"

"SHUT UP!"

Danny hung his head, breathing heavily. "Everyone," he started, his voice breaking, "everyone keeps telling me it can't work. That we shouldn't be together. If they don't say it, they're thinking it." He fought to swallow. "I thought you wanted this. I thought you wanted to be with me."

"I *do*, but—"

"But you'd rather die!"

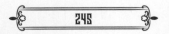

"What else do you expect me to do?" Colton said, raising his voice. That weight from earlier had broken open, flooding him with hopelessness and impotent rage. He pushed Danny down, putting his hands on his shoulders to have something to grip onto, to make sure Danny heard what he was saying. "I have two options, and neither of them are what I want. I *do* want you, but what am I supposed to do when you're gone? Or you grow so old you don't want to be with me anymore?"

"That—"

"Just think for *one second*, Danny. If you were a clock spirit, what would be going through your head right now?"

"I—"

"I lived a life where I couldn't afford to be selfish. And I'm glad for that, because it meant I could help others. Help you." Colton tightened his grip at the unfairness of their situation. "So this is the last thing I'll do for you, the last selfless thing."

"Don't bother," Danny growled. "Just waste away like the others, if that's what you want."

"That's *not* what I want! God, Danny—!"

"Let me go!"

"Just *listen*!"

Danny cried out, and his whole body jerked. Colton had squeezed his shoulder so hard the wound had reopened. Fresh, bright blood seeped from the tear.

"I-I'm sorry," Colton stammered, letting him go. "Danny, I'm so sorry—"

His body began to vibrate, and a strange, prickling sensation

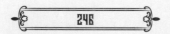

traveled over him. Looking down, he saw his hand was coated with Danny's blood.

As he tried to get up, the air around him crackled. The blood was hot. Too hot. The room warped, *tilted*. Whimpering, he fell from the bed as light exploded from his body, golden white and blinding.

"Danny," he called, frightened. He tried to wipe his hand on the floor, but the blood only spread. "What's happening?"

Ticks and tocks echoed in his ears, the movement of every clock and timepiece on the ship. Danny's timepiece was loudest of all, its ticks deafening, and Colton wanted to smash it against the wall if only to stop the sound.

Time writhed. Time pulsed. Time wrapped around him like a blanket, greedy and excited.

Colton crawled to the wall, shuddering. He couldn't feel his body, just the blood, strong and hot. Groaning, Colton held his head, smearing the blood into his hair.

The door burst open. Zavier first took in Danny, sitting on the bed and clutching his bloody shoulder as he stared uncomprehendingly at Colton. And then those penetrating gray eyes swung to him, and in a blink, Colton knew Zavier understood.

"That's it," he breathed into the light inching outward from Colton's body, his voice nearly drowned by the ticking. "That's how it's done. Blood."

Jo's voice crackled through the speaker: *"We're approaching Meerut. Landing party, prepare yourselves."*

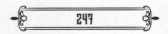

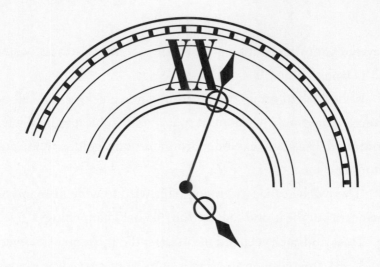

Danny sat on the infirmary bed as Charlotte stitched his wound closed once more. His eyes were glazed over with shock, his skin still tingling and his heart beating madly.

"Breathe evenly," Charlotte murmured. "In, one, two. Out, one, two . . ."

Elsewhere, crewmembers were making preparations for the landing, but Danny sat unmoving in the center of their activity, a boulder among the rapids. There was a flutter of fear in his stomach at the thought of what had happened. He knew Colton hadn't meant to hurt him; he was strong, and admittedly, he'd provoked him.

But that reaction . . .

Zavier had pulled him from the bed and forced him to dress. At Zavier's order, Edmund had brought Danny to the infirmary not twenty minutes ago. The last image Danny recalled was

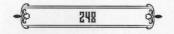

Zavier standing over a cowering Colton, bloodstained and glowing so bright he'd almost disappeared in the nimbus of light.

When Charlotte finished bandaging his arm, she came around to look into his eyes. "Danny, I don't think you should go down with the others. That wound is going to open again if—"

"Don't worry, he won't be coming." Zavier strolled into the infirmary, his eyes blazing in triumph. "He and Colton are going to stay on the ship while the rest of us go down and stop the Builders."

Danny began to stand, but Charlotte placed a warning hand on his uninjured arm. "Where is he?" Danny demanded through gritted teeth. "What did you do to him?"

"Dae is helping him. We've gotten the blood cleaned off, and Dae's making adjustments to the cog holder as we speak."

"I want to go to Meerut," Danny said. "I want to stop the Builders as much as you do."

"We can't let anything more happen to you." His eyes drifted to Danny's shoulder. "Especially when we have so much to talk about."

Liddy appeared in the doorway wearing a wide belt with a brace of guns and her taser. "Zavier, c'mon!"

"I'll be right there." He turned back to Danny. "This is monumental, you know. It may very well be the way to free Aetas, but it means something else."

"Like what?" Danny asked dully.

"A way to save Colton."

Danny's fingers twitched. Zavier gave him a cool smile before walking out the door.

Charlotte sighed before helping Danny back into his shirt. "Stay right here. I'm going to make you some tea."

While Charlotte was gone, Daphne and Meena rushed into the room.

"We felt it," Meena said. "What happened?"

Daphne took in the suture needle and cursed. "Your wound?"

He nodded, feeling as if he were in a surreal dream. "My blood got on his hand. Zavier saw the result."

The girls shared a knowing look.

"What's going to happen now?" Meena whispered.

"They're going to stop the Builders from starting a new Meerut tower," Danny said tonelessly. "And then they're going to free Aetas."

Meena came forward and lifted his chin. "Don't give up yet," she said. She'd reapplied her bindi, and he stared at it as she spoke. "We'll negotiate. We'll do something to stop them."

Charlotte came in with tea, followed by Felix.

"We have to go," he said.

Daphne and Meena gave Danny wary looks.

"I'll be fine," he said, though it sounded thoroughly unconvincing. "Be safe."

They reluctantly turned to the door as Felix took his wife in his arms, murmuring something in German. She responded in kind and they shared a kiss, Felix placing his hand on Charlotte's stomach. Charlotte noticed Danny's stare once Felix had left, putting her hand where her husband's had been a moment before.

"How long?" he asked.

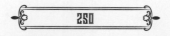

"A few months." She swallowed. "They'll be all right." But she sounded about as convincing as he had.

It surprised him how badly he'd wanted to go. Maybe for a chance to strike out at the villain, like in the stories—a chance to stop the people who were repeating violent history. Colton's history. If they got their hands on a Meerut mechanic . . .

He stood woozily, but the tea had helped clear his mind.

"Are you sure you should be up and about?" Charlotte asked in a disapproving tone.

"You're one to talk." She huffed in amusement. "I'm not going far. Thank you for . . ." He gestured to his shoulder.

"Of course. Come find me if you need anything else."

The ship always felt empty, but the silence and stillness now had an eerie effect. The corridors were dark, and his footsteps echoed off the walls.

Trying to ignore the pain in his shoulder, he found his way to Dae's workroom, one of the first places he'd visited after Zavier kidnapped him.

If he could go back and tell that version of himself what was about to happen, he wouldn't have believed it.

Danny pushed the heavy metal door open. Dae was at the forge, pounding at metal. He wore goggles and a thick apron and gloves, his dark curly hair falling toward his face, sweat running down his temples.

When Dae looked up, he pointed to the corner with his hammer, then resumed his work.

Colton was sitting on the floor playing with a metal

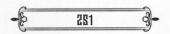

contraption. He was dressed and no longer shining like a newly born star. But his eyes were distant, as if locked on another world.

Danny knelt before him, placing his hands on Colton's knees. The spirit looked up, still playing with what Danny now saw was a brass model of a train car, complete with pistons.

"Are you all right?" Danny asked under the sound of Dae's hammer ringing on metal.

"You shouldn't be asking me that. I'm the one who hurt you."

"Not on purpose."

Colton looked down at the train car. "Zavier knows. I ruined everything."

"You didn't. He said there might be a way to use the power of our blood to save your tower." Remembering their argument, he winced. "If you still want that."

Colton nodded slowly. "I want that." He set the train on the floor, pulled it back, and they both watched as it chugged forward.

"I'm sorry," Colton whispered. "I keep making your life more difficult."

Danny pulled him closer. Colton rested his head on Danny's good shoulder. There were times, like this one, when Danny wondered how things got to be so complicated. In the end, it was simple: his heart beat for him.

"I'd rather have a difficult life with you in it than a boring one without you."

Colton smiled against his neck, then carefully drew the collar of Danny's shirt away, revealing the freshly stitched wound.

He traced it, making Danny shudder in pain and pleasure, then placed his lips solemnly against its sensitive edge.

"I'll never let you be hurt again," Colton whispered against his skin.

"If you wouldn't mind taking your canoodling outside my forge?" Dae said irritably.

But at that moment, they heard something in the ship move. It sounded like the hangar opening.

Danny stood, his arm wrapped around Colton. "They can't be back already."

Dae looked toward the doors, frowning. "Maybe they forgot something."

"I want to go with them to Meerut," Colton said, face set in determination.

"Me, too." After all, Zavier wasn't their only enemy. They had to unite against the true threat before the world was changed again, and for the worse.

Colton retrieved his cog holder from Dae and they headed toward the hangar. But even with someone else by his side, the ship still felt too quiet, too empty for Danny's comfort.

As they reached the hangar, Danny wondered how he'd go about convincing Zavier to let them help. It was ironic, really; all this time spent refusing to work for him, unwilling to go on missions, only to suddenly do an about-face.

The hangar door opened, and someone stepped into the hall. Danny opened his mouth, but his words turned into a strangled gasp.

A woman with short blond hair smiled at him, revealing her canines as two Builders appeared at her side.

Phoebe Archer.

"Run!" he yelled at Colton.

Danny grabbed Colton's hand and took off down the hall. The pounding of boots followed them.

"Is that the Archer woman?" Colton demanded as doors streaked past them. "Why is she here?"

"I don't know, just run!"

They raced deeper into the belly of the *Prometheus*, not toward Dae's forge, but toward a darker, less used section of the ship's maze. Where the hell were the others? Where were Jo, Sally, Charlotte?

Danny didn't have time to think. He ducked into an empty room, closing the door as quietly as his shaking hands could manage, then made Colton huddle with him in a corner behind a row of exercise equipment. While he struggled to catch his breath, Colton didn't make a sound. His amber eyes gleamed in the darkness, focused on the door.

The sound of running footsteps passed. Danny put a hand against his mouth, stifling the noise of his rasping breaths. One Builder paused outside the door for an unnerving amount of time; Colton tensed while Danny's heart threatened to burst from his chest.

A door banged open and they both jumped, but it wasn't theirs. Another crash echoed down the hall, then another, and another, moving closer.

"Come out, come out," the Builder sang. "We'll find you eventually."

Colton tugged on Danny's hand. As they crept toward the door, Colton picked up a metal rod coated in dust.

They waited in bristling silence as the footsteps stopped just outside.

When the door shot open, Colton jumped forward, slamming the metal rod into the man's head. The man was knocked to one side as he fired his gun, the shot missing Danny by a foot.

"Come on!" Colton pulled Danny into the hall, past the other Builder, who cursed as he grabbed for Danny's back and caught only air.

Danny's shoulder throbbed, his head spinning. Though he tripped and weaved, Colton kept urging him forward.

"What do we do?" Colton asked. "Where do we go?"

"I don't—I don't know."

Hurrying down another corridor, Danny grabbed Colton's arm to make him slow down. There was a shadowy mass on the ground that resolved into a body—Dae. He was lying spread-eagle, his eyes wide in surprise under the pulpy mess of the hole blown through his forehead. Blood spread in a halo around him, shining black in the darkness.

"Oh, God." Danny stumbled into the opposite wall. "Oh, God."

"Danny." Colton's voice was strangled as he tugged him along. "The others. We have to find them."

They ran into a familiar hallway, toward the plant nursery.

If Charlotte was there, they could warn her about the Builders' attack, and there was a radio they could use to contact Jo on the bridge.

But when they burst through the door, the room was empty save for the plants.

"There's a radio in here somewhere," Danny gasped as he held his side. Remembering how Charlotte had put a protective hand on her stomach, he was ferociously thankful they hadn't found her body. "We—"

The door opened and a Builder threw himself at Colton. The clock spirit grunted as he hit the floor.

"Colton!" Before Danny could kick the Builder in the head, his partner lurched into the nursery. Danny dove behind a bamboo plant, scrambling for something to use as a weapon. His hand closed around a potted lily at the same time the Builder grabbed his ankle.

The man dragged him closer, and Danny twisted and smashed the terra-cotta pot against the man's skull. Blood trickled from the Builder's hairline as he fell to the floor with a groan.

Danny frantically searched the room for Colton, but when he saw the spirit pinning the other Builder beneath him, he turned his attention back to finding the radio. *There*—on the other side of the ficus.

He fumbled with the controls. "Jo? *Jo!*" Nothing came through except static. "Jo, if you're there, Builders are on the ship. You have to get word to Zavier!"

Colton cried out. Danny whirled around, dropping the radio.

The second Builder, teeth gritted, had wrenched the cog holder from Colton's back and flung it across the room with a loud clatter. Colton sagged, and the men wasted no time tying him up.

Danny flung himself at the Builders. His shoulder blazed with pain, but he ignored it. He ignored the fist that connected with his jaw. He ignored the sound of the door opening behind him.

But he couldn't ignore the wet cloth pressed to his nose and mouth, or the tight grip of someone restraining him from behind. Immediately his vision swam and his knees buckled. A voice sounded in his ear, and he could tell the speaker was smiling.

"Now, now, Mr. Hart," Archer crooned. "No more of that."

He fell swiftly into darkness.

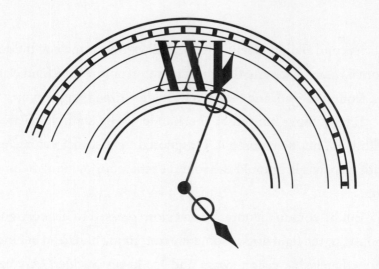

Every cough made Colton's shoulders tense, worsening the ache in his neck and upper back. He'd been carrying that ache for days, ever since the doctor had told them Abigail's lungs weren't working as well as they had the month before. Her breathing was labored, and sometimes her lips turned blue.

Their mother was at Abi's bedside day and night, barely eating, barely drinking water, barely sleeping. Colton had awoken that morning to find his mother slumped against the wall at the foot of Abi's bed, fingers still wrapped around the knitting needles that had gently *click-clack*ed him to sleep. When he shook her awake, she'd bolted up and resumed her knitting as if she'd never left off.

"Mum, you can't do this anymore," he'd pleaded. "Let me take care of her today. Instructor Beele doesn't need me, and Castor can come and help."

His mother had sighed and closed her eyes, which were now always ringed with dark circles. "I do need to go to the market, and your father said they might need help by the docks."

"I'll stay here with her, I promise."

So his mother had left to run errands and get some much-needed sunlight while Colton fed Abigail broth and told her a story about a princess with the power to turn anything to ice, while her brother could turn anything to fire. They looked after each other, the princess cooling off the wildfires her brother kindled when angered, the prince melting the icecaps his sister froze when sad.

Abi listened to the story without interrupting, her blue-tinged lips turned up. When she fell asleep, Colton crept downstairs to prepare lunch for himself and his mother, whenever she came home.

As Colton cut turnips from the garden, Castor opened the door. The moment their eyes met, Abigail coughed wetly above them. Colton winced.

"Water?" Castor asked immediately.

"No, I've already given her some. The doctor says she shouldn't have too much, in case it goes into her lungs."

Castor sighed and rubbed a hand against Colton's neck, fingers digging into the sore spots, as if he knew just where it hurt. As if they shared a body and a mind.

"What can I do?" he asked.

"Help me cut these?"

They worked side by side in a silence broken only by the snap of the vegetables and the occasional cough from Abi.

"It's not fair," Castor said at last. "She should be healthy. She should be outside with her friends, not cooped up inside all the bloody time. Can you imagine? Spending your entire life confined to one place . . ." He looked over and swore. "Colton, I'm sorry."

Colton set the knife down and choked on a sob. He put a hand against his mouth to stifle the sound, not wanting Abigail to hear, but hot tears kept falling down his cheeks and over his fingers, onto the sliced turnips.

Castor tried to wipe them away, but Colton waved him off, hiccupping a couple of times before forcing himself to stop. He couldn't let his mother or sister see him with red eyes.

"I'm fine," he said in little better than a frog's croak, picking up the knife again. "She'll be fine."

No, she won't. She's going to die.

"Colton, she's come out of these spells before. In another week or two she'll be back on her feet. You'll see."

Colton shook his head and returned to chopping. "But how long will that healthy moment last before she takes another turn? She can't keep going on like this. One day, it will be too much for her and—"

"Don't think like that."

"Why not? You keep telling me to be realistic. Or is that too real for you?"

Castor's face clouded. "I'm trying to help."

"Then maybe you should leave. I can take care of things myself."

"I just want to—"

"I can *handle* it."

"You can't! You obviously can't, or else you wouldn't be weeping over turnips!" He reached out to pull Colton's arm back from the table, to see his face. "Colton, if you just—"

"I said *leave!*"

With a pained hiss, Castor stepped back and cradled his hand. Colton dropped the knife stained with Castor's blood. He had forgotten he was holding it.

The cut wasn't deep, but blood welled on the side of Castor's palm and dribbled to the floor. Colton rushed to get a cloth and had Castor press it against the wound. As they waited for the flow to stop, tears stung Colton's eyes again.

"I'm sorry," he mumbled. "I didn't mean to hurt you."

"I'll be all right." Castor nudged Colton with his elbow. "I probably deserved it."

"Don't say that."

"I'm willing to do anything for you, Colton. Anything. But if I'm going to help, you have to let me. None of this pride and stubbornness anymore. Do I make myself clear?"

Colton sighed through his nose. "Yes."

"Sorry, what was that?"

"*Yes.*"

"And no more holding knives when you're upset. Although I think a scar will give me character, don't you?"

"Don't even joke about that. I feel terrible."

"Don't." Castor lifted the cloth to see if the bleeding had stopped. "If it does scar, at least it'll have been from you. That's a mark I can wear proudly."

Scars were memories. Colton didn't want to look at Castor's hand and remember when he'd been weak, or when Abigail was sick, or when, for just one second, he'd been glad that someone besides himself was suffering.

Colton opened his eyes, but he couldn't move his head. It was too heavy. His entire body was too heavy.

He was strapped to a wall with metal bars, two on each arm, one around his chest, one around his hips, two on each leg. He pressed himself against the restraints, but they stayed firm. His cogs were gone, the holder hanging by a heavily bolted door too far away to give him the strength he needed; even the cog from Big Ben was gone from his pocket.

The hum under his boots and the rush of distant air told him he was on an airship, but it didn't feel like the *Prometheus*.

The Builders.

Colton looked up and realized he wasn't alone. Danny was strapped to the opposite wall, unconscious. His chin fell toward his chest, his weight pressing into the metal bars. Without them, he'd have crumpled to the floor.

"Danny," Colton called, glancing at the door in case someone outside heard he was awake. *"Danny."*

Danny groaned faintly, shifting his head. It took a while for him to raise it and open his eyes, revealing that familiar glassy green. He looked straight at Colton with no recognition, then slowly let his gaze wander the dark, metallic room.

"What's happened?" he mumbled.

His confusion fed Colton's panic. What had they done to him? Had they addled his mind?

"The Builders," Colton whispered. "Do you remember that?"

Danny blinked a couple of times, flexing his fingers. "Yes. Damn it."

A minor tremor of relief ran through him. If Danny was swearing, his mind was probably sound.

"Where are we?" Danny asked.

"I think . . . I think we're on their ship."

The door opened with a scrape, and Archer strode inside flanked by Builders. Her eyes lit up at the sight of them.

"Well," she said as one of the Builders closed the door behind them. "It's nice to see you two awake at last. Have any pleasant dreams?" she asked, tilting her head at Colton.

"How did you get on the *Prometheus*?" Danny rasped. "What happened to the others?"

"Other than the one who got in our way, I didn't lay a finger on them. We waited for the landing party to enter the city before hijacking one of their planes, and then our contact opened the hangar for us."

She had said something about a contact in Dürnstein, but Colton hadn't suspected it was one of the *Prometheus* crew. "It

was a trap," Colton said. "You tricked us into going to Meerut so you could do this."

"I like this one," Archer said to her guards. "He's a sharp boy."

"How . . . How do you know who we are?" Danny asked slowly. "Why take us and not the others?"

She clasped her hands behind her back and tossed her head slightly to move a fallen lock of hair. "A cadet of mine reported encountering a rogue clock spirit in Austria with the *Prometheus* crew. A *British* clock spirit, who had the uncanny ability to travel outside of his tower. Now, let's think. What town in England is currently Stopped? It didn't take much research to find out the name of the town's mechanic, considering it's currently the talk of London."

Danny's eyebrows furrowed. "What's that supposed to mean?"

"It seems you've picked up quite an unsavory reputation, Mr. Hart. In any case, I heard the most peculiar report from one of my Builders when he was stationed in Dürnstein about a clock spirit out and about with members of the *Prometheus* crew." She gave an overly dramatized shrug with an exaggerated look of confusion. "Well, what on earth could that mean, I wondered—and besides that, how is it even possible? Since then, I've been eager to get you both on my ship."

"We won't tell you anything," Colton said. "Whatever it is you're looking for—"

"My dear boy, I have no interest in what you can or cannot tell me. I know everything there is to know about clock spirits and their towers. Then again," she went on thoughtfully, walking to Colton's cog holder, "it seems there is a touch I've yet to figure out. How this came to be manufactured, for instance."

"Then . . . why take us?"

"Hostages are always useful." She turned from the cog holder and flashed Danny a grin. "If I can ransom you two for the *Prometheus* leader, I wouldn't complain. He's become rather a thorn in my side, and we'd all prefer it if he'd stop with this Aetas nonsense. Still, I suppose I should have been clearer: I'm not interested in what you know, but I *am* interested in what you *don't*."

Colton and Danny shared a look of consternation.

"Adorable," Archer murmured. "Look how in sync you are." She turned to the guard on her right. The Builder nodded and moved toward Danny, key in hand.

"I've never had an opportunity like this before." Archer walked to Colton and touched his cheek, but he jerked his head away. "A spirit so far from his tower, and all thanks to a silly little contraption. A clock mechanic with a romantic bond to said spirit. It should be a fairy tale."

The guard began to unlock Danny's restraints; Danny flexed his arms, as if ready to pounce. Colton felt a deepening sense of dread.

"Alas," Archer said. "This is not a fairy tale. This is an experiment."

As soon as he was freed, Danny launched himself at the guard, but the Builder was much bigger and easily threw him to the ground.

Colton pushed himself against his restraints to no effect. Archer noticed and smiled.

"After I saw the hole you punched through Lalita's door, I couldn't very well give you an opportunity to break free. You're very weak without those cogs, aren't you?"

"What do you mean by experiment?" Colton growled. "What are you going to do to him?"

Danny, still weak and fighting off whatever he'd been drugged with, tried to crawl away. The Builder laughed and pinned him with a boot on his back.

Archer watched on, curious. "I know all there is to currently know about the spirits. I didn't lie about that. However, you symbolize everything I've yet to uncover—and not knowing something tends to make me cranky. I'm longing to know what can make you break. And . . ." She eyed his restraints. "What can make you stronger."

The Builder holding Danny down took a device from his belt. With a click, a many-pronged needle burst from one end, like a taloned claw. The device emitted a dull crackle, as if each needle held a bolt of lightning.

Danny's eyes widened and he fought to get away again, fingers scrabbling at the ground.

"Stop!" Colton shouted over the crackling of the device. *"Don't touch him!"*

But his plea went unheard. With a motion of Archer's finger, the man jabbed the needles into Danny's lower back.

The room filled with screams.

Colton fought against the metal strangling him, struggling to break from the wall. The cogs in the corner jerked and brightened, responding to his terror.

"Stop it!" he kept screaming, but he could barely be heard above Danny's wails of pain. After a moment, the Builder removed the needles long enough to kick Danny onto his back while the other man held him down. Danny weakly fought as they opened his shirt and pushed the electricity-crackling needles into his chest. He threw his head back and screamed, his heels thumping against the floor as his body twitched violently.

Archer hummed as she watched the cog holder rattle against the wall. "I had a theory that cogs were tied to a spirit's temperament. But perhaps the power in the spirit's body waxes and wanes with emotion, and the cogs tied to the spirit are therefore affected."

"Let him go!" Colton begged. "Please, I'll do anything! Just make them stop!"

Archer *tsked*, but lifted a gloved finger and the Builders paused, removing the device. Danny lay there gasping, his unseeing gaze fixed on the ceiling. Tears leaked from the corners of his eyes. Small red dots peppered his chest where the needles had pricked him.

"You must care for him quite a bit to react as strongly as you did," Archer remarked. "Ah, and the poor lad's already been through an ordeal." She indicated his bullet wound and the newer tear. "Shame."

"Danny," Colton called, trying to get his attention. Danny's eyes locked on Colton, so full of fear and pain that he had to bite his lower lip to pull back a sob.

"He'll be fine." Archer nodded, and her men roughly pulled Danny up. He struggled, and one of them smacked Danny across the face and he went down again. Danny grunted as the other kicked him in the ribs.

"That's *enough*," Archer barked. Sheepishly, they lifted Danny back to his feet and forced him back into the metal restraints.

"Whatever you're planning," Colton whispered, "just do it to me. Don't touch him again. I don't care what you do to me, but don't . . . don't hurt him again. Please."

Archer gave Colton a look of what might have been genuine sympathy. It was hard to tell, as the sharpness of her eyebrows gave her the appearance of constant displeasure. "Don't you worry; tomorrow will be your turn. That'll give the lad some time to rest."

"But—"

She raised her hand and the Builders followed her to the door. "I hope you don't mind, but we'll be taking this for examination." Archer plucked the cog holder from the wall, but then pulled a smaller cog from her pocket—Big Ben's cog—and tossed it at his feet. "Hopefully this will tide you over."

The door slammed behind them, throwing Danny and Colton into darkness and silence.

Danny's breaths were ragged, his eyes unfocused. Blood stained his lower lip. His shirt was still open, and Colton could see every wound, every scar. Those horrible memories, all carved into his skin.

"Danny," Colton said again, but the farther Archer carried his central cog away from the cell, the weaker he became. His vision darkened, his body sagged. He only had time to whisper "I'm sorry" before he sank back into his memories.

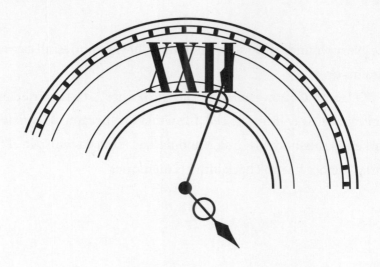

Danny was alone. It didn't matter that Colton was in the same cold, forbidding room; he'd been unconscious, semitranslucent ever since Archer had taken his cogs away. Only the small cog Archer had left kept Colton from turning completely seethrough. Danny wished he had the cog Colton had given him, but it was back on the *Prometheus*, and he'd probably never see it again.

Since Danny was alone, he didn't feel quite as ashamed to cry.

The shock from the needles had traveled across his body in waves of agony, setting every nerve on fire, jabbing into his brain like a thousand knives. He couldn't feel his back or chest. He could barely feel his heart pumping.

The pain had been worse than anything. Worse than the tasers. Worse than the bullet. Worse than having his shoulder torn open. Worse than his father's absence and Matthias's betrayal.

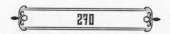

He wondered if Archer meant to kill him.

Impossibly, he fell asleep. It was a dreamless state, the kind where he couldn't be sure if he had slept at all. He thought he woke once to find a couple of Builders observing Colton and writing notes in ledgers, but when he opened his eyes again they were gone.

The next time he woke was with a half-hearted slap to the face. A Builder stood before him, short-haired and grumpy.

"Open your mouth," she ordered. He pressed his cracked lips together, trying not to wince; the bottom one had split.

The Builder grabbed his nose and tilted his head back. He struggled as she forced water down his throat, and it was either swallow or drown. He coughed and sputtered.

She stuffed a couple pieces of bread into his mouth and left without so much as a glance for Colton. As the door clanged shut again, Danny spat out the bread. For all he knew, it could have been poisoned.

"Colton," he called, but the spirit was still out cold. Every so often, though, Danny saw a finger twitch or heard Colton mumble. Once, he thought he heard the name *Castor*, and a dark emotion stole through him.

That's not important right now, he thought wearily.

He looked down at himself. Large, dark bruises bloomed on his chest. His lower back ached and his left shoulder was red and puffy, though the sutures were holding.

Had the *Prometheus*'s crew learned what had happened by now? Had Jo ever gotten his message? Had the Builders attacked them in Meerut? Had another mechanic been killed so a new tower could rise?

Over the next couple of hours, Danny faded in and out of consciousness. When the door opened, he jerked awake. Colton stirred and looked up, amber eyes hazy.

Archer came in holding the cog holder. The same two guards were with her, and at the sight of them Danny's stomach tightened. One wore the needle device at his hip. When he caught Danny looking at it, he grinned.

"Good afternoon," Archer said as if they were meeting for tea. She spotted the bread Danny hadn't eaten discarded on the floor. "Ah, Mr. Hart. It will not do to act the hero."

He ignored her, turning his attention to Colton. "How are you feeling? Are you all right?"

Colton lifted his eyes from his central cog, taking in the horrible bruises marring Danny's chest. "Oh, God. I should be asking you that."

"That's enough." Archer removed the central cog from the holder. "Time to get down to business."

Danny tensed. "What are you going to do with that?"

"I assure you, I don't plan on breaking it. It's only another experiment."

"I know firsthand the consequences of your experiments," he snarled. "Don't you dare lay a hand on him."

"I don't plan to." Archer regarded the cog in her hand, then smacked it suddenly—and loudly—against the wall.

Danny and Colton flinched as one.

Archer looked between them with interest. "Colton, would you mind telling me how that felt?" When he remained silent, she shrugged. "Have it your way."

She placed a boot against the cog and scraped it along the floor. Colton cringed.

"Uncomfortable?" she asked. "What about this?"

She drew out a gun and fired it at the cog. Danny yelped in surprise, while Colton groaned in pain. The bullet might have dented the metal before glancing off, but Danny couldn't be sure.

"Not quite enough." Archer held out her hand and a Builder passed her the needle device. With a click, it sprang out.

"Stop it!" Danny snapped at her. "Do you want to put the entire town of Enfield in danger? If you kill their spirit, that's what's going to happen!"

"My dear boy, I have no such plans. Your spirit will, by all means, live."

"Then why are you doing all of this?"

She regarded him for a lengthy moment, her brown eyes thoughtful under severe eyebrows. Finally, she clicked the needles back inside their holder and pocketed the device.

"I brought you two some light reading." She turned to the second Builder, who handed her a pack. Digging through it, Archer pulled out a book with a faded leather cover. "Nothing like a bit of context, hmm?"

"What are you talking about?" Colton asked.

She blinked at Colton over the top of the book. "You'll see."

Pacing the room, she opened the book and flipped through

yellowed pages until at last she let out a small "aha" and stabbed a finger to the paper. "Here we are. The English is a bit old-fashioned, but I've translated it as best I can. 'I have begun testing the theory and have uncovered some remarkable breakthroughs—'"

"What the hell is this?" Danny demanded.

Archer looked up, annoyed. "This, Mr. Hart, is a secret that has long been written out of any historical records: the last known documented proof of how the clock spirits came into being. I thought you, of all people, would be jumping at the chance to learn more."

Danny glanced at the book, confused. "But . . . how? Why would you have something like that?"

"It was written by my great-grandfather several times down, Henry Archer." The name triggered something in Colton, whose eyes widened. "Now, where was I?"

She strolled around the room, reading from the book. "'These breakthroughs, I believe, tie into the records we have stored regarding the issue of time and its measurements therein, and of the peculiar attachment between the time servant and its master. The master, in this instance, being Aetas, or being time itself. There have been certain issues, certain incidents, involving a time servant and the way in which time has been affected around his person as a result.

"'This affectation being the most prominent in the matter of blood.'"

Danny's own blood began rushing faster through his body, loudly whispering in his ears.

Archer flipped a few more pages. "'The first experiment is set. It has come sooner than we anticipated. Aetas's hold on us slackens, and as a result, time distorts around us. If we wait any longer, it may be too late. We have already chosen a subject. He is a time servant, a strong man named Stephen. We joke that he will be our martyr, our own St. Stephen, like his Christian namesake. No doubt that is what we will call his tower when construction has been completed.'"

Colton and Danny looked down at Big Ben's cog in horror.

"'It is done,'" she read on, turning the page delicately. "'The man was dragged like a pig to slaughter, poor beast, and bled over the cogs with which we will build the foundation of our first victory. The first clock tower will preside over London, and it will be a magnificent sight. Our emissaries are traveling now to the nearby towns and villages to repeat the process. Soon, the rest of the world will be regulated as London is. Soon, we will forget about Aetas and how he forsook us, condemning us to this hell.'"

She closed the book with a sigh. "It goes on for quite a few volumes, spelling out the procedures, the countries that converted and in what order, the meticulous journey of destroying all evidence in his wake. You must agree, he was very thorough. No one has known how to build functioning clock towers for centuries."

Danny tried to swallow, but his throat had gone dry. "How . . . How long have you known?"

"Many years."

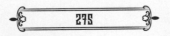

"And you never thought to *tell* anybody? What about when the Union tried to build the new Maldon tower?"

She shrugged. "It wasn't my responsibility as a member of the Archer family. My responsibility was to keep the world happy and ignorant. I wouldn't dare break hearts by revealing the ugly truth. And so the world's leaders celebrated the towers, protected them, funded people like you to care for them.

"But no one can stay happy and ignorant for long, isn't that so?" She ran a finger down Colton's cheek, and he jerked it away. "You know the truth about your demise, don't you? Other spirits are beginning to awaken to this knowledge as well, ever since Aetas's prison was located. We have your leader to thank for that—Mr. Holmes, is it? The Crown commissioned me to put a stop to his bothersome efforts, but I have grander plans than that. I'll protect my family's legacy, and the world can go on happy and ignorant."

"Except it can't," Danny snapped. "They know something's different now. Time continued on even after Zavier tore down those towers, and a new area of time was created when you rebuilt the Khurja tower. People will investigate. Mechanics are going to want to know the truth. And when they do—"

Archer laughed, cutting and dismissive. "Don't you understand, boy? Even if some of the mechanics found out, they wouldn't do a thing about it. No, such a discovery would cause too much panic. They'll keep any such knowledge out of history books. Millions of citizens will continue on as they always have, and people like you with your ability to sense time will continue on as clock mechanics, maintaining the order of the world. Weren't you happy as a mechanic? Didn't it satisfy a yearning deep within you? Aren't you fascinated by clocks and how they work, and so proud to understand them in a way ordinary people cannot?"

All she said was true, but Danny's connection to time had been forever tainted. The most fulfilling element of his life had proven to be nothing but a bloody secret.

"The Archer family understands this yearning. Henry Archer did everything in his power to nurture it, to manifest it into what it is today." Archer's voice had taken on a fervent note, though it was strangely angry. If Danny looked close enough, he could see the tick of her jaw as she clenched her teeth together, the flash of something half buried in her eyes. "I plan to do the same. No—*better*. The new tower in Khurja is only a prototype, the beginning of a new wave of time innovation, but now we can set our sights on London as our base of operations."

"Innovation? What does that even mean?"

"It means, Mr. Hart, that I will be the founder of a better world." She spread her gloved hands before her. "The clock towers as they are now are brittle and old. They fall into disrepair and put people in danger. But if we can find a stronger magic, a deeper connection between spirit and time . . . Imagine such a world. *Indestructible towers.*" She grinned in excitement, her eyes glazed with this vision of the future.

It was so similar to what Zavier had told him that Danny felt queasy. But whereas Zavier thought the solution was to do away with all towers, the woman before him wanted to rebuild their foundations.

Indestructible. Was such a thing possible?

She noticed the interest in his eyes and stepped closer. "Yes," she breathed. "Yes, Mr. Hart, what I say is achievable. You must want this for Enfield's tower, do you not? To stay forever with your spirit?"

He hesitated, glancing at Colton. The spirit was staring at the floor, dangerously still. Did he want Colton's tower to be indestructible? Of course he did.

But did Colton?

"Look at the new Khurja tower if you have any doubts," Archer continued when he stayed silent. "By using a higher concentration of blood, using two or even three times the servants per tower, the power we can eke out of the towers is that much stronger."

That snapped Danny out of his thoughts. Appalled that he had even been considering it, he scowled at Archer. "Unlike the Builders, I'm not interested in taking innocent lives."

Archer scoffed in amusement. "No life is innocent."

Danny opened his mouth to retort when Colton's voice broke in.

"How could you?"

They both looked over at the spirit. His amber eyes blazed as he glared at Archer, his teeth half-bared. There was something feral within him, something Danny had only seen a handful of times, which frightened him to his marrow.

"You knew," Colton said, his voice dangerously low. "You knew, and your father before you, and his father before. For years and years, your family knew. And still you did nothing."

"It wasn't our place to disrupt—"

"They *killed* me." His voice broke. "Your ancestor ordered men to hold me down and slit my throat. I died as my parents watched. My sister. My friends. I had to endure centuries trapped in that tower, alone. I was forced to forget who I was, *what* I was. And now you're doing the same thing. You killed Lalita. You've probably killed another mechanic by now, and are planning to kill more."

The sound of groaning metal filled the room. Danny realized it was coming from Colton's restraints. The cogs nearby began to glow with the force of Colton's rage, adding strength to the amplifiers Dae had installed.

Alarm crossed Archer's face as she realized the same thing. She threw the book down and swiftly moved to Danny's side, tugging the sleeve of his shirt over his injured shoulder. Without warning, she grabbed his wound and squeezed—hard.

Danny screamed, trying to shrink away, but his restraints wouldn't allow him to move. Colton froze, eyes meeting Archer's across the distance. The Builders by the door put their hands on their guns, wary.

"Get away from him," Colton said.

Archer released a shaky laugh. "Now, now. That's no way to behave, Mr. Bell."

Colton's head jerked back as if he'd been slapped.

"That *was* your family name, was it not?" she asked. "It's right there in Henry Archer's records. 'Colton Bell of Enfield, aged seventeen years and eight months, died on the evening of April—'"

"Stop it," Colton whispered.

"So long as you stop this foolishness, Mr. Bell." She squeezed Danny's shoulder again and he grunted. A bead of blood rolled down his chest.

Colton followed it with his eyes, the rest of him unmoving.

Archer released Danny, but eyed the wound with new interest. "Unfortunately, we will have to take those cogs away from you again. But first . . ." She picked up Big Ben's cog, still lying on the floor near Colton's feet. "Indulge me."

Before either of them could react, she pressed the cog to Danny's bleeding wound. He held back a startled cry as the air shivered around him. He could feel—*sense*—London. Smoke and steam and snow. It was so familiar that his eyes watered.

Time jumped over his skin and prickled at the back of his neck. He drew a breath through his teeth and tried to see if he could grasp hold of it, but the connection wasn't strong enough. The sensation fizzled away as soon as Archer removed the cog and wiped it off on her sleeve.

"Fascinating." She stroked her fingers through his hair, then held his face up with a strong hand, fingers digging into his cheeks. Turning to Colton, she shook Danny's head. "What do you think, should we feed his blood to the London tower? Should this be the new face of St. Stephen?"

Colton was utterly still. "Zavier is going to free Aetas and your secret will be revealed. You won't be able to kill anyone else and turn them into spirits."

Archer released Danny. "And you're willing to die, are you?"

"If that's what it takes to stop you."

She hummed in surprise. "No no no, we can't have that." Looking at the small cog in her hand, she thought for a moment, then smiled to herself. "I think, Misters Hart and Bell, there is time for one more experiment."

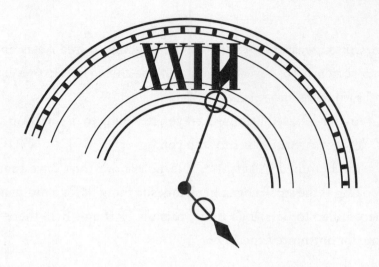

They were left alone for hours while Archer went off to plan her next "experiment." Danny watched Colton fade in and out, eyes opening whenever a tremor shuddered through the air as Archer and the others studied Colton's cog holder.

Likewise, he studied Colton. He remembered the human boy from those memories, the one with blue eyes, slightly crooked teeth, and freckles. The Colton in front of him was more perfect, more beautiful, and somehow lesser because of it.

I used to be so much more than I am now.

Colton Bell. Danny couldn't stop repeating the name in his head. He wondered if he'd been named after a relative, or if his parents had chosen the name at random. He wondered if Colton's mother had ever said his full name when Colton was in trouble, as his own mother had so many times before.

Daniel Alexander Hart, I swear if you take the mantel clock apart again—!

Colton Bell, do you see how much mud you've tracked inside? Clean it up this instant!

Danny tried to smile, but he couldn't manage it. Colton Bell was dead.

He closed his eyes against the tears, but they came anyway. He tried to breathe past the tightness in his throat, past the feeling that nothing could be done. That they'd been abandoned. That he was useless.

"I'm sorry, Colton," he whispered.

"Don't be."

He opened his eyes to find the clock spirit looking at him, tired and bleary.

Colton smiled weakly. "Nothing's over yet," he reminded Danny. "Just hold on."

"I wish I could do something useful. I wish I could help you."

"Danny," Colton whispered, "you're always helping me, more than I'll ever repay. This time, it's my turn."

The door opened and Danny braced himself for another assault. Archer strode in with Colton's holder slung over her shoulder.

"Good morning, boys," she sang. "Ready for another enlightening day?"

Danny licked his cracked lips. "What were you doing to his cog holder?"

"Simply adding a couple more amplifiers." She swung it around so they could see another band of metal crossing over the two Dae had added. Danny shuddered as he thought of Dae, of the bullet hole the Builders had blown through him.

Archer held up Big Ben's cog and inserted it into the new pocket. "Wonderful, no?"

"Why?" Danny asked, his voice flat. "You don't want to kill us—fine. But why go to these extremes? These *experiments*?"

"I certainly don't have to answer to you, Mr. Hart."

"You were a clock mechanic once, weren't you?" He flung the question at her like an aerial strike, and felt the briefest moment of satisfaction seeing her lips part in surprise.

"What are you trying to get out of me, Mr. Hart?" she asked softly. Dangerously.

Danny swallowed. Across the room, Colton watched the exchange warily.

"The truth."

Archer grinned slowly. It wasn't the grin of someone off-kilter, someone as perversely excited as she had presented herself these last two days. In fact, the startling awareness of that smile, the sheer intelligence of it, was even more terrifying.

"Let me tell you a bit about the Archer family," she said in a voice as carefully controlled as her stance—the stance of one who knew how to defend herself. "Starting with dear great-great-great-grandfather Henry. What a fascinating man. It's enough to humble the rest of us, trembling in the wake of the rock he dropped in history's ocean." She looked straight at Colton, her smile now gone. "The Archers are stained with blood, Mr. Hart. Imagine, if you will, what it's like to carry that burden, to be one of the only people who knows the morbid truth of this world." Archer blinked. "Well. I suppose you don't have to imagine, do you?"

Danny glanced at Colton's throat.

"The Archers are considered a *legacy*," she went on, quieter than before. "Each Archer harboring this precious secret, knowing how the sausage is made, so to speak. What a thing to be told. What an experience to read through Henry Archer's notes detailing every death he witnessed, how much blood he spilled across England. But this is our duty, you see? To keep the secret and to protect the towers. Did you know that Henry Archer helped establish the Mechanics Union?" She noted Danny's shock. "Yes, it's true. Several in our line were born with the gift of time, and many got to use it." She tapped her fingertips against Colton's cog holder. "Except me."

Danny shook his head. "You're not—you weren't a mechanic?"

"My father wouldn't let me study. Said it was too dangerous to link our name with the mechanics. Still, that didn't stop me from getting into the field, publishing reports and essays, going to clock towers to see how they ran. Knowing, in that locked part of me, the secret that led them to running in the first place."

She walked over to Colton, studying him the way one studies gearwork, its intricacies and its predictability. "When I told the prime minister I knew how to rebuild the fallen towers, they didn't hesitate. They gave me a small army and told me to go to India. But that Lead Mechanic of yours tried to intervene, and then there was that horrible business with the viceroy. The prime minister told me to rebuild the towers as fast as I was able, to put a stop to the growing unrest."

"I still don't understand. What do you get out of it?" Danny asked.

"I suppose money and power are fine things to have. But, more than that . . ." Again that slow smile, her gaze still fixed on Colton, who met it with steel in his own. "I finally get to use this gift. This connection to time that my father told me never to wield. I'm going to change the legacy of the Archer line, to turn us into heroes, by strengthening the towers and the spirits within—to revolutionize Mechanic Unions all over the world."

She handed the cog holder off to one of the Builders and drew something from the satchel at her belt.

When Danny realized what she was holding, he paled. The syringe flashed in her hand as Archer held it up and flicked a finger against the glass, making a hollow sound. She watched him with a hungry look in her eyes.

Colton struggled against the metal bands, but one of the Builders raised his gun to Danny's head.

"Your heroism is getting a bit repetitive," Archer said. "Well, Mr. Hart, let's see what you can do."

Archer tore away the sleeve of his shirt at his elbow, and he remembered the way the *Prometheus* crew had slid the needles into his veins. He tossed his head back in alarm, hitting his temple against the gun's barrel.

"Stop. Stop!"

But she didn't stop, and the needle broke his skin. The world rushed into a black tunnel around him and he groaned, heart fluttering. Archer drew the plunger and the syringe began to fill with his blood.

When it was completely full, she slid the needle back out and pressed a small cloth to the wound. "There, now. Not so bad, was it?"

"What are you doing?" he panted. "Why do you need that?"

"Patience, patience." She held up the ruby vial. "This is precious fuel. Just a few drops had the most interesting reaction before. And we all know what happens when the blood of a time servant is spilled onto a central cog."

She turned back to Colton. "But the blood of a time servant might have other uses."

Colton's eyes remained locked on Archer's as she approached him. She ripped at his sleeve, baring the smooth, veinless skin of his elbow.

"Don't!" Danny yelled just as she stuck the needle into Colton's flesh.

There was no visible reaction until Archer pressed the plunger down. Danny watched his blood disappear, flowing in spirals of reddish-golden light into Colton's body. At first, nothing happened. The room was silent. No one even breathed.

Then, suddenly, the room began to vibrate.

Archer stepped back, gaze eagerly fixed on the cog holder, which was now shining as bright as a sunburst.

Colton groaned and hung his head, his body trembling as a golden light flickered around him. He struggled to contain it, to control whatever reaction was happening within him.

But he couldn't hold on, and as Colton screamed out in pain, the light flared out, blinding them all. Danny shut his eyes and called Colton's name, but the room was chaos.

The ship lurched. Clocks sounded all around them, seconds quickening into furious *ticktockticks* in their ears. Then, the sound of shattered glass—the clocks, the timepieces, everything measuring time onboard the ship exploding into twisted fragments.

"Ma'am!" a Builder shouted. "We should evacuate! The ship—!"

"He just needs to control it!" she shouted back. "Feel that power! It's *beautiful*!"

Colton kept screaming, his body lost within the light. The metal of Danny's restraints twisted and snapped free, and he fell to the floor.

The Builder holding the cog holder yelped and dropped it as if the metal had burned him. Danny squinted into the light and saw Colton tear through his own restraints like they were made of papier-mâché. Before the Builders could react, Colton grabbed Archer by the throat and lifted her into the air, his teeth bared. Light was pouring from every inch of him, turning him into a second sun, a golden god of vengeance.

"How dare you?" His voice echoed and crashed like waves, from the lowest register to the highest trill and every timbre in between. "How dare you do this to us?"

Archer scratched at Colton's hand as her boots kicked feebly in the air. The other Builders clapped their hands over their ears and shrank toward the door as a sharp whistle cut through the room.

"Give me one good reason why I shouldn't kill you," Colton said in that horrible voice, those echoing words. He tightened his grip and Archer sputtered.

Danny struggled to his feet. His dizziness nearly made him fall back to the floor, but he focused on Colton, on this terrifying stranger who had replaced him. Gritting his teeth, Danny moved toward him, into the blinding light. Time wrapped around him, squeezing him like Colton's hand squeezed Archer's throat.

"Colton!" he yelled over the whistling. The clock spirit's body pulled him in, and he could feel his own blood singing in Colton's power. "Colton, let her go!"

"She would have killed us," he said in those many voices. "She plans on killing more mechanics. I won't let that happen."

"We won't! I promise, we'll stop them—but not like this!"

Colton bared his teeth again, his eyes blazing with golden hatred. He no longer looked human. He'd transformed into a being like the spirit guarding the Prague clock, a monster born of twisted power. He was no longer Colton Bell, or even Colton— only the rage of Time.

Danny had to stop him.

He staggered forward and wrapped his arms around Colton's torso. His body burned, the power driving into his skin like fire, but he held on. Colton felt rigid, distant, an entire universe away.

"Colton, you have to stop this. You can't allow this power to win you over. You have to control it." Danny closed his eyes and tightened his hold. "You said you'd never leave me. I can't find you anymore. Please come back. Please."

The room continued to shake, the whistle sharp in Danny's ears. Then Colton loosened his grip on Archer's throat and she gasped, her face a mottled red. The light eased inward, and the whistling gradually faded.

Slowly, Colton turned his head toward Danny. His eyes were still glowing, but after a couple of blinks, even they returned to normal. Danny breathed a sigh of relief.

"Danny," Colton whispered, and his voice, thankfully, was once more that familiar crystalline chime.

"Colton." He dropped his head onto Colton's shoulder. "Thank God."

Colton looked regretfully up at Archer, and the Builders who were regrouping behind her. Grabbing Danny around the waist, he turned and threw Archer against the wall. Dazed, she slid to the floor.

"We have to run," he said. "They're here."

"Who?" Danny demanded.

"The *Prometheus*. I felt the ship outside."

The other Builders rushed at them, but Colton pushed one back and kicked the other to the floor. His newfound strength buzzed across Danny's skin.

Colton put on his cog holder, and the power running wildly

through the air was suddenly focused into a small sphere around him. "Hurry!"

A Builder reached up and grabbed Danny's calf. Before Colton could do anything, Danny swerved and kicked the man between the legs. He wheezed but refused to release his grip, so Danny yanked the needle device from the man's belt and drove it into his chest. The Builder jerked and screamed as Danny and Colton raced out the door. Outside, Colton knocked a third guard against the wall.

"Where do we go?" Danny gasped, leaning into Colton. He could still hear screams behind them.

"When my power expanded, I was able to get a sense of the ship's layout." He looked at Danny, ashamed. "I'm sorry. I wasn't myself. Your blood, it . . . I can *feel* it. It's giving me so much power. It just took over, and I was so angry . . ."

"Let's worry about that later," Danny said as more Builders rounded the corner. "Right now, that anger could really come in handy."

Colton nodded and disappeared, reappearing in the midst of the Builders. The men and women barely knew what was happening before they were sailing through the air and into the walls, knocked out cold.

Colton popped back to Danny's side, a pained look on his face. "I don't like this. I don't want to hurt any more people."

"If we can just get to the *Prometheus*, we'll be fine."

They took off down the opposite corridor, alert for more

Builders. An alarm started blaring overhead and the lanterns along the corridor flickered. Danny had to stop to rest several times as his vision swam in and out of blackness; days without food and the loss of so much blood had taken their toll.

"Let me carry you," Colton pleaded.

"No. Need to—have—hands free. In case."

Footsteps rang down the corridor and the two of them ducked into the nearest room, which contained a bunk and a set of drawers, but thankfully wasn't occupied. They waited for the Builders to pass.

When Danny reached for the handle, Colton took his hand.

"Come here." He drew Danny to the bunk, then tore the sheet into strips. "You're still bleeding. Might leave a trail."

Danny watched Colton bandage his arm and shoulder. Although the look in his eyes was so familiar, there was still a troubling distance to him, as if he had to restrain himself with every motion.

Danny hadn't thought it was possible—a clock spirit receiving blood. Somehow, it made him feel as if he was within Colton's body, and Colton was seeing through his eyes.

He gently took Colton's face between his hands. "I know that wasn't you. I've seen what so much power can do to a clock spirit. You were just trying to protect us."

Colton ducked his head. "It was wrong of me. I hate her, but I . . . I didn't want . . ."

"I know."

"It hurts." He put his hand on Danny's chest, over the bruises. "I feel how much it hurts."

"I'll be fine," Danny said, taking Colton's hand and kissing his palm. "We need to get going."

Later. Later.

They stood up, ready to navigate the ship's corridors again, when the door opened. Danny stepped back while Colton tensed, but they both made sounds of relief at the sight of Daphne, Meena, and Liddy.

"I *knew* I felt you!" Daphne hooked an arm around each of their necks and held them fast for a few painful seconds. "What the hell happened to you?"

"Not now," Liddy growled, peering out the door, gun at the ready. "We have to move."

"Phoebe Archer's still onboard," Colton said. "We should take her and make sure she doesn't harm anyone else."

"No. Zavier's orders are to get you both out as soon as possible."

Meena noticed Danny's wounds. "What evil people. Will you be able to run?"

"He'll have to." Liddy took something from her belt and thrust it into Danny's hands. "We'll need to be fast if we want to get out of here alive."

Danny looked down at the gun, its weight cold and heavy in his hand.

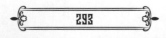

They had only been running—in Danny's case, limping—for two minutes when they heard a shout behind them.

"In here!" Liddy rushed through a doorway into a room large and cluttered enough to rival Dae's workshop. Glancing around, Danny now knew the source of the many clocks he'd heard before.

"What the—?" Danny turned, taking in the counters and shelves all filled with broken clocks, timepieces, gears, and cogs. There were even hourglasses, their glass shattered and their sand spilled across the floor that crunched under their boots, and a sundial cracked through the center. "What is all this?"

Colton began to glow again, but thanks to the amplifiers, he had only to close his eyes and focus to dim the light. Still, Danny felt time shiver around him, caressing his skin and something deeper inside, as if briefly cradling his beating heart and toying with the idea of stopping it.

"Less gawking, more moving," Liddy barked. "There's a hatch up ahead we need to get through before—"

The door banged open behind them. Builders rushed inside, firing their guns as everyone ducked behind the nearest counter. A shot fired dangerously close to Meena's head, and she growled before letting a random shot fly from her own gun. It bounced off a counter and into one of the broken clocks. Like a bomb going off, the clock whistled and glowed before it erupted into a lethal storm of gears and springs.

Time warped around them, bringing the Builders closer within a blink. Colton concentrated on fixing the tiny rift as

Daphne pulled him and Danny toward the opposite side of the workshop. Liddy and Meena still fired behind them, dodging bullets and throwing any available objects at the Builders to keep them at bay.

"Hold on!" Danny grabbed the nearest timepiece and smashed it against the counter. Time warped again, a sudden current that slowed the Builders' bullets, suspending them in the air. The Builders, surprised, tried firing again, but their bullets moved as fast as flies swimming through porridge.

Abandoning their guns, the Builders charged instead. Colton lifted a hand and one of the women froze mid-motion, her eyes wide. She couldn't move a muscle.

Another Builder threw a coil from his belt. It wrapped around Daphne's legs, yanking her to the ground. Meena threw another clock at the Builder's head, bringing him down. The man struggled to his feet only to be struck with the clock again, and again. They watched in horror as the man entered a strange time loop, standing and being struck over and over.

Danny unwound the coil from Daphne's legs as Liddy sent an electric jolt through another Builder, sending him to the ground.

Colton was shaking. "I can't hold it for much longer," he said, his voice strained. "And more are coming."

More Builders swarmed into the workshop but drew up short, gaping at their time-affected comrades. Daphne jumped to her feet and pushed Danny and Colton into the hallway. Meena and Liddy followed.

"Now what?" Daphne panted.

"You're looking for a hatch?" Colton pointed to their right. "This way."

"How do you—?" Liddy waved her gun in agitation. "Never mind, let's go."

They took off again, but Danny knew he couldn't match their pace anymore. His body started to topple, and he stumbled into the nearest wall.

Meena put a hand on his back. "Maybe Colton should carry you."

Danny shook his head, as much to deny the offer as to clear his vision. Her worried face swam back into focus. Danny was tired of that look. He was tired of everyone needing to take care of him.

"I'm *fine*," he rasped, pushing away from the wall.

Colton frowned. "Danny, they—"

"Shh!" Liddy held up a hand. Two sets of boots could be heard running toward them from the direction of the hatch. Liddy and Meena readied their guns, and Daphne raised her fists.

Edmund and Astrid rounded the corner and skidded to a halt, out of breath and sweating.

"Oh, good, you found them," Edmund gasped.

"Is the plane still waiting?" Liddy asked.

"Still there. But we have to hurry."

"Not before we find 'er," Astrid snapped.

"Her?" Colton looked between them. "Who? Archer?"

"No, Sally," Edmund said.

Danny's fingers twitched. "Zavier's sister? I thought he never let her go on missions."

They all looked at him as if he'd sprouted a third eye. All except Colton, who looked just as confused.

"You don't know?" Daphne asked slowly. "They didn't tell you?"

"Tell us *what*?"

"Sally was captured along with the pair of you," Edmund said, worry tightening his eyes. "We found out too late that one of us has been working with the Builders. Ivor. He let their plane in for Archer to steal you three, but Jo stopped him from leaving with Archer. We'd hoped to find you lot together, but it seems they've locked Sally elsewhere."

Danny felt his legs buckle again, and leaned his shoulder against the wall. "We never saw her."

All this time, while they were being tortured and experimented on, Archer might have been doing the same to Sally, who shared her brother's connection to time.

"Leverage," Danny muttered. "Archer said she needed leverage against Zavier."

"Well, she bloody has it," Liddy snapped. "We can't leave without Sally. Zavier will come charging in himself, and we can't risk losing him. It was bad enough having to drug him."

"You *drugged* him?"

"'E was ready to chew a door through the Builder's ship otherwise," Astrid said with a flip of her hair. "If we cannot find 'er, what do we do?"

"Split up," Edmund said. "Liddy, you take these two to the plane. Daphne or Meena should go with you—"

"I'll help you find Sally," Meena said, reloading her gun. "Daphne, if Akash doesn't see one of us soon, he's going to come barging down here on Zavier's heels."

"*He* should have been drugged," Daphne grumbled. "Are you sure? I can go with you."

Edmund shook his head, patting her shoulder. "Help them to the plane."

A couple of Builders turned the corner. Without missing a beat, Astrid threw one of her knives, which found its target in a Builder's chest. Edmund fired a shot that took out the other.

Colton stared at the bodies. "You . . . You killed them."

"They killed Dae." Edmund nodded to Liddy and took off running, Astrid and Meena just behind.

Colton looked after them as if he'd never seen them before.

"Remember what they've done to our own," Liddy reminded him, her voice surprisingly soft.

Colton closed his eyes. "There have already been too many deaths."

"As much as we all want to hold hands and sing hymns, that's just not in the cards." She flashed a meaningful glance at Danny. "The hatch is just ahead."

Daphne and Liddy checked around each corner before ushering Danny and Colton forward. Colton supported a now-flagging Danny, though with the spirit's new strength, it was more like dragging him. With each step, Danny's chest and back flared with pain, his shoulder throbbing angrily.

Liddy turned the next corner and froze. "Oh, damn."

In a square-shaped hub, six Builders stood guard before the hatch. They opened fire and she scrambled back behind the wall.

"Now what?" Daphne yelled over the noise.

Colton leaned Danny against the wall, then disappeared. Danny heard more shots, some grunts, and a garbled yell. Liddy wasted no time rushing back around the corner to join the fray, while Daphne and Danny crept toward the hub, anxious to see what was happening.

Colton had knocked out three of the guards, and Liddy had shot another in the arm. The man went down with a shout and a spray of blood, but his partner grabbed Liddy from behind. Colton stopped circling his next target and appeared suddenly behind the Builder, yanking her off of Liddy and throwing her over his head to slam her into the floor. The Builder coughed and wheezed, too stunned to move.

But as Liddy recovered and Colton hesitated over the Builder he'd thrown—Danny could see the remorse on his face even from where he stood—another man aimed his gun at Colton's head.

Danny was barely aware of lifting his hands. He'd nearly forgotten about the foreign weight he held, the unfamiliar grooves of a pistol. It didn't matter in that mindless moment as he acted only on impulse and pulled the trigger.

He wanted to misfire, to scare, maybe to injure.

The bullet crashed through the Builder's head.

They all watched, even the last Builder standing, as the man tottered on his feet. The gun he held clattered to the floor, slowly followed by the thud of his body. His head squished as it hit the hard ground, a dark pillow of blood oozing beneath him.

"Jaime!"

The cry came from the last Builder. He stared at Danny with wide, wet eyes. Mouth twisted into a grimace, he yelled and came at him with only his bare fists.

Danny didn't move. He almost welcomed the man with open arms.

Then Colton was between them, catching the man by his shoulders. "I'm sorry," he said before he twisted and knocked the Builder's head against the wall. The man slid down to the floor, unconscious.

Colton turned to face Danny. He expected to see disgust. Shock. Fury. What he didn't expect was guilt.

Danny dropped the gun. Daphne retrieved it and put a hand on his arm.

Liddy was already climbing the ladder toward the hatch above. "More will be coming," she said, grunting as she turned the hatch door open by its wheel. "Come on!"

Daphne gently tugged Danny forward. His eyes landed on the ruined mess of the Builder's head, and something deep inside his stomach lurched.

"Don't look," she whispered. "Eyes up, Danny."

She climbed up before him, Colton supporting his weight from behind. Danny's left arm was difficult to move, but he bit his cheek and forced himself to climb hand over hand until

coppery blood spilled in his mouth. Colton made a slight sound of pain below.

Daphne and Liddy half-pulled him into a storm of blustery wind. They were standing on the very top of the Builders' airship. His open shirt flapped madly, his eyes stinging at the force of the wind.

"Akash!"

Danny squinted through the light refracting off the clouds. The *Silver Hawk* had attached itself to the airship like a barnacle on a whale's back using odd tubular suckers. Not four feet away from the ship, Akash and Anish were fighting a pair of Builders.

Anish had his Builder in a headlock, but Akash was having more trouble. Someone had given him a gun, but he must have run out of bullets, because he was using the butt to try and knock the Builder on the head. As he turned, the Builder hooked his leg, taking him down.

Daphne ran forward. Liddy trained her own gun on the man and cursed.

"I can't get a clear shot!" she yelled above the wind.

The Builder descended on Akash, drawing a knife from up his sleeve. Daphne reached them just as the Builder's head snapped up, giving her the perfect angle to smack it with the butt of the gun she'd taken from Danny.

A shadow appeared in the corner of Danny's eye. The *Prometheus* lurked just above them, off the starboard side. Something sprang from the side of the airship, careering toward the Builders' ship: a metallic grappling rope.

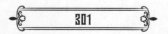

The grapnel tore into the hull. The ship lurched and they all scrambled to keep their footing. The Builder Daphne had hit clawed at the smooth metal under him as he listed to the side. She and Akash threw out their arms, but the Builder slid off with a scream.

Anish had grabbed hold of the *Silver Hawk*'s wing. The Builder he'd been fighting, now passed out, rolled off the side to join his partner. The ship righted itself, connected now to the *Prometheus* by an umbilical-like cord.

"That rope's for the others!" Liddy yelled. "They must not've been able to get to the hatch. Come on, we have to go!"

She ushered them to the plane as the ship's hatch banged open behind them. Akash pushed Daphne before him into the *Silver Hawk*. Colton helped Danny up, followed by Anish, then Liddy, who managed to fire off two bullets at the approaching Builders before falling inside and slamming the door shut.

"Go!"

"Where's Meena?" Akash demanded even as he flipped through his controls.

"She's coming with the others, now GO!"

They separated from the Builders' ship with a loud *pop*. The plane teetered as it took to the air, small pings in the hull alerting them that the Builders were still firing.

Danny wanted to look out the window. He had to know that they were free, that they were going to be all right.

He also needed to be sick.

But none of that compared to his urgent, overwhelming need to pass out. He tried to warn Colton, but even as he grabbed a fistful of the spirit's shirt, he found himself giving in to the roar of darkness that rose up to claim him.

He thought he heard screams. Someone saying his name over and over. Guns. Yelling. He smelled blood, thick and metallic, and tasted it on his tongue.

When Danny opened his eyes, he was greeted by a slate gray ceiling. The one in his room on the *Prometheus*.

Turning his head, like a compass arrow pointing north, he saw Colton sitting on the edge of his bed. Colton smiled, but it didn't touch his amber eyes. He reached out and smoothed back Danny's hair.

They stayed in silence a while, needing no words to understand that they were both too tired to process what had happened. Too, too tired.

Eventually, Colton met his eyes again. *Are you all right?*

Danny struggled to swallow. *I'll be fine. I think. And you?* He

couldn't shake the image of Colton wrapped in his furious power, seizing Archer by the throat.

I've been better. And I've been worse.

They sat in mutual weariness for a moment, then tensed. Their gazes locked.

"What?" Danny asked, his voice strangled.

"Did we just—?"

"You spoke to me. In—" Danny tried to lift his hand, but found it was too heavy. "In my mind. You spoke to me *in my mind*."

"I heard you, too." Colton put a hand to his forehead. "I thought . . . I thought it was just me."

"What do you mean?"

"While you were unconscious, I kept hearing things—words and broken sentences . . . My name. It was all in your voice." Colton moved his hand to Danny's forehead, fingertips tracing the arch of one eyebrow. "And I can feel something here. An ache."

Danny looked at Colton's arm. "It's the blood. It has to be."

"Do you think so?"

"What else could it be?" *Can you really hear me?*

Yes.

Danny shuddered and wondered if he was dreaming. "My blood is linking us, like how you were able to connect to Lalita."

Colton stared at Danny's chest. "I can feel your heart beating. It's distant, but I can hear it. And your blood. It's . . . soothing."

It all came rushing back. Blood. The Builder's head. The bullet.

He choked.

Colton shot to his feet, grabbing the rubbish bin just in time for Danny to retch over it.

All that came up was bile, and it seared his throat. When he was done, Colton handed him a cup of water. "Danny," he said, settling beside him, "it wasn't your fault. You were trying to protect me."

Danny downed the water and tossed the cup away. Resting his head in his right hand—his left shoulder hurt too much to move it—he pressed his pounding forehead against his clammy palm. Colton moved the rubbish bin away, then rubbed circles over Danny's bare back.

"I killed a person," Danny whispered. "Doesn't matter if it was an accident. His heart stopped beating because of me." He couldn't shake the image of that other Builder, the horror and hatred and tears in his eyes.

"Danny—"

"How can I go home like this? How can I ever face my parents? How can *you* even stand to be near me right now?"

Colton gently moved Danny's hand away. "I know how guilty you feel. I know it's twisting you apart. But it wasn't your fault." He leaned forward until their foreheads were resting together. "Remember what they did to you. What they threatened to do to you. If the situation were reversed, I'd have done the same. Besides, we escaped. Try not to think about it anymore."

That's easy for you to say, Danny thought, before recalling that even his mind was no longer private. "I can't just forget about it."

"We have more pressing things to think about."

He leaned back. "Like what?"

"Well . . ." Colton looked down at his hands, picking at his fingernails. "I told Zavier what Archer said. Everything she said."

Danny stiffened, the hairs on his arms standing on end. "You did what?"

"He wanted to know what they did to us. After he realized that our blood holds power, I didn't see any reason to keep the whole truth from him any longer. I told him Archer's plan, too, and how she's trying to build stronger towers by using more clock mechanic blood. I think—and he thinks—that Archer could have been right about one thing, which is that this might be a way to save my tower."

Danny took a deep breath. He was shaky and nauseated, his mind spinning too fast to grasp onto a single thought. "What else?"

"I think he wanted to know more, but he's been . . . distracted." Colton hesitated, biting his lower lip. "They didn't find Sally."

Scenarios flashed through Danny's mind. Archer torturing Sally. The Builders dumping her body once they were through with it. Archer using her to lure Zavier into a trap so she could recapture them.

Other images crept in, unfamiliar. He saw himself on the floor, writhing under the needle device. That was what Colton remembered, what could end up being in their futures. What could be happening to Sally at that moment.

Archer would be furious that he and Colton had escaped. What else was the woman capable of?

"The others?" he whispered.

Colton shook his head. "Edmund and Astrid were able to get back to the ship. Meena . . ." His voice faltered. "She was reaching for the rope when the Builders grabbed her. She's still on Archer's ship."

Danny wanted to see Daphne and Akash, but Colton insisted he eat something first.

"I can eat later."

"You haven't had anything in three days and you're weak as a newborn kitten. Besides, I can feel how hungry you are, and it's driving me mad." Colton shoved a small tray of toast and eggs at him. "*Eat.* And not too fast."

He grudgingly gnawed at a piece of toast, washing it down with water. Placated, Colton fetched him his clothes. Rising from the bed proved to be a challenge; the world went tilting in all directions. Danny hung his head and fought off vertigo, clutching at the edge of the pallet.

"Danny, are you sure . . . ?"

In answer, Danny tugged on his clothes, wincing whenever he moved his shoulder. His chest was dark and mottled with

bruises, and his lower back felt like someone had strangled his tailbone.

The announcement system crackled before Zavier's voice, cold and rough, filled the halls.

"Everyone to the B-side hangar. Now."

Danny frowned at Colton. "What's that about?"

Colton seemed just as troubled. "I don't know."

He turned to move to the door, but Colton stopped him, holding out a cane. "Charlotte said it might be good to use if you get dizzy again."

"I don't need it."

You're being stubborn. Danny felt the wave of Colton's irritation like heat escaping a just-opened oven door. He wondered if he would ever get used to this new connection.

Then he wondered if that had been Colton's thought or his own.

"I'll be fine," Danny said, heading for the door again. Colton pressed the cane against his chest.

"If you just—"

Danny grabbed the cane and threw it against the wall with a loud *bang*. He turned back to Colton, who stood watching him, expressionless. But the irritation deepened, linked to something else—worry and sadness.

Opening the door, Danny started down the hall. Soon enough, though, he realized he'd overestimated his strength. Each step cost him a little more until the corridor swam before him. He stumbled a couple of times, pressing a hand against the

wall to steady himself. Perhaps he should have taken the cane after all.

When he stumbled a third time, Colton caught his arm. Danny yanked it away.

"*Don't* help me!"

He hadn't meant to yell, but the words came from a pit in his chest that was steadily devouring him from the inside out. Colton must have felt it, too, that empty helplessness. He only met Danny's eyes with that same sad look.

Colton didn't try to help him again as they made their way through the ship with painstaking slowness. Danny stopped frequently to catch his breath, and Colton remained his silent shadow.

When they reached the hangar, Danny saw most of the crew there, but Daphne and Akash were absent. There was no landing plane in this hangar—it must have been the one the Builders stole—and the large, metal room was cold and barren, minus the cluster of nervous people at its center.

Danny limped up to Prema. "What's going on?"

She turned to him, her eyes pinched. Astrid, beside her, was stone-faced.

"Punishment," Astrid said.

That's when Danny noticed Ivor on his knees before the hangar door. His hands were tied behind his back, and there was a large bruise at his eye and temple, his lower lip split. His hair was lank and unwashed, his skin sallow, as if he'd been living in the cells the past few days. He very likely had.

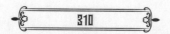

Zavier paced before him, holding the controller for the hangar door in his metal hand, connected by a long cable. His face bore an intensity that made his eyes crackle, trembling with the sheer force of his rage. Jo stood by the wall, hugging herself as she watched her nephew pace. Her eyes were red, her body swaying as if drunk.

Finally Zavier paused before Ivor, who refused to look up at him.

"You were a part of them all this time," the young man said, his voice hollow despite the anger tightening his shoulders. "Working for *her*. Working *against me*."

Ivor looked up then. Although his face was stoic, Danny saw a glimmer of fear in his eyes.

"You were workin' against what I wanted," the man answered.

"And what is that?"

"Archer promised to make me Lead Mechanic of the Scottish Union," Ivor said. "With complete autonomy. I couldna very well pass that up, aye? Not when the English insist on stickin' their noses into every matter. As if they have the right, after the thousands they slaughtered."

"There will be no Scottish Union when I succeed," Zavier said. "There will be no English Union, either. Your treachery was for nothing."

Instead of being cowed, Ivor grinned. "Ah, but ye haven't succeeded yet, have ye?"

Zavier's nostrils flared as he pressed the button for the hangar door. The lower section opened with a blast of air that made the crewmembers scramble to grab purchase. Colton held onto Danny as a patch of white light grew behind Ivor, whose hair whipped in a frenzy.

"You betrayed me and you betrayed my aunt!" Zavier yelled above the sound of the wind. "Dae is dead because of you! They have my sister because of you! They could *kill her* because of you!"

Ivor's gaze slid to Jo, who huddled now in the corner. Danny saw his flinch, the genuine regret that passed over his face.

"I—"

Zavier placed his boot on Ivor's chest and kicked him out the hangar. They only heard the first sharp note of his exclamation before it was eaten by the wind.

Jo slid to the floor, weeping silently as Zavier closed the hangar door. He threw the controller to the ground and stormed out, yanking his arm away from Prema as she reached out to comfort him. Charlotte crouched by Jo, murmuring softly to her.

Danny leaned against Colton, shaken. He knew he shouldn't feel bad for Ivor's fate—he was the reason he and Colton had suffered, the reason why Meena and Sally were probably suffering right now—but he did anyway. Another death. Another senseless loss of life.

Because of Archer.

"Let's go," Colton whispered.

When Daphne opened her door, her eyes were red, her long blond hair free of its usual braid. Her tattoo stood out starkly against the rest of her pale face.

"Danny," she said in surprise, "what are you doing up? He's not supposed to be up." That last remark was directed at Colton, who shrugged in resignation. "You look awful. You should be in bed."

"You don't look much better," he grumbled, limping past her. As he suspected, Akash was there, sitting at a small table by the porthole. He turned and saw Danny, but his blank expression didn't change. His dark eyes were bloodshot and his mouth was pinched. His entire posture had changed, as if resisting gravity's attempts to pull him toward the floor.

Danny made it to the table and collapsed in the other chair. Daphne allowed Colton in and closed the door.

"Akash," Danny said, "I'm so sorry. If I'd known Meena was still on the ship when we left—"

"You couldn't have done anything," Daphne interrupted. "You'd fainted."

Danny clenched his jaw. "I still would have tried. We'll . . . we'll do what they did to us. We'll lure them into a trap, pretend we're prepared to offer a treaty between Zavier and them, and then we'll sneak onto their ship and get her out."

Akash stared at the tabletop. Finally, he cleared his throat. "How bad was it, Danny? What they did to you?"

Danny couldn't help but glance at Colton, quiet and solemn at Daphne's side. He saw the images again, not his own, but from Colton's point of view. Shaking his head, he turned back to Akash. "She can survive whatever I did and more."

Akash dropped his head in his hands.

"It's not hopeless." Daphne placed her hand on Akash's shoulder. "We can still save her and Sally. The Builders want to use them as leverage to get to Zavier. Maybe Danny's right. Maybe we can lure them into a trap, say we'll exchange them for Zavier."

"That did sound like what Archer wanted," Colton agreed.

"I told her not to go." Akash rubbed his eyes and dropped his hands. "But she was so stubborn."

Colton gave Danny a withering glare. "I know what that's like."

"Stubborn people are the most resilient," Daphne reminded Akash, gently shaking his shoulder. "Especially Meena. You know she'll hold her own. And if she doesn't take over the Builders' ship herself, I'll be floored."

That managed to nudge a tiny smile onto Akash's face. Meena was strong enough to endure everything they had. But that didn't mean she should be going through it at all.

"Zavier wanted to speak with you, Danny." Daphne glanced at the clock spirit. "He's already spoken to Colton."

"I figured as much." He really didn't want to talk to him, though. Not after what he'd just seen.

"Is it true?" Daphne asked. "The blood . . . connected you?"

Danny and Colton exchanged a look. It was still such a new thing, as invasive as it was comforting. Some part of him didn't find it strange at all, as if it had always been this way.

Danny pinched his own arm—hard. Colton jerked.

"*Ow.*"

Daphne narrowed her eyes. "That doesn't prove anything."

"I'm really not sure—" Danny began.

"—what else you're looking for, then," Colton finished.

Even Akash was paying attention now. Daphne went to her bedside table, returning with a sheet of paper and a pencil.

"Here. Danny, you write down three words. Colton, go in that corner and close your eyes."

Danny sighed and did as she asked. As soon as he put down the pencil Colton announced from the corner: "Kettle, Agra, bell."

Daphne grabbed the list from Danny. Her eyes widened. "God, it's true. It's like you share one mind."

Colton ambled back to the table, his eyebrows raised at Danny. *Bell?*

Later.

"I've seen some peculiar things lately," Akash mumbled, "but this by far is the strangest."

"It's better than radios, anyway," Daphne added. "Maybe this new trick will come in handy. Speaking of . . . Danny, you should really talk to Zavier. The others are worried."

"I'll go." He gritted his teeth and stood, Colton twitching as if to help him.

Stay with them, Danny told him. *They need someone, too.*

Colton hesitated, then nodded with some reluctance. Danny heard him say, "Would you like me to make tea? Mrs. Hart taught me how," as he closed the door behind him.

By the time Danny reached Zavier's office, he was out of breath, black spots swimming before his eyes, and desperately in need of something to dull the pain in his shoulder. One look at Zavier through the open door told him the young man needed something much stronger for his own suffering.

He looked as if he hadn't slept in weeks. The fury from earlier had fled from him, his gray eyes now dull and sunken, his skin pale, his hair limp and uncombed. Someone had pulled apart the strings of his person, leaving him unraveled.

Danny knocked on the doorframe. Zavier raised his head from the book on his lap. From where Danny stood, it looked like it was written in Latin.

Zavier wordlessly put the book aside and turned his chair around. He gestured for him to sit. Danny suppressed a groan as he lowered himself into the chair.

"Look . . ." What the hell could he say? Danny shifted in his seat. "I didn't know about Sally. Archer told us she'd only taken Colton and me."

Zavier ran a hand through his hair. "I know. It's not your fault. Aunt Jo's been beside herself ever since it happened, but it's not her fault, either. After the Builders stole our plane down in Meerut, Ivor let them into the hangar, and Jo let him because she thought it was us. But then she heard you on the radio. Ivor tried to run, and she caught him. Knocked him out before he could join up with Archer. When she found out what happened, and that you and Colton and Sally were gone, and Dae was . . ." His voice grew uneven, and he waited a moment before continuing.

"She called us all back. Thank goodness we had the *Silver Hawk* with us, or else we'd have been stranded. Of course, by then, it was too late."

Zavier took a sip from a tumbler on his desk. Judging by the color of the liquid, Danny guessed it was whiskey.

"Aunt Jo's been drinking herself sick since," Zavier said, noticing Danny's gaze. "She can't even bear to come apologize to you. She's too ashamed."

"She doesn't have to be," Danny said. "She couldn't have known."

Zavier shrugged, and even that motion seemed sloppy for him. "I do what I can to calm her nerves. As soon as we get Sally back . . . and Meena . . ." He paused and downed the rest of his drink.

Danny knew what was coming, and made sure not to look away when Zavier found his eyes.

"Tell me every single detail."

And he did. The cell, the Builders, Archer and her journals, the experiments, the torture—everything. There was no need to hold back any longer.

"I'm sorry for what they did to you." Zavier took a deep breath. "Maybe this is hubris. Maybe I wasn't meant to be Heracles and free Aetas." He laughed, but it was a hollow sound. "I'm such a fool. Brought down by my own self-importance."

Danny shook his head and leaned forward. "You can't just give up."

"They have my *sister*, Danny. And Akash's."

"We can find a way. I've always drawn a line between the possible and the impossible, but every day that line is shrinking. I'm—I'm connected to a clock spirit. A bloody *clock spirit*. Don't rule anything out as impossible."

Zavier looked down at his metal hand, clenching and unclenching it.

"Have you ever read *Paradise Lost*?" he asked. Danny nodded. "Shelley once compared Prometheus to Milton's Satan. They were both considered heroes, Prometheus because of his rebellion to better serve the needs of humanity and his courage to steal fire. But Satan? How could he have fallen so far? He also wanted rebellion. He had his own heroic struggle, his own brand of courage in facing hopeless odds. If they were both so similar, then why is Prometheus lamented and Satan scorned?

"Think about what happens to them. Prometheus chained to a rock, enduring endless torture." Zavier glanced at Danny's chest. "Satan was punished, yes, but he wasn't noble about it. He turned to revenge. He turned to hatred. Everything in him that would have once appealed to our humanity grew distant, cold. He lost his ability to be a hero."

Zavier licked his dry lips, thinking. "So if I turn myself over, and accept my punishment, will I be a hero? Or if I lash out and swear revenge, will I simply become the villain?"

Danny didn't have the answer. He'd always thought of Zavier as the villain, but now, right before his eyes, that line was again becoming blurred.

And maybe that was enough: being the line between, instead of standing on one side or the other.

He opened his mouth to say as much when a knock sounded at the door. Prema opened it slowly, a guarded look on her face.

"We found something."

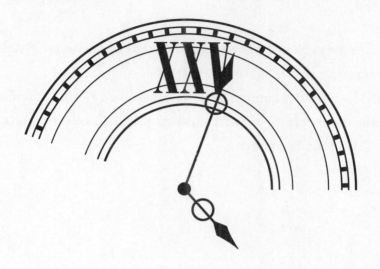

They stood on a flat plain near the Bay of Bengal called the Northern Circars, a division that had long since fallen into British control. The plains here were wide, growing as green as any in England, but the sky was different. Back home, sunset was a layered dish of grays, blues, and purples. Here, it was a starburst of oranges, reds, and yellows, making Daphne feel as if she were witnessing the creation of a new universe.

They walked from the *Silver Hawk*, casting long, dark shadows across the ground before them. Akash, Edmund, Liddy, and Astrid waited by the *Silver Hawk*, on the lookout for Builders or British soldiers.

Near her, Danny was pale but upright, Colton standing attentively at his side. Zavier had insisted on coming, along with Prema, perhaps to make sure Zavier didn't do anything rash. He had a feral look in his eyes Daphne didn't like.

They approached the plain's new addition, a ramshackle blemish on its beautiful surroundings. It leaned slightly to one side, the wood hastily whitewashed, as if someone had abandoned the task halfway through. The boards creaked under the weight of the plaster roof, which had been clumsily applied, drying unevenly into a lumpy mass.

The only clue that this was supposed to be a clock tower was the bright yellow face at the top, its hands little more than crude rods. That, and the feeling that skittered over Daphne's body when they got close enough.

The tower was creating its own area of time.

Daphne rubbed her arms. It was humid in the Northern Circars, but she felt chilled from the inside out.

Zavier stared up at the tower like it was a gallows. Danny glanced at him, then caught Colton's eye. They were having one of their strange mind-talks again.

"I'm going inside," Danny said. He moved to the open doorway—there wasn't even a door—and Colton followed. Swallowing, Daphne forced herself to do the same.

Grass crunched underneath their boots. Above their heads stretched a second story, reachable only by a ladder that rose through a square-cut hole in the middle of the room.

Daphne wanted to tell Danny not to climb if his shoulder still hurt, but she knew it would be futile. Danny gritted his teeth and ascended, Colton's worried eyes on his back the entire time. The clock spirit scaled the ladder easily, and Daphne, Zavier, and Prema followed.

Standing on the second story's slanted wooden floor, Daphne took in the low-ceilinged room as sunset's coppery light filtered through the clock face, draping them in a muted sheet of gold. Gears and cogs circled slowly before them, and a pole attached to the mechanism turned the hands of the clock at a steady pace.

The golden light sparked off Danny's green eyes. For a moment, Daphne thought he looked like he could be the spirit of this tower. Then he drew a deep breath and the illusion was shattered.

Colton turned and froze.

"Look," he whispered.

Sitting on a wooden box labeled PARTS was a golden figure with its back to them, staring plaintively at the clock face.

As Daphne took a step forward, the figure sensed them and turned its head, cocking it to one side. Daphne felt her body lock, her lungs incapable of drawing another breath. A word burst from within her, as explosive and red as the sky outside this godforsaken tower.

Meena.

The clock spirit stood, letting her yellow braid fall over her shoulder. She wore what Meena had been wearing last: a long tunic and loose trousers, her traditional salwar kameez. But everything else was off. Her skin was bronze instead of brown, her eyes the same amber shade as Colton's.

Behind them, Prema sobbed. Someone ran to the ladder, but Daphne couldn't make herself look to see who. She could only stare at the new spirit. Her friend.

"Meena," she whispered. The word barely escaped her lips.

"What did they do to you?" Danny's voice was almost too faint to hear. "God, what have they done?"

Colton hadn't moved an inch, but now he forced himself to walk toward her. "Meena? Do you . . . can you remember anything? Do you know us?"

She looked between them, her face politely inquisitive. "Aap kaun hain?"

Colton shook his head and responded, speaking Hindi almost too fast for Daphne to follow.

"She doesn't remember us?" Danny asked. Colton must have been translating the conversation in his mind.

"It's how it was with Lalita," Colton explained. "She has no memory of how she got here."

Someone scrambled up the ladder behind them. Prema had run to fetch Akash.

"Meena!" He staggered forward. "Yeh kya kiya hai? Meena!"

She frowned slightly and repeated her earlier question. *"Who are you?"*

Akash stared at her, then looked madly between Danny and Colton. "Why is she saying that? Why is she like this?"

But no one wanted to say the truth out loud.

They killed her, Daphne thought, recalling the bloody memories Colton had shown her. *They held her down and . . .*

She turned away as her breath hitched. Zavier had retreated to the corner, his face slack.

"Why can't she remember me?" Akash demanded. "Meena, it's me, tumhara bhai."

Colton bit his lower lip. "Meena? Main tumhara haath pakar sakta hoon?"

She nodded and held out a hand. Colton took it in his own, then closed his eyes. She watched him calmly, a small smile on her face. Then something changed. Her smile disappeared. Her amber eyes grew large and her mouth opened. She was seeing something beyond the tower, something beyond all of them.

She screamed.

Akash rushed forward and grabbed her in his arms, speaking in rapid, desperate Hindi. Daphne could only make out a few words. He was saying he was sorry. He was saying he had failed her.

It's not true, Akash.

"What did they do to me?" Meena sobbed, though no tears came. "That woman, she—!"

Danny put a hand over his mouth. Colton tried to touch her shoulder, but she backed away from him and her brother like an animal being cornered.

"I'm . . . I'm like you now." Her wide eyes were fixed on Colton. "They did this to you, too. They killed you. They . . ." She put a hand to her throat. "There was so much blood. It's all around me. I feel it pulling—"

She spun around and noticed Daphne. "Make it stop. Please. I don't want this."

Akash tried reaching for her again, but she vanished, reappearing in front of Zavier, who started backward.

"Take it down," she demanded. "Take this unnatural thing down."

Zavier opened his mouth, looking at Akash over Meena's shoulder. Akash stood stricken, watching his entire world fall away before his feet.

"I can't," Zavier mumbled. "Not without your brother's consent."

"Am I not my own person? Am I not capable of making my own decisions?"

"You aren't tearing it down!" Akash finally grabbed her arm. "Don't you know what that will do to you?"

"Look at me, Akash!"

They stared mournfully at her, the spirit of a girl sacrificed to time. The work of a blade had turned her into this, and Meena the girl had left, leaving only Meena the clock spirit in her wake.

She turned to Colton. "You know what sort of life this is. If you could choose to live this way, would you?"

Danny stared at him, but Colton couldn't meet his gaze. He focused on Meena as, slowly, he shook his head no.

"This isn't a life, Akash," Meena whispered. "They *took* my life. They took me from you. You have to accept that. You have to let go."

"Wait," Danny said. "What about blood? If we took someone's blood—a mechanic's blood—and put it into Meena, she'd be strong enough to leave this area, wouldn't she?"

"But time here will Stop," Zavier said quietly.

And if Aetas was freed . . .

Daphne crossed to Meena, clutching her by the shoulders, looking straight into her now-amber eyes. Trying not to let her own eyes water. "Even if there were a way to take you from here, would you want to go?" The girl shook her head. "What do you want, then?"

Meena's gaze traveled the room, shifting from Zavier and Prema to Danny and Colton, both wrapped in fear and guilt, to Akash, who moved his head a fraction as though he could stave off what was coming.

"I want to sleep," Meena said.

They waited outside the tower as Felix and Zavier set up the equipment. No one spoke. No one looked at anyone else. Sunset darkened into dusk, murky and stagnant. It reminded Daphne of when she was little and would throw the covers over her head, certain that there were monsters in her room. With the dark blanket shielding her, the monsters wouldn't see her. They couldn't touch her. And she had felt safe.

She couldn't tell if Danny and Colton were mind-speaking, but they stood off to one side holding hands as if to keep from drifting apart. Daphne felt sorry for them, but her heart, her attention, was all on Meena and Akash standing just inside the tower doorway.

Daphne moved closer to hear them. They were speaking in Hindi, but she understood most of what they were saying.

"*Please don't leave me, Meena. Don't make me go home without you. What will I tell Mother and Father?*"

"*Tell them I married a British boy and ran away to his country. That will make them happy.*"

Akash made a sound as if he were trying to laugh, but it came out as a sob. He held his sister tighter, burying his face in her hair.

"*I wasn't there for you. I couldn't protect you. This is all my fault.*"

"*None of this is your fault. I made the decision, and this is my choice. I want to die on my own terms, Akash. They took my life, but I have control over this, at least. You have to let me go.*"

Akash cried harder, and Meena rubbed his back as if he were a small boy. Daphne turned away, pressing a sleeve to her eyes.

Zavier and Felix walked out of the tower, their faces somber. "It's done," Zavier said, "but we'll need to use the water. There's just enough left on the ship."

Meena stepped back and took Akash's face in her hands. "Main tumse bahut pyar karthee hoon."

He whispered the phrase back to her, kissing her on her forehead, where her red bindi would normally be. Then he turned and walked back to the plane, forcing himself not to look back.

Meena silently watched him go. "Please take care of him," she whispered to Daphne.

She took the girl's hands in her own, time shivering through her. "I will. I promise."

Meena managed a smile, but the devastation in her eyes filled Daphne with sorrow and helpless rage. Meena reached up and wiped away Daphne's tears, such a loving, sisterly gesture that Daphne only cried harder, kissing Meena's hand before she slipped away.

Then Meena turned to Danny and Colton. "If there's a way to save your tower, Colton, I hope you find it."

Daphne saw the boys' hands clasp tighter together.

It took Danny a couple of attempts before he could speak, and when he did, his voice was low and hoarse. "I'm sorry, Meena."

"There's nothing to be sorry for."

"I'm going to stop her," he whispered, a dangerous glint in his eye. "We're going to find Archer, and I'm going to make her regret everything she's done. I promise."

Daphne expected Meena to protest, to scold him for instinctually turning to violence.

Instead, she said, "Good."

Finally, Meena turned to Zavier and gave him a single nod. He opened his mouth, hesitated, and ducked his head. "I'm sorry." He walked away, back to the *Silver Hawk*, before she could respond.

The others followed. When they reached Akash's side, they turned back. Meena put her hands together and bowed over them in prayer, or maybe in farewell.

Then she disappeared.

Everything that is born must eventually die.

That's what Meena had once told Danny, when she had taken him to the temple in Meerut. She'd explained to Danny that Shiva had created the world, but that one day he would destroy his own creation. It was a cycle that would be repeated throughout time, birth and life and death and birth. That was simply the way it was.

He watched from the *Prometheus*'s observation deck as Felix flew the water over the small tower. In five seconds, the tower crumbled. A golden glow radiated outward from its center as time was restored. Birth and life and death.

Akash cried out, falling against the window. Daphne held him from behind, hiding her own tears against his back. Danny turned and walked away, feeling nothing; not his body, not his thoughts, not even Colton behind him.

"Danny." Colton reached for him, but Danny pulled his arm away. *Danny.*

Danny walked through the corridors. He might have passed the others, but he couldn't be sure. There were tears. There were whispers. He was numb to it all, sheltered by a screen they couldn't penetrate. He just kept walking, looking for nothing, hoping to find something, anything, to fill the yawning emptiness inside him.

He stopped and leaned his shoulder against the wall, savoring the new flash of pain that ran through his body like an electric shock.

I want to die on my own terms.

Everything that is born must eventually die.

He didn't remember sliding to the floor, or when he'd started crying. He took every little thing from inside that pit in his chest and pulled it out, piece by painful piece, opening a fresh wound inside himself—gaping, raw, bleeding. He sobbed and punched the wall, the floor, the spirit before him who tried to grab his wrists.

"You're hurting yourself!"

That's what he wanted. To hurt himself on his own terms. To not let people—not let others like Archer—make his pain for him. He wanted to choose for once. He wanted to say whether or not he wanted this pain.

"Danny, that's *enough*." Colton pressed Danny's arms to the wall. "I know you're upset. I know you're hurting. I know you're afraid that will happen to me, too. But it won't, because I won't let anything touch my tower. We can still stop the Builders. This isn't the end of us or the others. We can still find a way."

Danny couldn't stop the tears, or the hemorrhaging inside of him. He kept seeing Meena, golden Meena and human Meena, and the knife they'd pressed to Colton's throat.

Colton put his lips to Danny's cheek. He kissed up to his eyes, kissing the tears away. When their lips met, Danny tasted his own grief. He tasted the ocean.

I won't leave you. I promised.

Promises can be broken.

Not mine.

Colton kissed Danny all the harder, drawing him in so tight he couldn't breathe. He didn't need to—wasn't sure he wanted to. Colton swallowed his small broken sobs, stanched his internal damage, placed a hand upon his chest to remind him that his heart still beat. He let Colton sew him back together with a promise in the thread, the only one that mattered. The one he would fight to keep or die trying.

Danny found Zavier in a small sitting room far from his office. Prema had said Zavier didn't want to talk to anyone, though questions flew about the ship. *Where to now? Will the others leave? Are we still freeing Aetas? What about Sally?*

But Danny had remembered something when he woke after hours of dreamless sleep, something he hadn't told Zavier before.

The young man barely looked up as Danny entered. Zavier held a paintbrush in his hands, and all of his attention seemed to be focused on it.

"Sally's," Zavier croaked. "She's quite good, but too shy to let anyone but me look at her paintings."

Danny sat across from him. Zavier closed his eyes, releasing a shuddering breath.

"I'm sorry about Meena," Zavier whispered. "What happened to her is my fault. All of this is a product of my vanity. My impatience. They kept telling me I was losing sight of what I wanted, and they were right. Now an innocent girl is dead, and my sister could be next. She wasn't trained, but she can still sense time. They knew that. That's why they took her."

"That's what I came to warn you about."

Zavier looked up, his eyes darkening like clouds before a storm.

"Archer said something to me when I was on her ship. She touched my blood to the small cog Big Ben had given Colton. She said . . . She asked Colton if—if I should be the new face of Big Ben." He fought to swallow. "Zavier, I think they're going to turn Sally into the new London tower. We have to go back to England."

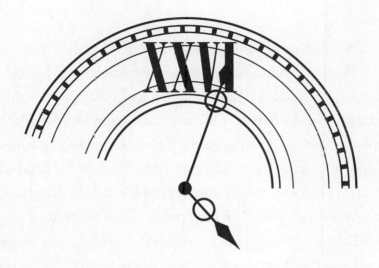

Colton felt pain every single minute. Whether it was the throb in his side, the ache from Danny through their bond, or the hurt that permeated the very air of the ship, he was at its mercy with no means of escape. But that pain was nothing compared to what they were about to face.

The possibility that the Builders would attack London scared him, but it scared Danny even worse. They spent hours discussing with Zavier what they might expect and what they should do.

"We should forget London altogether and free Aetas *now*," Edmund said at a meeting.

"What about Sally?" Jo demanded, hand clenched around a brandy glass. Dark circles were under her eyes. "We can't just let them butcher her!"

"Not to mention," Zavier said, tapping a file on the table, "that there are reports of the *Kalki* near London."

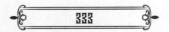

Danny's head shot up. "The Indian rebels?"

"Their mission was aborted when you intervened. Enfield is Stopped, true, but that didn't put much of a dent in the British armory. My guess is that the Builders formed some sort of alliance with the rebels after we dropped our ties." He looked pointedly at Akash, who stared at the tabletop as Daphne held his hand. He hadn't spoken a word since Meena's tower had been destroyed.

"Will they try to attack Parliament?" Daphne asked.

"Danny said that Archer mentioned something about using London as their base of operations. If they've betrayed the Crown, that means their only method for accomplishing that is through sheer force. Therefore, we should set our sights on London. We can piece together a more cohesive plan in the next twenty-four hours."

Colton heard Danny's thought before he spoke it. "Could . . . Could Colton and I visit Enfield? I want to see how it's doing. I want to see Colton's tower."

Zavier looked as if he wanted to protest, but thought better of it. "Yes. But you can't take too long."

Which was how they landed several hours later, beyond the forest on the western side of Enfield. Colton still felt as if he were in India, so taking his first step off the plane onto British soil was like a slap of cold wind. Literally, as the air that greeted them was chilly and damp.

Danny stopped beside him, overcome by the same sudden, bizarre feeling of homecoming. They looked around in awe, taking in the gray sky, the lush field, the smell of rain and peat.

"We're back," Danny whispered. "We're actually back."

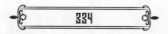

Edmund stepped out of the *Prometheus*'s landing plane and drew in a deep breath. "Ah, cow dung. Had to have missed that. All right, I know it's hard to gauge time in there, so take this." He attached a small timepiece to Colton's cog holder. "Colton should have enough power to create his own little area of time, so stay close. Zavier wants you back in two hours."

They had asked Daphne if she wanted to come, but she'd shaken her head no. She needed to be with Akash and wanted to hear the plans Zavier was spinning. So they struck out, just the two of them, toward the gray dome that had once been Enfield.

Colton hesitated beside the road.

"We only have two hours," Danny reminded him.

"I know." He shifted on his feet, the timepiece on his back ticking. "What if they hate me? I've been away for such a long time. I don't even feel like I'm *here* right now."

"Trust me, I know." Danny held out his hand, and Colton twined their fingers together. "We've been threatened, kidnapped, and tortured. I doubt they'll hate us for being a few months late."

Colton squeezed his hand. "I hope not."

They were able to walk through the barrier together—Colton because he was a clock spirit, Danny because he was a clock mechanic touching him. Colton remembered walking through that barrier six months before, desperate and afraid. They'd both been desperate and afraid when they had first passed through the barrier when Enfield had Stopped because of Matthias. Colton was *still* desperate and afraid, but at least he had Danny at his side, and that was worth the world.

Time warped around them. Colton could feel it **stretching** and **pulling** about him like taffy, unsure what to make of him and his new power. The timepiece ticked louder and his cogs grew hot. Danny reached into his pocket with his free hand and clutched the small cog. Colton touched the time threads he could reach, as familiar to him as his own fingers. With some tampering, time flowed smoothly across their bodies as they pressed through the gray barrier.

On the other side, Danny gasped. Colton would have, too, had he been able.

It was Enfield. It was *home.*

Colton could see the wide village green, the parish church, the quaint squashed-together homes that lined the dirt road. Relief, warm and strong, ran through their bond, but he couldn't tell who it came from. Maybe both of them.

Two people were walking away from the barrier as they entered. At the sound of Danny's gasp, they turned and gasped themselves. One was Mayor Aldridge, the other his assistant, Jane.

"You're back so soon?" the mayor wondered at the same time Jane exclaimed "Danny!"

The two of them had walked him to the barrier, Colton realized. Half a year ago.

"My boy, I thought you'd gone to India," Aldridge said.

"We, er . . . did." Danny exchanged an awkward look with Colton. "It's been a little while."

Their faces fell. "How long?" Jane asked.

"About six months."

The mayor groaned and rubbed his forehead. "We can handle that later. The important thing is: can we fix the tower?"

"Show me."

Colton didn't want to see it, but kept hold of Danny's hand all the same on the awkward walk to the tower. Awkward, because time sometimes made them backtrack to where they'd been, or propelled them farther down the road. Annoyed, Colton grasped the Enfield threads again, weaving them until time around the four of them eased to normalcy. Aldridge and Jane couldn't feel it, but Danny did, and he sent Colton an impressed look.

The pain in Colton's side grew worse. By the time they stood before his tower, he was pressing a hand to his ribs, trying not to make a sound.

"Oh, no." Danny dropped Colton's hand and stepped forward. He took in the slanted building, the shattered glass, the crumbling brick. The gaping, open wound in the tower's right side. He looked back at Colton, his eyes going to where he pressed his hand against the scar.

"Can it be fixed?" the mayor asked, wringing his hands together. Danny blinked at him, and through the bond Colton felt a dizzying sense of déjà vu.

"Er . . . yes. Yes, it can be fixed." Danny examined the hole again. "I hope."

Colton and Danny went inside. The stairs were broken in the middle. Colton reminded Danny to be careful, that he was still weak, and if he fell from this height—

"Calm down." Danny hopped easily over the break. "Time is Stopped. It's not going to fall out from under me."

As they climbed higher, the damage grew more severe. Broken beams slanted through the ceiling, two of the four bells had fallen—one had rolled down the stairs—and gears and cogs were scattered everywhere. It was eerily silent, too; the normal sounds, the whirs and clicks and tocks, were gone. It was just them, and the sound of Danny's breathing.

The central cog on Colton's back pulled him toward the clockwork. Colton kept far away from it.

Danny turned in a circle, taking in the damage. They could see a sliver of Enfield through the massive crack in the limestone. Danny put his hand over it, running his fingers over the edge. Colton felt those fingers against his side and shivered.

Danny was remembering Meena's tower. Watching its destruction from the safety of the *Prometheus*. Colton walked up behind him and slid his arms around his waist, putting his forehead against the back of his neck.

"I'm sorry, Danny. I know she was your friend. She was mine, too."

"Look at it, Colton. This tower—this *thing* they built with your blood." He turned suddenly and kicked a gear away. Colton winced.

"It's going to fall." Danny faced him, breathless. "The way the structure is damaged, it can't hold once time restarts."

"But time will Stop again when it falls," Colton pointed out. "Maybe the tower can be rebuilt then."

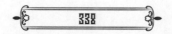

"Maybe." Danny rubbed his eyes. "What do I tell them? How do we give them hope?"

"Just tell them the truth. It's the simplest thing to do."

So that's what Danny did. He and Colton returned outside and explained to the mayor and the other Enfield residents who had gathered on the green that the tower might not be able to stand once time was restored, but that they would still try to rebuild it. The news wasn't welcome, but no one seemed surprised. Some of the townspeople crowded around Colton, asking if he was all right, what the cog holder was, where he had been.

He answered as best he could, all the while keeping track of the time through the timepiece on his back. He wondered if he should tell them what they'd discovered about Aetas, about the sacrifices, about the true nature of his existence.

Don't, Danny thought at him. *They'll find out eventually. There's no need to do it now.*

"Will Danny go to London and come back with more mechanics?" Jane asked.

"Yes, I expect he will. I need to go with him, though. He won't be able to pass through the barrier otherwise."

When he turned, Danny was talking to another one of Enfield's residents. A bolt of displeasure hit his stomach; it was Harland, an admittedly attractive young man who had once kissed Danny. Colton had long since dropped the matter entirely. Or so he'd thought.

He went to Danny's side, trying not to glare at Harland. The

young man smiled at him, but he looked nervous. He was tall and well built, with thick brown hair and dark eyes.

"Colton, hello. I was just telling Danny that it was good to see you. I mean, good that nothing's happened. Nothing's happened, has it?"

"A little of this and that," he replied coolly. Exasperation trickled through the bond.

"Harland was asking if he might help with repairs when we return from London," Danny said in a tone that commanded: *Be nice.*

"Oh. Yes, that would be . . . nice."

Danny rolled his eyes, but Harland nodded.

"I'm sorry about the tower, but I think with some adjustments—"

They let him talk a little longer while Colton felt Danny's exasperation growing. Finally, Colton tugged on Danny's sleeve.

"Our two hours are nearly up," he muttered.

"Right. Erm, thanks, Harland. We'll be back as soon as we can."

"Of course. I suppose it'll be no time at all until I see you again."

"No time at all," Colton mumbled.

Danny sighed as Harland left. "Will you let it rest? He's just trying to help."

"He still looks at you oddly." When Danny raised his eyebrows, Colton scowled. "You're being a hypocrite, you know. What about Castor?"

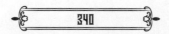

Danny's face reddened. "Castor has nothing to do with it."

"Castor?"

Harland had turned around, a puzzled look on his face.

"Does the name mean something to you?" Colton asked slowly.

"Well, sure." Harland kicked at a pebble with his boot. "Castor's the name of my father."

With time swirling normally around Colton, the three of them were able to walk to Harland's house near the edge of town, somewhere near the factory. They were quiet, and Harland must have sensed something amiss, his shoulders tense as he led them to his front door.

"Mind the step." He ducked inside, heading to the back of the house. Danny and Colton hovered in the doorway by the kitchen.

It can't be a coincidence, Danny thought. *Castor isn't a common name.*

Unless his father is hundreds of years old, I doubt it's the same Castor, Colton replied. But a little leap of impossible hope betrayed him all the same.

Harland returned carrying a large book. He let it fall onto the kitchen table with a *thud*.

"This is our family history," he explained, opening the cover. Colton and Danny drew nearer, peering down at the spidery

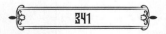

handwriting on the first page. The pages were yellowed with age, and the binding was coming loose. "It's been kept for hundreds of years on my father's side. There've been a lot of Castors down that line."

He flipped the pages in the back until it came to the early 1800s. "There's my father. There weren't any Castors for about two generations, but . . . yes, there's a great-great-great uncle named Castor, and"— he flipped through more pages—"a great-grandfather named Castor as well."

Colton reached out to stop him. "May I . . . Is it all right if I look?"

"Of course. Just be careful, my dad'll have a fit if anything happens to it."

Colton felt Danny hovering at his shoulder as he slowly turned the pages back through history. He almost didn't want to know what he would find. But then Danny's hand was on his lower back, supporting him, and it gave him the strength to keep going.

When he stopped near the beginning of the book, a folded sheet of paper slipped out. Colton was reaching for it when he went still. His eyes focused on the spidery handwriting on the book's page before him, on the one name that had meant so much to him—that still meant so much to him.

"Castor Thomas," he whispered. "That's him."

Danny looked up. "It is?" He gaped at Harland, who shifted nervously on his feet.

There were dates above Castor's name; his birth and death

dates. Colton's legs grew weak. He knew without a doubt that Castor was long gone, but seeing it here, on paper . . .

Danny pulled out a chair just in time for Colton to sit down hard. He ran his fingers over Castor's name, over the dates.

Forty-nine, Danny told him.

"Forty-nine," Colton said out loud. "He lived until he was forty-nine."

Danny put a hand on his shoulder and pointed at a line attached to Castor's name. "That's not all."

Colton followed his finger across the line, to the other side of the page. If he'd had a heart, it would have stopped.

Abigail Thomas, née Bell.

"He . . ." Colton moved his face closer to the page. But there it was in old ink, inscribed on even older paper. "He married her. Castor married my sister."

Castor had always told him he would help take care of her. With him gone, Castor had made good on that promise. The date of their marriage was just two years after Colton's death. And Abigail . . .

"How long?" Colton whispered, unable to do the math.

"Sixty-one," Danny told him softly.

She'd lived sixty-one years. The sickness hadn't gotten the better of her after all.

His eyes traveled past their names, to the ones attached to their marriage line. They'd had three children: Jacob, Eliza, and . . . Colton.

They were all right. They lived. They were happy.

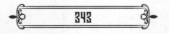

343

Colton put his head on the book and tried to let it sink in. Danny kept his hand on his upper back, radiating sympathy through their bond.

"Is he all right?" Harland asked faintly. "Is something wrong?"

"No, it's just . . . hard to explain."

As Danny tried his best to fill Harland in, Colton forced himself to sit up. The sheet of paper that had fallen out of the book was lying on the floor. Written across the front were the words *Beloved Brother.*

Hands shaking, he picked up the sheet, old and delicate paper with a crumbled red wax seal that had been broken by a curious descendant. When he saw the first line, he has to suppress a shocked cry.

Abi had written this letter. Though they hadn't been able to read or write, she must have found someone to take it down as she dictated, for the voice was surely hers.

My Dearest Colton,

Words cannot begin to describe the sorrow that haunts me to this day. Since those men came, since you died, Castor and I have not been the same. Mama and Papa have been quiet, so very quiet. The whole town is quiet.

I do not know how to process this grief, except to put it into words that you will never see. Some days, it feels as if the grief will kill me as well. The sickness comes and goes, but my heart keeps beating, none the weaker. You would be pleased to know that, at least.

Castor has asked for my hand. We know it is not the joyous moment it should be, but neither is it unwanted. There is simply no one else who understands this heartache. He has been close, so close, and he has confessed what you two were to each other. I am glad, Colton, that you had one another. I hope you can forgive me for having him now.

He says he wants to take care of me, to take me to London. We cannot stay in Enfield any longer, not with your grave stark and gleaming before us. It is too much for us to bear.

I decided yesterday to walk into the tower. It was admittedly late at night, and I should have been in bed, but Mama and Papa were asleep and did not hear me steal away. I went to the tower, because I wanted to feel some part of you again, wanted to hope that your spirit lingered in that horrible mechanism.

At first there was nothing, only the sounds of the clock, terrible and accusing. It felt so empty and airless, reeking of oil and copper. I wept for you. I thought that would be enough to provide me relief.

But as I turned back for the door, I saw . . . it would not be fair to say I saw you, but I did. Or, perhaps it was only an apparition made by grief, a kindness. A mercy. You were golden, fair and golden like a fey prince from Papa's stories. You tilted your head and smiled, as if confused. You asked if you knew me.

I cried, my dear brother, to hear that question spoken from your lips. You did not know me, not as I knew you—or the boy you had been, the boy Castor and I had so loved.

I told you that I loved you. That I was sorry. Still, you did not understand. And so I said goodbye and fled back home, weeping until Castor had to come and calm me. I told him the horror of that forgetting, and then he cried, too.

We will go to London soon. I regret leaving you, but I must. I hope you can understand.

Maybe, in my secret heart, I still hope you will see these words one day, and remember how much and how fiercely you were loved.

Your sister,
Abi

Colton stared at the letter for some time, reading and rereading until he could conjure Abi's voice from his waning memories. He had seen her, all those years ago, and not recognized her. His chest tightened with despair.

"Colton?"

Danny and Harland were watching him.

Carefully, Colton tucked the letter back into the book. Then he stood and looked at Harland, really looked at him. Of course, he had nothing of Castor in his appearance; too much time had thinned his blood. But he didn't just come from Castor. He came from Abi, too. Harland was part of his family.

"You're my . . . nephew."

Harland blinked a couple of times. "Uh?"

Danny told him about Castor and Abi, but by the end

Harland still looked as if someone had stirred his brains with a mixing spoon. He kept looking between Colton and the book.

"So, my great-great-several times great-grandmother is your sister? *Was* your sister?"

Colton winced at the emphasized word. "Yes."

"But that means—"

"That he died and became a clock spirit," Danny said. "I told you, it's hard to explain, but I think this can work in our favor." He turned back to Colton, his green eyes shining with some of his old fervor. "Remember what Archer said? That there may be a way to make the towers indestructible by using more blood. Maybe we can use *his* blood to keep you alive after Zavier frees Aetas."

Harland held up his hands. "Excuse me, what?"

"Oh," Colton said, eyes widening. "Yes, because he'll have some of my blood in him, since we're related."

"Did you say *blood*?"

"Maybe if we put it on your central cog," Danny said.

"Or around the tower, do you think?"

"Oy!"

They both turned to Harland, who looked uneasy. "I don't understand. You want to use my *blood*?"

The timepiece on his back warned him that two hours had passed. "Danny, we have to go."

"I promise we'll explain later," Danny said. "And it would be better if you didn't tell anyone else about this."

"But—"

They ran from the house back to the edge of town. The mayor called after them, but they only lifted their hands in farewell and didn't stop.

"Now what?" Danny panted. "Should we tell the others?"

"Yes. The more Zavier knows, the better our chances." Colton grabbed Danny's hand and they crashed into the barrier. Time spasmed again, but they made it through to the other side.

Edmund was waiting by the plane. "You're ten minutes late." He saw the looks on their faces. "Did something happen?"

"Something," Danny agreed breathlessly. "Is Zavier back on the ship?"

"Yes. He's just radioed that I'm to fly us to London."

"London? Now?"

"He needs to get reports from his contacts about the Builders and such. While he's doing that, you're allowed to do as you please." He jostled Danny's uninjured shoulder. "Which means you ought to prepare for your homecoming."

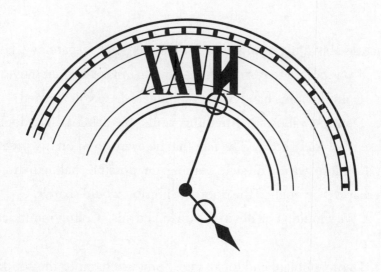

XXVII

Danny stared at the same green door he'd known all his life. When he was little, he would beg his father to give him the key so he could be the one to unlock it, thinking it was an important ceremony only adults could do. Christopher would solemnly hand him the key, struggling to keep a straight face as Danny stretched up as high as he could on his tiptoes to reach the lock. Frustrated and unable to get to it, he'd have to give the key back to his father, who had grinned and ruffled his hair.

"You'll get there, Ticker."

The day he'd finally been able to unlock it on his own, Danny had been so proud of himself. Proud for something as simple as turning a key in a lock.

Today, he faced an even greater challenge. He was more than tall enough now; he could reach the lock, even reach up to the

mantle above his head where his mother kept a spare key. His hand was poised to turn it, but he couldn't make himself move.

Colton put his hands on his shoulders. "Are you worried?"

Danny swallowed. Anything could be behind that door: absence, blood, scorn. The fact that he even stood on his street, in London, was a miracle verging on possible hallucination. Perhaps, if he opened the door, the illusion would shatter.

"We shouldn't be out in the open like this," Colton reminded him.

Danny blinked and looked up. Somewhere far to the southwest, the *Prometheus* prowled the cloud-covered sky. Somewhere even closer, they had landed the plane in a private hangar owned by a woman who had tipped her hat at them. Zavier had multiple contacts throughout the city, products of his aunt and late uncle's money and influence. Danny wondered if some of them were in the Mechanics Union.

"It's getting late," Edmund had told them when they got off the plane, "so feel free to stay the night. Zavier has loads of work to do."

He had given them a radio, which Colton attached to his belt. Zavier would call them back in the morning after he'd heard from his contacts. Danny needed to use the time between now and then wisely.

Instead, he was standing on his front step like a fool. A scared fool.

A rumble sounded above their heads. The sky was a hazy purple, and scudding through the clouds was an army-issue airship, searching the skies for ships like the *Prometheus* and the *Kalki*.

"Come on," Colton whispered, eyes fixed on the airship.

Danny nodded and turned the key. Just as it had the first time, the small gesture nonetheless felt momentous.

He crept into the dim hallway, Colton at his heels, and closed the door softly.

"I feel like a burglar in my own house," he mumbled.

They walked through the kitchen, the sitting room, and went upstairs to check the bedrooms. Danny had the strangest sensation that he'd never left. Everything was the same: the faded green wallpaper with water stains near the floor, the telephone in the hall, the blankets on his bed. Maybe no one had lived here in all the time he'd been gone, and the house was simply waiting for his return to come back to life.

"My parents must still be at work," Danny said, trying not to be disappointed. "I guess we'll have to wait."

Even so, his head was full of nightmarish scenarios—his parents tied up and awaiting ransom, headlines of Mr. and Mrs. Christopher Hart dead in a tragic traffic accident, or simply deciding to leave London and their son behind.

"None of those things are true," Colton said as Danny walked into the kitchen and turned on a gas lamp. "You shouldn't think that way."

"I can't help it." Danny put the kettle on to boil. "After all that's happened, do you expect my mind to filled with innocent things?"

"I don't think your mind has ever been innocent, Danny."

Danny turned to glare, but stopped when he saw the small,

sad smile on Colton's face. Colton was trying so hard to keep strong, despite everything they'd just learned.

"It must have been a shock," Danny said, carefully watching his reaction. "About Castor."

Colton looked toward the ceiling, as if the genealogy lines were etched in the plaster and wood. "You could say that."

"I'm sorry."

"Don't be." Colton looked into the cold box and took out a packet of fish. Someone must have bought it that morning. He handed it to Danny before going to the pantry. "I'm glad, actually. I've spent all this time worrying, thinking the worst."

"And you tell *me* not to worry," Danny scoffed. "Hypocrite."

"It's a happy thought, though. Castor marrying my sister. Providing for her. Giving her children. Giving her a long life."

Colton held a carrot in his hand, staring at it blankly. Danny walked over and took it from him.

"It hurts, though," Danny said. "You can say it."

It hurts, Colton thought instead, the words safer in his own mind.

Danny read his other thoughts, the what-ifs that had sprouted since they'd found out. Had Castor really loved Abi, or had he made his choice only out of obligation? Had Abi been happy? Had they forgotten him?

"They would never forget you," Danny protested. "They named their child after you."

Colton winced and looked away. *It was a burden.*

Danny touched his cheek, then turned back to prepare dinner, allowing Colton a few minutes to think.

Eventually, Colton came to help. Danny remembered Colton saying that he had helped Danny's mother cook during the months he'd been holed up here. He wondered if Colton remembered cooking for his sister and parents.

As the fish was frying, Danny peered out the window. He thought he saw a dark shape across the street, but it could have been the hedge.

"I'll need to ring Cassie and tell her I'm back." His stomach flipped with anticipation. She would either smack him with a wrench or kiss him. He wasn't sure which would be worse.

He ate at the table while Colton sat beside him. But after enduring Colton's stare for a while, he lowered his fork. "What?"

"I've noticed I can sort of taste what you're eating. All these things I've tasted before. It's odd. Like tasting a memory."

Danny pushed his vegetables around, suddenly self-conscious. "This connection will never stop being bizarre."

"Do you think it will stay this way when Aetas is released?"

Danny felt his face harden. Ever since they had taken down Meena's tower, something had been shaken loose in him. That desperate hope he had clung to was being shed, revealing the vulnerable, inescapable truth underneath.

He had been so sure that Colton's tower could be saved. But now . . .

"We can use Harland's blood, and yours is already inside me,"

Colton reminded him, sensing Danny's thoughts. "It should be strong enough."

"But what if it isn't?"

"It will be. It has to be."

A flash of pain jabbed Danny between the ribs as he reexperienced the bombing of Meena's tower. Danny grunted and doubled over, breathless.

"Danny—"

"Shut up," Danny said through gritted teeth. He swallowed the tears back. "Just don't, all right?"

"I made a promise to you," Colton whispered, touching his shoulder. "I'm going to do everything I can to keep it."

Danny got up with a scrape of his chair legs and grabbed his plate, his dinner barely touched. "I don't want to talk about this now."

"Danny—"

He slammed his plate onto the counter and whirled around. "I said—!" He stopped short, mouth hanging open.

His father stood in the kitchen doorway.

The bag Christopher held slipped out of his hand and onto the floor. There were already tears on his face, slack with disbelief.

"Danny," he breathed.

Danny couldn't move. He stood there, mouth still parted, as his father strode across the kitchen and wrapped him in his arms. He was a child again, reaching desperately for the lock above his head; wanting to be small, to be safe, to have his father lift him off the floor and tell him everything would be all right.

"Oh, God, Danny." Christopher's words were muffled in his hair. "I thought I'd never see you again."

Danny didn't want to let go, but his father leaned back and lifted his face. He looked older, the crow's feet at his eyes now matching his mother's.

"What happened, Ticker?" Christopher asked softly.

The question unstoppered the well of emotions he had been trying to keep down. He was only dimly aware of resting his head on his father's chest, of smelling the familiar scent of oil and wood shavings. Of hands rubbing his back, and a soothing voice whispering in his ear.

He didn't deserve it, any of it. He had helped destroy clock towers. He had been helpless to save a friend. He had killed a man. His body was covered in his failures, betraying him with scars.

"Danny!"

He was hit by a waft of cigarette smoke before he found himself looking into his mother's dark eyes. She was incomprehensible, babbling questions as she kissed his cheek, clutching him and crying as she stroked his hair.

"They said you were taken," she kept sobbing. Her brown curls were coming undone from her coiffure, tickling his face whenever she leaned in to kiss him again. His voice bubbled over a laugh and he hugged her back, feeling too large and awkward beside her thin, narrow body.

"Leila, let the boy breathe." But his father was grinning from ear to ear. "I don't think he's said a single word yet."

Danny opened his mouth, but couldn't find any words. A rustle in his mind reminded him that Colton was there, and he looked to him for help. His parents followed his gaze and started.

"Colton!" Leila shouted.

"Where the hell were you?" Christopher demanded, but Danny grabbed his father's arm.

"He came to find me. To save me. Please, don't be angry with him."

Colton had stood up from the kitchen table to watch the reunion. He lingered in the doorway, his eyes uncertain, his posture defensive. Danny ached to see him that way, especially in his own house.

He felt his father's body relax. Christopher sighed. "You caused a lot of trouble when you wandered off." Colton lowered his eyes. "Will you both please tell us what happened?"

"And make it quick," Leila said, peeking out a curtain.

Danny found this ominous, but he would ask later. "There's one thing I have to do first."

A minute later he was hunched over the telephone in the hall as his parents prepared tea, murmuring to each other in the kitchen.

"'Lo?" answered the person on the other end. The voice nearly made his heart stop with happiness.

"Cass," he said. There was silence on the phone except for a faint crackling, then the sound of the other receiver being slammed onto the handle. He looked at his own receiver, frowning.

"Give it a moment," Colton said, looking at the door. Sure enough, a minute later it boomed under the weight of Cassie's fist.

"Open the bloody door you good-for-nothing bastard!"

Leila clucked her tongue as she headed for the sitting room. "Really, she needs to calm down." Said the woman who still had red-rimmed eyes.

Danny bounded to the door and yanked it open. He had just a second to see Cassie's freckled face before she flung herself at him. They laughed, staggering into the hallway and nearly falling to the floor. Colton wisely jumped out of the way.

Then Cassie started punching Danny's arm. "Don't—you—ever—leave—again!"

He uttered small *oomphs* with every jab, but when one landed too near his chest, he nearly crumpled. Colton was there in an instant to support him. Cassie froze with her fist still in the air, horrified.

"Dan! I'm so sorry. Are you hurt?"

"It's nothing," he mumbled, but when he looked up, he saw his father lingering worriedly at the end of the hall.

Cassie's eyes filled with tears. She hugged Danny again, gently this time. "I missed you."

He rested his cheek against her hair and closed his eyes. Colton was there in his mind, within and apart from him. Danny could feel his sorrow, deep as a crack in bone.

As if she could feel his isolation, too, Cassie attacked Colton next. Danny smiled as Colton held her back.

"All right, boys," Christopher finally said, gesturing to the sitting room. "Time to explain."

They didn't tell them everything. Not about their arguments, or the man Danny had killed, or the torture—although they did explain Colton being injected with Danny's blood. By the time they were finished, their small audience sat stunned, absorbing the story in silence.

Danny felt wrung out. Exhausted. Although Colton had spoken at least half of the time, it had taken everything inside him just to listen. Images kept flashing through his mind. His limbs were heavy. The past six months had seemed like years.

"Does it hurt?" Cassie asked, her eyes on his injured shoulder.

"It's not too bad," he said under Colton's "It reopened recently, so it's still healing."

Leila looked at Danny like she was trying to figure out where the last piece of a puzzle went. His father stood.

"Colton, may I see your cog holder?"

He nodded and slipped it from his back. Thanks to the new power of Danny's blood, he wasn't quite as weak without it, but his overall appearance dimmed slightly.

"These adjustments are fascinating," Christopher murmured, sitting back down with the device in his lap. As he poked at it, Leila got up and wrapped her arms gingerly around Danny's shoulders, kissing the top of his head.

"I'm so sorry," she whispered. "I knew you never should have gone."

But thinking back on it, he wondered what would have

happened if he hadn't left. Maybe Enfield would still be Stopped. Maybe Aetas would have been freed by now, or Zavier and the others killed by the Builders. In some strange way, he was glad he had gone. He just hated what had come of it.

"May I see?" Leila asked, hand hovering over his injured shoulder. "I want to make sure it isn't infected."

She's your mother, Colton thought at him when Danny hesitated. *Let her worry over you.* He saw a brown-haired woman with dark circles under her blue eyes, pale and hunched over the bed of a young girl. Colton's mother.

Danny nodded. Leila inhaled sharply when she unbuttoned the top of his shirt. The wound was red, and it felt hot. Thankfully, Danny had no fever—she put her hand to his forehead to check—but his shoulder still ached.

"Oh, Lord." She saw the bullet wound and the bruises across his chest. "What have they done to you?"

From across the room, Christopher caught sight of the scars and paled. Danny buttoned his shirt back up, feeling like a spectacle. Colton put a comforting hand on his leg.

Leila combed her fingers through his hair, like she had done when he was little. It eased some of the tension from him, and he found himself leaning into her touch. "They just keep hurting you," she whispered, a tear rolling down the side of her nose. "I can't . . . I feel like I can't protect you. From any of it."

"You don't have to, Mum."

"I do. That's what a mother is supposed to do." Leila rubbed her eyes and sniffed. "I'll—I'll go get a compress." She scurried from the room, but Danny could still hear her sobbing in the hallway.

Christopher gave Danny a helpless look before following her, first giving Colton back his cog holder. Cassie sat on Danny's other side and held his arm. He relaxed for the first time since he'd stepped foot in the house. Colton on one side, Cassie on the other; he hadn't realized how badly he wanted that.

"So Zavier's trying to find out if the Builders are in London?" Cassie asked. Both he and Colton nodded. "I wouldn't mind a shot at them myself, after what they did to you two."

"Cass, what's it been like here?" Danny asked, picking up her hand. "We didn't hear anything on the ship, but it feels like London's changed. Like the entire city is on guard."

She bit her lower lip and fidgeted with his hand, pulling on his fingers, flexing them back and forth. It was something she used to do when they were little. Whenever their families were out, their mothers told them to hold hands so that they wouldn't get lost. Cassie wouldn't be able to stand still; she'd twitch and fidget and play with his hand. Back then it had annoyed him, but now he was thankful for the distraction.

"Well, the news that Enfield was Stopped got out," she said. "People started panicking again, like when Maldon was Stopped. Then there were reports of other clock towers in India being destroyed, as well as Prague, and some idiots over here tried to blow towers up in nearby towns—"

"*What?*"

"—so there've been a lot of guards about, cracking down.

There were a couple of riots. Religious nutters going on about God enacting justice over our sins. People saying we should go back to following the Gaian gods again, while the religious nutters say that was paganism. A couple of fires broke out near Westminster. Big Ben's been shot at. Clock mechanics jumped in the street."

Danny rubbed his forehead, the ache there deepening into a sharper pain. "Damn it. This is worse than I thought."

"There've been sightings of foreign airships nearby, too, so sky patrol's been heavy. Some were even saying it was the Indian rebels starting the riots."

"That may very well be the case." It would be easy enough for the Builders to win over the rebels after Zavier had cut ties with them. If the Builders won, they would run London through the new clock tower. They'd have control over the entire city. Archer would have her base of operations, her capital from where she could begin her campaign for stronger, blood-soaked towers.

Danny wondered if she considered herself a hero.

His parents returned to the parlor. Leila had composed herself, though her eyes were redder than before. She handed Danny a compress that smelled sharply of antiseptic. He tucked it between his shirt and shoulder, flinching at the sting.

"Thanks, Mum."

She shared a look with his father, the one that was usually a precursor to a lecture. "Danny, you aren't going to help these *Prometheus* people, are you?"

"What do you mean?"

"It's not safe out there," Christopher said. "Just going into the

Mechanics Affairs building is a risk. The Lead is this close to a stroke."

"Which is why something has to be done," Danny argued. "Look, I know Zavier seems like a bad person—"

"He *kidnapped* you!" Leila nearly shrieked.

"Yes, but—"

"And held Colton captive," Christopher added.

"Well, that's true—"

"And you probably wouldn't have been hurt at all if it weren't for him," Cassie pointed out.

"His mother's trapped!"

They all went silent. Danny met his father's eye.

"His mother's trapped in a town on the continent, one that Stopped a long time ago, and no one can fix it. And his sister . . . the Builders took her. They're planning on killing her. I can't just sit here and let them."

"But why are you so willing to help him?" Leila asked. "After everything he's done?"

Danny was silent for a moment. Why *was* he so willing? He felt Colton's heavy gaze, asking the same question. Danny had saved Zavier in Prague, and now he wanted to take down the Builders alongside him. What had changed?

He's me. Before Danny had met Colton, before he'd freed his father from Maldon, he had been exactly like Zavier: distant, aggressive, desperate to the point of failure. Willing to go to any lengths to get what he wanted.

Colton squeezed his leg. He felt a warm rush of sympathy through their bond, along with exasperated fondness.

"I have to do this," Danny told them. "I need to help in any way I can."

"And me," Colton whispered.

Cassie shook her head. "Count me in, I suppose. Whatever you need, Dan. I'm here."

His parents looked less certain, but Christopher gave a slight nod. "I'll help, too. But . . . there's something you ought to know first."

Leila made an anxious sound. "Something terrible happened while you were gone. We didn't want to tell you, but we have no choice."

"What is it?"

"You . . . well . . . they're saying you're a—a traitor to the Crown." Leila gulped. "They searched the house, your room. I tidied it up, but you should have *seen* the mess—" Christopher cleared his throat pointedly. "They said you Stopped Enfield on purpose, and that you were part of some ridiculous scheme to kill the viceroy in India!"

Danny slowly collapsed onto Colton's shoulder.

"Wonderful," he muttered.

"The Lead's been working to have your name cleared, but it's a bit difficult, what with you missing," his father said. "We can get this all sorted out first thing tomorrow, though. Or"—he glanced at the radio on Colton's belt— "whenever this whole affair is over."

It was getting late, so Cassie made to leave, stopping at the door to kiss Danny's and Colton's cheeks. "Ring me in the morning," she said. "I'm scheduled to be at the shop, but I can give Morris my shift, he's been slacking."

"I'll call when we know more," he assured her.

He closed the door and turned to Colton. There was still a fractured sadness in him, but the spirit managed a smile. Their hands met, singing the same song, holding the same blood.

I don't belong here, Colton thought.

You belong wherever I am. Danny leaned forward and kissed him, slow and soft. The pain lessened, but the sadness lingered.

A small cough made them draw apart. Leila stood with blankets piled in her arms.

"Danny, why don't I set you up a bed in the sitting room? It's warmer down here, anyway. Colton can take your bed."

"Mum, he doesn't sleep." Danny sounded angrier than he would have liked.

"It's all right," Colton said. "I can stay down here. Danny can have the bed."

Leila tried to smile, but her usually pursed mouth trembled. She turned and made her way into the sitting room. Christopher, who had been watching from the stairs, cast them a baleful look.

"It's been difficult for her, Danny," he said. "Be kind to her."

Danny thought about his mother's poor health while his father was trapped in Maldon, the terrible hope, the cruel doubt. She'd gone through all that again—because of him.

When she came back into the hall, he wrapped his arms

around her. Surprised, she returned the embrace after a slight hesitation.

"Thanks, Mum. I missed you."

She exhaled a tearful breath. "Oh, Danny. I missed you, too." She clutched the back of his neck, as if refusing to let him go. "I love you. Just the way you are."

The words sounded simple, but they were anything but. Danny felt his throat closing, his eyes prickling, and tightened his arms around her before stepping back.

"No more heartache from now on, all right?" she said, wiping her eyes again.

"I'll try."

In his room, Danny stared at the walls. This room had known him since he was a child, his crib exchanged for a bed, his toys replaced with gutted timepieces and screwdrivers. Suddenly, he had the strangest feeling that these walls no longer knew him. That he was no longer tied to that child.

He found a nightshirt in his dresser. The sounds of his parents getting ready for bed were muffled through the wall, peppered with their low murmurings. He slid under the cold sheets and rested his head on a pillow that smelled like their familiar lavender soap.

The house fell silent. He couldn't sleep. His mind was blank, but his heart kept racing.

He stood and crossed to the door. When he opened it, Colton was already on the landing. Their eyes met, and they relaxed at the same time.

Danny held out his hand and drew Colton inside, closing the door behind them.

There were no layers between them other than the sheet of moonlight across the floor, which turned their skin to pearl and silver. Fingers skimmed sides and dragged across chests, but only one set of lungs breathed.

"Shh," Colton whispered as he traced the incline of Danny's hips. "You have to be quiet."

"I am quiet," Danny argued before Colton caught his mouth.

A tiny, bright seed pulsed in the center of Danny's mind. He knew this presence now, recognized it as something apart and within. His chest was lighter, his stomach heavier.

"I can feel it, too," Colton whispered. His eyes were bright and feverish, golden like the flames of twin candles. "What you feel."

Danny sensed his wonder. His desire. They read it in each other's bodies, minds. For a moment he saw through Colton's eyes—saw his own face look up at him, unrecognizable. It was something in the eyes, he realized. Something in the way he looked at Colton.

He pushed a hand into Colton's hair, watching the golden strands shift and part between his fingers. It was so soft, and bright, like just-spun gold. All of him was made of gold, from the tips of his eyelashes to the glint of amber in his eyes, the faint glow of his

skin. Danny's thumb brushed over Colton's jaw, over his cheek. Colton's eyes fluttered and closed as he leaned into the contact.

Danny brought his other hand up to frame his face. He reached up and kissed him again, feeling the trembling strain in Colton's chest and stomach, the arch of his neck, the urge for his body to follow Colton's, striving to get closer. Colton lowered himself and deepened the kiss, nudging Danny's lips apart with his own. A shallow, curious brush of his tongue. Danny shivered. A deeper exploration, stroking Danny's tongue with his, eking out a small sound from Danny's throat.

It was in these moments the world fell away. It was just the two of them, one heartbeat, two bodies, soft whispers. Danny's heart was bigger than himself; it crowded the room, the house, the town, all of this island on a cold battering sea. He drowned in it, starved for air and enjoying it—this terrifying surrender, the idea that someone could tie themselves so closely to him that there would be no life without that connection. That gentle reminder, and sometimes not so gentle, a pounding pain in his heart that expanded it and weakened it at the same time.

Colton traced the arc of Danny's ribs as if they were a pathway to another world. Then his arm reached around, hugging him, bringing him close. Their bodies pressed flush together, their mouths still attached, Danny shuddering at the horror and the wonder of it. His hands still framed Colton's face, digging into his hair. His lips shaped his name around kisses that stole his mind and his breath. He heard it in Colton's voice, that singing sweet voice.

"Danny."

He clamped onto it, needing it to survive. Again, his name. Again, a reminder he was here, lost and found in the middle of his beating heart, with someone who held it reverently between his palms.

They didn't have to say anything, because it was all spread out before them. Spoken on fingertips, read in goosebumps and shivers, heard in soft gasps. There were secrets older than the universe between them, in the places they touched. How stars were born and died, and how the dust from those celestial bodies had formed their bones, fragments of a galaxy long forgotten. Colton murmured something against Danny's stomach, but he was already breathing the truth into his lungs and exhaling Colton's name like it was the only word he had ever known.

He still saw the thought blast across Colton's mind like a firework. The raw sparks landed on his skin, singeing them both. Danny pushed him back and straddled him. They arched and dug fingers into the sheets as moonlight bathed them, turned them pure, washing out their sins. For just a moment. For just a night.

In the light, they burned into new stars.

They lay awake as the night pulled onward. Colton was too busy tracing the soft curve of Danny's shoulder to pay attention to time passing. Too intoxicated by the pliant press of his mouth.

He wanted everything. He was so full of want that it pooled in his belly and nestled in the hollows of his collarbones. It limned the creases of wherever they touched.

Colton leaned their foreheads together and closed his eyes. It was an easy bridge to Danny's mind, a simple turn like glancing out the window for a different view. Danny let him in; there was no resistance. Just a long sigh and letting go.

And that easily, he was there. Surrounded by a familiar voice that seemed somehow both magnified and quiet at the same time.

—*strange*. He caught the tail end of a thought.

Colton fell in deeper. Gently exploring. Felt doors opening willingly, none of them locked, everything bared. The sound of clocks. A man and woman laughing. The kiss of snow on his cheeks, the sting of cold air. The smell of oil. The taste of gingerbread. The shape of tools in his hand, a simple pride in knowledge. Chasing after an auburn-haired girl in the rain. The glowing face of Big Ben. Cool fingers sweeping the hair off his forehead. The sound and weight of water, gray raindrops rolling down a windowpane.

The gray had a taste, a shape in his mouth, something heavy and aching. A hole, or a ridge, a falling off into something too deep to explore.

Loneliness.

It was there, a looming presence in mind and body. He wore it like a shroud. Even with Colton, even surrounded, it was unshakable. Unmistakable.

I'm here, he thought into Danny's mind. He felt it echo across him, and Danny's lips parted in surprise. His voice traveled into the grayness, making it ripple. Turning it a shade lighter.

Yes, Danny thought back, and relaxed against him.

Colton kissed him awake the next morning. Danny smiled and pulled the spirit closer, wanting to stay like this forever. No thoughts of the world outside, or the stirring in the next room.

"I need to go downstairs," Colton protested between kisses.

Danny leaned back with a sigh. He watched Colton dress and then reach for his cog holder. At the door, Colton smiled over his shoulder, sending Danny an image of the night before that made him blush.

After readying himself for whatever the day would bring, Danny joined Colton and his parents downstairs.

"I can't just *leave*," Leila was arguing.

Christopher put a hand on her arm. "There's nothing we can do from here. If something happens, I'll come get you."

Danny easily read what was underneath those words: his father wanted her to be away from any danger.

He bent to kiss her cheek. "I'll be all right, Mum. We all will."

"Just be safe. And ring me if anything happens," she insisted before reluctantly departing for work.

After a small breakfast, Danny put the dishes away and turned to his father.

"I'm going out."

"What? Why?"

"I want to find Brandon. He might be willing to help us." Danny also wanted more information about the state of the city. "Maybe I can find the Lead and—"

"It's not safe," Christopher cut in. "I should at least come with you."

"And leave Colton here by himself?"

"I can go, too," Colton argued, but Danny shook his head.

"You need to wait for Zavier to radio."

Christopher scrubbed a hand through his hair. "Cassie can stay with Colton. I'll go with you."

"I'm not a child," Colton muttered. "I'm perfectly fine here by myself."

"Dad—"

"That's final, Danny. Give me a moment to get ready," he said before disappearing up the stairs.

"I'm going," Danny whispered. "It'll be easier to move around on my own."

Colton nodded, trying to mask his disappointment. Danny gave him a quick kiss.

"I'm sorry. I'll be back as soon as I can."

He snuck out the front door and into the street, keeping his head low. Once around the corner, he broke into a run.

He breathed in the cold, brittle air. It felt good to be outside, to stretch his legs. There was an omnibus stop a few streets down. If he made it there—

Someone grabbed his arms. Danny barely had time to cry out before a hand covered his mouth. Remembering the ether the Builders had used, he thrashed in panic, but he felt no drowsiness—just fear, hot and potent in his stomach as his captors dragged him into the nearest alley.

"Knock the wrigglin' bleeder out already," a man grunted by his ear.

Another loomed before him. He only had an instant to recognize the uniform of a London constable before a baton crashed into the side of his head.

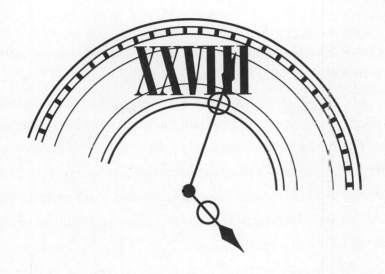

The house looked abandoned. And for good reason—it *was* abandoned. No one had lived there for at least six months. The windows were dark, the paint of the frames peeling from the recent harsh winter. The hedge beside the brick entryway had grown wild, reaching for the road with its bloated branches. Unread papers sat deteriorating on the front step.

Daphne walked through the front door. It stuck a little, but opened to reveal a dim interior crowded with dust and memory. Both made her eyes water.

"I'm home," she murmured to no one.

She set her bag on the receiving table by the door. She tried not to look at the dried, brittle flowers in the blue and green vase her parents had bought at a boutique shortly after marrying, or the dusty round mirror hanging on the wall she hadn't been able to reach until she was nine. Ghosts tugged at her arms, wanting her to slow down and acknowledge them.

The stairs creaked under her boots. Her bedroom was straight ahead, but she turned left, toward her mother's room.

The hinges protested loudly as she nudged the door open. Her mother hadn't lived in the house for a couple of years, but Daphne had kept the room clean all the same. Maybe it had been hope, or impulse. Maybe she couldn't stand seeing more of her life fade into nothingness.

A doily was draped over her mother's vanity table. On top sat an old hairbrush, a mostly empty perfume bottle, and a container of stale face powder. Daphne lifted the perfume and pressed the pump, spraying some into the air. Faded roses.

Daphne skimmed her fingers over the white and cream counterpane of the bed. When she was much younger, she used to run into this room when she had a nightmare, crawling under the safety of the sheets. The counterpane had often served as a shield during games of hide and seek with her father. She had run her fingers over the embroidered edges until she had memorized the whorls and lines.

Shaking her head, she took a small jar from her mother's vanity before going to her own bedroom. She'd put away her childhood possessions long ago; they sat in a box in the closet downstairs. Now, the room was sparsely furnished, only a mirror above her dresser and a painting of foxgloves serving as a contrast against the salmon-colored paint.

The jar of whitening mixture in her hand was crusted around

the edges, though still gelatinous inside. Sticking her tongue out in disgust, Daphne swirled the cold cream with her finger and applied a dab to her tattoo.

She knew she'd been labeled as missing for months now. There were probably plenty of people out there who knew her face and name. Yet despite the restlessness of London, she had pleaded to come to the city to check on her mother.

"I've been gone for months," she'd told Zavier when he hesitated. "If Danny can see his parents, I should be able to see to my own affairs, too."

"Just make sure you aren't seen. We can't afford anything happening to any of you."

She'd asked Akash if he wanted to accompany her, but he insisted it wasn't wise.

"I'll draw too much attention."

Which was true after the events at Victoria's camp, but she had still been disappointed. Lately, he always had a glassy look to his eyes and barely said a word. Meena's death hadn't been easy for any of them, but for Akash it was as if someone had ripped a piece of his soul from his body; without it, he was directionless.

Daphne had hoped—

Well, it didn't matter what she hoped. They had a job to do. Still, she ached for him. And for Meena.

Rubbing a knuckle under her eyes, Daphne sniffed and then rose, going to her closet. She picked out bulky clothes, finishing off the ensemble with a scarf she could wrap around her lower face.

Downstairs, she took the keys to her motorbike from the peg by the door and stopped. On the wall was a portrait of her family. Her mother's blond hair curled elegantly around her shoulders as she stared out at the viewer with a wide smile on her face. She looked happy. She looked like a stranger. Beside her stood her husband, tall and broad and dark, his brown eyes intelligent even in a painting. And between them, a younger version of herself, entirely unaware of all that would happen to her.

Daphne touched her fingers to her lips and rested them against her father's cheek. Taking a deep breath, she walked outside and around the back to the shed.

At first, her motorbike wouldn't start. She fed the condenser water and changed the oil, but even then it stuttered with neglect. After a swift kick to the side, it finally purred to life.

She blew out the dust from her helmet and strapped it on, then grabbed goggles and wheeled the bike out to the street. Straddling it, she kicked the bike into drive and sped off.

She'd almost forgotten how exhilarating it was to zoom through a congested London. While other passersby were stuck in their steam cars and omnibuses and horse-drawn carts, she glided easily between them, dodging pedestrians and piles of horse manure, breathing deeply the steam and smoke and fog.

Stopping for a traffic automaton, she took in her surroundings. She was near Blackfriars, where people clogged the roads, the curb, the shops. A group armed with picket signs nearby protested with upraised voices. She thought she heard "God's judgment" being chanted before the automaton dropped its arm and she was forced to speed on.

Following a growing suspicion, she drove toward Westminster. The closer she got, the more she could feel the familiar pull of Big Ben. But as she turned the corner, she gasped. The tower was still there, bright and golden, but before it—and before the Mechanics Affairs building—even more protestors had gathered.

She slowed to a stop across the street to watch. People were yelling up at the building, demanding answers. Demanding the resignation of the Lead. Demanding that the clock mechanics fix things. Someone had thrown a brick through one of the lower windows; another threatened to set fire to a nearby tree. Constables had erected barriers around the tower, and the disapproving eyes of the London police swept over the panicked crowd.

How long has this been going on? What have we started?

Throughout her time on the *Prometheus*, all she had wanted was to come back to London, to walk through the familiar halls of the Mechanics Affairs building and resume the job she was so good at. Zavier had threatened to erase that, and now the result was before her eyes.

She had wanted consistency, normalcy. She had turned a cold shoulder on the truth: nothing could ever stay the same for long.

Shaken, Daphne turned her motorbike around and headed for her mother's asylum. She parked and removed her helmet, rearranging her cap so that most of her blond hair stayed hidden.

Heart beating a nervous rhythm, she entered the building, ducking her head as she approached the receptionist. Thankfully, she didn't recognize the woman.

"I'm here to see Mrs. Richards."

"She should be in the garden. She likes sitting there in the afternoon before she has her medication."

Daphne knew that, but it was nice to have confirmation of an old routine. That at least one thing hadn't changed. She walked down a hallway with a polished wooden floor to the rear of the building.

The garden wasn't large, but there was enough space for four main plots: a hedgerow, flowers, vegetables, and herbs. Her mother sat with an attendant on a white bench near the hedgerow, taking in the flowers.

As she moved toward them, the attendant politely rose and stood off to one side, giving them privacy while still keeping an eye on her charge. Daphne sat beside her mother and looked her over. Her hair was more white than blond now, her wrinkles deeper around the mouth, her eyes more sunken. Her knobby hands twisted an old handkerchief into knots.

"Mother," Daphne whispered.

There was no response.

"Mum, it's me. It's Daphne, look."

Her mother blinked, then glanced at her. "What?"

"It's Daphne. I'm here to see you." A sudden fear pierced her stomach. "You . . . You do remember me, don't you?"

"Daphne. Yes, of course." Her mother bit her lower lip and kept twisting the handkerchief. "Daphne, where is your father? Where's James?"

"He . . . He'll be by later."

"I hope he's not flying again." Her mother squinted upward. "That ratty old plane. He'll kill himself."

Daphne swallowed back the lump in her throat. "Mum, I'm sorry I've been away so long. I wish I could have called you, or written. Something terrible has happened—several terrible things, to be honest—but I'm back for good now, all right? I won't leave again."

Her mother just kept staring at the sky.

"Mum? Did you even know I was gone?" *Did you even care?*

"Rosemary," her mother whispered. "That's what I'll use. A nice stew, and rosemary from the herb garden."

Daphne drew away. "Mother . . ."

"Where is that girl?" she muttered. "Daphne? Daphne!" she called into the garden. "Fetch me some rosemary!"

The attendant stepped forward. "Pardon me, miss, but I think it's time I bring her back in."

"Wait." Daphne grabbed her mother's hand, forcing their eyes to meet. "Mum, please, just say something to me. Say you missed me. Say you were worried. Just tell me you knew I was gone!"

But the woman before her was no longer her mother. Only a shade of her. She shook her head slightly, pale hair swaying.

"I didn't say crimson silk, I said *blue*."

The attendant gave Daphne an apologetic look. "Let's get you up, Mrs. Richards. There we are. Would you like a nice cuppa?"

As her mother shuffled back inside, Daphne was left sitting on the bench while clouds churned above her head. Left to contemplate how one's existence could be erased within the span of several months, how the only life you had ever clung to could be ripped from your fingertips.

She thought about that empty room in her parents' house, preserved only through her own stubborn efforts.

It would always remain empty.

She found Jo at the hangar where she had been dropped off. Parking her motorbike, Daphne asked the woman in charge of the hangar if she could look after it before they returned to the *Prometheus*.

"How was your visit, dear?" Jo asked, but Daphne remained silent.

Once aboard, Daphne went in search of Zavier. She found them in the mess hall, having returned from the city himself to gather information. Zavier saw her and opened his mouth to ask a question, but decided against it at the look on her face.

"What's the plan?" she demanded.

He cleared his throat. "Builders have been seen throughout the city. Some have been involved in, or even started, the riots.

They're gearing up for an attack, and soon. My contacts believe they want the city distracted while they target the tower."

"Nothing about your sister?"

Zavier's face tightened and he shook his head.

"There's still time," she said.

"About that. I was thinking . . ." Here he turned to include the others. "I wanted to go after Archer and rescue Sally, but I need to free Aetas. Alone. I think I know how, and Oceana will allow me to pass. The rest of you will be in charge of getting Sally back."

Prema's eyes widened. "Alone? Zavier, that's not a good idea. What if Builders are there? What if something happens?"

"And let's not forget these are *gods*," Edmund added. "I reckon they're not exactly the chummy sort."

"It'll be too dangerous," Felix agreed.

"Then he should go. By himself."

Akash stood in the doorway. His eyes were bloodshot, as though he hadn't slept in days. His flight suit was wrinkled, his hair mussed. His dark eyes were fixed on Zavier, stabbing through him.

"He put my sister in danger," Akash said. "He doesn't deserve protection."

Daphne took a step forward. "Akash—"

"This happened because of *you*." Akash pointed a shaking finger at Zavier, who stood frozen to the spot. "She died because you took her. Because you forced her—and me—to play your game. You British are all the same, making people work for

you, getting their hands bloody so yours can remain spotless. Wouldn't want those polished boots of yours to get dirty, right?"

Zavier exhaled slowly. "You're right. It is my fault. But I plan to make this right. Hopefully, by freeing Aetas—"

"Make it *right?* It's too late for that!"

Daphne caught Akash's arm as he made for Zavier. "Wait! I know you're upset. I know you're grieving. But instead of blaming him, we can make sure no one else needs to die."

She turned back to Zavier. "I'm going with you. To see Aetas."

Zavier looked her over. "Why?"

It wasn't a dismissal, like he'd given the others. "I have nothing more to lose. I want to go with you, to end all of this. I don't want anyone else to suffer. If that means helping you free Aetas, then that's what we'll do."

"No," Akash said loudly. "I'm not letting you go with *him.* He'll have you killed to save his own sorry skin."

"I plan on no such thing," Zavier said coldly. "Akash, I'm sorry about Meena. But this isn't only about her. This is about the world. About time itself."

Akash grabbed Daphne's arm. "I'm not letting you go alone with him. I'm coming."

"Akash—"

"I can't lose you, too," he whispered. His gaze was desperate, fierce. It made her insides writhe and catch fire. He radiated a raw sort of power, as bright as it would be short-lived—a rage fueled by loss. A wick on its way to burning out.

She placed her hand against his cheek, his jaw rough with

stubble. "You won't lose me. I'm not going anywhere without you."

Edmund shifted. "If they're going, I—"

"No," Zavier said, cutting off all further protests. "I need the rest of you here in London to stop Archer. We'll draw up a plan and monitor the city."

Edmund and the others nodded reluctantly.

"Now, I was thinking—" Noise crackled from somewhere in the room. "Ed?"

"Oh." Edmund pulled the radio from his hip. "Hello? Danny?"

More static. The group listened as a voice came through, crackling but recognizable.

"Not Danny. It's Colton."

"I was just going to give you two a nudge. We're drawing up plans for the Builder showdown. What say I come get you? Surely you have some ideas for bashing heads?"

"I think that'll have to wait." Even through the static, Daphne heard the worry lacing Colton's words.

"Why, what's happened?"

"Danny left this morning to find Brandon, but he hasn't come back, and now his parents are worried and won't let me leave. I can't even see into his mind." The static nearly ate Colton's next words. "I think he's in trouble."

XXIX

It wasn't the cold that woke him, or the hard stone at his back. It was the yelling.

DANNY.

He started awake, his head pounding. Danny moaned.

"What?" he slurred, moving his head. "Colton?"

Danny! Where are you?

"Uh . . ." He tried opening his eyes, but it made his head hurt worse. "God. Ow."

Are you hurt? Who hurt you?

"I don't . . . Just give me a minute."

Danny touched the bump on his head. Wincing, he struggled to keep his eyes open as he took in his surroundings. Vague memories came in flashes: men muttering, a police car, struggling against handcuffs, blacking out. A large stone fortress.

"Oh, no," he muttered.

The room they'd left him in—he had to be honest, it was a cell—was old. Old discolored stone crumbling in the corners, an old bed with a rusting frame shoved to one side, old stale air with a horrible draft. Danny pressed his palm against his cold nose, trying to warm it. His entire body was shivering.

"I think I know where I am," he said to the dripping walls.

"Oy, settle down in there. Who you talking to?"

Danny forced himself to his elbows. He peered at the steel bars that separated him from a dank, stone hallway flickering with torchlight. A man clad in a constable's uniform with his helmet slanted to one side stood watch, twirling a baton in boredom.

"Can't a bloke talk to himself once in a while?" Danny asked.

"An unhinged one, I s'pose. And judging from the reports, you're a little more than unhinged."

Who is that? Why is he saying you're unhinged?

"Just some fool with second-rate insults."

The guard banged his baton against the bars. "Stuff it, you!"

Danny lay back down with a soft laugh. It wouldn't do him any good to argue with his captors; he knew that from experience.

I think I'm in the Tower of London, he thought to Colton.

What? You mean the prison?

No, it's a merry place full of flowers and rainbows. Yes, of course it's the prison.

Irritation leaked through the bond. *I radioed Zavier because I couldn't find you. I need to tell him where you are.*

Colton, wait—

There was a small severing, like Colton had slammed a door

between their minds. Danny sighed and closed his eyes again. His head was killing him.

The Tower of London. If he lived through this, he would have quite a few stories to tell at parties.

He rolled onto his hands and knees, fighting off the roaring in his ears.

"Cold in here," he told the guard, who scowled in reply.

"There's a blanket on the bed."

Danny reached out to touch it. "It's damp."

"Well, that's all you get."

Danny tried to stand, but his legs collapsed beneath him. He leaned his weight against the bed frame instead. "Do I get to plead my case?"

"The Chief Inspector is on his way from Scotland Yard as we speak. Until then, shut your bleeding mouth."

"Do you *really* think an eighteen-year-old clock mechanic could orchestrate a terrorist attack and assassination?"

"I think there's things you know you're not saying."

Fair enough.

Danny rubbed his head, then combed his hair down with his fingers. "You had people watching outside my parents' house, didn't you?"

"Who knows, mayhap mum and dad'll be joining you down here."

Panic jabbed at him, but Danny kept his face neutral. "You just want more people to practice your insults on, don't you?"

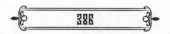

Colton, he thought, trying to reopen their connection, *make sure no one sees you. Police might be watching the house.*

They're already here. Danny took in a hazy image of dark wood and the smell of dust. *I'm hiding in the attic while they question your parents. The men are threatening to arrest them for hiding you.*

Danny cursed.

The guard looked entirely too smug for Danny's liking. "You know this place is haunted, right?" Danny said. "I bet the ghost of Anne Boleyn is floating around here somewhere, looking for revenge . . ." He suddenly pointed to a spot over the man's shoulder. "Watch out!"

The guard whirled around, baton raised. Danny snorted.

"You little shit," the man growled. "Careful, or I'll bash your head in!"

"You'll do no such thing."

Danny craned his neck, trying to locate the owner of the new voice. A portly man appeared before the bars, throwing the guard a less-than-impressed look. The constable snapped to attention.

"Sir! I was merely trying to intimidate the prisoner."

"And doing a rather poor job, by the sound of it," the new man observed. Judging by his sharp outfit and the badge at his breast, this was the Chief Inspector.

The police want to search the house, Colton thought at him.

Hide. They can't know you're there.

"So." The Chief Inspector wrapped a hand around one of the bars, examining Danny with more curiosity than suspicion. His jowls spilled out of his high, stiff collar, and his head was bald save for the thin hair at the sides, which tapered into wiry mutton-chops. "You're the one who supposedly Stopped Enfield, fled to India, joined the rebels there, and took part in the destruction of several well-known clock towers. Not much to look at, that's for certain."

How did they know about his connection to the towers? He thought about all the people who might have seen his face in Lyallpur and Prague.

Then another terrible question sank its claws into him. Were the London police tied to the Builders somehow?

Danny, the police are coming up to the attic.

He tried to arrange his features into an expression of implacable calm. "The Tower's a bit much, don't you think? Downright melodramatic, actually. Who's going to show up next? The Queen?"

"Her Majesty is otherwise engaged," the Inspector drawled. "Trust me, she would very much like that you be sentenced with a proper punishment."

"I haven't done anything," Danny said. *Colton?*

I hid in a box. They didn't see me. Your father's yelling at them to leave. He sent Danny a memory of his power on the Builders' ship, the one he could unleash now, if he chose to.

No, don't. Just make sure the police leave. Then wait for Zavier.

"We'll be the ones to decide if you're guilty or not," the Inspector said. "And as for who's to show up . . . Well, why don't you come with us and see?"

The nasty smile on the Inspector's face turned Danny's stomach. The guard unlocked the cell door, which opened with a shriek of metal on metal, then snapped handcuffs around Danny's wrists. He was forced to his feet and out into the hall. He stumbled into the wall.

"What's the matter? Not gentle enough?" the guard simpered, poking his baton into Danny's back. "Get on with you."

Torches flickered in their sconces as the group traveled down the narrow halls, Danny flanked on either side. He had always wondered what the inside of the Tower looked like, but hadn't expected just how dreary it really was. The walls were thick and dark; Danny couldn't help feeling that they might swallow him into the earth.

They passed a couple of walls with graffiti carved into the stonework—prisoners' names, coats of arms, and a large circle with intersecting lines connecting to smaller circles around the perimeter. It almost looked like a clock face.

Colton, what's happening?

There was a pause that stoked Danny's worry until the clock spirit's voice filled his mind. *They're gone. But they threatened to bring your father in for questioning. They warned your parents not to run. What's going on? Why are you underground?*

They're leading me somewhere to interrogate me. I think they have a higher officer waiting.

Don't worry, we'll get you out. Just be patient.

Like he could do anything else.

The Inspector stopped before a wooden door studded with

iron nails. Nodding to the guard to open the door, the Inspector gave Danny another of those nasty smiles.

"After you, Mr. Hart."

Danny narrowed his eyes and walked into the room, head held high. Whoever was waiting, he could face them. He'd faced Zavier and Archer; what was one more antagonist?

But it wasn't an unfriendly face that greeted him in the small stone room. A man stood from the table, his mustache bristling with excitement.

"Daniel!"

"Sir," he said, too stunned to manage anything more. The Lead hurried forward and drew him inside.

"I told them this was all a mistake, that you couldn't have been involved in any of this willingly, but they simply won't listen. We'll get you a lawyer, and—"

"That won't be necessary," the Inspector said. "Not for this particular conversation, anyway."

It was only then that Danny noticed another man in the room, who had remained seated on the other side of the table. His brown hair had grown long and hung in unwashed locks on either side of his gaunt face. His blue eyes, once bright and intelligent, had dulled, but still flashed in recognition as they landed on Danny.

Matthias smiled grimly. "Hello, Danny Boy."

Danny's blood turned to ice. He stepped back and nearly trod on the Inspector's foot.

"You—What the hell are you doing here?"

"Why, I thought you were friends," the Inspector said with false brightness. "After all, you share a penchant for terrorism."

"I'm nothing like that bastard," Danny growled. "He betrayed me and my family. He lied to me for years and nearly killed me!"

Danny, what's going on? Why are you with Matthias?

I'm about to find out.

"We'll sort through all that in a moment." The Inspector gestured for Danny and the Lead to sit.

Reluctantly, Danny settled into the chair. The Lead sat on his right, glowering at the Inspector and the guard at the door. Matthias watched Danny. Prison hadn't been kind to the man. His jaw was dark with stubble, there was gray in his brown hair, and his face had grown sharp. His clothes were gray rough-spun garb, and when he shifted in his chair Danny heard the clink of chains.

Matthias had once been strong, indomitable. In the eyes of a younger Danny, he'd been a hero—the model clock mechanic. All that had changed when Danny had learned the truth: that Matthias was harboring Evaline, the clock spirit of Maldon, trapping both the town and Danny's father within it.

Matthias had planned to kill Colton so that Evaline could make his tower her new home. When Danny had stopped him, he'd discovered how his blood could control time. But that day, he'd lost as much as he had won. He had lost a mentor and a friend. A second father.

"You've grown again," Matthias said, his voice rough. "You're barely a boy anymore."

"Shut up. Don't talk to me."

The Inspector *tsk*ed as he sat at the head of the table. "None of that, now. We need you both to shed a little light on our current situation."

"He isn't involved in this," Danny snapped.

"We'll see. Is it true you planted bombs in clock towers a year and a half ago?" the Inspector asked Matthias, who nodded with a small sigh. "And you kept the clock spirit of Maldon at your place of residence?" Another nod. "And you stole the central piece of clockwork from Enfield's tower?" Matthias almost rolled his eyes before giving another nod.

"We've already been through all this," the Lead cut in. "Yes, Matthias committed those crimes. And this young man stopped him from making a terrible mistake. He saved Enfield. He *lives* in Enfield, for God's sake! Why would he want to Stop it?"

"That's what we're going to find out." The Inspector turned back to Matthias. "You've known Mr. Hart for quite some time. Do you have any inkling of what his motive may have been?"

Matthias hesitated, and Danny felt his stomach drop; Matthias knew about Colton. He could easily out him right here, in front of the Lead and Chief Inspector.

"There is no motive, because I *didn't do it*," Danny said

quickly. "But I can tell you why Enfield is Stopped and who's responsible."

The Inspector linked his hands together on the tabletop. "I'm listening."

"There's an airship controlled by Indian rebels called the *Kalki*. They were trying to start another rebellion in India, but their plans failed. They tried to assassinate Viceroy Lytton, but botched the attempt." Danny struggled at his shirt, hands clumsy above the fetters around his wrists, and ripped off the top button to pull the collar down far enough to reveal the bullet wound. "They shot me instead—while I was trying to save him."

"And as for Enfield, the rebels were targeting the factory, the one that produces guns for the soldiers in India. Stopping the town meant that no more guns could be made."

Everyone was staring at him, the Lead with horror, the Inspector with interest, Matthias with remorse.

"And just how did you come by all this information?" the Inspector finally asked.

"Because I met some of those Indian rebels and tried to stop them. Because I was kidnapped by an arse who wanted to help their cause as cover for his own."

"The towers?" the Inspector guessed.

"Yes. I was kidnapped in Meerut and forced to help him. I only just escaped. Can you blame me for wanting to go home?"

The Inspector snorted and sat back in his chair. "This is all very convenient, Mr. Hart. Do I really need to point out that you've been involved in both plots to demolish towers?"

"I wasn't part of his plot!" Danny waved his hands in Matthias's direction with a rattle of his shackles. "I *stopped* him!"

"Maybe. But I can't ignore the fact that you were at the very heart of this man's scheme to take out Enfield."

"I think your take on matters is the convenient thing here, Inspector," the Lead remarked. "You've read the reports. Daniel had nothing to do with the Enfield affair, short of putting an end to it."

"Then let me ask one more thing." The Inspector leaned forward again, staring intently at Danny. "How did time keep running in those Indian cities with the towers little more than rubble?"

The silence could have smothered someone. Danny tried to meet the Inspector's eyes, but found the act difficult.

"I don't know," he finally said. "It just did."

The man smirked and turned to Matthias. "And you? Why didn't you use this method while you were running amok?"

Matthias shook his head. "I don't know how they managed to destroy the towers without affecting time's influence on those cities." But it was clear from the look he was giving Danny that he was eager to find out, his clock mechanic's curiosity still intact.

"This is uncharted territory," the Lead said. "Obviously, we need to apprehend the man who took Daniel and forced him to do these things. For that matter—where's Miss Richards? Is she a captive, too?"

Danny nodded. "She's still with him. But don't worry, he won't hurt her."

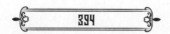

"How do you know?"

"I just . . . do."

"What is this man's name?" the Inspector asked.

"I . . . I think he used a pseudonym. He never told me much."

"Well, where is he now?"

"I don't know."

"Where is he going next?"

"I don't know."

The Inspector stood with his hands flat on the table. "I've had enough. Mr. Hart, you know something, and you're going to tell us what it is. Kidnapped or not, you've been involved in the terrorists' plans. For all we know, you are now one of them. We'll find them—and Miss Richards—and stop these attacks once and for all. If these terrorists think they can take out Big Ben, they have another thing coming."

Danny's heart stuttered. "No, they're not—that's not what he's going to do. Listen, these aren't the people you need to be looking for. There's a group who call themselves the Builders—"

"We know about the bloody Builders. They were assigned to put a stop to the terrorism, but they went right off the rails and ran off with the Crown's money. Trust me, they're next."

"They should be *first*! They're more dangerous than Zavier—"

He bit his tongue, but the Inspector had already latched onto the slip.

"Zavier? Is that your kidnapper's name?"

"I—no—it's a fake—"

"Bring Mr. Hart back to his cell," he ordered the guard at the door. "I'm going to get this information from you, young man, even if it means spilling a little blood."

"Now hold on just a minute!" the Lead snapped as he stood. "He's only a boy, and he's been through a terrible ordeal!"

"I serve the Queen," the Inspector said. "My only concern is the welfare of this country. If this *boy* holds the key to protecting our citizens—"

"I know."

They turned to Matthias. He stared at the still-exposed bullet wound on Danny's chest, then lifted heavy eyes to the Inspector.

"I lied. I do know how they tore the towers down and still managed to keep time running, and I know what they're planning next. I was part of their group for a while. Until I was captured." He held up his chained wrists.

Danny shook his head. "That's not true. You weren't with them."

But Matthias cast him a glare that made him shrink back. He knew that look. Matthias had taken care of him as a child all the time. When Danny refused to go to bed, or didn't eat his vegetables, or threw a tantrum, Matthias employed that look. It worked every time.

The Inspector grinned. "I knew it. Dutton! Get him out of here." He waved dismissively at Danny. "I'll need to wire the Commissioner."

"I insist we find another way," the Lead was saying, but the Inspector ignored him. The guard seized Danny, shoving him roughly toward the door. Just before it closed, he locked eyes with Matthias. The old mechanic's eyes were now as clear as they had ever been, their intensity restored. He knew exactly what he was doing.

And so did Danny.

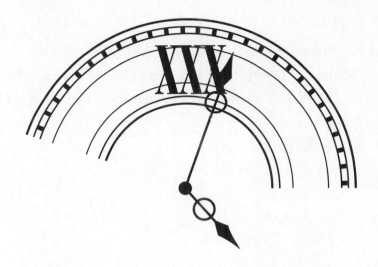

They're going to interrogate him for information he doesn't even have. They're going to torture him.

Danny paced his dank cell, rubbing a finger over the scar on his chin. Matthias had caused that scar when he'd rigged explosives in the Shere clock tower Danny had been assigned to repair two years before. The explosion had sent the tower's central cog flying, slicing Danny's face, creating a permanent reminder of Matthias's betrayal.

But none of that seemed to matter now that Matthias was in danger. The police were going to interrogate the man because he'd lied, because Matthias had protected him.

Why, though?

He realized he was waiting for a response and received none. He prodded the connection between Colton and himself.

Can you hear me? Where are you?

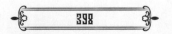

Nothing. Either Colton was too busy to pay him any attention or something had gone terribly wrong.

"Oy, stop pacing about," Dutton ordered, banging his baton against the bars. Danny wondered if this was what animals in the zoo felt like.

"I'll stop pacing if you get me some water," he said.

"I'm to stay right here. And don't even try to talk your way out, because it won't work."

"Why, has it happened before?"

The guard's jaw twitched. "Of course not."

"You'll just have to put up with my pacing then."

Danny turned on his heel, his mind still churning. How long would it take for the commissioner to get to the Tower? Who else was coming? What would they do to Matthias?

Footsteps announced the arrival of another guard coming down the hall. He was expertly swinging his baton in one hand, his dark mustache slicked with wax. He tipped his helmet to Dutton.

"Evenin'. I'm to relieve you."

Dutton frowned. "There weren't supposed to be no shift switches. Did the Inspector send you?"

"I was just with him. Said he needs you right away."

"For what?"

The mustached man shrugged. "Can't read his mind, can I?"

"Where did he say he was transferring the prisoner?"

The other guard hesitated, and Dutton brandished his baton. "You lying—"

Dutton didn't have time to get out another word as the second guard got him in a headlock and knocked him out with his baton. Dutton sank to the floor as the mustached man bent to retrieve the keys at his belt.

Danny approached the bars. "Who are you?"

"Temporary friend."

"One of Zavier's contacts?"

The man unlocked the cell door with a wink. "His aunt has deep pockets."

Danny hurried from the cell as soon as the door creaked open. The new guard used the key he'd nicked from Dutton to unlock Danny's handcuffs.

"Where to now?" Danny asked, rubbing his sore wrists.

"Follow me."

They stole down the corridor and made a left, their breathing loud against the cold stone. Danny didn't know how many guards patrolled this place, or how many prisoners were being held within these ancient walls.

Danny!

He nearly collapsed in relief. *Colton! Where are you?*

Here. The spirit sent him an image of a waterlogged chamber with a large double gate half-submerged under an arch. Traitor's Gate.

The gate was situated under St. Thomas's tower, an entryway once used to transport criminals from the Thames by boat. Apparently, the plan was to leave as so many of the condemned had once entered.

Danny followed the guard out into the cold night air. They ran alongside a building that Danny thought must be the Bloody Tower, where he had been held.

"Melodramatic bastards," Danny grumbled. Maybe the ghost of Anne Boleyn really was gliding the hallways, her severed head tucked under her arm.

They reached the top of the stairs just as a small group was ascending.

Colton cried out and hugged him in relief. Danny looked around and spotted Zavier pressing a purse into the guard's hand. Daphne was there as well, and Liddy and Astrid. They were all out of breath.

"Thought there'd be more of a challenge," Liddy grumbled, shoving her gun back in its holster.

Daphne grabbed Danny's arm. "Are you all right?"

"I will be once I get out of here."

"Then let's not waste time," Zavier said, turning back toward the stairs.

"Wait!" They all turned to face Danny. "They have Matthias. They think he has information about you. We have to get him out."

Colton frowned. "After everything he did to you?" He glanced at Daphne, who had gone pale. "To both of you?"

"If he hadn't put himself forward, it would be me being questioned right now. I can't just leave him here."

"Danny," Zavier started, but Astrid flicked a throwing knife into her hand, balancing the tip between two fingers.

"I need to stretch my legs," she said. Liddy grinned and drew her gun again.

Zavier pinched the bridge of his nose. "Fine. You and Astrid go find Matthias. Norris"—he slipped the guard another, smaller purse—"please go with them."

The guard took a coin from the purse, bit it, winked, and ran off after the girls.

Zavier crossed his arms, leveling a look at Danny. "What have you told them?"

"Nothing. Well, I accidentally said your name." Zavier sighed. "They're on the lookout for you—for the entire crew."

"That's not important right now. The Builders have been skulking around the city, causing riots. It's all a big distraction. They're gearing up for an attack, and one of my contacts believes it'll happen tomorrow morning."

So soon, Danny thought, his breath catching with sudden panic. "What do we do?"

"I'm going with Zavier to free Aetas," Daphne said.

"And you're coming with us," Zavier added.

"*What?* I can't possibly—"

Yells broke out nearby. Daphne and Zavier slipped their pistols out as four guards ran at them. A bullet hit the stone by Danny's leg, making him jump.

"Christ!"

Zavier shot one guard in the arm and Daphne nicked another's shoulder, but it barely slowed their advance. Stepping

forward, Colton began to glow. Taking the taser from Zavier's belt, he disappeared.

He reappeared behind one of the guards to yank him back by his collar. Winking out again, he appeared in front of the other two and knocked their heads together.

The fourth looked around, wide-eyed, gun shaking in his hand. "What the hell is that? Where did he go?"

Colton winked back into view at the man's shoulder. "I'm right here," he said sweetly before he jabbed the taser into the guard's back. The man went down jerking and choking.

"You are truly frightening," Zavier said as Colton walked back to them, passing the groaning bodies of the downed guards, to hand him back the taser.

The sound of running echoed through the courtyard, but it was only the others with Matthias in tow. The man was unfettered, but he ran with a limp and blood stained his forehead.

"Let's go," Zavier ordered. They hurried down the stairs to Traitor's Gate, trying not to trip. Danny was swallowed in darkness, but held onto Colton as he glowed faintly, lighting the way.

As the group reached the bottom of the steps, Danny laid eyes on Traitor's Gate, a sunken stone chamber filled with green water. It smelled damp and foul, the sound of the water lapping at stone magnified in the small space. The gate had been thrown open, revealing a crescent moon of freedom leading to the Thames beyond.

Danny heard guards descending from above. Zavier splashed

into the water to steady the boats they'd paddled into the chamber.

"Hurry!"

A bullet pinged off the bottom of the stone stairs, another hitting the water. Danny allowed Colton to hoist him into one of the boats before clambering in himself. They reached out to pull Matthias inside as the girls piled into the other boat.

Zavier shot twice into the stairwell and a body tumbled down the steps. Another guard stumbled out of the shadows of the staircase and launched himself at Zavier. The two of them fell into the green, murky water with a resounding splash.

Liddy jumped out of the boat to pull the guard off of Zavier and use her taser on him, making him flounder. Zavier came up soaked and sputtering. Astrid flicked two knives through the air, sinking another guard. His body toppled into the water, creating a small wave that rocked the rowboats.

Daphne scrambled for the oars, but one slipped off the side of the boat, sinking below the murk. "We have to get through the Gate before more guards come!" she called out.

There was still one guard left, who had lingered at the foot of the stairs. He shot now at Danny's boat, and Colton shoved Danny down before he disappeared again. He reappeared in front of the guard, knocking away his gun before tossing him into the water.

"Get in!" Colton yelled at Zavier and Liddy, who each climbed into a boat, sending them rocking. Colton jumped nimbly into Danny's boat and closed his eyes, sending his body up in a blaze of golden light. He pulled on the time threads near his hand, and—

In the next moment, they were bobbing on the surface of the Thames. Danny gasped, looking around as his heart raced. He didn't remember paddling, yet here they were, several yards from the entrance to Traitor's Gate. Colton had managed to transport them with his heightened power.

Fragmented moonlight glinted off the water. They rowed toward the dock opposite, where schooners and rowboats were already tied. Zavier's neck and shoulders strained with each rotation of the oars, his teeth bared in determination. Since the other boat was missing an oar, Colton hung off the back of theirs to hold onto the prow and tow them along.

Zavier and Colton jumped out to pull the boats onto shore. They all tumbled out into the shallows of the Thames, and Danny's boots filled with freezing water.

They climbed up the shore, toward the street above. Zavier, soaking wet, ran to one of two black autos waiting for them and hopped into the driver's seat. Danny and Colton dove into the back as the girls rushed to the other auto, but Matthias hesitated. He was looking back at the imposing fortress that was the Tower.

"Move your arse," Danny snapped. Matthias started and shoved himself into the last remaining seat as Zavier took off, tires squealing, before the door was even closed.

Danny shut his eyes, fighting not to be sick as they sped along, the streets of London tilting drunkenly. Fifteen minutes later, the car stopped abruptly, causing his head to bounce against the seat in front of him.

They were in the hangar where two of their planes were

parked. The woman who ran it came out of a back office with her arms crossed.

"I wasn't expecting auto chases when Jo asked me for this favor," she said as they got out.

"We'll be out of your hair as soon as we can," Zavier assured her. "Sorry for the trouble."

Danny circled a hand around his wrist where the handcuffs had left a red welt. "They'll be looking for us. They might even go after my parents."

"I called Cassie before Zavier picked me up from your parents' house," Colton said. "I told her to take your parents someplace safe."

Danny reached for his hand and squeezed it. "Thank you."

"If we want to stop the Builders, we need to get moving," Zavier said. "Let's get back to the ship and finalize our plans."

"There's something I need to do first." Danny glanced at Matthias, who stood off to the side. Daphne noticed him and scowled. When Matthias opened his mouth to say something to her, she turned her back on him. The man used to be her mentor. Now he was only a disappointment.

"We don't have time for you to run errands," Zavier snapped.

"I need to take him somewhere so he's out of the way," Danny argued. "I should be back by dawn."

"We can't wait that long," Zavier insisted. "You're coming with us."

"He doesn't have to," Daphne interjected. "I'm more than enough to be your backup."

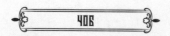

"You shouldn't be going with Zavier in the first place," Danny said. "Not under these conditions."

"What do you expect me to do, then?"

"You could stay here with me and Colton and—"

"Actually," Colton broke in, "I'll need to go back to Enfield. I'll use Harland's blood and my new power to reattach my central cog, and create a web of time around Enfield strong enough to block Aetas's power. Once I establish my own time around the town, I should be able to prevent my tower from falling."

Danny stared at Colton, trying to read his thoughts, but his own were too jumbled. Colton gazed back, steady and sure. Everything Danny wished he could be right now.

"Whether you come with us or not, Daphne and I need to go now," Zavier said. "We'll need a head start if we're going to reach Aetas's prison by tomorrow."

Don't go with them, Colton whispered in his mind.

I won't. I'll come with you to Enfield.

No. I don't know what my area of time will do to Enfield. I need you on the outside, just in case.

Then where did that leave him? Suddenly Danny thought of Meena, the cruel permanence of her end. He thought of how much she deserved to be here still, tugging on her braid and muttering quips under her breath.

Now Sally faced the same fate.

"Zavier." Danny approached him, staring into his gray eyes. The young man had been his kidnapper, his enemy, his distorted reflection. It was past time he became an ally. "I won't go with you, but I'll help the others get Sally back. I promise I'll do everything I can to save her."

Zavier's eyes widened slightly, but Danny could have sworn he saw relief under the surprise. Zavier nodded, then held out his hand—the one made of flesh. There was a lingering pressure between their palms before they separated. "The others will meet you here in the morning," Zavier said. "That should give you enough time to do what you must. But be careful. We can't break you out of the Tower again."

"I'll do my best."

Zavier hesitated. "I'm sorry. For everything."

"Those words will sound better when you've returned and I've saved your sister."

Zavier's smile was fleeting. He moved toward one of the planes, Astrid and Liddy trailing behind him, but Daphne lingered. Danny knew he should try to stop her, but everything was happening so fast that he couldn't find the right words.

"I didn't want this, you know," she said softly. "I did what I could to resist it."

"I know. This . . . all feels inevitable, somehow. Still, you don't have to go."

"I never thought I would." She stared at the plane, its engine idling, waiting for her. "I didn't want Zavier to win. But now that I've come home, I've realized that it can't stay the same. If freeing Aetas is the only way to prevent more deaths from happening, to stop Archer, then I have to help him."

"Be careful, Daphne," Colton said. "Please. I've felt Aetas's

power, and it's . . . strong. He might be dangerous. Oh!" He snapped off Big Ben's cog from his holder. "Take this. It might help."

Daphne accepted the small cog and slipped it into her pocket. "Thank you, Colton." She looked at Danny, waiting for him to protest more. When he said nothing, she gave him a brief, hard hug, and then another to Colton. "I don't know what will happen tomorrow. Promise me you two will stay out of trouble."

"We can't promise," they said at the same time.

She laughed, but the sound caught in her throat. Pressing her lips together, she looked between them, her eyes lined with silver tears. "I'll see you," she said, as if trying to convince herself. She turned to the plane and hopped in after Zavier.

They watched the hangar doors open and the plane wheel around to the small tarmac outside, where it lifted into the night sky to rejoin the *Prometheus*.

Danny stared after it. His mind was crowded with concerns—Sally, Aetas, his parents, Colton's tower. A girl who had long ago been his enemy, now his friend. A boy who had very recently been his enemy, now an ally.

The proprietor of the hangar closed the doors. "Quite a night, eh?"

"You could say that," Danny said. "Are these your autos?"

"That they are."

"May I borrow one? I promise I'll return it."

She raised her hands in resignation. "Might as well."

Danny turned to Matthias. The man was looking pointedly

at the ground, arms crossed. Danny's stomach twisted, even as he knew what he had to do.

"I'll go with you," Colton whispered, but Danny shook his head.

"I need you to find Cassie and Brandon. One of them can take you to Enfield."

Colton nodded and touched Danny's arm. "I'll wait for you to come back before I leave."

Colton was always waiting for him.

Danny opened the driver's side door and looked across the bonnet at Matthias. "Get in."

The man eyed him with confusion. "Why? Are you having second thoughts and bringing me back to the Tower?"

"No. We're going to Maldon."

Shock etched its way across Matthias's face. Slowly, he opened the door and slid into the seat. Danny started the engine and gave Colton a small wave before he turned the auto around and out of the hangar.

They drove in silence, passing under the sodium glare of gas lamps along cobblestone streets. Few autos were out this time of night, but those that were left ghostly trails of steam in their wake. The city felt restless, excited, like a breath being held before a plunge into water.

Danny passed through Charing Cross and out of London. It was much darker as they neared the countryside, in the middle of the inky unknown. He thought about Daphne leaving with Zavier and Akash, heading toward a question mark. He thought about

Colton leaving for Enfield, another question mark. Somewhere between them was where he stood.

"Why are you doing this?"

Matthias's voice was low and rasping. He stared out the window, up at the stars he probably hadn't been able to see from his prison cell.

"Why did you protect me in the Tower?" Danny countered.

Matthias sighed. "Do you honestly think I would sit back and let them interrogate you? I may have made mistakes, but I'm not a monster. I watched you grow up, Danny. Believe it or not, I care about you."

"Cared about me enough to betray me, apparently."

"If that's what you want to think." Matthias sounded tired. Older. "Also, the guard who walked me to the interrogation room told me to stall long enough for your friends to break you out."

Danny started. Matthias had known Zavier and the others were coming for him, and lied so that Danny would have a shot at escaping. His guard must have been the same one who had freed Danny from his cell.

"I answered your question, now answer mine," Matthias said. "Why are you doing this?"

Danny chewed the inside of his cheek, still reeling from the night and all its revelations. "You probably overheard," he said, "but the others are going to free the god of time."

"Aetas is dead."

"That's what we've been taught, isn't it? But I felt him. Colton's seen his prison. Chronos trapped Aetas under the

ocean, and now Daphne, Zavier, and the others are going to bust him out, just like they did us."

Matthias frowned. "But that would mean . . . The spirits would . . ."

"Yes." Danny swallowed hard. "I figured you would want to see her. Before . . ."

Evaline and Matthias had parted over a year ago, and not on good terms. But Danny had seen her longing, her guilt, her inability to stop loving the man who'd lied to her just so they could be together. He thought it might be cruel, to reunite them one last time before Matthias experienced such a loss again, but Danny had a suspicion he would always regret not giving the man the chance to choose for himself.

Matthias curled his hands into fists. "Why aren't you stopping them? Why not just leave Aetas in his prison if he's been there this long?"

"It's a long—"

"Story, I know. And it will take some time to get to Maldon."

Danny sighed. Slowly he unraveled what he'd learned over the past months, and all he knew about the sacrifices. He heard Matthias draw a sharp breath once, but otherwise the man was quiet.

"So now the Builders want to turn more people into spirits to fuel the towers," Danny finished. "But we can't let that happen. Freeing Aetas still seems wrong to me, but letting Archer create these new towers would be even more wrong. At least this way, the clock spirits can rest in peace at last."

"What about Colton?"

"It's . . . complicated. We might have a way to save him, but it's not a method we can use for the other spirits."

They fell back into silence. Danny wished there was no rift between them, no sullied history. He could have comforted any other man in this situation. But not Matthias.

Maldon came into view up ahead and Danny rolled to a stop. They stared out the windscreen as the engine idled, steam spiraling up to join the murky stars above.

"Does he make you happy?" Matthias asked quietly. Danny nodded. "I wish you luck, then. I wish for you to have what I cannot."

Danny tried to respond, but the words wouldn't come.

"Whatever you're about to face, remember that you're far from powerless. I know that firsthand." Matthias opened the door. "Your father . . . Tell him I'm sorry for what I did. I never did get to say it."

"Just go," Danny whispered.

"I never meant for everything to get so out of hand."

"Don't! You—don't." Danny's hands tightened on the steering wheel. "Just leave. Please."

Matthias nodded and climbed out of the auto.

Danny took a few rattling breaths, trying not to think of the man who snuck him sweets, sang old sailor songs, and bought him his first drink.

"Matthias," he choked out. "Thank you. For tonight."

The man was nothing more than a dark shadow, but Danny

saw his teeth flash in a sad smile. "You've been through enough. Try to remember the good in me, Danny Boy."

He watched Matthias head toward Maldon like a man sleep-walking. Danny turned the auto around and drove away, leaving that part of his life behind him for good.

He was headed to whatever awaited him next. To the last question mark.

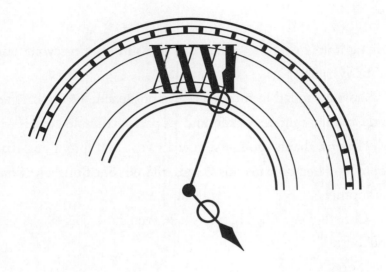

He came to a stop in the hangar sometime in the middle of the night. The old woman had fallen asleep on a stool, so Danny turned off the ignition, leaned back, and also fell into an uneasy sleep.

The sound of the hangar doors opening jolted him awake. He rubbed his face and got out of the auto. The woman raised an eyebrow at him, then jerked her thumb toward the approaching planes.

"Your friends are back."

Danny opened his mouth to reply, but his stomach answered for him with a loud gurgle. The woman laughed and said she'd fetch him something.

The *Prometheus* planes minus the *Silver Hawk* taxied into the hangar. As their propellers slowed to a stop, the crew—or what was left of them—hopped out. Edmund was directing them,

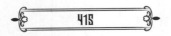

talking loudly over the others to make sure that everyone was properly armed.

An auto rolled in through the opposite side of the hangar, and Colton, Brandon, Cassie, and his parents tumbled out.

"Danny, thank goodness!" Leila swept him into a hug that could have fractured his ribs. "God, if it's not one thing with you, it's another!"

Christopher ruffled his son's hair, then cuffed his ear. "I told you to *wait*."

"Sorry."

"I'm just glad you're safe, Ticker."

Brandon nodded in greeting. "Danny. Thought I'd never see you again."

"I'm glad to see you, too, Brandon." He turned to Cassie. "Thank you for taking care of them."

"Don't worry about it. We *should* be worrying about what's going to happen next. Erm . . ." She looked at the *Prometheus* crew. "What *is* going to happen next?"

Edmund finally noticed him. "Danny, c'mere and get yourself situated. We have to head out."

Danny took a step forward, then stopped. Colton had been watching him throughout the reunions, his face a storm of longing and fear and resolve. Something in his eyes threatened to shatter Danny. Remake him.

Danny drifted toward him as if he had no other tether, ignoring the sounds of prebattle at his back. Colton was trying to be stoic, trying to be a player in this morbid game, but Danny wouldn't allow it. He took his face in his hands and brushed his thumbs over Colton's cheeks.

"You're going," Danny said. It was only half a question.

Colton nodded. "I have to be in Enfield when it happens. If I'm here . . ."

"I know." Danny slowly dropped his hands to Colton's shoulders, his chest, his waist. He had the dual sensation of giving and receiving those touches, the both of them working in harmony.

"Danny, you have to be careful. You know what they're capable of."

"I'll be fine." *It's you I'm worried about.*

"Danny, come on!" Edmund called.

Danny tightened his hold on Colton's hips, refusing to let go. He remembered the first time they met on the scaffolding outside Colton's tower. Colton had shown him not to be afraid. That there could be no possible reason to be afraid as long as he was there.

Colton touched Danny's face, his lips, his throat. He leaned in, and Danny desperately closed the distance between their mouths. Warmth, safety, and the ticking of a distant clock. Time seemed to stop around their bodies, a moment of privacy from the rest of the world. They were apart and the same, connected by blood and something thicker. Something both fleeting and permanent.

Edmund called his name again. They broke apart and broke the spell, but Colton dug his hand in Danny's hair, looking him straight in the eye. Danny leaned their foreheads together.

Tried to find himself there, next to the boy who had changed everything.

"Wait for me," Danny whispered.

"I always do," Colton whispered back.

Then Colton was slipping away, getting back into the auto as Brandon made for the driver's side.

"I'll look after him, mate," Brandon told Danny.

"I know you will."

The auto turned out of the hangar. Colton stared out the window until they disappeared from sight, but even then Danny still felt him firmly lodged in his chest, crowding his bones and muscle with the memory of him.

Danny was turning back to the others when he thought he heard a whisper in his mind.

I'm sorry.

He whirled back to face the road, but Colton was long gone.

"Danny." Cassie tugged on his sleeve. "Those people are waiting for you."

"Right." He shook his head and finally joined the *Prometheus* crew.

"Have Zavier and Daphne gone?" he asked Edmund. The boy nodded. "When do you think they'll arrive?"

"They left eight hours ago, so I suppose it'll take them a couple more hours."

The hangar proprietor returned with a thick slice of bread slathered with butter. "Here you are, lad."

"Thank you." Danny took a bite as he eyed the equipment strapped to the others. "What's all this?"

"Gotta be ready for anything." Liddy pointed out the various weapons on her person. "Gun, second gun, taser, rope, knife, and a nice little device that shoots out gas when you throw it. Dae made it before . . ." Her expression shuttered, but she quickly composed herself. "Oh, and Felix has a couple of bombs, too," she added as he lifted his grenadier bag. Danny was glad to see that Charlotte hadn't accompanied him, likely staying with Jo back on the ship.

"There's plenty for you, too," Prema said, handing him one of the metallic discs that shot out rope, a tin canister probably holding more of the aforementioned gas, and a small gun. Sighing in resignation, Danny strapped the holster to his belt and pocketed the other weapons.

"My son isn't carrying a gun," Leila argued, but Christopher placed a hand on her shoulder.

"It's going to be dangerous with those Builders and rebels out there."

Cassie held up a hand. "Anything left for me?" Never mind that Danny saw the imprint of a wrench in the deep pocket of her coveralls.

"You're not fighting," Danny said firmly.

"I'm going wherever you are, whether you like it or not."

Astrid flicked out one of her throwing knives and handed it to Cassie while Liddy tossed over her second gun.

"I like these people," Cassie said.

"Ugh. By the way, Cassie, *Prometheus* crew. *Prometheus* crew, Cassie. And these are my mum and dad." He gestured at them. "Mum, Dad, meet my kidnappers."

Christopher scowled, but Edmund held out a diplomatic hand.

"May I just say, sir, that I'm terribly sorry for any distress we've caused your family. However, today there are much bigger fish to fry."

"As much as I hate to admit it," Christopher grumbled, ignoring the proffered hand, "I agree. But I'm going to be handing each and every one of you over to the police when this is finished."

"Fair enough. All right you lot, I think first off we need to—"

Something boomed through the air, rocking the building. The proprietor shrieked and ran into the office, returning with an old rifle in her arms.

"They tracked our planes," Edmund shouted as mortar dust rained down on them.

"Well, don't just stand here!" Liddy cocked her gun and ran toward the street. Cursing, Danny fumbled with his own.

"You're not going out there," his mother said, holding his arm in a too-tight grip.

"Mum, I have to! I need to get to Big Ben!" That was where the Builders would be—and Sally.

There was another small explosion, followed by screams. He shared a desperate look with his father, who nodded for Danny to go.

"Danny!" Leila screamed as he tore from her grip, running out into the street with the others.

There was too much dust and smoke to see clearly. Coughing, he held his sleeve over his mouth and squinted through the murky dawn air. Shots echoed as people darted in blocky shadow, avoiding cracked cobblestone, while others rushed from nearby buildings in search of safety.

Danny identified the blue jumpsuits of the Builders. Some wore justaucorps jackets that must have denoted rank, as if Archer had turned them into her own private militia.

He ducked as one of the Builders shot at him, answering in kind but missing widely. Then Liddy was at his side. With a sweep of her arm, she hurled an object that sang through the air and cut straight into the Builder's neck, downing her with a spray of blood, before whizzing back into Liddy's palm.

"Neat, eh?" she called to Danny over the sounds of fighting, showing him a curved wooden handle attached to a wicked blade.

Anish charged two fleeing Builders, grabbing the backs of their suits and smashing their heads together. Edmund stayed to one side, firing the rifle he'd had slung on his back. Astrid weaved in and out of the crowd, using the smoke and debris as cover to throw her deadly knives.

Someone gasped behind Danny. He turned and saw his parents standing horrified in the hangar door, the proprietor shooting down the blue coats nearby.

"Get back inside!" he yelled to them.

But Leila hurried toward him instead, her hand outstretched.

"Danny, get out of the street! Come with me, we'll get you away from here!"

"I can't, Mum, I—"

Felix yelled somewhere nearby. Danny turned to help him when his eyes locked with a Builder across the street and he stopped dead in his tracks. The world seemed to fall away until it was just the two of them: Danny and the man who had seen him kill his comrade on the Builders' airship.

The man's face twisted in loathing. He opened his mouth, but whether he was shouting words or just screaming in rage, Danny didn't know. Danny couldn't even lift his gun. He was frozen, watching the man approach through the smoke and grit like an angel of retribution.

Leila reached Danny and grabbed his arm.

The man lifted his gun and fired.

Danny staggered against the heavy pressure. He remembered what it felt like, being shot: the slam of the bullet, the second of numb shock before the pain tore through muscle, limb, every bodily cell. This didn't feel like being shot.

Danny turned his head and met his mother's eyes. They were dark and wide, too large for her face. She opened her mouth and coughed. Blood splattered his face.

Danny didn't see Prema take down the Builder. He was too focused on the circle of crimson spreading at his mother's stomach, the dampness soaking through her clothes, the scent of her blood hot and metallic between them.

"Mum," he whispered.

He caught her as she started to fall. Turning her onto her back, he stared at the growing halo of blood that pooled from the bullet wound.

"Hurt?" she wheezed, fumbling for his arm. "Are you—?"

"Leila!"

Danny had never heard his father scream that way. Christopher fell to his knees beside her, grabbing her hand, tilting her pale face to look at him. "What did you do?" he asked, eyes flitting between her and the blood and Danny. "What did you do, Leila?"

"Safe," she whispered, seeking out Danny again. "He . . . Danny?"

"I'm here, Mum." The words barely came out; he doubted she could hear him. Taking her other hand, he pressed it to his face. "I'm here. I'm not hurt."

"Thank . . . God." More blood bubbled in the corner of her mouth. Danny wiped it away with a knuckle.

"Leila, no." Christopher framed her face, just as Danny had framed Colton's minutes ago. "No, no."

"I wanted to . . . protect you," she struggled to say around rattling breaths, tears slipping into her curly mess of hair. "I'm sorry. I'm sorry. Chris, help . . ."

She tried to look at Danny again, but her head lolled toward his father. Her dark eyes were glassy, vacant. Her lips were parted, awaiting her next word.

Danny waited, too. Waited for her to blink and sit up. To fiddle with her hair, give that nervous laugh of hers.

But as he stared, she transformed from his mother to a woman's body sprawled on the ground. His knees were damp with blood. The air smelled thick with it, and the acrid tang of nitrate.

A hand touched his shoulder. He looked up at Cassie. She was sobbing quietly.

"I'm so sorry. She just—she just ran. I couldn't stop her."

Christopher kept shaking his head, sobbing and murmuring Leila's name as the fight died down around them. Danny lifted a hand and closed her eyelids. It was the only thing he could think to do.

He stood and stumbled away, bracing himself against the nearest wall while the world spun around him.

Danny? It was the faintest of calls. *What happened?*

He curled his hand tighter around the gun still in his hand. *My mother is dead.*

A gasp—almost a sob—escaped him, and he pressed his forehead to the brick. He couldn't do this now. It hadn't happened; it could continue not happening, so long as he didn't look back over his shoulder, so long as he just kept moving.

Shoving back from the wall, he ran a sleeve under his nose. The others were watching him sadly, warily, Prema wiping tears from her eyes. Builders, dead and unconscious, littered the street. Aside from a few scratches, everyone else was all right.

Everyone except the woman lying in the street, who had taken the bullet meant for him. The woman who had been his mother only minutes ago.

"We need to get to Big Ben," he said, his throat raw. "Archer will be there."

Edmund glanced at the others and stepped forward. "Danny . . . are you sure?"

"Yes."

Cassie took his free hand and squeezed it. "I'm coming with you."

Christopher had stayed kneeling on the ground, but he was quiet. He looked like . . . nothing. The numbness within Danny given a face.

He looked up. "I'll go to the office." His voice was hollow. "I'll help the Lead and the other mechanics."

Danny nodded. He didn't ask what would happen next. He wasn't sure it mattered. He could only think about what Zavier had told him about *Prometheus Unbound*, about Satan, about what turned a hero into someone no one could humanize.

Colton had once told him he was a prince, the hero of a story. But now hatred boiled in his gut, that same inhuman rage he had seen on the Builder's face, the intangible hunger for revenge.

If Zavier was right about the difference between gods and monsters, then Danny would have to become the villain.

XXXVI

The *Silver Hawk* landed clumsily on the South African coastline. Akash nearly crashed them into the rocks and trees framing the beach before they came to a bumpy stop and Daphne could release her breath.

Akash kept his hands tight on the controls, staring out the window at the churning sea. Zavier wasted no time and opened the door, letting in a strong breeze that smelled of salt.

"Come on," he called over his shoulder.

The wind tugged on their hair and clothes, invisible hands that pulled them toward the water.

"No Builders," Akash said, looking around. "Do you think they're hiding?"

Zavier shook his head. "No. This is the one advantage we have: we know where Aetas is imprisoned. They don't. And no one followed us." He took a deep breath. Daphne had seen Zavier

like this before, determined, brittle, unmovable. "For now, this corner of the world is ours."

He walked toward the ocean like a man beckoned. Akash started to follow, but Daphne put a hand on his chest. "You should stay by the plane."

"Why?" The word was sharp, but she knew he wasn't angry with her.

"Zavier and I are clock mechanics. We know what to look for. I don't want anything happening to you down there."

His eyebrows furrowed. "And I don't want anything to happen to you."

"What if the Builders *do* come? Who would warn us if we were all down below?"

His face softened. With his hands on her waist, he kissed her. A thrill shot through her as their lips touched, as she held him back just as fiercely. She felt his bones and muscle and strength, the solid foundation of all she had left.

She didn't know how long they stood like that, but when they broke apart, she knew she had to get away from him—that one second more and she'd lose her nerve. So she kissed him one more time, hard, and turned to the water. She felt his eyes on her back, counting her steps.

Her boots crunched against the sand as she joined Zavier at the water's edge. The ocean was bluish-gray, like liquid pearl. The waves were restless, splashing over black rock. The sky overhead brooded with storm clouds.

"He knows," Zavier said.

Daphne shuddered. She sensed the same sharp power she had felt before. It made her lungs crackle with every breath.

Her pulse started racing. She didn't know why until she blinked and saw the image of a woman amid the waves. Daphne stepped back, but Zavier didn't seem fazed.

"Oceana." He swept her a bow.

The woman was the most peculiar thing Daphne had ever seen. She seemed to float on top of the water, her hair a tangle of seaweed, her skin the same pearlescent shade as the sea. Her eyes were emerald, cerulean, turquoise, constantly shifting. Her dress waved gently in the wind, making the seashells and cockles hanging off of it clatter together like wind chimes.

The god inclined her head to Zavier. *You have returned.* Daphne didn't see her blue lips move, but she heard the woman's deep, fluid words inside her head all the same.

"We've come to free your brother. Will you please allow us in?"

Oceana swept her eyes over them, taking in Akash at the far end of the beach. *The two of you?*

Daphne felt a chord plucked within her, as if the god had tapped her soul. She gasped and nearly buckled, but Oceana nodded as if she'd found exactly what she sought.

Yes, both of you. Come. He grows impatient.

The woman disappeared. Daphne put a hand to her head. Perhaps the plane really had crashed. Perhaps this was a dream.

"Zavier—"

"Hold on."

They waited. The sea began churning harder, frothing and

roiling like water bubbling on a stove top. Then, miraculously, it parted. Daphne's heart pounded as the ocean yawned, the two walls of water stretching farther and farther apart.

"So this was how Moses felt," Zavier said. He almost sounded happy.

"This is mad," Daphne whispered. "Absolutely mad."

"The only thing madder is going down there." He looked at her with a half smile. She couldn't help but give him an incredulous one back.

Slowly, carefully, they descended the slope into the belly of the ocean. The sand was wet and hard to walk through, but Daphne paid little mind to how far her boots sank into the muck as she gawked at the corridor, the top roaring like a waterfall, their sides like aquarium glass. Dark shapes darted by, making ripples in the walls. The ocean floor was littered with flopping fish and drying coral; Daphne nearly stepped on a crab that scuttled furiously toward the nearest wall of water.

It was the most amazing thing she had ever seen.

After they'd gone a mile along the corridor, Oceana reappeared, pointing ahead.

This is where he lies.

They continued forward. The sand was harder here, a circular rim around the prison where Chronos had banished the god of time so long ago. The latticework of bars looked as if they'd been crafted from the strongest stone. A bright golden light shone around them, much like the glow that encircled Colton when he used his power. Darkness, deep and eternal, waited beyond.

Release him.

Oceana's face was still arranged in that serene, unbreakable expression.

Zavier put his hand to his chest. "I've sworn it to you."

Daphne took a shuddering breath and looked at the prison again. The sharpness was almost unbearable here, the air pricking her skin, time seeping through her pores.

"So?" she asked. "What do we do?"

Zavier took out a knife, studying it a moment. Daphne wondered if he would turn it on her.

Instead, he walked to the outermost edge of the prison, where the golden glow lit his face like a surreal vision of immortality. Zavier raised his arm—the one of flesh—over the bars and put the knife to his wrist, opening the veins, allowing the blood to dribble into the darkness.

"We give him an offering."

Brandon parked the auto just outside Enfield and got out, but Colton sat there a moment longer, trying again to contact Danny. It wasn't working. Something had happened—Danny had said *My mother is dead*—and then the connection became like static. He caught flashes of pain, of rage, of smoke and blood.

Danny, please, what's happening?

Nothing.

"We have to go," Brandon urged.

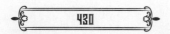

Colton reluctantly got out. Brandon was right; he needed to focus on Enfield. But when half of him was still in London, it was proving difficult.

Colton took Brandon's hand, pulling him through the barrier. Brandon's fingers tightened in surprise, but Colton kept pressing forward, weaving a small web of time around them.

"Bloody hell," Brandon muttered when they were through to the other side. "Can't believe Danny's done that twice."

"Four times, actually." Colton looked around. The mayor and Jane were walking away from the barrier, as if they'd just sent him off six months before.

He called out, and Jane gasped as they turned.

"You came back!"

"Of course. Don't you remember? Danny and I were just here."

Mayor Aldridge blinked. "Oh . . . Oh, yes, that did happen, didn't it?"

In a Stopped town, time played wildly inside the barrier, but Colton didn't have any to waste. "I need to speak to Harland. Where is he?"

When they said they didn't know, he left them with Brandon to explain the plan while he went to find him. Harland was near his house, stuck in a loop of walking out the door. Colton watched him take three steps then disappear, only to open the door and take the same three steps.

As Colton drew closer, Harland stopped. The young man looked around, dazed, before his eyes finally landed on the clock spirit.

"Where did Danny go?" he asked. "You two just ran out. I was trying to follow—"

"Danny's in London. I'm here because . . . because time is going to start again. But I think I know a way to keep me and my tower safe."

Harland's face darkened. "That rot about my blood?"

"Right." Colton studied him, wishing he could find any hint of Castor or Abi. "I know it's a strange request, but it's our only chance."

Harland looked down at his feet, chewing on the inside of his cheek. "You and Danny . . . ?"

"Yes."

Colton expected annoyance or defeat, but Harland smiled. "I knew it."

"I'm not just doing this for Danny, but for myself, too. If you don't want to help, I won't blame you."

"No, I . . . I'll help. What do I need to do?"

Colton brought him back to his tower, his poor pathetic tower. There, Brandon caught his eye. "I explained, but they're a bit confused."

Colton turned to the mayor and Jane, and a few others who'd drawn close to listen. "Aetas, the god of time, is going to be freed. Time is going to be a loose thing again, and you won't need the clock tower anymore. If . . . If you don't want me to try and save my tower, I'll understand. You should have the right to be like the rest of the world."

Aldridge shook his head and placed a hand on Colton's shoulder. "No, son. That's not what we want."

"You belong in Enfield as much as any of us," Jane agreed. Those who were listening nodded in agreement.

"Do you mean it?"

"Of course. We've lived this long with a tower. Do whatever you need to, Colton."

He dropped his gaze, unsure how to thank them. "I'm going to try."

He entered the tower, Brandon and Harland following behind. Before the clockwork, Colton examined the makeup of his existence for the past several hundred years. How long had he spent staring at this mechanism? How long had he wondered what it would be like to not exist?

"Harland? Would you please hold out your hand?"

The young man looked frightened as he raised his palm. Brandon rolled up Harland's sleeve and cast Colton a wary glance. "Is this really what we need to do?"

Colton took off his cog holder. "It doesn't have to be much."

Brandon frowned and nicked the edge of Harland's wrist with his pocket knife. Harland flinched, and Colton couldn't help but think of Danny's injuries, how little this was in comparison. He pulled his central cog from the harness and held it below Harland's arm.

A few drops of blood fell onto the metal. Castor's blood. Abi's blood.

His blood.

The cog flared. Colton stepped back, power vibrating through the cog and through his body. Enfield shuddered around him. He felt as if he could control it with a whim.

As calmly as he could, he lowered the cog and focused on the other boys. "You should probably wait outside."

Brandon opened his mouth to argue, but Colton pointed at the cracks running through his ruined tower.

Brandon sighed. "Yell if you need help," he said. He plucked Harland's sleeve and they both turned toward the stairs. They hesitated at the top.

"Good luck," Harland said.

Colton watched them leave, feeling more alone than when he'd been locked up on the *Prometheus*. Turning back to his clockwork, he held the thrumming cog to his chest and closed his eyes. So much power. His fingertips buzzed with it.

Danny, he called out, *where are you?*

The connection faltered, flickering like a guttering candle. Then a scene began to emerge, transmitted from Danny's eyes into his mind. Colton's own eyes flew open and he nearly dropped the cog.

"No," he whispered.

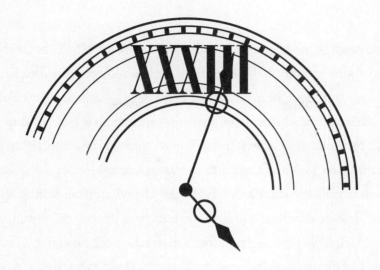

Everything had descended into chaos. As soon as Danny and the others reached the perimeter of Westminster Abbey, they could see just how much of a head start the Builders had gained.

"God," Cassie whispered.

Danny severely doubted God could help them now. Crowds were fighting on the green, the noise of the skirmishes reaching them with all the clamor of a battlefield. Rioters pressed against terrified citizens trying to escape. Builders attacked the London Metropolitan Police with the help of the Indian rebels they had recruited, blue coats a blur.

Across the street, flames licked at the government buildings. The Mechanics Affairs building stood slightly apart, but was still seething with people. Clock mechanics had taken up arms—even the apprentices—and fired guns out of windows on the upper floors while older mechanics joined the fray outside. Everything was illuminated red, the entire square washed crimson with fire, blood, and the light of dawn just breaking.

Airships flew overhead, blasting cannons that echoed down like the bellowing of leviathans. Danny spotted the *Prometheus*—manned by Jo—and the *Kalki*, as well as a couple other ships that looked military standard. They fired at one another and at the people below. Screams erupted as bullets peppered the ground.

Archer had certainly crafted a distraction for herself.

Cassie shook as she took in the scene. Danny wrapped a hand around her wrist.

Strangely, he didn't feel afraid. He didn't feel like he ought to be. At his core was a void he had to fill with other things: running, shooting, revenge. There was no time to be afraid. All he knew was that this chaos had to be stopped.

Distantly, he felt Colton reach for him. The connection opened briefly, like a floodgate, and Danny knew that Colton was ready. But he couldn't stand to let Colton watch what he was about to do, so he did as Colton had before—he shut the door between them.

But not before Colton called his name, desperate, frightened. All the things Danny couldn't be.

The rest of the group hovered on Broad Sanctuary, just around the corner from the square.

"We have to get to the tower," Danny shouted about the noise.

"How?" Liddy demanded. "Shall we just stroll through the masses?"

Danny looked around again. Snipers dressed in Builder uniforms were poised at the top of Westminster Abbey, taking down policemen. Danny watched in morbid fascination as a gearwork gargoyle leapt onto one of the snipers' backs and dug its sharp talons into the man's eyes.

"The church," Cassie shouted in his ear. She pointed to the right, where St. Margaret's stood in the shadow of Westminster. "The square is overrun, but if we go around the church, we can avoid most of the fighting!"

Edmund studied the path and nodded. "It'll connect us to Parliament Street. We can reach Big Ben from there."

Danny wanted to cross the square to the Affairs building. The Lead would be there. His father, too. He wondered what the Lead had done after Danny had escaped from the Tower, if he'd remembered Danny's warning about Big Ben and summoned all the mechanics he could to stand against the Builders.

But the others were already running, and he had to hurry to catch up. They raced across the façade of the Abbey, passing each arched window. Two of the windows were already blasted open, revealing glimpses of the columns inside.

Above their heads, a plane took a hit and wavered, listing to one side as its right wing was consumed by flames. The plane spiraled and slammed into one of the Abbey's towers with a dull crash of stone and steel. The *Prometheus* crew jumped back as huge pieces of stone rained down, and Cassie grabbed Danny around his waist, pressing him into a nook just before a jagged piece fell right where they'd been standing.

"Damn!" Edmund yelled. "That was close!"

Gunshots rang in their ears and pinged off the building beside them; they had been spotted by Builders. Danny pulled Cassie down as Liddy and Edmund swung their guns around and fired back.

Prema beckoned to Danny and Cassie. "The church!"

Astrid took down a Builder and went to retrieve her knife from the corpse. Prema gestured for her to hurry and follow them.

But Astrid didn't see the Indian rebel behind her. The man raised a machete-like weapon above his head—

"Astrid!" Prema screamed.

Cassie shrieked as the shot went off. Danny hadn't even realized he'd been the one to fire. The rebel staggered back with a pained sound, clutching his side. Liddy threw her bladed boomerang, snagging the artery in his neck and ending him quickly.

Prema sobbed as she rushed forward, grabbing Astrid and holding her tight. Astrid gaped at Danny over her shoulder.

Cassie was wild-eyed. "Was that the first person you've shot?" she asked.

Danny swallowed. "No."

She gripped his wrist, just as he had gripped hers moments earlier.

The plane that had crashed into the Abbey's tower fell with a sickening screech of metal. The resulting explosion made them stagger back as fire consumed the rest of the plane. The pilot inside was already dead.

They darted around the skeleton of the plane toward St. Margaret's. Several Builders turned and charged toward them. Edmund shot one down, but another grabbed Liddy just as she threw her bladed boomerang.

Felix took out one of his tin canisters and let it fly, cloaking the path in a thick miasma of smoke that sent their pursuers to their knees, clutching at their throats.

Liddy kicked back with her heel and hit her assailant between the legs. He buckled and she broke away from him as Edmund fired a bullet into the man's head.

"Tetchy son of a bitch," Edmund said as Liddy rubbed at her arm. "You'd think—"

He never got to finish the sentence. The bladed boomerang came back and sliced through half his neck.

"ED!" Liddy caught him as he fell. His face was frozen in shock as blood gurgled up through the gap in his throat. He tried to speak, but only coughed out more blood before falling still.

Cassie looked away, heaving. The others could only stare, horrified, as Liddy hovered over Edmund's body.

"Oh, God," she kept saying. "Oh God oh God. No. *No*."

Felix put a hand on her shoulder. "We'll come back for him. We have to keep moving."

Three more Builders rounded the corner, trailed by rioters.

Liddy pushed herself to her feet, aggressively wiping at her eyes. "No. I'm staying here." She took up Edmund's rifle and looked straight at Danny, the rage of loss making her seem raw, stripped. "Go get Sally."

Liddy started firing at the advancing Builders as the others headed around the church, toward the street.

Danny's stomach contracted, his numbness turning brittle and hot.

Dae, Meena, Edmund, his mother. He wanted to turn around and kill as many of the Builders as he could—ten of them for every life they'd snuffed out.

But when he saw Big Ben, he knew his mission lay ahead. The tower was bathed with the same red that stained the sky, the reflection of flames flickering over its plated iron exterior. A mass of people swarmed its base.

"We can't get through there," Astrid called. "Felix, we need a distraction."

The man nodded, fumbling with his grenadier bag. Shots tore through the air overhead as a plane zoomed by, pounding the street with bullets. Felix went down with a shout as a bullet got him in the arm, the bomb in his hand rolling away.

Danny dashed forward and kicked the bomb as far as he could, shielding his face from the heat as it erupted down the street amid screams.

Prema dragged Felix to the shelter of the church's wall.

"I'm all right." Felix was panting as he clutched his arm in a white-knuckled grip, dark blood pooling on the ground below him. "Go on without me."

Prema ripped away a piece of her shirt and made a quick tourniquet. "Don't be ridiculous, I'm staying right here. Charlotte would never forgive me otherwise." She picked up a fallen rifle

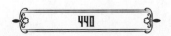

and primed it, ready to fend off attackers. She met eyes with Astrid, who clenched her jaw and nodded. She knelt and pressed a quick kiss to Prema's mouth.

"We can't waste any more time," Astrid said as she turned back to the others. "Come on." She ran straight for the tower. Another bomb went off in the square. Bodies were blasted back, a couple of people running by with their clothes on fire. Danny peered through the smoke and saw a familiar figure at the base of Big Ben.

Archer.

White-hot electricity ran through his body. He started forward, but Cassie threw out an arm to block him.

"You can't! There's too many people!" Soot was smeared across her face, and a fleck of blood—he didn't know from whom—had dried on her chin.

He gritted his teeth as Archer disappeared into the tower. Everything inside his body screamed. His blood called for hers.

"We can't go through that way," Astrid agreed. She looked Danny up and down. "If we give you a distraction, will you use it?"

At first he wasn't sure what she meant. Then he touched the metal disc in his pocket. "Yes."

That was all she needed. She shared a small nod with Anish before racing forward, firing into the mob, seeking out Builders and rebels. Cassie looked as though she were ready to join them, but Danny held her back.

"Spot me."

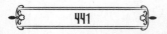

They hurried toward Bridge Street, along the river-facing side of Big Ben. Time seemed to flicker before him, and he shivered. The clock tower was the source—there was a panic to its threads that offset his own.

Only a couple of Builders were stationed on Bridge Street, and they lifted their guns when they saw Danny and Cassie. Danny raised his own, but the Builders went down before he could even shoot.

Looking over his shoulder, he saw a group of clock mechanics around his father's age, faces he recognized from the office.

"Christopher said you'd be out here," one of them called; Danny thought her name might be Joan. "He sent us to protect the tower."

"Where is he?" Danny called back.

"Helping the Lead back at the office. Come on, you lot," she yelled to the others. They ran toward the mob teeming in front of the tower. "Be careful, Danny!"

He swallowed and approached the clock, trying not to look at the bodies scattered across the ground.

Cassie touched his back. "Are you sure this is safe?"

"No." He laughed, the sound wild and uncertain. "But this is the only way I can get up there."

Removing the disc from his pocket, he flung it up with all his strength, as he'd seen Zavier do in Prague. The rope extended far enough to snag on one of the spires of the Parliament Building right beside Big Ben. Danny yanked the line to be sure it was secure, then pulled Cassie close.

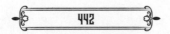

"I have to go alone," he whispered in her ear. "Stay safe. Keep by the other mechanics."

She wrapped her arms around him and hugged him tight, kissing him at the corner of his mouth before stepping back, eyes shimmering with tears.

Taking a deep breath, Danny began to climb. He knew it would be difficult, but he hadn't expected just *how* difficult. He focused hand over hand, one foot before the other, though his shoulder ached and his body was already weak. He focused on Archer. On the image of his hands around her throat.

Reaching the top of the Parliament Building, he paused on the roof to catch his breath. Then he stood back up and flung the disc again and again until it caught the edge of the clock face's dial.

Pulling himself higher, the air warped downward over his body in a shudder. He had to hurry. Danny fought the fire in his arms, the shaking of his upper body. His shoulder started bleeding. Tears stung his eyes as cold wind made him sway on the rope, and smoke invaded his lungs.

Just a little more. Just a little farther. Danny bit back a scream of pain, trying not to look down. Trying not to loosen his grip. Trying not to let Colton in to see.

Groaning through his teeth, he reached the bottom dial, searching for the door the mechanics used to hang the scaffolding. It was just above, and he reached desperately for it with one hand.

The clock face shattered.

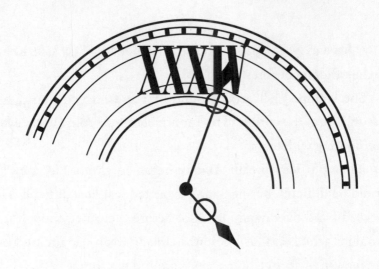

As Zavier's blood dribbled into the prison, a guttural groan emerged from the earth itself. It didn't sound human. It was the sound of the impossible.

Daphne hugged herself, shaking. Time drifted in curious tendrils, snaking through her hair, winding around her legs. The small cog in her pocket began to vibrate.

Zavier didn't seem to notice any of it. He stood at the lip of the prison, staring into its bottomless depth, watching his blood feed the power that was growing all around them.

"How much does he need?" she asked.

"I don't know."

She looked up. The clouds were darker than when they'd first arrived, the ocean more restless. Lightning flickered in the distance.

Oceana's serene face was now marred slightly with a frown, like the thinnest crack in a bowl.

He knows, she said.

"Who?" Daphne asked. "Aetas?"

No, Chronos.

If Zavier had heard, he didn't react. Daphne shook his shoulder. "Didn't you hear her? If Chronos knows what we're doing, he might try to stop it." It sounded implausible when she said it out loud, but here was a Gaian god before her, another beneath her, and another about to descend from the heavens.

Zavier's brow furrowed, but he kept concentrating on the prison. Just as Daphne was about to shake him again, one of the bars began to crack, then crumble. His face lifted in triumph.

"It's working!"

His words were nearly drowned by a clap of thunder that echoed around them. Daphne whirled around, finding that Oceana had disappeared. In her place stood another being.

Chronos was blazing with a molten light. His eyes gleamed crimson, his hair redder than blood. He stood taller than Oceana, his stance wide, his large hands folded into fists. His glimmering tunic was woven with dark blues and silver streaked with winking reds and oranges, as if he'd wrapped himself in the cosmos.

STEP AWAY.

The booming voice made Daphne stagger back, clamping her hands over her ears. But the voice was all around them, inside them. There was no escaping it.

"Aetas has done you wrong!" Zavier shouted above the crashing waves and the thunder that cracked above them. "He merely went against your wishes in giving humans power to manipulate time!"

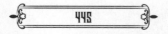

Chronos didn't move, and yet he seemed to do nothing but move. As Oceana's movements had been constant and flowing like water, Chronos's body blazed and faded, both opaque and transparent.

IF YOU KNOW OF HIS WRONGDOING, the terrifying voice boomed, *KEEP HIM IN HIS CELL.*

Zavier shook his head. Daphne was impressed that he had the courage to face down a Gaian god, but as she looked closer, she saw his body trembling, his nostrils flaring in panic.

"I cannot, in good conscience, do as you say," Zavier shouted back. "Aetas has served his sentence, and I believe he is ready to be freed. My people face terror even as we speak because Aetas cannot guide us. Release him, and we will be eternally grateful to you, Lord Chronos."

Chronos's light waxed and waned, but his eyes harbored the fire of a dying star. There was a horrible pounding in her ears, and Daphne realized Chronos was laughing.

MORTALS NO LONGER TRUST IN OUR POWER. THEY NO LONGER PRAY OR FOLLOW THE OLD WAYS. IF I KILLED ALL MY CREATIONS, WHAT WOULD YOU MORTALS DO, I WONDER?

In all of the tales, Chronos was the creator of time, the reason why humanity advanced. To hear him speak in such a way, that he could disregard the people he had once protected, rattled Daphne to her core.

Oceana appeared again. She looked so small compared to her

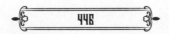

creator. *Please, Chronos. Allow my brother to be freed. I will see to it that he will never disturb your rest.*

Chronos made that grating laugh again. *MY REST HAS ALREADY BEEN DISTURBED, AND FOR THE LAST TIME.*

Daphne didn't see him move, but suddenly Chronos was standing before Zavier. With a sweep of his great hand, the god knocked Zavier away from the prison and sent him flying.

"Zavier!" She made to run to where he'd landed, but Chronos blocked her path. Daphne stepped back, her eyes fixed on the burning holes of the god's eyes.

Shots rang out, hitting Chronos in the chest yet doing no damage. The god turned his head, and so did Daphne. Akash was racing down the slope, slipping and sliding over the wet sand, firing at the Gaian god.

"Get away from her!"

"Akash, no!" Daphne screamed, but Chronos had already disappeared, rematerializing in front of Akash. The pilot tried to skid to a halt, but Chronos lifted him by his throat. The gun fell to the sand.

"Akash!"

Oceana lifted her hands and water arced out of the walls on either side of them, pounding Chronos's back. He lifted a hand and bonds of shimmering black rock pinned her to the ocean's floor, locking her into her own aquatic prison.

All the while he maintained his grip on Akash's throat. Akash kicked out, gasping for breath.

Daphne couldn't move, couldn't think of what to do. A god who had always been little more than myth to her was going to kill her, kill Akash, kill Zavier. Aetas would remain trapped. Colton might survive, but Danny and the others . . .

"Daphne."

She glanced over her shoulder at the prison. Zavier had dragged himself back to the edge, half of his face newly bruised, his lip split and bleeding.

"Distract him," he wheezed.

Distract a god? How? Her heart was the roar of the water all around her, drowning her.

Then she felt the cog in her pocket as a small pinpoint of heat. Daphne drew it out, and it lay buzzing against her hand. Big Ben's cog. She gripped it tight in her fist, tighter, tighter, grunting as it punctured her palm.

And felt it: London. Steam, smoke, smog. No matter how it changed, she would recognize it anywhere.

Home.

A bright starburst of power flared up around her. Her body felt light, hollow, filled with heat.

The bloodstained cog secure in her fist, she advanced on Chronos.

"Put him down," she ordered.

Chronos turned to her, but the power pulsing from the cog made him shy back. A groan rumbled from the earth. Lightning and thunder battled high overhead.

HOW DARE YOU USE THIS POWER. MY POWER.

"Let—him—go!" she screamed.

She strode forward, the power moving with her. Chronos backed away and dropped Akash, who fell to the ground in a spray of sand, coughing and sucking in air.

Daphne knelt beside him, keeping her bloody hand extended and her eyes on Chronos. "Are you all right?"

He nodded, his breathing harsh but evening out.

The god's light was flaring again, the heat from his body evaporating the water closest to him. Desperate, Daphne spared a glance back toward the prison.

Zavier had reclaimed his knife. He met Daphne's gaze, the golden power of Aetas flickering in his gray eyes.

"If you want to help the world," he said, "there must be sacrifice."

Daphne watched in horror as he dragged the knife across his arm. Blood sprayed and poured into the prison. The cog in her palm went still as the light grew blinding, shooting up into the sky like a beacon under the sound of crumbling stone.

NO, Chronos yelled, the anger in his voice rattling Daphne's bones.

She clung to Akash and shut her eyes against the light. As it began to fade, she turned again and gasped.

The figure of a man knelt beside the broken bars of the prison. He was tall and otherworldly, with golden skin. Everything about him was golden: his hair, his eyes, his tunic. The air swirled and spun around him, caressing him with beams of sunlight. It hurt to look at him.

And there were time threads connected to his body. Dozens, perhaps hundreds of them, all thin and gleaming with potential. With power.

Now, said Aetas, standing to his full height, *we may finish what we started.*

And with that, he launched himself at Chronos.

Something flickered in the distance. Colton looked up, though he couldn't see beyond Enfield's barrier except when he concentrated on the occasional flashes he got from Danny.

But this new feeling, this crawling sensation across his body, was a warning. It was already happening—Aetas was escaping.

He stared at his central cog, still glowing like a furnace. If he installed it now, time in Enfield would return. His tower would crumble, and he along with it.

But if he installed the cog, and kept time locked firmly around Enfield with his blood-enhanced power, he could wait out Aetas. The god's power would pass Enfield, and Colton could then release the barrier, keeping the town in his own bubble of time. He could stay here forever, in the last tower-run town in the world.

He thought of all he had seen, the freedom of leaving Enfield and adventuring to foreign lands. The excitement of standing by Danny's side. Feeling normal. Being equal. Remembering the human boy he'd once been.

Castor had always spoken of traveling, of taking Colton to see new sights. He wouldn't want this for him: trapped in a tower, unable to enjoy life the way he once had. But he also didn't want Danny to think he'd failed, to be left alone. He'd promised he would do whatever it took.

Colton knelt before his clockwork, the gears and chains eerily still. He hesitated until another wave swept through the barrier. He needed to make a decision.

He reinstalled his central cog.

For a terrifying moment, the barrier disappeared and the tower wobbled. Colton flung his hands out on either side of him, as if he could physically hold up the tower walls through sheer will. His new power—Danny's blood, Harland's blood—blasted out of him. He felt it again, that amazing rush of strength, the ability to control time down to the barest fraction of a second.

Laughing in delight, Colton pressed the power further. It enveloped Enfield in a barrier of gold. For the first time in months, the people moved normally, spoke normally, cheered as their imprisonment ended.

This was another type of imprisonment, but one they had chosen. One they were willing to preserve.

Once again, Colton tried opening his connection with Danny, wanting him to see that their plan had worked. But something was wrong. In the distance, London wavered. Time skewed over the city. He sensed it here in Enfield, and felt it as Danny felt it, wrong and sick and threatening to collapse.

Colton needed to make another decision.

He spread the power out farther, farther, pushing the energy out as far as he possibly could. He shook and clenched his jaw as he touched London's time, trying to connect to Big Ben. Gold merged into the gray, tendrils running over the chaos of the city.

Finally they overlapped, Enfield's time connected to London's. Colton stretched his power out, steadying London's time, but still it wasn't enough. Something else must have been happening, something in the London tower.

Something was happening to Danny.

Danny ducked his head as shards of glass sprayed out in all directions. A sliver cut his cheek, but he could barely feel it.

A Builder was thrown from the clock face and screamed as he plummeted toward Parliament's roof. His scream ended when he was skewered on one of the spires.

Danny held tight to the rope. The spirit of Big Ben stood on the lip of the clock dial, above the Latin inscription that was also tattooed on his arm. As the spirit caught Danny's eye, he knew that Big Ben had been the one to throw the Builder to his death.

Although he kept flickering, Big Ben knelt down and hoisted Danny through the broken clock face.

"You're just in time, mechanic," the clock spirit said. His amber eyes were fearsome, his golden beard bristling.

"Yes, you are just in time, Mr. Hart."

Danny turned at the sound of that hated voice. Archer stood

on the other side of the room, illuminated by the glow coming through the opposite clock face. Her hands were clasped behind her back, her posture relaxed. At her feet sat Sally, bound and gagged, tears streaming down her face. Sally's gray eyes locked onto Danny and she shook her head.

"Let her go," Danny demanded, but Archer only laughed.

"Come to take her place, have you?"

"Yes. Let her go, and take me instead."

"I'm afraid I'm not in the mood to negotiate, Mr. Hart. We're already well underway with our renovations."

Big Ben lunged forward, fists clenched, but flickered again and dropped to one knee with a hiss of pain. A familiar sensation crawled up Danny's arms; he looked out the gaping clock face to confirm his fears. Time had shuddered to a halt. A gray barrier had replaced London's red skies.

A Builder ran up the stone steps, clutching the tower's central cog in his arms. "I have it!"

Big Ben clutched his chest and groaned. Time threads were spread throughout the clock room in a golden, messy web, all attached to Big Ben's body.

"Don't just stand there, destroy it," Archer drawled.

"You can't do that!" Danny yelled as the Builder fell to his knees, retrieving a chisel and hammer from his pack.

"On the contrary, we can." She unstrapped something from Sally's back: another central cog. "This will belong to the new London tower. Nice and shiny, isn't it? We had some lovely data from Colton's cog to work with."

"Stop them," Big Ben growled, flickering at an alarming rate.

Danny hesitated. Outside, the sounds of fighting had entered a chaotic loop, the same shots being fired over and over, the same screams escaping throats. An explosion across the square burst up in a deadly flower of heat and fire before shrinking back into a bud. Time was out of control. Repeating.

Then something trickled through, something familiar and golden and warm. Danny looked north. Toward Enfield.

"Colton," he whispered.

I don't know how long I can hold it.

The gray barrier was streaked with veins of gold. Time moved, but oddly, jerkily.

Danny had to move.

He drew the gas canister from his pocket and hurled it at the center of the room. It burst in a noxious cloud that made three of the Builders choke and stagger back. Archer cursed, covering her mouth with a sleeve. The Builder still holding Big Ben's cog did the same.

Eyes watering, Danny moved toward one of the downed Builders, pressing his arm to his nose as he held his breath. He fumbled at the man's belt and found the device he was looking for. He stood and faced Archer. Pressing the button, the needles sprang out, crackling with electricity.

Danny risked lowering his arm from his nose. "Your people killed my mother. You killed Meena, and Lalita, and Dae, and probably other mechanics we don't even know about." He brandished the needles at her. "I'm here to make sure no one else suffers the same fate."

Archer lowered her arm with a smirk. He didn't know why until he felt arms seize him from behind.

White-hot rage filled him again. Danny stabbed backwards, jabbing the needles into the Builder's face. The man screamed and fell back, jerking on the floor. Danny pulled the needles out with a sickening squelch and ran at Archer. Her eyes widened right before he knocked into her.

But she was strong. Before he could sink the needles into her chest, she grabbed his wrist and squeezed until he dropped the device. He butted his head against hers, fumbling with his other hand to reclaim his only weapon. She nearly had him pinned when he seized the device and shoved the needles into her side.

Her scream echoed across the clock room, reverberating against the opal glass of the clock faces. Danny was lunging at Sally to undo the rope around her hands when Archer caught his hair and dragged him away. He grunted and squirmed, but it only worsened the burning pain along his skull.

"You little brat," Archer gasped. She flung him to the floor and rammed a boot into his stomach, winding him. She yanked the needles out of her side with a suppressed groan. "I've changed my mind. I'd like to negotiate after all."

Time skittered around them. A crack sounded across the room, followed by Big Ben's cry of pain. Danny tried to crawl to the spirit, but Archer gave him a swift kick to the ribs.

"How close, Michael?" she called.

"Almost done, ma'am!"

While Danny curled into a ball on the floor, Archer retrieved the new cog and came back to stand over him, all sweet smiles again.

"Well, Mr. Hart, I'd *hoped* this young girl's brother would show up, but I can deal with him later. Perhaps I'll make him the new Enfield clock spirit, hmm?"

Danny glared up at her. "I won't let you do this."

"It's a bit too late for that, lad."

She knelt by his head and yanked his hair again, forcing his neck into an arch. Archer lifted her hand, firelight glinting off the knife she gripped.

Danny closed his eyes, expecting her to slit his throat. But the blade descended, sharp and searing, into his shoulder, reopening the wound wider and seeping fresh blood onto the tower floor. Danny screamed.

"Ohhh, that hurts, doesn't it?" Archer crooned above him. "Let's see what happens when we spill more."

She lifted the knife again, its tip dripping with his blood.

The Magician. You are on the path to something momentous. It will show you how much power you possess.

Remember that you're far from powerless.

Danny delved deep into his power, focusing on the wet warmth of his blood as it oozed onto the clock tower floor. He sensed the time threads there, static and shivering, and grasped at them furiously.

The knife began its descent—then stopped. Archer's grin dropped as she stared at her frozen hand in bewilderment.

"What are you doing?" she demanded, her eyes wide. "How are you doing this?"

Danny used all his strength to hold onto the time threads keeping the knife in place. "Ben!" he yelled through gritted teeth.

One second Archer was there, and the next she wasn't. Through a haze of pain, Danny turned his head and saw Big Ben, flickering, using all his remaining strength to lift Archer into the air above his head.

"Put me down!" she screeched. "Put me down *right now*!"

"If you say so," Big Ben grunted before he threw her through the broken clock face. Her scream faded as she fell, until Danny imagined her body hitting the ground far below, crumpling into a bag of broken bones.

Another wave of distorted time rippled through the room and Big Ben threw his head back with a yell. He flickered once, twice, then faded entirely.

Time scattered, seconds spilling like grain. The Builder holding the hammer and chisel gaped at the open clock face, Big Ben's central cog lying in pieces before him. Everything compressed around them, through them, as searing as the knife.

Sobbing with desperation, Danny dropped the knife and fumbled for his gun. He shot the Builder in the chest. The man slumped against the clock face behind him, leaving a crimson smear on the glass. The shadows of the clock's hands were spinning frantically. Danny watched as they stopped, quivered, and switched directions.

Time ran backward.

Archer smirked at him.

He was climbing the rope.

The Builder fell and hit the spire.

Edmund died.

His mother coughed blood.

He blinked and found himself back in the clock room. Sally was crying, looking at him in terror. To the north he felt Colton, struggling to maintain his grip on London's time. To the south, he felt the boiling rage of the sea.

Aetas.

He realized he was mumbling something over and over:

"I have to."

It came out as gasps, as pained wheezes. Forcing himself to stand, he took the new central cog Archer had prepared and limped to the broken clock face, his left arm hanging useless at his side, trailing blood in his wake.

Danny stared out at London. The people swarmed like insects below him, fighting for survival. Somewhere down there were his father, Cassie, his mother's body. Somewhere out there was Colton, fighting for him. Risking everything for him.

He had to.

Cradling the cog in his uninjured arm, Danny leaned forward and dripped his blood onto its untarnished surface.

Everything rushed in at once.

Danny screamed.

Yet he was no longer Danny. Nor was he Big Ben.

He was Time.

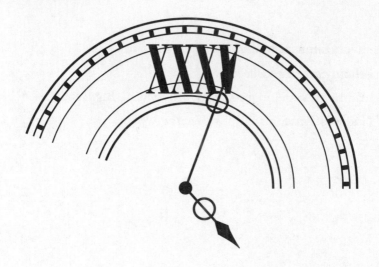

Sunlight slanted through the clock face and stained the floor-boards. Colton watched the dust motes dance lazily in the beam, bored. Everyone was bored today. The entirety of Enfield was bored.

But he was due for a maintenance check; he had long since memorized the schedule. It was said the Lead Mechanic in London, a woman by the name of Archer—descended from a long line of Lead Mechanics named Archer—demanded the strictest of schedules for her workers. Colton was never really sure why. His memory was fuzzy. He couldn't remember that far back.

Sure enough, an hour later a sleek auto came rolling up the street. A young man stepped out and took something from his pocket. Colton had seen others using them before: strange, bright devices called mobiles that allowed people to speak to

others who were far away. The young man yawned and checked something on the device, then pocketed it again and headed for the tower.

Colton made himself disappear when the young man came to the clock room. He was tall and lanky, with dark hair and light eyes. The mechanic sniffed and looked around, probably gauging how much work was required and how little he could get away with.

Something about him was familiar. Curious, Colton waited until the young man's back was turned to reappear. When the young man turned around again, he started.

"Holy hell! Where did you come from?"

Colton shrugged.

"Hold on . . ." The young man looked him over. Up close, Colton saw his eyes were blue. That disappointed him. He'd thought they were green.

"You're the clock spirit, aren't you?" the mechanic whispered.

Colton smiled.

"I know we're not allowed to speak with you, but . . . you're the second one I've ever seen. The spirits are usually so shy. What made you come out to say hello?"

Colton thought about it, cocking his head to one side. "You remind me of someone."

"I do?" The mechanic scratched at his head, making a mess of his hair. The image pulled at Colton's memory even more. "Can't imagine who."

"I . . . don't remember." He wished he could. "You said I'm the second spirit you've seen. Who was the first?"

The mechanic grinned. "Big Ben! You know what's funny, though, is that he isn't even all that big. He's about as tall as I am, and just as thin. You'd think a name like that would be meant for a bigger bloke, wouldn't you?"

"Yes," Colton murmured. "I would think so."

Danny climbed the last of the stairs and rested the package containing the new Roman numeral II on the floor. Out of breath—it had been a while since he'd climbed so many stairs—he took off his coat and examined the clock face before him.

Just as they said: a missing two o'clock. Shuddering, Danny wondered who could possibly do something like this to a clock tower. Was it a prank? An accident? He touched the scar on his chin and hoped this wasn't a prelude to anything like what he'd recently experienced. One tower bombing was enough to last him a lifetime.

He thought he heard something and turned, but no one was there. Frowning, Danny prepared for the installation of the numeral. The apprentice never showed up. *Typical.* Then again, it was probably better that he work alone, considering how nervous he was.

Everything was a mess: the scaffolding, the installation, the way he dropped one of his tools to the ground below. He groaned and prayed for it to end. He used to love the clock towers. He used to love doing this work. But now, all he wanted to do was run far, far away.

By the time he was finished, he was sweaty and useless. His arms shook and his head was pounding. And to make matters worse, he kept feeling eyes on him. Not just the ones of the Enfield citizens below, but somewhere above him, too.

He left the tower, barely stopping to accept the mayor's thanks. He just wanted to go home and lie down. Before he got into his father's old auto, he looked back up at the clock face he'd just repaired, feeling a certain amount of pride.

Movement caught his eye at the window. He thought he saw a face, but when he blinked, it disappeared.

"Losing my bloody mind," he mumbled as he slid into the driver's seat. No matter; he was never coming to Enfield again.

The time servants were huddled in the back of the church, waiting for news, waiting for *something*. Colton felt Castor trembling beside him and pressed their shoulders together.

"What do you think they're going to do?" Colton whispered.

"I don't know. Damn it, I'm scared. I've never been this scared before."

"Calm down. We'll find a way out of this."

The man in the green coat returned at sunset, followed by the mayor's aide. Henry Archer walked up and down the line of time servants, eyeing each one critically.

"You all hold the power to connect to time. Some might even say the power to *control* time." Colton heard Beele's sharp intake of breath. "This power is pivotal to us all, now. If time runs rampant, it'll only be a matter of days until we destroy ourselves." Suddenly, time warped and Archer was an old man—a skeleton wrapped in a leathery wrapper of skin. Some of the children yelped.

Then Archer was himself again, slightly off-kilter. He shook his head to clear it before continuing on. "I only need one of you to put our plan into motion. Does anyone volunteer?" None of the time servants moved. No one made a sound. "It'll be much easier with a volunteer."

Castor stirred, but Colton nudged him hard with his elbow. Their eyes met, and Colton shook his head. Castor bit his lip.

"Lucius," Archer drawled, "you know these people well. Tell me, which do you think is the best choice?"

The mayor's aide shrank back, shaking his head. "I-I'm sorry, but I—No. I'm sorry."

Archer gave a dramatic sigh. "I suppose I'll have to choose myself." He went down the line again, his eyes skimming over the smallest of the children and the oldest of the seasoned time servants before falling on those in between. Everyone dropped their eyes, trying to disappear into themselves.

Only Colton defiantly met Archer's gaze. The man stopped before him, his upper lip curling. Then he went on down the line, sighed again, and walked over to a guard to whisper in his ear.

"I've been told," he said, "that some of you show great prowess in the field of time."

Castor stirred beside him.

"This isn't easy, but it's the only way. I can only hope our God in Heaven will forgive us."

Then he pointed straight at Castor. "Take him."

"No!" Colton made to get up, but the guard coming to take Castor kicked him, and Colton crumpled back to the ground. "No, stop! Take me instead!"

"Colton!" Castor screamed, struggling against the guards. *"Colton!"*

"Don't take him, please! Take me!"

They wrestled Castor from the church, his screams fading into the violent blossom of sunset beyond the doors. People were yelling. Time was skipping, warping, *hurting*. Colton closed his eyes tight and tried not to sob.

Within ten minutes, they felt time smooth out like wrinkles being melted by heat. Colton opened his eyes and gasped, looking around the church. All the time servants felt it. They were murmuring, crying, some even passing out.

Archer returned, wiping blood from his hands. "Release them," he ordered the guards.

As soon as he was free, Colton ran at Archer. "What did you do to him? *What did you do?*" He was weeping and barely understood his own words as they tumbled from his lips. A guard escorted him from the church. He was still weeping when his parents wrapped him in their arms, told him not to look, not to see what had been done.

But there was no way Colton could escape the truth. Castor was dead. These men would build a clock tower over his grave. A tower that controlled time.

It should have been him.

The time fibers unravel around him. They twist into knots. Danny plucks at them, weaving them into patterns, into different shapes.

He is back on that street outside the hangar, watching as his mother is shot over and over again and helpless to stop it, this fixed moment in his past. The spurt of blood on his face. Her last words. The way the life leaves her eyes. Over and over and over and over and over

and

over

and

then he sees Cassie in the crowd below as she fires her gun. Her aim is messy. She runs from a Builder and trips. The Builder

is about to shoot her. Danny plucks a thread of time and the bullet stops midair. It drops, harmlessly, to the ground. The gun

d

i

s

a

p

p

e

a

r

s

There is Liddy, fending off anyone who comes near Edmund's body. She screams and shoots blindly, tears on her face, until a Builder riddles her with holes. Liddy's body lies slumped against Edmund's, her tears drying.

Revenge, he thinks. It's a sweet-sounding word.

He repeats his trick with the bullet. Stops a handful of them, five points across the square like a star, and turns them against their shooters. The bullets fly. They slam into chests, throats, heads.

Danny grins.

It shouldn't excite him, the sight and smell of blood. But flowing from these bodies, it's something to be savored.

He begins to laugh.

Everything that is born must eventually die.

There is a sorrow too deep to touch. A loneliness that can't be relieved. He uses it to fuel his desires, turning bullets, striking hearts, forcing breaths to stop.

Wrong, says the sorrow, says the loneliness. *Wrong, wrong*.

Danny sees and hears and tastes and wonders.

He can't do anything about what's happened.

He can do something about what's happening now.

At least, that's what Colton thinks. His time is tapped to London's, to Big Ben's. When it went out, it tapped into something else.

Danny.

Everything was colliding. Everything happened all at once, and never happens at all.

Aetas brooded.

Colton focuses on London, on the connection, blood and power alike. He sees the jagged remains of the clock face, the shape of a boy framed by shards and death. The boy is tall, with dark messy hair, blood flowing from his shoulder onto a cog he holds in one arm as the other extends toward the city.

His eyes are amber.

Danny, he thinks. *Danny, what have you done?*

This city is mine now, Danny thinks back. He sees Colton in Enfield, kneeling before his clockwork, eyes turned toward London. He's always been beautiful, but lit with gold and power, he is even more so. *I can control it for as long as I want.*

No, you can't, Colton argues. *You're bleeding out. Danny, you're dying.*

And just like that, it slams into both of them, the knowledge: they are dying.

I can still make this right, Danny thinks. *If I can make it all go away—if I can stop it—*

Stop what? Aetas will be free. If you become a clock spirit, you'll go away. Just like me.

Danny shakes his head, not even sure he has a head anymore. He can't feel anything but power. *I can keep Aetas locked away. I can make us live forever. You and I can be together.*

Colton wishes he could cry. *No, Danny. That's not what I want, and it's not what you want, either.* He feels the life leaving Danny's body and panics. *Danny, you have to let go. Please.*

I can't. If I let go, the time around Enfield will start. Your tower will fall. Aetas—

Don't worry about that. I'll be fine.

They both know it's a lie.

Danny is shaking. He's lost too much blood. His heartbeat is getting slower.

Let go, Colton urges him. *Danny, it's time to let go.*

I can't.

You have to.

Danny is swaying. His skin is turning from pale to bronze. His hair is fading to gold.

Danny, Colton pleads, reaching out his hands, his voice, his heart. *Let go.*

Danny lets go.

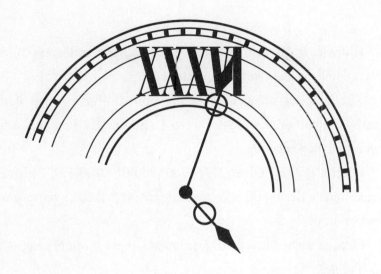

The two gods clashed together with a warlike blast, the sound ripping through the air and echoing through the water corridor. The golden form of Aetas seemed to almost merge with the galactic entity that was Chronos, emanating a spiral of multicolored light.

Daphne was crouched above Akash, leaning protectively over him as she watched the titans fight. Aetas was shot into one of the walls of water with a swift attack from Chronos, but he reappeared not a second later, holding fistfuls of golden time threads in his hands. He tied one of them into a knot as Chronos advanced, and the god froze mid-step, uttering a wordless roar of fury as a golden band held him in place.

Aetas broke another thread, dissolving the bonds around Oceana.

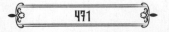

Hide, sister, he told her in a voice like the soft creeping of dawn. *I will not have him harm you.*

This has been both of our fight, she replied. With a sweep of her hands, she gathered whips of water in her hands. *I will not have him imprison you again.*

I WILL WIPE YOU BOTH FROM THIS WORLD, Chronos yelled before flaring up and breaking through Aetas's temporary hold on him.

Oceana turned briefly to Daphne. *Gather the rest of your mortals and flee.*

Aetas burned bright and shot into the sky, Chronos chasing after. Oceana rose to the surface of the ocean as the sky overhead roiled with the storm, the water walls shivering and threatening to collapse. Chronos called down that storm, enveloping Aetas in a swarm of lightning-laced black.

The god of time multiplied. Five images of him charged at Chronos as the original fought against the lightning, twisting the time threads around him. Oceana used her water whips to latch onto Chronos's legs as the five images of Aetas attacked with a boom that shuddered across the sky.

Daphne could only watch, stunned, until Akash grabbed her wrist.

"We have to get away," he said, his voice hoarse. "We've done all we could."

She nodded, running back to the prison where she found Zavier lying unmoving beside the broken columns of stone. His arm was sliced down the middle, and he'd lost enough blood that his skin was pale as moonlight.

"Zavier." She patted his cheek, wincing at the crashing sounds overhead. "Zavier, please!"

He opened his eyes, glassy and faraway, and in them she could see the reflection of the gods' light. As they came into focus, he gave a strangled gasp as he realized what was happening above them.

"He's . . . here," he croaked. "Freed."

"Yes. You did it, you freed him." She glanced up in time to see Chronos come at Aetas with a sword of lightning, which Aetas dodged and Oceana countered with a spear of coral. "We have to get away from here before—"

Before Chronos won? Before Aetas or Oceana could be slain?

But even as she tugged at Zavier, she felt the cold weight of his body and knew. Heart stuttering, Daphne shook her head, wanting to deny the limits of mortality as the strength of immortals was tested above her.

Zavier had been watching the fight with awe, but now his eyes fluttered, as if he couldn't keep them open any longer. His mouth moved, and she had to bend her ear close to hear him.

"Sally . . . tell her I'm sorry."

"You can tell her yourself!"

His throat bobbed as he fought to swallow, his breathing shallow. "My . . . mother. I'll never . . ." A tear escaped the corner of his eye, rolling down his temple. "Mama . . ."

His pulse faded to nothing beneath her thumb.

The battling powers overhead surged brighter than the sun. Daphne shielded her eyes and felt Akash pull her back.

"We have to go!"

"But his body!" She fought to get back to Zavier, but Akash kept driving her forward.

The water rippled on either side of them as the gods continued to fight. As Daphne and Akash raced toward the distant shore, the earth beneath their feet erupted and knocked them onto their backs. Daphne yelped as her ears rang.

Chronos! Aetas yelled. *Your fight is with me, not the mortals.*

THIS ONE IS YOUR PET, IS IT NOT?

Hands of water wrapped around Daphne's limbs, wet and firm. Akash was too slow to grab her as she was pulled into the air with a scream.

WILL YOU LEACH YOUR POWER OUT OF HER? Chronos boomed. Daphne hovered between the walls of water, struggling against her bonds. WILL YOU RECLAIM WHAT I GAVE YOU, AND ONLY YOU, TO PROTECT?

The mortals have done their fair share of protecting time, Aetas said. Daphne craned her neck and saw Aetas approach his creator, a sun against the cosmos. *I will do it now in their stead. They have suffered in my absence.* He turned his burning gaze to Daphne, to Zavier's body. *They suffer still.*

YOUR COMPASSION MAKES YOU WEAK. THEY HAVE NONE TO SPARE YOU.

So be it.

A dagger of lightning formed in Chronos's hand, behind his back. Daphne sucked in a breath, but water flooded her mouth a second later, choking her.

No, she thought, tightening her hand around the bloody cog she still held. *NO!*

She felt the time fibers around her like a loom, ready to be woven. Reaching desperately for those nearest her, she grabbed hold and *yanked.*

The water fled her body, and she crumbled back into the corridor. Akash gathered her in his arms as she coughed, fighting to get to her feet.

Chronos had been aiming the dagger at Aetas when Daphne broke his hold on her, distracting him long enough for Aetas to weave his own time threads, stopping the dagger in its fatal path. Chronos flickered and staggered back, seething.

YOU HAVE CHOSEN, THEN, the Gaian god rumbled under the growling thunder.

I chose a long time ago, Aetas replied, keeping his time threads at the ready in case he attacked again. *You did not like my choice then, either.*

MORTALS HAVE SHOWN ME ONLY THEIR VANITY AND GREED AND DESTRUCTION. IF YOU WISH TO CONTINUE YOUR LONG LINE OF DEGRADATION, I WILL NOT STOP YOU. BUT I WILL WATCH NO LONGER.

Before Aetas or Oceana could respond, Chronos disappeared. The storm still churned, and the water walls began spilling their waves.

"It's collapsing!" Akash took her hand and made again for shore. "Hurry!"

They slipped over the sand as the water poured back in, filling the corridor Oceana had created. They had just reached the beach when they were dragged under. Daphne grabbed Akash's arm and pulled them to the surface, struggling to get to the beach.

Gasping and shivering, Daphne looked behind her, but the gods were gone. There was only the long stretch of the sea with its silver-tipped waves. Underneath all that water was Zavier's body.

Time's last sacrifice.

She stood on the shore and let it all build within her, a swell of *ending*, of something started so long ago that the idea of it being over now was unfathomable.

She wept when she thought of Zavier's mother, free now, and what she would say when she found out her son was dead. That he had died, that he had upended the world, all to rescue her. That he had died knowing he would never see her again.

Nothing more than memories that would fade over time.

Akash grabbed her arm. "Daphne!"

She looked up. Standing before them was Aetas.

The cog in her hand grew so hot she had to drop it. Daphne's lips parted, but she couldn't find the words to speak.

The god did not look happy, didn't wear his victory in any perceivable emotion, but there was still a glimmer of determination when he looked at her. In that brief moment, Daphne felt all the warmth and power she had come to associate with clock

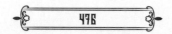

towers, that uniquely singular connection between heartbeats and seconds.

And then it waned. It left her like blood dripping from a wound, something within her renting open. Daphne staggered against Akash, who caught her.

It wasn't all her power the god took. She could still feel him there before her, could still perceive the tentative thread between her and the cog at her feet.

Aetas bent his head to her. *He will be remembered.*

Then he was gone. They were left standing on the beach as the god's light left their eyes. Slowly, the clouds dissolved, and the brightness of morning began to sparkle on the ocean's surface. It all seemed fake. Unnatural. But Daphne's eyes were still clouded in darkness. Part of her was still under those waves.

Akash held her to him. She rested her head on his chest, and thanked every god she knew that his heart still beat.

A gentle ripple went up her back. "Time is returning," she whispered.

Danny blinked and saw London. His London. No barriers. No time threads. Dawn gave way to morning light, and it was as effortless as breathing.

Time felt natural. No woven tapestry of controlled order; nothing pulsing from the tower in which he stood. A complex pattern, like a skein of yarn. Like a ball of twine.

Danny dropped the bloody cog to the floor. He turned and saw Sally on the opposite side of the clock room, staring at him in wonder. He took a step toward her, but his knee buckled and he fell.

When he opened his eyes, Cassie was leaning over him. She was crying.

"Thank God! Danny, can you hear me?"

He groaned. His body was heavy, and he could barely lift his head.

"When we came up, you were bleeding all over the floor! That Archer woman is dead—she fell somehow—and there was some sort of cog . . ."

Danny reached for her, pulled her closer.

"Enfield," he whispered. "I have to go."

"*What?* No. You're lucky you're alive right now. You can't even—"

He rolled onto his side and sat up with Herculean effort. His shoulder throbbed grotesquely, and he threw up.

"That's what you get," Cassie mumbled.

His shoulder had been bandaged. He couldn't move his left arm. Looking around, Danny found he had been laid out at the base of Big Ben, the broken clock face gaping above him. The injured were being tended to by nurses. Policemen rounded up the last of the fighters. The dead had been lined up—were still being lined up—in the middle of the square.

Several of those bodies held bullets he had fired

Christopher was standing nearby, in conversation with a handful of other clock mechanics. When he saw that Danny was awake, he excused himself and ran to his son's side. "Danny!" He planted a messy kiss on Danny's forehead. "You're all right, thank God."

"Will everyone stop thanking God and take me to Enfield?"

Prema saw he was awake and came to join them, Astrid wearily holding her hand. Not too far behind them were Anish and Felix, the latter being tended to a weeping Charlotte who couldn't stop planting relieved kisses over her husband's face. The only survivors.

"Will you please tell them I have to go to Enfield?" Danny pleaded with Prema.

She knelt and checked his eyes, his pulse. "You've lost too much blood. You need to wait here until the ambulances come."

They didn't understand.

Danny turned to Cassie and grabbed her arm, as much to keep himself sitting up as to gain her attention.

"I have to go," he said, his voice breaking. "Please. I have to. He's waiting for me."

Cassie's face softened. She touched his cheek, nodding.

"He really shouldn't," Christopher began, but Cassie looked up at him with an expression Danny had never seen her wear before, something like resolve mixed with grief.

"I'll take care of him, Mr. Hart. I promise."

Christopher took another look at Danny, and sighed. "All right."

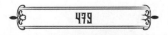

Cassie took Christopher's auto. Prema helped her get Danny situated before Cassie took to the driver's seat. Danny sat back and closed his eyes, his head too light, his body too heavy.

"Sally," he whispered to Prema through the open window. "Is she . . . ?"

"She's safe. A nurse took her away from the square, to someplace quieter. Jo is with her." Prema reached inside the auto to grasp his hand. "Zavier will be so relieved when he returns."

Danny wanted to feel relief too, but it eluded him as he kept reaching out to Colton with no reply.

He didn't know what he did in that hour of pain and uncertainty as Cassie drove, but when he next opened his eyes, Enfield spread out before him. His heart gave a violent jolt.

Cassie rolled the auto to a stop, but before she could shut off the engine Danny had already opened the door and tumbled out.

"Danny—!"

A crowd had gathered at the edge of the village green. He'd seen the sight so often before, curious Enfield citizens hovering around Colton's tower.

But this time, there was no tower.

The space was empty.

Brandon paced near the crowd. When he saw Danny, he raced over and made to take his arm, but Danny yanked it away and dove into the throng.

A few people turned and recognized him. They nudged their neighbors and the crowd parted before him. When Danny finally reached the front, his breath caught.

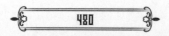

The tower was in ruins. It lay in a mound of rubble, dust still floating in the air from broken mortar and plaster. The minute hand stuck out from the wreckage like a black arrow, pointing accusingly at the sky. Glass lay in millions of shards and fragments, glittering like discarded diamonds, crunching beneath Danny's boots.

The mayor stood off to one side, speaking to a boy. Or rather, the ghost of a boy. Colton was nearly see-through, flickering just as Big Ben had. Mayor Aldridge noticed Danny, and like the others, quietly stepped aside to let him by.

Danny met Colton's eyes. The spirit smiled, but it was one of his small, sad smiles, one that tried to preserve whatever strength he had left into the tender curve of his mouth.

"You let go," Colton said. Even his voice was faded. "You did as you were told. For once."

Danny couldn't stop staring at the rubble that had been Colton's tower. "We . . . We can rebuild it. We can start right now." A new hope, bright and painful, burned in his chest. "We have to get a carpenter, and—and that bloody ironworker, what was his name?—but we have to start right now. We don't have much time."

"No, Danny." Those two words doused the hope that had flared so suddenly within him. "You have all the time in the world, now. But I have none left."

Danny shook his head. "No. No, there can still . . . I can't . . ."

Colton flickered. He lifted a hand and put it on Danny's cheek, or tried to. His fingers passed through him, fog and dust and the memory of starlight. "The best decision I ever made was showing myself to you."

"Stop," Danny pleaded.

"When I think about what could have happened if I hadn't, if I had just stayed lonely and forgotten in my tower . . ." Colton glanced down at the remains of that tower. "It was all worth it, Danny. Every minute. Because I had you."

"Don't," Danny whispered. "Don't talk that way."

"You have to promise me, Danny. Promise you'll live for me."

Danny shook his head, but it passed right through Colton's hand.

"You said you'd never leave me. You promised."

Colton closed his eyes. He flickered.

"I wish I could have done the easy thing. I wish I could have thought only of myself. But I couldn't. And you'll get to live such a full life, Danny—"

"Stop."

"—and meet someone special, and visit all those places you've dreamed of seeing. You won't be tied to Enfield. You won't be tied to me."

"I wanted to be," Danny sobbed, reaching out for him, but his hand passed through Colton's chest. "I wanted to be tied to you."

"You still haven't promised me."

"Colton . . . God . . ."

"Just say you will. Please."

Danny stared at Colton, fighting against the bitterness in his throat, the agony crushing his heart. "I will."

Colton locked relieved. He flickered again. "I'm sorry, Danny. I'm sorry." Flicker. "I wish I could have stayed."

Another flicker as their eyes locked, as they tried to find themselves in the other.

"Danny," Colton whispered, "I would have chosen you."

In the next blink, he was gone.

Danny drew in a broken breath. He lifted his hands, but there was nothing but air and dust and sunlight. Everything that was left at the ending of the world.

"Colton," he called, but his voice was feeble, barely audible. "Colton."

No one answered.

He staggered into the rubble. Slowly, he fell to his knees, clutching the nearest piece of debris and pressing it to his chest.

It was all he had left.

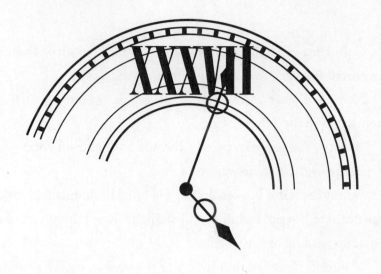

There was once a golden boy who lived in a golden tower.
And then the tower fell.

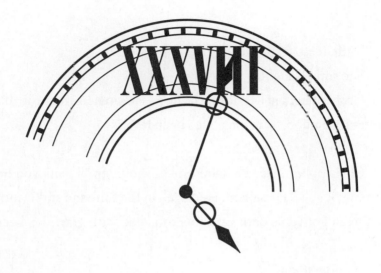

XXXVIII

Daphne made sure the address was correct before knocking. The door opened to reveal a middle-aged man, the current head of the Mechanics Union after the tragic shooting of the former Lead Mechanic. Now that clock mechanics were no longer a necessity, there had to be someone in charge of who was reassigned to what, and what trades they could transition into now they were all technically out of jobs.

Christopher Hart gave her a weary smile before ushering her inside. "Daphne, hello. I didn't expect to see you."

"I thought I would drop by before I leave. I'm going to be away from London for a while."

"Are you? Probably for the best." It was a nightmare, cleaning up after the Builders had attacked. Only a week had passed, and so little had been accomplished. "May I ask where you're off to?"

"India."

"Ahh. It stole your heart, did it?"

She smiled slightly. "In a way."

Christopher led her down the hall. "He's in here. It's probably better if you don't stay long. He's been feverish."

"I'll try not to upset him."

Christopher placed a hand on her shoulder. "Thank you for coming. It's . . ." He sighed. He'd aged in the time she and Danny had been gone, his dark hair now threaded with gray. "It's been difficult."

"I understand."

She walked through the door, bracing herself for what she would find.

What she actually found was relatively tame: Danny was sitting at the end of the couch, the sunlight from the open window slanting across his legs. There was a book propped open on his lap. His left arm was heavily bandaged and held in a sling.

He didn't look up at the sound of Daphne's footsteps, or when she sat down beside him. He just kept staring at a spot beyond the book's pages.

Much like his father, Danny looked tired. Distant. His green eyes were glassy. *Feverish*, Christopher had said, and it was true; there was an unhealthy tone to his skin and his body radiated too much heat.

Daphne put a hand on his arm. "Danny, it's me. It's Daphne." He didn't respond. She was now glad she hadn't brought Akash, though he'd wanted to see Danny before they left. "How are you feeling?" It was a silly question, but it was the only one she could summon.

He didn't answer. Trying not to sigh, Daphne looked at the book in his lap.

"Greek myths? I think we've had enough of those for a lifetime."

Danny closed his eyes.

"I'm sorry, Danny. I'm so sorry." They sat in silence. After a while, she said, "I'm going to India. With Akash."

He finally looked at her. There was nothing behind his eyes; they were flat. Empty.

"My mother is being taken care of, and there's nothing tying me here. He wants me to come with him to see his family," she explained. "To tell them about Meena. It was difficult, telling Jo and Sally about Zavier. I'm not sure if I can handle going through that again."

She took a deep breath. "But I will. For him."

Danny slowly moved his good hand until it was grasping hers.

"Be happy," he whispered. "With him."

Her eyes filled with tears. Leaning over, she kissed Danny on the cheek. "I will. And I'll be back, you know. I'll come and kick you into shape."

That managed the barest of smiles, but it was gone too quick for her to tell.

Akash was waiting for her at the house. Daphne had become so used to bracing herself before opening the door, to be greeted by emptiness and silence, that the sight of him nearly knocked the air from her lungs.

She supposed not all change was bad.

He took one look at her face and came to hug her. She sank into his embrace, into the sheer relief of being able to do so.

"How's Danny?"

"He's . . ." Daphne swallowed. "I wonder if maybe I should stay here a bit longer, just in case."

He ran his fingers through her hair and didn't say anything. He was leaving it up to her, despite the fact that his family waited for him back home.

You can have more than one home.

London would still be here for her when she returned. Her mother would be cared for; Danny would be cared for. It was time for her to care of herself.

She leaned back and caressed the side of Akash's face, his dark eyes somber yet warm.

"Let's go home," she said.

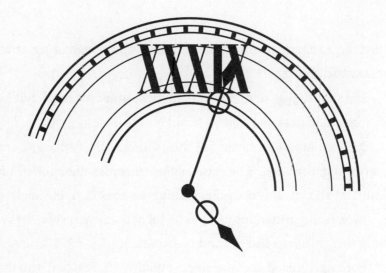

Danny breathed in fire and exhaled knives. Every movement hurt. Everything turned dizzily around him. He was stranded, adrift.

He found himself on the landing, calling for his father. But the word only came out as a thin wheeze. He fell, banging into the wall.

A door whisked open. "Danny!"

He welcomed the black when it came.

He woke to heat and pain. Distantly, he thought he felt his heartbeat—a dull thing, inconsequential. Each pump fueled the ache in his head and stomach.

Danny opened eyes that were dry and scratchy. He didn't

have the strength to rub them. He just lay there, staring at an unfamiliar ceiling.

His mouth was so dry. It was an effort to tilt his head, but he was rewarded with the sight of a cup beside him.

A low groan escaped as he shifted. Everything hurt. Everything pounded. The ache exploded across the back of his skull and shot down his spine, making his toes curl. He sobbed in a breath and gritted his teeth as he turned onto his side, everything *thump thump* and red and black.

Forcing himself to take deep breaths, he reached for the cup. Nothing happened. Danny lay with half his face buried in the pillow, staring blankly where his left hand should have been. But even as he felt he was moving it, he couldn't see it. The cup remained untouched.

Danny turned onto his back and looked down.

Empty space where his left arm once was.

He stared at the emptiness, the phantom limb, invisible flesh. The swath of bloody bandages over the stump of his arm, hot and sickly and pulsing with every beat of his heart. Red and black and *thump thump*.

It still felt like a part of him. Until he tried moving again, and the cold air rushed in. His shoulder an empty socket, his side exposed to the world. Something ripped away, flesh torn from his body, removed like time—no longer there, no longer a sensation he recognized, no compass or guidance or fibers or ticks or tocks or mother or Colton and *oh God Colton I can't feel him I can't—*

He didn't know when he started screaming. People rushed

into the room, crowded his bedside as he kicked at the covers and slammed his head back on the pillow.

Broad hands held his head still. "Danny! Danny, calm down, please—"

His father's voice. He looked up, dazed, to seek out his father's green eyes, wide and swimming with tears.

"Thank God," Christopher choked out. "Thank God you're alive."

The doctors were poking and prodding, and there was pain. Danny whimpered and tried to turn away, tried to turn back to where the other sensations waited. Time and his mother and Colton and *my mind is so empty.*

"He's going into another fit."

"It must be the fever. He's burning up."

They held his arm down and prepared a needle. Panic rose through him and he started screaming again. He was back on the *Prometheus*, looking into Zavier's eyes. But those gray eyes belonged to a boy who was dead. Everything was dead and his arm was gone and *Colton*—

The needle clattered to the floor. Someone swore. Before Danny could try to heave himself up, a wet cloth was slapped on his face and his eyes fluttered closed, throwing him back into the void.

He woke to the sound of his father yelling. The door was closed,

but Danny still heard Christopher's raised voice and the shouting of others trying to defend themselves.

The door opened. "—don't care about your bloody regulations! This is my *son*!"

"Mr. Hart, please—"

The fingers of Danny's right hand peeked out from underneath the covers. His mouth shaped a word.

"If you don't think I'm going to report this, think again. You could have made everything worse."

Danny tried shaping the word again. This time, the barest of sounds came out: "Dad."

Remarkably, Christopher heard. He rushed to his son's side, grabbing his hand. His face was pale and gaunt.

"How do you feel, Ticker?"

Sick. Weak. In pain. Nothing.

His eyes traveled down to the nothingness of his arm.

Christopher brushed Danny's hair back and sighed. "The blood infection was going to spread to your heart, and they had to take it at the shoulder. I'm so sorry, Danny. I asked if there was anything they could do to save it, but . . ."

He wondered where his left arm was right now. Lying in a rubbish bin, incinerated in a burner, being fought over by dogs in an alley?

"But don't worry." Christopher's voice was fading, growing thinner and fainter as it stretched across the distance. "We have a solution. It'll be all right, I promise. Danny?"

But he was already sinking into the hollow place again.

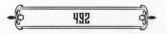

It took a while for the shoulder to heal sufficiently. Once it was decreed stable, and Danny's fever had burnt away—or mostly away, he couldn't tell when his body was constantly numb—he sat on the edge of the hospital bed with his father at his side.

They showed him the arm. Long and chrome, with an elbow joint that allowed easy motion. The fingers were round, not skeletal as Zavier's had been. A few days before, they had fixed a metallic holder to Danny's shoulder socket, a process that had been so taxing he had passed out.

"This will be painful," the doctor warned, looking at Christopher instead of Danny. "Especially the first fusion."

Christopher nodded, securing an arm around Danny's back.

Danny was unmoved by the warning. He almost welcomed the thought of pain. The chance to feel something.

He was unprepared. When the doctors suctioned the joint to the metal fuser in his shoulder, his nerves snapped and crackled and sent pure white agony across his synapses. His scream flooded the room. He grabbed his father's shirt and pressed his head into his chest. Christopher clutched him tighter, murmuring that he wouldn't let go, he would never let go of him again.

When the pain finally subsided, Danny doubled over and vomited onto the floor.

Someone laid him back down when he was done. The room spun. His body was so hot. He was going to burn here, turned to ash and the bitter reminder of pain.

He faded in and out of consciousness. By the time he knew he was awake again, the doctors were long gone and his father sat sleeping in the chair beside his bed.

He looked down at his new arm. It shone weakly in the lamplight, chrome and cold. He tried to move it and bit back a whimper; it was sore and stiff. Focusing on the fingers, he concentrated until one, then two, then all the metal appendages moved.

Breathing out a sigh, Danny leaned his head back and closed his eyes. He felt no relief.

Only disappointment that he'd survived.

When Danny's mother had died, part of him had died with her. The child he'd been was lost. He couldn't find him. Probably never would.

He still felt time, but it was more distant than it had ever been.

He hadn't been out of the house except for his stay at the hospital, so he knew nothing about Big Ben's current state. His father told him the clock tower would stay, along with the name, but there were reports of towers around the world being demolished.

The truth had spread. Christopher Hart had seen to that. When people learned about the sacrifices, the true history of the clock towers, they'd been appalled. Angry. Intrigued. No matter the reaction, the overwhelming consensus had been: thank goodness that's all behind us now.

Danny couldn't share in the sentiment.

Every night, he woke up screaming. He dreamed he was time, controlling people, controlling nations. Stopping bullets. Burrowing them into muscle and tissue and organs. Watching his mother die. Colton telling him to let go. When he woke, he huddled in the corner of his room and held his head, his metal fingers snagging in his hair, yelling at himself not to let go, don't let go, you shouldn't let go, *why did you let go*? His father came in and sat with him, whispering to him through the worst of it.

Danny suffered the fevers and infections and dreams. He hallucinated seeing Leila in the kitchen, making eggs. She asked him how many he wanted. He stood in rooms for minutes at a time, silent, staring at nothing.

An invisible hand covered his eyes, his mouth. It was like seeing out of a shadow. He didn't know what to name this emptiness, this excess weight that shrank inward like a black hole.

They gave him medicine for the pain that pulled him into thick, dreamless sleep. He wasn't sure what was worse: the nightmares or this constant state of unbeing, his senses swallowed and smothered every night and leaking into the next day, so that it seemed as if he'd never feel anything again.

Most of his days were spent lying on his bed. Not thinking, not remembering. Just staring at the same whorl in the ceiling above him.

One day, he couldn't concentrate on the whorl due to an incessant ticking in his room. He got up and searched, growing more and more frantic when he couldn't find the source. He had to make it stop, he couldn't stand it anymore, that God. *Damn.* TICKING.

He found the culprit: his timepiece. He smashed it against the wall, against his dresser, pounded it with the thickest book he owned. His father found him ripping apart the gears and bloodying his fingers.

His blood was useless.

When he wasn't staring at the whorl, he was sitting in the back room. People came to see him there. Cassie, Brandon. Friends of the family, friends of his mother. He could barely make himself speak to them.

But three weeks after he'd received his new arm, when his father came to the back room and told him he had a visitor, Danny's heart began to race. He saw familiar faces over his father's shoulder.

Jo and Sally offered polite smiles, but he could tell they were forced. He didn't even attempt one of his own. They'd brought with them a willowy woman with brown hair, a strong chin, and gray eyes.

"Hello, Danny," Jo said. "May we sit?"

He nodded. They settled on the opposite couch.

"Daphne told us about Zavier's final moments," Jo said. She faltered and pressed the backs of her fingers to her mouth. After composing herself, she continued on. "I know you might not agree, but it was a courageous thing he did."

Danny nodded again. "It was."

"Sally said you were very brave yourself, at the clock tower. We wanted . . . wanted to thank you."

Jo finally gave in to tears.

The other woman continued for her. "I've heard what my

son did to you," she said, her voice high and clear, like a flute. "And I'm sorry for it. He always was headstrong."

"It doesn't matter now," Danny said.

"It does. My Zavier is . . . was . . ." She let her own tears flow. Danny recognized the hollow acceptance of grief in her eyes, so much like her son's. "He was a good boy, but lost. Thank you for trying to help him. None of this would have happened if it hadn't been for me."

Danny had a feeling she was wrong, but didn't say so.

They were sorry for his loss. Jo told him she would miss Colton tremendously. Danny suspected Jo had been the one to pay for his new arm, but he didn't have the strength to thank her. He could only manage a few more polite words before they rose to leave.

Sally stopped before him, her eyes filled with tears, and signed something before she bent down and kissed his forehead.

He knew she had said "Thank you."

Cassie tried to take him to the park. It was too loud, too messy, too colorful, too *everything*. He dissolved into wordless panic, pressed against a tree, unable to breathe. Convinced that everyone could see him, that they would *know*, that they would rip him apart and make him pay for everything he'd done.

"It's all right," Cassie said in the auto on the way home. "I'd hoped it would help, but . . ."

Danny only pressed his forehead against the cool window, watching London roll past.

"I didn't know what to do after William died." He heard her swallow, her voice nearly breaking on her brother's name. "I pleaded with God every damn day to bring him back, because what else could I do? The world didn't seem fit to live in without him in it." She sighed, then reached over to pat his knee. "We'll try again another time."

But Danny stayed in the house.

One day, his father received a phone call that put an odd look on his face. Shortly after, he announced that he was taking Danny to Enfield.

The panic returned. "No." *Never again. Not there, please.*

But his father insisted, putting Danny in the auto and driving to Enfield. Danny didn't know why they were bothering. He didn't want to see it. He didn't want everyone looking at him when he broke down, when he screamed and thrashed and relived the worst moment of his life.

When they arrived, Danny automatically looked for the tower and expected to see nothing. He could already feel the emptiness inside himself expanding.

But when he looked across the green, something else filled the emptiness: disbelief.

There was a tower.

It looked nearly identical to Colton's. Danny got out of the auto and drifted toward it, as drawn to the structure as much as he was repelled. He expected to see a face in the window, but the tower remained still. Lifeless.

Of course.

He turned to face his father. "What the hell is this?"

Christopher put his hands in his pockets. "The mayor told me they were rebuilding it. He wanted you to come."

Danny trembled with rage. "It's not going to bring him back."

"I never said it would."

He turned back to the tower, wanting to ruin it, wanting to break it down piece by piece, stone by stone. He remembered the Taj Mahal, the emperor's last gift for his beloved wife. Maybe he also thought it could bring her back.

This wasn't a clock tower. It was a grave marker.

"Take me home," Danny said.

Christopher sighed. "Danny—"

"Take me *home*. Please."

Neither of them spoke about it again.

Danny started to move more. Started to talk more. He found the small cog in the pocket of a pair of his trousers. Instead of throwing it away, he kept it there.

"I'm sorry," he said to his father late one night as they both sat in the back room, reading. "For how I acted."

His father merely shook his head. "Don't apologize. You had every right."

Danny forced himself to swallow. "I miss Mum."

Christopher sat by his son's side, one arm around his

shoulders, turning him back into the boy he thought was gone. It was all they needed.

The silence was a little easier after that.

One day, Danny made himself drive to the coast. It took a while, and by the time he reached the shore, it was nearly dark. The dim sky was painted with solemn blues and purples, but in the distance a strip of yellow still streaked the horizon, all that remained of the sun.

Danny walked onto the beach, thankful he was alone. Cold wind swirled past him, whistling in his ears, making them numb.

He stared out at the dark ocean for several long moments. When the thinnest strand of sunlight remained, he began to wade into the water.

Waist-deep, he shivered and closed his eyes. He wanted to feel Aetas there. The more he concentrated, the more he was sure he felt him, a dark mass of energy and power connected to the tangled ball of time. The method of keeping all of time in order with the clock towers seemed so foolish now that he sensed it this way, the way it was meant to be. Everything was interconnected. Past, present, future.

I pleaded with God every damn day to bring him back, Cassie had said.

Breathing even and deep, Danny took the small cog from his pocket. He stared at it on his palm, just an ordinary piece

of metal now. It had once connected him to something greater. Something thicker than blood.

Danny rested the spokes of the cog against the underside of his nonmetal wrist. He nicked his skin again and again until blood welled.

He distantly thought that Zavier had died this way. A hero, not a villain.

Danny was still unsure what he was.

Only that he'd found his way to the end of his story with nothing more than a question mark.

Blood dripped from his wrist into the water. He held his wound under the surface, letting the blood drift from his veins, savoring the sharp sting of salt against the wound.

"Aetas," he said softly to the water, "I don't know if you can hear me. Or if you care. But I have an offering for you."

Something churned deep within the water. Brushed against his leg.

He inhaled. Exhaled. "You took someone from me, and I want him back. I'm prepared to bargain, though. So here it is: my offering. I'll give you half my life. Half, because he has the other half."

Danny's lower lip trembled. "Take them from me, those years. I don't want them. If you can give them to him instead . . . if you can bring him back . . ."

He started to cry, because he knew it was impossible. He started to sob, because of how badly he wished it weren't.

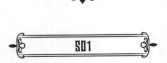

Danny started to eat more regularly. He could tell his father was relieved by the change.

His father was also relieved when Danny's name was officially cleared by the Chief Inspector. A witness from Victoria's camp had been called in to back up Danny's story, and a prime piece of evidence—the telegraph Danny had sent from Delhi to Agra—had been provided by Major Dryden.

Now that he had a clean slate, he began to wonder what to do with his life. He couldn't be a clock mechanic anymore, but there was nothing else he was good at. Cassie said she could get him a starting position at her automotive shop, but he declined. It just didn't feel right.

He was looking through job postings when the telephone rang. His father wasn't home—he was busy with the disbandment of the Union—so Danny answered.

"Hart residence."

"Ah, Danny! Good, I hoped you would pick up."

The voice belonged to Mayor Aldridge. Danny frowned, wanting nothing to do with him or his town.

"Is something the matter?"

"Well . . ." There was an awkward pause. "I was wondering if you could come to town. Today."

No.

"I don't think that would be a very good idea."

Never again.

"But . . . well . . . The clock tower's gone a little iffy and we were hoping you could fix it." There was a note of desperation in the mayor's voice.

"You do realize you don't need it anymore, right? Time's not going to Stop."

"We would still very much appreciate if you'd come and have a look."

Danny's eyes sought the portrait of his mother hanging by the telephone. He wondered what she would say to him. Berate him for being rude, most likely.

Danny closed his eyes. "I'll be there in an hour."

Making the familiar drive to Enfield felt surreal. He didn't sense his own body. He thought of himself as the auto, mechanical, functional, with no real attachment to the world. That's what he would be today. And after this, no more clock repair. Never again.

When he arrived, Aldridge greeted him. He was clearly excited, babbling a mile a minute. Danny patiently stood through the stream of chatter until Aldridge at last asked Danny to follow him. Danny warily followed the mayor's steps, clutching his tool bag in one hand. They passed the tower.

"Er . . . sir?"

The mayor stopped in front of his office. There were a few people lingering nearby, talking amongst themselves and glancing in their direction. Harland was among them. His eyes brightened when he saw Danny.

"There's another matter I thought you might help us with," Aldridge admitted. "Late last night, a young man wandered into

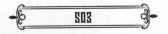

town. No idea where he was, but he said he thought he was going somewhere in particular. I thought . . . we thought . . . you could help him."

This entire affair was getting stranger by the minute. Maybe being in a Stopped town for so long had altered their minds.

"I really think I should be going," Danny said, turning back to his auto.

"Just see him," the mayor begged. "Please."

Danny sighed, then nodded. The mayor opened the door and Danny stepped inside, ready to deal with whatever hapless wanderer had had the misfortune of stumbling into Enfield.

A boy was leaning against the mayor's desk. He had brown hair that wisped gently around a pale face spotted with freckles. When Danny walked in, the boy straightened and looked directly at him.

Danny dropped his tool bag.

Not amber eyes. Blue.

But still the same.

"Colton," he breathed.

He knew him. The shape of his face, the arch of his eyebrows, the bow of his lips.

The boy frowned, confused. Danny rushed forward to grab his arms, but the boy shrank back, eyeing him distrustfully.

"What are you doing?" the boy demanded. Even the voice was the same, but not—it was more human.

Danny stood there, breathless, unable to believe it. The scab on his wrist began to tingle.

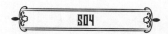

"I'm sorry, but do I know you?" the boy asked.

And there it was. The catch.

Danny's lips quirked up. He laughed faintly. That laugh turned louder, until the boy began to back away again.

"They said they called someone who might know who I am," the boy said weakly. Wearily. "Are . . . you him?"

Danny put his head in his hands. "Aetas. You bloody bastard." At some point his laughter had turned into tears. He wiped them away and looked back up at him, at Colton. Human Colton. Beautiful and unreachable.

"You don't know me," Danny said. "Do you?"

The boy shook his head.

"Danny. You don't remember Danny." Another shake of the head. "What about Castor? Do you remember him?"

Another shake. It was like Colton had been born a second time. No memories—starting from scratch.

Tabula rasa.

Danny should have rejoiced. He should have been glad. But he didn't feel those things. He felt betrayed, spat on, laughed at.

The tears flowed again. He couldn't stop them. Danny held out his hands, shaking and desperate. "Do you remember a boy named Colton," he whispered, "who had a sister named Abigail and who loved the sea? Who read fairy tales and wanted to see the world?"

Colton looked close to tears himself. "I'm sorry," he said again.

Danny couldn't do this. Not now. Not when everything else had been taken from him.

He fumbled in his pocket and took out the small cog. "Here." He pressed it into the boy's hand, trying not to feel how warm it was, how human. "I don't need this anymore."

He turned and picked up his tool bag before walking outside. The mayor tried to ask him questions, but he brushed past him to his auto. He couldn't stop the angry sobs that climbed into this throat, the terrible burn of being cheated, once again, by the gods.

But if he had stayed in that office, he would have seen the boy looking at the cog balanced on his palm, head cocked slightly to one side.

He would have seen the questioning glance the boy gave the door.

He would have seen the boy grow frustrated with himself, scared that he knew nothing when he clearly should have.

He would have seen the boy form a fist around the small cog and wince when it dug into his palm.

He would have seen the boy open his hand, surprised to find his blood touching the metal.

And he would have seen the boy's blue eyes flash amber.

Danny fumbled with his keys, shaking too much to unlock the auto door. He wiped his eyes and kept trying, cursing under his breath when the key wouldn't go in.

Someone shouted his name.

He turned.

Colton stood in the doorway of the mayor's office, looking at him as if he'd just climbed the stairs to his tower.

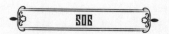

As if he had been waiting all this time.

"Colton," he whispered.

They were running, and then Colton crashed into him, sending them sprawling to the ground. They laughed and rolled, kissing every spare inch of skin, counting every freckle, saying each other's names like invocations.

"Danny," Colton kept saying, kissing him over and over. "Danny, Danny, Danny."

"How did you know?" Danny asked. "How did you remember?"

Colton pressed the bloody cog to Danny's chest in answer.

This close, Danny saw how dark eyelashes framed his blue eyes, the way his teeth were slightly crooked, the real, human tears that slid down his face. He could feel the warm breaths leaving Colton's body.

He was a miracle.

Danny slid his hand under Colton's shirt, pressing his palm to Colton's chest just as Colton pressed his own to Danny's. And there it was, the most beautiful sound he'd ever heard.

Two heartbeats.

EPILOGUE

They didn't go back to London just yet. They stayed in Enfield that night while the villagers fawned over them, peppering them with questions they didn't know how to answer. Tables were dragged out onto the green, lanterns were lit, and as night fell, the celebration began.

Danny could barely pay attention to the food and the noise and the music. All his focus was on Colton, the way he moved, the way he spoke, reconciling a clock spirit with the ghost of Colton Bell.

Colton took in the festivities, the lights winking in his blue eyes, the glow of the fires curling against his skin and threading his brown hair with gold. A boy within their world, so familiar and yet so different. Danny saw the boy he knew there—the small smile, the warmth of his eyes. And yet, he also saw a new boy, a new awareness, a new presence.

It wasn't *his* Colton, not quite, but it was enough.

An entirely new world was spread across Colton's face. Danny never wanted to leave it.

In a blessed moment to themselves, Danny explained what had happened during and after the battle at Parliament. His words were weighted with a sorrow too deep to touch, even now, with a miracle sitting beside him. That sorrow would likely always be there, a shadow at the edge of the light.

When he reached the part about his arm, Colton leaned over

and took it. He drew up Danny's sleeve and worried off his glove, gazing at the mechanics of it, his eyes somber.

Danny expected him to say something. But Colton only stroked his fingers over the metal, then lifted the arm to kiss the back of Danny's hand.

A portrait of the things he'd lost, returned in different ways.

"Things will be different," Danny warned him. "Everything will be new."

"Then we'll start at the beginning," Colton said.

Danny kissed him, forgetting they were in full view of the townspeople until they started cheering and whistling. Danny jerked back, flushed. Colton, equally pink, met his eyes and started laughing.

And there he was—his Colton. The boy who had changed everything.

The next day they made a detour to the ocean.

Danny parked by the beach as the sun was setting. The sand was cool, but their hands were clasped above it, warm and safe.

Colton sat studying the small cog in the fading light. It was so odd to take him in, Colton and not-Colton, an image of two people joined as one.

Colton noticed Danny staring and unleashed that slightly crooked smile. "What?"

"It's strange seeing you with brown hair."

"Would you rather it were blond?"

"No. Yes. I don't care. As long as it's still you under there, it doesn't matter."

Colton grinned. Danny leaned in until their smiles meshed. The thrill of time was gone from their touch, but another thrill remained, one just as strong. Thicker than blood.

He slipped his hand under Colton's shirt, feeling his heart beat under his fingertips. It was a sensation Danny thought he'd never get enough of.

"This time I waited for you," Danny whispered.

Colton touched his cheek, then the scar on his chin. "I know you did. You'll never have to again."

Danny knew that he would have to tell him soon, what he had done to make this possible. But not now, not this moment. It could wait.

They didn't have all the time in the world. But they had time enough.

THE END

ACKNOWLEDGMENTS

As I sit here thinking over the last several years, it is so remarkable to me how much this trilogy has been a part of my life. I first drafted *Timekeeper* in 2013—a very horrible, horrible draft—and now, almost exactly five years later, I'm putting the finishing touches on *Firestarter*.

I have had so many people help me these last five years. First and foremost, thank you to my fantastic editor Alison Weiss, without whom I would be a puddle of tears and anxiety on the floor. Alison, you saw the potential in this weird story about clocks and ghosts that, by all means, *should not have made any sense*, and yet you knew just how to encourage me to make it shine, and for that I'll be forever grateful. We both know the real ending is Danny and Colton grabbing some Chipotle.

A big thanks to Laura Crockett and the folks at TriadaUS, who first took on this project and continue to help boost it to the world. *Big* thanks to Nicole Frail and Johanna Dickson for helping shuttle this book to publication, as well as everyone at Sky Pony who had a hand in its production. Thanks also to Sammy Yuen for that amazing cover.

Thank you to Victoria Marini for being so supportive and gung ho about everything. Please continue to hold my hand forever, even when it gets sweaty and gross.

Hearing my words come to life is *super embarrassing* but also *super cool*, so thanks are in order for Pamela Lorence at Forever

Young Audiobooks, as well as Gary Furlong for being such an awesome and enthusiastic narrator.

Thank you to Sona Charaipotra for helping me with the Hindi. All mistakes are mine.

Being an author would mean nothing without the friends I've made on this journey so far, who get me through every single day and read my atrocious first drafts without cringing too much. To Emily Skrutskie: yelling at/to/with you is pretty much a daily ritual that I hope never ends. To Jessica Cluess: when we begin to sing the same song and/or say the exact same thing at the exact same time, I know we are drift compatible. To Traci Chee: you were one of the first author friends I ever made, and to this day I'm so thankful that you weren't creepy (and didn't find me creepy). (Thank you also to Cole Benton for having proficiency in bag carrying.)

A huge hug for the writing cult: Akshaya Raman, Katy Pool, Meg Kohlmann, Kat Cho (also known in some circles as Goxikeh), Amanda Foody, Christine Herman, Melody Simpson, Axie Oh, Clairbel Ortega, Amanda Haas, Mara Fitzgerald, Janella Angeles, Ashley Burdin, Ella Dyson, Joan He, and Alex Castellanos. You are all wonderful and talented and beautiful.

To TJ Ryan: your *Timekeeper* fan art brought us together, and I am so glad it did. You have been such an amazing friend and *strums guitar* I love you, bitch.

My publishing journey has resulted in a lot of new friends, but I'd be nowhere without some of my oldest. To Ellen Gavazza and Carrie Gratiot: you've known me since we were tiny things and yet you're still somehow friends with me. Thank you for your friendship and understanding and alcohol. To my Hollins family: I wouldn't be the person I am today without you, and you're forever in my heart.

To the booksellers, book bloggers, and book reviewers: thank you for all that you do to spread the word about books!

To my readers: you have played such a huge part in my journey. Thank you for picking up copies of these books and reading them, loving them, reccing them, hand selling them, reviewing them, making fan art for them, and overall making me proud to have written them.

I would like to *not* thank my cats for distracting me and biting my notebooks, but I do thank them for being cute.

And last but certainly not least, huge thanks to my family, especially my parents. Without you, I doubt I would have gotten this far, and it is through your love and support that I find the strength to keep going. Mama, I remember the look of horror on your face when I told you I wanted to be an author when I grew up, and the memory is made even better by the look of pride I see on your face now. Father, in that same memory you weren't surprised at all, because you always knew this would be my future. You're as much a part of these books as I am.